Michele Renae is the pseud[...] author Michele Hauf. She ha[...] novels in historical, paranormal and contemporary romance and fantasy, as well as writing action/ adventure as Alex Archer. Instead of writing 'what she knows' she prefers to write 'what she would love to know and do'. And, yes, that includes being a jewel thief and/or a brain surgeon! You can email Michele at toastfaery@gmail.com, and find her on Instagram: @MicheleHauf and Pinterest: @toastfaery.

Hana Sheik falls in love every day, reading her favourite romances and writing her own happily-ever-afters. She's worked in various jobs— but never for very long, because she's always wanted to be a romance author. Now, happily, she gets to live that dream. Born in Somalia, she moved to Ottawa, Canada, at a very young age, and still resides there with her family.

FAKING IT
WITH THE BOSS

MICHELE RENAE

ANOTHER SHOT
AT FOREVER

HANA SHEIK

MILLS & BOON

First published in Great Britain 2025
by Mills & Boon, an imprint of HarperCollins*Publishers* Ltd,
1 London Bridge Street, London, SE1 9GF

www.harpercollins.co.uk

HarperCollins*Publishers*, Macken House, 39/40 Mayor Street Upper,
Dublin 1, D01 C9W8, Ireland

Faking It with the Boss © 2025 Michele Hauf

Another Shot at Forever © 2025 Muna Sheik

ISBN: 978-0-263-39673-7

02/25

FAKING IT WITH THE BOSS

MICHELE RENAE

MILLS & BOON

For Mary and Lois.

We basically rock.

CHAPTER ONE

ASHER DANE STROLLED into The Art Guys' London office, inhaling the subtle scent that always calmed him yet at the same time seemed to sharpen his senses. Lemon. It was the receptionist's doing. A tiny terra-cotta scent pot sat on the corner of her desk. She—Maeve—commandeered front and center of the circular office space, with three private offices and the large meeting room curving along the back. The curvaceous area enhanced the appeal of their product, which was art.

Even more so, the receptionist gave good curb appeal as she looked up, nodded, then spoke to whoever it was on her headset. That tiny smile of hers, barely there, always managed to capture his attention. Because at the corners of her mouth were perfect little apostrophes. They enticed him. Made him want to trace them. With his lips.

Asher caught himself before he walked into a Grecian amphora displayed on a pedestal. A five-hundred-thousand-pound deduction from his paycheck should the vase shatter. He swerved, but his gaze snatched one more glance. That intriguing grin. It said there was more to the woman than met the eye.

And yet, he rarely spoke to her save for long-distance office calls. Not because he didn't have an interest in learning more about the petite dark-haired woman who had worked for them for two years. She'd been hired six months after he'd rejoined Krew and Joss here as a permanent broker. Rather, those almost-smiles she cast him made him believe she wasn't interested or impressed by him. Perhaps even judging him for things he'd rather not think about but tended to consider at odd times, like when he was brushing his teeth or sitting with a paddle in hand waiting for an art auction to begin.

For heaven's sake, he didn't know what to do when in the same room as her. Not a feeling he was accustomed to. And that annoyed him.

"Ash!" Joss Beckett poked his head out of Krew's office and waved him inside. "Excellent timing. Get in here!"

Passing by Maeve's desk, Asher slowed, and she glanced up at him with glittery green eyes surrounded by the lushest black lashes. He winked at her. Her mouth, deliciously dark cherry and curvy, dropped open. Whoever was on the other end of the line prompted her to a flustered apology.

Wrong move, man! He'd spoiled her concentration.

Asher darted into the office. Why did he assume idiot mode around that woman?

"Good to see you, Asher. Have a seat."

Krew Lawrence leaned back in his chair, feet up on the desk. A tidy tweed vest worn over white shirtsleeves rolled to his elbows was his usual garb. His nickname for the show? The Brain. Fitting. Asher had met him at university, and they had bonded over their love of art. Krew handled the legal and accounting for the trio's billion-dollar empire.

Over the last decade, the university friends had come together through their love for all manner of art and formed a brokerage. They bought, sold, discovered and appraised, and had acquired an A-list of celebrity clients and accomplished artists. Halfway through that decade though, Asher had been forced to leave the trio to care for his ailing parents. But after finally finding them the proper care, Asher had been able to return to the team almost three years ago. It had been right before Krew and Joss had been approached by a major television network to do a short-run series. Last month, they'd wrapped filming on their second season. Six episodes that followed their quests for rare artwork, the travails of high-stakes auctions, and even that one episode that had featured him and Joss helping a ninety-year-old woman go through a Highgate apartment that had been locked and preserved since before World War II—that had netted millions in rare and previously unknown artwork.

Asher loved being in front of the camera. When others were watching he was at his best. The way to garner attention was to flash his pearly whites and give them what they expected: a surface glamour that no one cared to see beneath. They hadn't nicknamed him The Face for the show for nothing. The label didn't bother him. He'd always been called handsome, and hell, he knew how to use his looks to get what he wanted. Yet sometimes he got so focused on the outer glamour and what it could get for him that he wasn't even sure anymore who Asher Dane was.

He veered his attention back toward reception. Apparently, no matter how much he utilized his patented charm, some things were unattainable. Such as Maeve's interest. How she frustrated him! And those bold colors and mismatched prints she always wore. There were days it hurt his eyes to even glance in her general direction.

"We have a job for you, Asher." Krew, ever on a schedule and always the first to spot a forgery, wasn't one for hellos or pleasantries.

"I've been on the road two months, and the first time you see me, you shove another job in my face?" Asher teased.

Then he laughed, meeting Joss with playful punches to one another's shoulders. "How you doing, man? Did the trip to Brazil take it out of you?"

"Almost got squeezed to death by a giant python," Joss said, nicknamed The Brawn for the show for good reason. The man had the muscles and the fearless audacity to rush headlong into adventure, be it a scuba diving mission to search for a lost ancient sculpture or tackling a swarm of bees that had overtaken a castle's art room. "You look good. But then, you always do."

"It's a curse." Asher sat on the velvet chair before Krew's desk. Everything in the office was curved and no hard lines. The decor had been Asher's doing. He loved the romantic aesthetic. Yes, he was a sucker for the Pre-Raphaelite period. Modern, blocky, light-starved Mondrian and Picasso? He'd leave the geometric stuff to Krew. "What's up with this new job? And don't I have a thing in Bangladesh soon?"

"You do. But I think you can squeeze this one in." Krew turned his laptop around.

The screen displayed an article about Tony Kichu, "relationship coach to the stars." Asher skimmed the text, which detailed the eccentric man's methods of coaching via Zoom. None of his clients had ever met him in person, though he was a billionaire due to his cultlike following.

"Apparently," Krew said, "the man is also an artist. His clients want to buy his work but he won't sell."

"What's his style? His medium?" Asher scrolled the page but there wasn't any mention of Kichu's art.

"No one knows beyond that he paints."

Asher diverted his attention between both men's gazes. Each was thinking the same thing. "Then how does anyone know they want it?"

"Because of his fame," Joss said. "Isn't that how it always goes?"

"Fair enough. So what?" Asher leaned back in the chair. "You want me to talk to the guy?"

"Yes, and get a look at his work. If we can snag him as an artist…"

"We could use another buzzworthy artist to introduce to the world," Krew said.

"Buzz is always good," Joss added. "And…" He sighed.

Yes, yes, the unspoken rang loudly in Asher's head. He'd yet to bring in his own artist. Sure, he handled a list of elite clients, and he could buy and sell at auction like no one's business. But he'd been out of the business those years he'd been taking care of his parents, and when he had been here at the beginning his focus had been garnering publicity and making a name for the trio.

But now? Whether the guys ever said it out loud—and he knew they never would—bringing in an artist would finally prove Asher's true worth to them. That he was the entire package. That he contributed as much talent and skill as his two colleagues.

A gruff voice from his recent past muttered in his thoughts.

You're subpar, Dane. There's no substance behind the pretty face.

A comment that had gutted Asher not once but over and over, as it had been recorded and shown on the TV series.

It wasn't true. He wasn't subpar. He could hold his own alongside Krew and Joss, but… He hadn't a stable of artists to nurture and hone and bring to the world to show that The Art Guys really was the number one brokerage with the most unique and talented artists.

"And," Joss added, "nabbing Tony Kichu would be another notch for your social media."

"It's not a notch, Joss. Just another post and tons more followers for *our* socials."

Asher spent time enhancing his online presence and that of the brokerage. He had over five million followers. That kept The Art Guys in the news. He was providing value to the team in that manner.

But to finally bring in an artist? That was paramount.

"I can do it," Asher said. "Where's the guy at? And if he doesn't meet personally with his clients… I really hate to do an appraisal via Zoom."

"You won't have to. Kichu holds a couples' spa retreat once a year at his home base just out of Reykjavík."

"Iceland? Nice place to visit this time of year. And a spa? Swing in. Soak in the geothermal pools. Then finagle a meeting with Kichu. No problem."

"There is one problem." Krew turned the laptop back around and stood. "It's a couples' retreat so you'll need a significant other on your arm. You dating anyone at the moment?"

"That's a stupid question," Joss said. "The Face always has a woman on his arm."

True. Dating beautiful women made for good content on his socials. Though it never seemed to fill his emotional content bucket. Currently, Asher was between women.

Honestly? The surface-level connections he made were not cutting it anymore. He craved real connection, and something that lasted longer than a weekend. At thirty-two, he wasn't getting any younger, and much as he'd never admit it to his proudly single business mates, he did want to start a family.

"Totally single right now."

Both his coworkers stared at him in disbelief.

Asher shrugged. "What can I say? Sometimes even The Face needs a break."

"Well, you need to get a woman. Fast," Krew said. "I've already had our Maeve book a flight and tickets for the retreat. Plane leaves tomorrow evening and the retreat begins the next day."

He expected nothing less than last-minute orders from Krew. "Well…" Asher rubbed his jaw.

He did have a few regulars he tended to hook up with, but the idea of spending a week with someone he wasn't close to? Iffy. And while he had a type—sexy, smart, independent, usually had their own influencing gig—none had ever felt like go-the-distance girlfriend material. Like someone with whom he could share a future.

That shouldn't matter if he intended to fake being in a couple.

"Why not bring along our Maeve?" Joss suggested.

The other two men cast their gazes toward reception.

Asher smirked. "You guys do know that calling her *our Maeve* makes her sound like some kind of Jane Austin character?"

"I rather like Jane Austin," a female voice said.

Asher turned as Maeve entered the office and set a bulky folder on Krew's desk. She wore a slim-fitted Maxfield Parrish blue dress that emphasized her long legs and tiny waist. It had a wide green paisley collar and matching turned-back cuffs at the short sleeves. Some kind of retro look, he decided. It suited her. Even if the paisley clashed wildly with the striped blue fabric. But those severe black bangs. Another retro style, perhaps. He preferred his women with long lush locks and silk shirts beneath a business suit.

Yet, oh, those apostrophes hugging her lips. And the way the afternoon light beamed across her pale skin…

"Did I hear my name?" she asked.

"She's *our* Maeve," Krew said, smiling at her, "because we love her. And Maeve is family."

"Family?" Asher looked to the receptionist to see how she would react to that overly familiar label.

"I like it when Krew calls me our Maeve," she offered succinctly. "He's like my smart big brother who watches out for me. And when Joss says it, it's also nice. He's my little brother who would fight a guy to protect me."

"Damn right I would," Joss agreed.

Really? They were a family? When and why had *he* been left out of this secret office alliance? Sure, he traveled a good ninety percent of the working calendar, but he stopped in at least once a month for in-person meetings.

"Maeve, would you like to accompany Asher on the spa trip?" Krew asked. "As you booked the reservations, you are aware it is a couples' retreat. Asher doesn't have a partner to go along with him, so if you'd like to…?"

Asher sat upright. The guys were rushing ahead with a plan they hadn't discussed with him! And sure, he wouldn't mind a little get-to-know-you time with *our Maeve*, but he didn't want them to push her into it. Or him. Because there was that issue of not knowing how to breathe around her or act, or talk, or—

"You need me to…" She paused, glancing briefly to Asher. Was that panic on her face? "Fake being Mr. Dane's partner?"

"It's just for show," Krew said. "It would look a bit odd if he showed up alone."

"A week holiday at a spa?" she asked. "Paid for by the company?"

"All expenses," Krew reassured. "You've been wanting us to consider you for fieldwork. This might be a good chance to watch Asher in action, get some tips and see how you can assist. He can assess your talent and give us feedback."

Assess her talent? Oh, he'd assessed her. Plenty of times. And—what was going on?

Maeve nodded eagerly, but when she again glanced to him, her smile fell. Gone were those enticing punctuation marks. "Is that all right with you, Mr. Dane?"

Why did she call them Krew and Joss while he was always Mr. Dane? What had he done to alienate the one person in this office who seemed to fascinate and confuse him at the same time?

"It'll work," he offered. He was used to putting on a show, charming the clients, saying whatever was needed to win the deal. Over the years, it had grown much easier to be The Face than Asher Dane.

"Can you be ready to leave by tomorrow evening?" Krew asked Maeve.

"Of course! That'll give me most of the day to take care of any office work that needs attention over the next week."

Even as she spoke she strolled around Krew's office, tugging open a cabinet drawer and pulling out a big file. That slim-fitted skirt hugged her slight curves and… Assess her? Oh, he was up for that job.

"Joss is due in Las Vegas next Tuesday," she said. "And you, Krew, have the DeSevre's auction in town. I'll make sure everything is prepared. And if you need me you can always call." She left, breezing toward her desk, answering a call on her headset even as she sat.

Asher turned to face his friends. Both wore cat-snuffling-cream smirks on their faces. "What?"

"We know," Joss said conspiratorially.

Krew wore one of those sneaky smiles that indicated *I know things you think I don't.*

"You don't know," Asher defended. But what it was they thought they knew, he wasn't even sure about.

"Oh, we know," Krew said. He met Joss with a fist bump. "We know."

Asher spun on the chair to spy Maeve sorting through a file folder while simultaneously speaking with a client. Her long legs were crossed gracefully and her body tilted forward. She wore the Parrish blue dress like the artist himself had mixed the vivacious color especially for her.

He was to spend the next week with her at a couples-only private spa?

Maybe they *did* know.

CHAPTER TWO

MAEVE MET HER FLATMATE, Lucy, at the front door of their two-bedroom flat in Fulham. The West London neighborhood had been an ideal landing spot for Maeve when she'd moved there from Dublin five years earlier after landing her first job with a local art gallery. The neighborhood was filled with colorful Victorian houses and pubs, and the food shops offered delicious cuisine. And it was a short walk to nearby Bishops Park, where she liked to linger in the rose garden on weekends.

Lucy had parlayed her gregarious and slightly theatrical charm into a cushy job as a makeup influencer, so she was always home. In her bedroom, sitting beneath perfect lighting, doing her thing. Maeve could tell that she was looking forward to having the place to herself while she was away because it would allow her to pack. Lucy was getting married next month, which would leave Maeve in need of a flatmate to cover the rent that sucked up a third of her income.

Maeve had met Lucy the day she'd arrived in London. She had been sulking in a coffee shop because the idea of staying with her dad in his open studio, along with his snooty girlfriend, had given her a gut ache. She and Lucy shared a common love for natural history nonfiction, sugary breakfast pastries and weird decorating aesthetics. Lucy had encouraged Maeve to go wild when decorating the apartment and they both agreed the flat looked like "Martha Stewart meets Cottagecore meets Alice in Freakin' Wonderland." Color was Maeve's means of expressing herself.

Another instant bond had been their shared dreams of owning a shop. Maeve had been the idea woman; Lucy was the accounting, marketing and all-that-financial-stuff woman. They'd opened their shop almost a year to the day after that auspicious meeting over coffees. Calling it Fuchsia, the shop had sold color in every form, from kitschy home decorations, to paints and markers. Colored papers and fabrics. Anything to add color to a person's life. Maeve's ultimate dream was to eventually parlay the shop into a consulting business in which she would help people design rooms or entire households through color.

It had been lovely, exciting, and…one month after the official opening the pandemic had hit. They'd had to close two months later. Their inventory had been sold to pay lenders—namely, Maeve's mother—but Maeve's dream to own a shop, this time specifically related to color consultation, still shone brightly in her heart.

Maeve had admired how Lucy had pivoted like a pro. She was a marvel with makeup, and even did occasional "look-alike" posts where she transformed her face into that of a celebrity. Her Adele look was spot-on. Her fiancé was a world traveler, so she intended to wave goodbye to London and head out on an adventure.

Lucy nudged Maeve's hardshell suitcase, purple with white skull polka dots. "Are you sure you can do this, sweetie?"

So much in that simple question. Maeve knew that Lucy was aware of her desire to reopen her business. And that she needed to increase her earnings to do so. And that she would never again ask her mum for a loan. Mariane Pemberton's oft-repeated epitaph for her daughter was "you've failed."

Recently named one of the top fifty investors under fifty, Maeve's mother was a go-getter multimillionaire who had built her own investing firm geared toward women. If a person wasn't working or thinking about work, or moving up the corporate ladder, they had failed at the game of life. Which was why Maeve's dad had divorced his wife eight years ago. Maeve was much more her father's daughter when it came to tackling life as it was thrown at her. Of course, her father was currently a kept man—his girlfriend had a trust fund—so that's where the comparison stopped.

Maeve grabbed the handle of her suitcase. "Of course, I can luxuriate in a spa for the next week with no cares but to look at some art, Lucy!"

"Those hot springs are supposed to be the fountain of youth. Not that you need it, you and your porcelain skin. Lord, I wish I had cheekbones like yours." Lucy fluttered her fingers over her face. "I wouldn't have to contour!"

"You don't need to," Maeve said. "You are beautiful with or without makeup."

Lucy gasped. "No one will ever see this face without the war paint."

"I have."

"And you will take that knowledge to your grave." Lucy touched Maeve's bangs, adjusting them. Maeve ruled the decorating; Lucy had free rein over all hair and makeup decisions. "I know you'll enjoy the vacation part of the adventure, but you *know* what I'm really asking you."

Maeve sighed heavily. Never in a million years would she have thought one of her fantasies would come true. And to be literally thrust into a quasi-relationship with the one man she lusted over?

"He's my boss. He needs a fake girlfriend. I need the points with my other two bosses if I'm to move up in the company. My dream to reopen the shop as a consulting business will never happen unless I increase my finances."

"It'll happen. You have a gift, girl. You need to spread the color around. But seriously. You slyly bypassed the fact that you have crushed on The Face since day one."

"The whole world crushes on Asher Dane. There's nothing special about that. He's handsome. He's also…a little cold, I'd say. He rarely speaks to me unless it's directly related to the business." She made to step around Lucy. Asher had texted he'd pick her up for the airport in ten minutes.

Lucy sidestepped to block access to the doorknob—clear crystal set against a lavender-painted wood door with pale pink stripes.

"Yes," Lucy said, "but the whole world does not dream about staring at artwork with Mr. Dane. Just…lolling there. Looking at it. I don't get it," she said of the oft-visited fantasy Maeve had once divulged. She shook her head and gestured dismissively. "I'll never understand you art people."

"Says the woman who literally creates art on her face."

"So true."

"As for my fantasy… Mr. Dane sees things in art," Maeve said. She'd watched Asher lose himself in a painting. Often. It was remarkable to behold. It was exactly as she did when she viewed a beautiful piece of art. She fell into the story of it. "Don't worry. You know Mr. Dane never gives me the time of day. This week at the spa is pretend."

"You pretending to be his girlfriend? I know exactly where that's headed." Lucy winked. "If you're lucky."

"Please, Lucy. It's not going to be like one of those silly romance movies we like to watch over popcorn and beer."

"Yeah? Sweetie, you know those stories always end with the girl getting the guy."

Maeve sighed. If only the same could happen to her. But she was a realist. And Asher was not the sort of man who would date a girl like her. He dated models and celebrities. She was weird and color-crazy Maeve, a displaced expat from Dublin who had dreams of owning her own business.

Of finally proving to her mum that she could be a success.

"I already know the ending," she said to Lucy. "And the credits are not going to roll *happily ever after*. Besides, I'll be on the clock. I need to study Mr. Dane's style to see how he gets the job done if I'm ever to impress the other bosses."

"Oh, we both know you've studied his *style* far too much already."

"Lucy!"

Her friend narrowed her gaze at her, capped by perfectly sculpted brows, and leveled her with a firm, "Maeve."

Lucy was right. As well as being incredibly alluring regarding his passion for art, the man was not terrible to look at. Maeve crushed on him. Hard. And so maybe she had plans to enjoy this week of pretending she was in a relationship with him. Why not? It would be the closest she ever got to the fantasy. But she'd be careful not to let her heart into the deal. Her mum always said love complicated things. It's why she and Maeve's dad couldn't make it work. Mariane Pemberton had chosen success over love.

"Something good will come of this," Lucy said with a glint in her eye.

"Me being promoted?"

Lucy tilted her head, assessing. "Maybe."

"I don't know what else could come of it." Yes, she could dare to dream that Asher Dane would fall madly in love with her, drop to his knees and propose to her.

"Exactly," Lucy decided, as if reading Maeve's wildly fantasizing thoughts.

Keep it fantasy, she warned inwardly. *Business not pleasure.*

Checking her texts, Maeve opened the door and fled, calling back, "I'll see you in a week!"

Lucy's call echoed down the hallway, "At the very least, get a kiss out of the deal!"

Rolling her eyes as she entered the lift, Maeve pressed the button for the main floor and clutched her suitcase handle. She had no intention of crossing any work boundaries, especially when she wanted to prove herself to Krew and Joss. This week must be nothing more than a relaxing—and learning—vacation.

Once out of elevator, she stepped outside into the warm July air as a limo pulled up. The back window rolled down and Asher Dane winked at her.

Maeve's stomach flip-flopped like a giddy guppy. Her cheeks flushed as well. Mercy, this was not going to be a relaxing vacation if the man released one more of those electrifying winks on her.

Keep it together. It's just pretend.

And she had best keep her fantasies to herself.

The three-hour flight allowed them to do a bit of homework on one another. Over wine provided by first class, they shared highlights of their university info. He'd attended the Royal College of Art and had majors in art history and social sciences. Maeve had taken a year of art from Westminster, with a side of business management thrown in.

Asher's suspicion Maeve had grown up in Ireland was confirmed. Her accent was faint. Her father was British but her mother was Irish. Both parents had initially traveled for their jobs. After her parents divorced and her mum had permanently relocated to New York, Maeve had moved to London to try her feet in the business world and she'd lived there since.

Asher had lived in London all his life. He'd always strove to stay close to his parents. He hadn't explained to Maeve about his parents' conditions. It wasn't necessary for their one-week fake relationship. And no one wanted to hear the real-life stuff that tended to throw a wrench into the fantasy of reality. Besides, having retired to a quiet country home in Bath, Mr. and Mrs. Dane were doing well so long as they stayed off the grid.

"So you and Krew and Joss met at uni?"

She had turned on the seat and tucked up her legs to face him. Her petite frame was all black hair and peach linen. It would easily be possible to fit two of her in the seat. She'd slipped off her strappy green heels to reveal tiny violet toenails. Yet it was her lipstick that drew his gaze. Deep red, almost like velvet, with tones of blood-dark crimson. And those two tiny apostrophes that always gave the appearance of a smile even though her eyes often said otherwise. He wondered what her mouth might taste like…

"Mr. Dane?"

She had caught him looking. When he noticed the stern glint in her eyes, he shook himself from his foray into a kiss and composed himself.

"You should stop calling me Mr. Dane if we're to appear as a real couple."

"Good call. Asher." With a lift of her chin, she asked, "And do you remember *my* name?"

"What? Of course."

"Really? Last week you called me Marsha. And I've heard

you mutter Minnie, Morgan and even Alice as you march past my desk to your office."

"I do not march. I never *march*," he insisted. More like a careful stroll, ever cautious he might trip or do something ridiculous to completely humiliate himself before the remarkable and mysterious Maeve.

There was something about using a person's real name that weirdly flustered him. It was intimate. Most of the time, with men, he used their surnames. And women he could easily name darling or babe, or some nonsense. But naming *her* felt intense. Like he was claiming her. Making her his own.

You have to play along for this fake-a-week adventure.

"Minnie is a nice name," he said. "So is Margot, Morgan and Estelle."

She gave him that disapproving smirk he was so accustomed to receiving from her. Admittedly, he did like to tease. Get a reaction. It was how he gauged people's interest. It was a tool he utilized to move through life.

Her mouth compressed, which curled those apostrophes even more.

"Maeve," he stated. He liked the feel of her name in his mouth. Short, simple, but like delicate artwork that required study. "Very close to *mauve*, which is about the best color ever. And don't get me started on its invention in the nineteenth century."

"William Perkin, a chemistry student was synthesizing quinine from coal tar for a malaria treatment when he happened upon the mauve dye."

Asher snapped a look at her. How did she…? "Right, an art student. A lifelong love?"

"Since I used to scribble with coloring crayons and markers. Still do, actually. An intense love for color lives in me. Mauve, carmine and emerald run through my veins."

God, he loved that statement. And to imagine? Such a lush manner of speaking about one's passion. Truly, why had he never dared to converse with *our Maeve* before?

"One day I will own a Maxfield Parrish lithograph," she stated proudly.

"Love the saturated colors that man utilized. Such whimsy. And the curves."

"Your artistic preferences do tend toward the curvy."

Asher crooked a brow, but she didn't notice his curiosity as she handed her empty wine goblet to the passing flight attendant. How did she know what he preferred? He was rarely in the office.

"So how long have we been dating?" Big green eyes peered at him from beneath lush black lashes. "It'll be helpful to know what the intimacy level should be. If we don't want to send up any red flags, we'll have to act as if we've known each other awhile."

"A year?"

"Oh." She tugged in her lip with her teeth, and the action drew his attention intensely. Those perfect white teeth. Yet, she was worried?

"Too long?" he wondered.

"That would imply we know each other quite well and might have to…"

Was she afraid they might have to hold hands or kiss? Best way to convince others they were a couple. Did she have anything against kissing him? He supposed it was a lot to ask of an employee. Perhaps she worried about employer/ employee fraternization?

"A few months," he tossed out. "Long enough to know a little about one another and to have googly eyes for each other, but not so long that we've, you know."

"Yes, I know."

Did everyone know? Apparently, they did. Thinking back to Joss and Krew stating as much in the office, Asher had to laugh. And before he could answer Maeve's question about why he was laughing, the pilot announced their landing.

He clasped her hand and gave it a squeeze. "Ready?"

A genuine smile beamed in her eyes, and it grabbed him by the heart and squeezed. Quite unexpected. What was it about the deliciously intriguing yet weirdly colorful Maeve Pemberton?

"Not completely ready," she said with a brave inhale, "but let's do this anyway."

"Less sure than I would expect from you, but allowable."

"I don't have it completely together," she said. They'd talked briefly about her masterful control of the office and everyone's schedules. He certainly wouldn't have survived without her background control of the little necessities that made his life simply work. "But I want to show you and the other guys that I'm worthy of taking on assignments beyond the reception desk."

So her plan for the week was to impress him? Done. Onto the next plan. Which was…? Locate the elusive relationship coach and charm him into becoming Asher's first official artist.

"Shall we?" she asked.

Asher realized he still held her hand. It felt like some kind of anchor to a reality he rarely touched. He wasn't sure if that was a good or bad thing. But something told him he was going to find out soon enough.

"Sure, honey," he said.

Maeve wrinkled her nose.

"Honey doesn't work for you? Babe?"

A vehement head shake.

"Sweetie, darling, lover?"

She cracked a terrified grimace.

"Just Maeve?"

She exhaled and nodded.

Just Maeve then. But not our Maeve.

How about *his* Maeve?

At check-in Asher played the suave boyfriend in dark sunglasses and a designer suit who sweet-talked the receptionist into a room facing the steaming geothermal springs behind the resort. Meanwhile, Maeve browsed the glossy flyer detailing the week's schedule. What was life without a proper schedule? Lots of classes, instructive sessions and spa moments but—what was that subtitle below the title of Reconnecting Romance? She'd not noticed that detail when booking tickets.

"It's late, but do you have time for the entrance interviews?" the receptionist asked. "They take about fifteen minutes and will help us to fine-tune your schedule for the week."

Asher glanced at her and shrugged.

Maeve grabbed his hand. "Just a second. I need to talk to my boss—er...boyfriend." With a forced smile to the receptionist, she then tugged Asher aside near the fountain bubbling in the center of the pristine Prussian-blue-tiled lobby.

"What's up, sweetie? Sorry. Maeve."

A momentary thrill of hearing him say her name swept through her like a cyclone, only to be followed by an even bigger, and more harrowing, disaster. "It's this." She waved the flyer between them. "This is not just a couples' spa vacation."

"What? The signs say Reconnecting Romance. Kind of cute."

"Right, it is a spa, and about romance, but it's also focused on this." She turned the flyer toward him and tapped the top line.

Asher read, "Relationship *rehab*?"

Maeve swore under her breath. "I'm so sorry, I didn't notice this when signing up. I can't believe I let that slip by me."

"What does it mean exactly?"

"It means that not only are we faking being a couple, now we're going to have to fake relationship issues. We're here to *fix* our relationship, not relax and rejuvenate."

Asher winked at her. "Guess I'm calling you sweetie, after all."

He turned and told the receptionist they could do their interviews now.

CHAPTER THREE

MAEVE ARRIVED AT the room before Asher. She rolled in her suitcase and walked beyond the bed, dressed in natural linens, to the patio doors to look over the landscape. Other than her weekend strolls through Bishops Park, she so rarely saw unrestrained nature. Outside the room, lush forest hugged one side of the resort with emerald, olive, sepia and glints of azure, and a mossy rolling plain hissed with pearlescent steam billowing from various geothermal pools. The main pool behind the resort featured a wooden walkway circling it and a shower house.

The plan was to settle into that pool as quickly as possible. Though, she understood they'd have to attend the classes to not stick out and look like a pair of art brokers skulking about to find the reclusive owner. Reception had said they'd email a schedule within the hour. It was late, so she'd unpack and…

Turning, she took in the room. Much smaller than she'd expected for a luxurious resort. Just the one low platform bed. It did not offer a lot of stretching-out space. Not even queen-size?

"Bother," she muttered. What would she and Asher do about the sleeping situation?

There wasn't even a sofa or easy chair. Two wood stools were placed before a narrow natural wood bar situated to look out the patio windows. And on the wall opposite the bed hung a large mirror. A person could not lie in the bed or make any movements on it without having such motions reflected to them. Like a kinky—no, she wouldn't go there.

Well. She could, but she must not.

"Double bother."

Peering into the bathroom, she was relieved to see it was larger than most hotel offerings and featured a deep soaking tub, separate shower and two small mirrors above two sinks. About the same size as the bedroom.

"Weird," she decided of the setup.

Then she crossed her fingers that whatever was involved in a relationship rehab did not involve… She glanced to the mirror and shook her head. Not wise to think too far into that one. She was nervous enough now that she stood in this room, waiting for the one man she had admired for years.

More like ogled and secretly swooned at as he entered the office and filled the air with his easy charm and barest hint of intriguing cologne. Asher Dane captured her attention with nothing more than that discerning crimp of brow and his innate confidence. And those stunning glacier-blue eyes that were framed by earthy brown hair. And while he always wore the most expensive suits, tailored to fit his tall frame, she did schedule gym dates for him twice a week, no matter what country or city he was in. When he called and listed off the various outdoor activities he wanted to try in his spare time while on a business trip, she'd look them up and schedule a session for him.

Maeve had been running Asher's life for the last two years, and he'd never even acknowledged it. Of course, he had a private life that she wouldn't attempt to dabble in. On the other hand, most of his life was posted to his social media pages. Accounts she wasn't allowed to handle. Fine with her. She'd seen enough of his *woman holding his hand and looking toward some fabulous sight* shots that she'd rolled her eyes so far back into her head there were days she wondered if they might get stuck. It was his thing. A gimmick. His followers always gushed and liked and hearted the posts. The women's faces were never shown. They were props in his art.

"Just another of his harem?" she muttered as she unzipped the suitcase and took out the book lying on top of her clothes. A copy of *A Natural History of the Senses* by Diane Ackerman. A dog-eared comfort read.

Never would she want to feel such a way while dating a man. So, yes, that confirmed her fantasies were simply that—dreams. The Face had shown her who he was—an egotistic attention-seeking influencer—and he wasn't her type.

Until she got to the cerebral and inner life of Asher Dane. The way he got lost in a painting...

She clutched the book to her chest and closed her eyes. So many times she'd found herself leaning over the back of her chair, chin in hand, as she'd watched Asher standing in the main conference room, alone but for a recent acquisition—whether painting, sculpture or antique—and realized he lost himself in the observation of another person's creation. It never ceased to thrill her, to give her a zing of shared appreciation and an even deeper swell of admiration for his passionate interest.

Maeve spun abruptly as the door opened and in walked the man of her daydreams. "Mr. Dane!"

She instantly adjusted her thrill level.

Don't act like the rest of the swooning women so happy to be in his presence. Just chill. Be normal.

As normal as a twenty-seven-year-old woman with a penchant for wild colors, copious daydreaming and a desperate need to increase her income could be.

He narrowed his gaze at her. She couldn't tell if that was a smirk or a curious smile. "Were you expecting someone else?" He made a show of looking around him as he rolled in his suitcase.

"No. You surp—doesn't matter. How did your interview go?"

He plopped his Louis Vuitton suitcase on the bed and sat beside it. "They wanted to know what one relationship issue we have that I didn't think we'd overcome while here. I mean, what? I don't even know you!"

"You didn't tell them that?"

"Don't worry. I can play the fake better than most." He lay back, stretching his arms out, and Maeve saw the bed was not going to fit them both comfortably. Was the size purposeful? Force the couple having relationship issues to sleep close?

Mercy, she was in too deep. Was it too late to run screaming for the safety of her tidy office files and accept her life would be forwarding phone calls from here on?

"I told them we're have trouble communicating," she offered, then tugged his suitcase from the bed and rolled it to the wall next to hers. "It's been rolling across the ground and the wheels are dirty," she offered to his silent query. "I figured that's what most couples have issue with, yes?"

"I suppose. Good call, Marsha."

She spun and gaped at him.

He winked. "You see? I already know what you're going to say to me. I'd say we're pretty good at communicating."

"Hmph. Every time you call me Marsha I'm going to call you Windfield."

"Where did that one come from? Sounds like a stiff-lipped butler."

"He was the principal at my primary school. It's a very pompous name."

"So you think I'm pompous?"

"No. It's just…" A tease. She didn't want to start out with an argument. This week was going to be stressful enough if they introduced real miscommunication. "I think we'll manage to convince them well enough that we're not on the same page." Her phone pinged, and, setting the book on the bed, she checked the screen. "Reception sent the schedule that starts tomorrow morning at six."

"Not going to work for me. My brain doesn't start functioning until seven or eight at best."

"Then you'll miss breakfast and…a crystal bowl chakra clearing."

Asher closed his eyes and smiled. "Bring me back a cinnamon roll if they serve them. So what are we going to do about the sleeping situation?"

Maeve opened the closet and surveyed the contents. "There's extra blankets and pillows in here. I can sleep on the floor."

Asher sat up, regarding her for the first time since he'd walked into the room. His soft gaze tripped from her shoulders, down her skirt and then back up to what felt like her lips. Suddenly she felt unclothed. Like he could see every line of her body beneath the fitted dress and was calculating…things.

Things she wouldn't mind doing a few calculations on herself.

Seeming to catch himself, he inhaled and looked aside. "You think I'm going to do the chivalrous thing and argue that I wouldn't dream of allowing you to sleep on the floor?"

She could hope for as much. Maeve shrugged.

He made a show of considering it for far too long. "We can share the bed."

"Not a good idea. You take up the whole bed!"

"Yeah, but you're a pixie from the land of Eire." He tried for an Irish accent at the end of the sentence, and it set Maeve's heart to a flutter. "You'll only require a sliver of mattress."

She'd never imagined his attempt at an accent could affect her as if he'd touched her. Right there. On her—

"What's this book? You think you'll have time to read while here?"

Shaking out of a familiar fantasy, she took the book from him. "I never go anywhere without a book. But back to the bed situation, I'm a stretcher when I sleep. Arms out, legs this way and that. There isn't room for both of us in that bed." She tugged down the blankets and a pillow from the closet shelf and tossed them to the floor. "It's late, but I'm still a bit buzzed from the wine on the flight. I think I'll take a walk and check the outside amenities."

"Might I join you?"

Maeve twisted a look over her shoulder. He seemed genuinely interested in accompanying her. And what woman could honestly say no to those glacier blues? "I suppose that is what couples do."

"And we are a couple. I need to walk off the flight and decide whether to take the floor or the bed."

"Maybe we take turns?"

"Possible." He stood before her like a god rising from the depths to command the space and air around her, hair curled haphazardly about his ears and neck—his utter *presence* enveloping her.

Maeve sighed.

Asher quirked a brow, and then there was that knowing wink. Darn it! She'd swooned, hadn't she?

"I'm going to wash up," he said with a nod toward the bathroom. "I'll meet you outside in ten."

"Sure." She pulled out a bright violet sweater from her suitcase, and squeezing by him in the narrow entry, she made it out of the room without another mutinous sigh.

For the next few days she was stuck in a small room that offered only a single bed, with the sexiest man alive. This was either going to be hell, heaven or the worst kind of crazy that would try her every nerve, erogenous zone and mental fortitude.

The sun shone above a stretch of volcanic lava that had hardened over decades to a craggy obsidian frosting. Steam rose up from geothermal pools of assorted sizes and locations across the landscape. The earth and air mixed a heady verdant scent that Asher realized he missed living in the city. The light here was ethereal, at times ineffable. Nature did things to a man. *It cured.* And he was in for the benefits.

"That sky view is not going to stay there forever. I have to get a shot."

He tugged out his phone from an inside suit coat pocket that his tailor had lined with protective material. While Maeve wandered to the railing that edged the vast walkway that meandered throughout the resort grounds, he lined up the shot. "Faking aside, we're going to have to hold hands for this. You've seen my shots." His followers loved the shots of a woman looking toward the scenery while he held her hand. They were sort of his trademark.

Maeve, her choice of purple and peach clothing inadvertently matching the sunset, crossed her arms and shook her head. "I'll pass."

Asher stared at her, agape, then realized his mouth was open and shut it.

"Much as I adore your eye for preserving the perfect shot," she added, "I don't want to be another faceless prop."

She wasn't to be... A prop? How rude. Why wasn't she as amiable as, well—the women in his photos were not... Hmm...

Very well. The fact that he never showed their faces *did* make them into a kind of prop. But they always consented. They understood his medium and were always thrilled to be included when he shared the photos with his followers.

The defiant curve of Maeve's lips softened and she shrugged. "There you go. We've established a relationship issue."

Meager, but it could be useful. Lifting his phone and framing the shot, he took a few, sans Maeve, then turned off his phone and tucked it away. He hadn't plans to post anyway. They'd decided The Art Guys' followers didn't need to know that Asher was at a relationship retreat this week. There would be questions.

He didn't need those questions. The Face was all surface and no depth. And he preferred it that way.

"Your phone is never on," she noted. "I can't count the times I've tried to contact you and you never answer."

"It's..." The thing he'd learned to do after years of watching his parents suffer from the debilitating effects from radiation and electronic frequencies. Thus, the special protective material in his suit coat pockets, and turning off electronics when he wasn't using them. He wanted to be smart. And really, his life was busy enough without being a slave to the constant ring or ping of texts. "Just my way."

He willed her not to question him further. The last person he wanted to spill his guts to was the receptionist who already knew too much about his life as she organized his trips and daily life on the road.

"I've decided to only carry my phone when necessary this week," she said. "I did tell Krew and Joss I'd be available if they had issues. But I've emailed detailed instructions to each of them, along with a schedule, and I also set up daily phone alerts."

"You do like schedules," he noted without realizing that it could be an accusation.

Maeve lifted her chin. "What's wrong with being orderly and respecting others by being on time?"

Was that a dig? So he had a tendency to show up ten or twenty minutes late. Often.

"It's…" she continued. "I know how to do certain things and I like them done my way. Krew and Joss seem to appreciate my assistance."

"They do," he offered, knowing he'd cut her, and angry at himself that he'd done so. "As do I."

"You rarely give me a glance when you're in the office. And my texts go unanswered for days."

"But you always manage to get me to where I need to be and make my life easier for the details you attend to. I'm aware of all you do, sweetie." He winked then because it felt necessary to lighten the mood.

"Thanks, Windfield. I appreciate hearing that."

Touché. Well, they were headed in the correct direction— a couple in need of romance rehab—so he wouldn't let it bother him.

Asher crooked his arm toward her. "I noted the dining room is open all hours. How about we end the day with something decadent."

"More wine? Cheese and crackers?"

She hooked her arm through his, and he felt as if it were

a gift he would be wise to tender carefully. He smirked at her simple pleasures. "I was thinking chocolate and Chantilly cream. I sneaked a look at the menu while on the flight. Thought to preplan an excursion or two. Are you in?"

"You said the magic word."

"Chocolate?"

"Preplan."

It had been a long day with the flight and the anxiety of learning they had to fake being an arguing couple. All Maeve wanted to do was take Asher's arm every chance she got and swoon over him. But to remain undercover they had to assume the ruse—or risk getting kicked out.

In the dining room, Asher sat on a cozy window seat, one leg stretched the length of it and leaning back to study the starry sky through the window that curved from over their heads down to the floor. His suit coat strewn aside, shirt cuffs and top two buttons undone, he raked his fingers through his earthy hair and looked absolutely…

"Stunning," he said.

"Yes," she agreed, and then caught herself in the daydream of tangling her fingers in his hair and inhaling him. *Pay attention!* Maeve glanced upward where he pointed. "Oh, yes, the stained glass." A half circle of stained glass topped the large window that dominated the farthest end of the dining room. It wasn't a scene but rather geometrical shapes in finely detailed arrangement. "The colors are amazing. Royal blue and eggplant. It's a bit too modern for your tastes, yes?"

"It is." A smirk crimped his cheek. Caught her mooning over him again?

Oh, Maeve, control yourself.

The plate she had propped on her lap held a half-eaten

chocolate lava cake surrounded by an ocean of Chantilly cream. She'd eaten all the thick melty chocolate from the middle.

"So." She sat up straight and set her plate on the table. "What's our plan for…" She glanced around the vast dining hall. No cameras in sight, but one never knew. "…talking to you know who?" she whispered.

Asher swung his legs down and patted the cushion beside him. "Slide over, Margo, this sounds conspiratorial. And I do love some intrigue."

While she loved his fanciful nature, she still wasn't sure if his use of incorrect names was all in play or if he really didn't remember hers. He'd called her Maeve on the plane and once at reception. She'd give him a pass for now.

Sliding up beside him, she plucked up his suit coat in the process, folded it and carefully laid it over the back of the seat. Then she cast another look around the dining area, which was elegant and Nordic in design, while the space toward the front of the room was more cafeteria, walk-up and self-serve style. One other couple stood by the ice cream machine talking quietly.

When Asher leaned in she felt him sweep over her like warm sun. His scent, his body heat, his presence. It wasn't like cologne or spice, or any of the tired scents men wore. It smelled like royal violet swirled in earth and rain. She could imagine the color and thought it would suit him well, what with his lightly tanned skin and dark hair.

He whispered, "We are talking about Kichu, right?"

"Yes. And who knows if we're being watched."

"Gotcha. I can do the sly."

"I read the schedule." Lifting her chin straightened her body. The heat wafting from him shimmered through her being, teasing at her self-control. "All classes headed by Mr.

Kichu are taught via Zoom. He only makes a live appearance on the final day."

"That's not going to work for us. We need to get to him sooner. Charm him."

"I'm going to leave the charming to you. I'm the student, remember? But you're right. We can't leave this until the last day. If he's so averse to selling his art, we need to work on him. And see the art. Is it even worth the effort?"

"All art is worth the effort."

"Even Mondrian?" she asked, knowing his utter disgust for the artist's works.

"Such basic colors. So…geometrical." The last word he spoke as if naming a foul substance.

Maeve laughed softly. She did share his penchant for the lush and beautiful. She didn't mind some of Mondrian's less geometric, landscape works, but the colors were *pedestrian*, as she'd once heard Asher state.

"We need to explore the resort, locate his private rooms," she suggested. "Maybe we'll catch him walking somewhere?"

"The resort is huge. Much bigger than I'd expected for the dozen couples staying. It could house hundreds. And there's an underground space. I noticed the drive going down toward the carport. There's a lot of area to cover."

"We can't be caught skulking about."

"Probably not, but if we go as a couple there's always the excuse that we got lost."

"A person can get lost on their own." Why was she trying to talk him out of sharing a sleuthing adventure? Any time spent with him racked up points in her fantasy.

He leaned forward to look at her. "I know you don't need anyone to do your exacting and precise work, darling, but get into character, will you? Love of your life here, remember?"

If only he knew how true she wanted those words to be. And how difficult it was to fake being in love with Asher when really she was a little in love with him already, yet they were at odds, but not really, and, oh—this was getting complicated.

He took her hand and kissed the back of it. All the body heat she'd been feeling emanate from him now gushed from his lips to the back of her hand, infusing her with a giddy inhale. Though, she'd seen him perform the same chivalrous move many a time when introduced to a female client at the office. A tool in The Face's charming arsenal. But still, Maeve was pretty sure his atoms had permeated her skin to forever entangle in her molecular makeup.

"Relax," he said. "We've got this."

Oh, he had some part of her, that was for sure.

Please don't blush, please don't blush!

"We do?"

"We'll case the joint early, before classes begin, and then again late after they've finished."

"Good plan. But you are not an early bird."

"For you, I'll set my alarm. And, you can have the bed tonight. I have occasion to sleep on the floor. It's good for my back."

"Are you sure?"

"I'm not sure about much, but I am sure about one thing. I need this artist to prove my worth to the other guys. And that will require your help." He stood and held out his hand for her to take. "You in?"

She clasped it. "I'm always in for secret spy stuff."

He tugged her to her feet and she tipped forward, catching her palm against his chest. They both looked to the couple by the ice cream machine, who did not notice their awkward and surprise embrace.

"Even couples having difficulties are allowed some intimacy," he offered.

His eyes traced hers, and she relaxed her curled fingers against his shirt, noticing that his heartbeat thundered under her palm. Maeve nodded, unsure what to say that wouldn't see her blurting "I love you!" like some lovesick teenager.

She didn't love him. She admired him. She respected his art aesthetic. And she fantasized about him in a manner that involved shedding clothing amidst tangled sheets. None of that required love.

He tipped up her chin and tilted his head in wonder. "So much in there."

"In where?" she asked innocently.

"Your eyes. They are like paintings. The light is…ever changing. And don't even get me started on your mouth. I like to…well…"

"You see stories in paintings," she rushed out.

"How do you know that?"

She shrugged. "I've seen you stand before a piece of art. I know that feeling. It's the best kind of lost."

"Lost in the story of the paint." He kissed the back of her hand again. "Best we be careful we don't graduate this rehab too quickly, eh, Penelope?"

Was he implying they were getting along? That they had a common interest? Of course they did, and why couldn't that be enough for him to fall to his knees, propose and live happily ever after with her?

Oh, Maeve! She told herself that she should be focusing on her own needs. She must do what she could to show Asher she was a valuable asset to The Art Guys so he could bring a positive report back to Krew and Joss. Increased wages meant the dream of her color consulting business could become a reality. She must not fail!

"Course not." She dropped his hand and smoothed a palm down her skirt. "Until you can remember my name, we've nothing to worry about, Windfield. I'm going back to the room for a shower. I'd appreciate you giving me ten minutes of privacy. I'll take the bed, as offered. See you in the morning?"

He called after her as she strolled off, "Remember, I like cinnamon rolls!"

Already feeling so at ease with her to request she serve him? The notion didn't bother her at all. She'd serve him sweets to sweeten his affections toward her. And she would also prove to him she knew her art, as well as what it was that pleased him. When it came to art, that is.

And maybe her?

Business before pleasure, she reminded herself. Mariane Pemberton would shake her head severely if she saw her daughter kissing up to the boss to gain momentum at work. A woman who relied on a man to achieve success would never truly be an independent force.

Maeve knew she could be that force. And she would find her way to her dreams this week. And if that required kissing up to the boss? Her mother would never have to know.

CHAPTER FOUR

THEIR EARLY-MORNING spy mission was dissuaded by a bright-eyed employee carrying an old-fashioned walkie-talkie. Maeve and Asher had slipped down a dimly lit hallway that didn't appear to lead to any guest-friendly parts of the resort. After they'd tracked in about fifty feet, Maeve realized someone else was in the hallway. She tugged Asher around, and they both looked the smiling employee in the eye.

"Just trying to find an exit," Asher summoned up the lie quickly. "I think we're lost, aren't we, sweetie?"

"I told you we should have turned left back there." Maeve tugged the small backpack the resort had provided over her shoulder. When she noted Asher held his hand open near her thigh she slipped hers into it. "Honey."

Asher's demeanor changed quickly. "You are always picking the wrong way. Why should I take your word?"

Shocked, but suddenly aware of what he was doing, Maeve played along. "You never listen to me. You didn't even get my name right the first weeks we were dating!"

"Oh, come on, Marsha, don't be like that."

"Uh, I'll show you to the outer door," the young girl in green khakis interrupted. She twirled around, expecting them to follow. "The resort is a bit twisty at times. There's nothing down this way but storage rooms."

"He's always getting us lost," Maeve added as they

MICHELE RENAE 45

rounded the turn and the obvious light from outside shone
down the hallway. "Of course, that way."

They thanked the girl and headed outdoors. The employee
called after them, "Stick with the program, guys! It'll get
better! I promise!"

They walked outside to the brisk morning air, which
would warm to a cozy seventy degrees before noon. Maeve
wore a yellow sweater with tiny violets appliquéd around
the neckline above ankle-length green-and-brown-striped
chinos. Around her neck she had on a bright fuchsia scarf
because the day had felt promising, if not daring.

"Failed," she muttered.

They wandered the wood pathway toward a vast patio
area that overlooked a former volcanic field covered in a
soft blanket of emerald moss. It bumped and cragged and
dipped and curved. The terrain was very Seussian. Yet a sign
warned them to stay on the path. Lava fields were fragile
and sharp lava could be concealed by moss.

"Not a failure." Asher slung his suit coat over a shoulder, keeping it in hand with a fingertip. "We ruled out that
section of the resort. We're narrowing down our options."

"You're quite the optimist, Windfield."

"I thought we managed that fake argument well."

"We did," she said with a big smile.

He met her renewed enthusiasm with a fist bump. "As for
my optimism, it comes in handy when standing in an auction room vying against a determined bidder who wants the
one item you need most."

"So it's optimism that nets million-dollar artwork?"

"Always. I rarely lose a piece."

"I think it's that patented charm of yours. You deploy that
toward the opposing bidder and they lose all logic, forget
what they're doing, and you win the bid."

"You think? Can't say I've tried it on a man, but the women…"

She knew he would be as successful charming a man as he was with the women. Asher had a unique appeal that she felt sure most would succumb to. She had, after all. The man had a certain ease that could make anyone feel comfortable, and that was a rare quality to possess, let alone utilize to one's advantage.

Herself, she tended to speak with her clothing and exacting work. She wasn't an extreme introvert. She liked to mingle and talk amongst small numbers of people. It was groups and intense conversations that tended to ratchet up her anxiety. Those were times when she wore jewel colors because they made her feel as if she wore a protective shield.

"I do have to give you credit for seeing me on my feet before seven in the morning." He strode ahead to a bench that overlooked a volcanic spring posted off-limits for bathing, and which captured the rising sunlight in a metallic sheen across its glossy surface. He sat and she joined him.

"It's because of this, isn't it?" She pulled out a box from her backpack and handed it to him. Breakfast was already available at the dining room.

Opening it, he lifted the oversize pastry to his nose to smell and chuckled gratefully. "Oh, you are good."

The cinnamon roll was so fresh it still steamed when he pulled it apart, and she could smell the sugary frosting.

"Did you bring one for yourself?" he asked as he bit into it and moaned with pleasure.

"You're not going to share?"

He paused in his enjoyment and studied the treat, then glanced at her. Was that actual indecision pulling at his face?

"Don't worry." She pulled out another box to reveal inside a fresh *pain au chocolat*. "I'm a chocolate girl."

They toasted with their pastries then sat quietly eating them. Maeve could get used to scenery like this. She'd always lived in a city. Had grown up in Dublin. Then moved to London. When she'd been a child, her parents would pack up the caravan every summer for a week and they'd head off on an adventure, seeing the sights across Ireland. Eagle Point in West Cork had been her favorite because her dad had taught her to fish there. But those blissful summer trips had ended when her mum had rocketed to investing mogul, divorcing Maeve's dad to fulfill her dreams.

Winners never fail, was one of the Mumisms that Maeve could never pry out of her bones.

Maeve had failed with her small business. And her mum wouldn't let her forget it.

Oh, Maeve, maybe now you'll do something sensible. Art is so...subjective. Ethereal. You belong in a solid job where you can rise through the ranks and prove yourself. Marketing, investments, hell, even real estate. Forget about the silly color stuff. See where it got you? You need to apply yourself!

Which meant *prove* herself. Her mum tended to dole out her love and affection through gold stars and ratings for a job well done like some kind of online ordering service. Physical affection was not in Mariane Pemberton's wheelhouse. Likes and dislikes were.

"What are you thinking about?" Asher wiped his fingers on a napkin from inside the box.

That she needed to succeed without asking her mum for another loan.

Maeve set down her empty box. "This scenery is like a painting. It's got an amazing story to it."

"What story does it tell you?"

She closed her eyes, inhaling. Fresh green mixed with a dry rocky tone and a spice of salt from the ocean that was but an hour's drive away. When she opened her eyes, for a few seconds everything was more vivid. It was in that split-second fresh look she discovered so much in art.

"It's an old tale," she said. "Steeped in myth and legend but threaded through with truths." She caught herself in the mad fantasy that had been ingrained in her since she'd learned to read. Most definitely a gene she'd inherited from her bookworm of a father. "Silly of me."

"No, it's not. I like your scenario for this place. Makes a guy imagine things."

"Like what?"

"Like fairy warriors marching along the horizon and ancient evils rising up from the bogs."

Enamored at the man's fantastical musing, she could only nod. Was there more to Asher Dane than being The Face for a billion-dollar art brokerage?

"I should snap a shot," he said.

Maeve's shoulders dropped.

"But I won't." He propped an ankle over his knee and leaned back to look at her. "I'll remember it. Can I ask you something?"

"Go for it." She took the box from him and nestled it in her lap, setting their refuse aside on the bench.

"I assume you don't have a significant other since you are here on this playdate with me. Can't imagine any boyfriend would be happy with such a situation."

"You assume correctly."

"Why is that?"

"What do you mean?"

"You're very pretty. You're smart. You seem to have your wheels on the track, heading in the right direction. What man wouldn't want to date you?"

Hearing her dateability assessment from Asher lifted her, but she wasn't going to read it the wrong way.

Just here on a fake date, she reminded herself. *Don't let your heart get involved.*

"I don't need to always be in a relationship to enjoy my life."

"Nor do I. But having someone to share life with does make it more fun. Interesting."

It did. Because had she been sitting here on the bench alone the landscape wouldn't have been quite so vibrant or her mood so light.

"I've recently had some bad luck on the dating front," she confessed. "I know it shouldn't put me off, and it doesn't, but I guess a streak of caution colors my life lately."

"Anyone who broke your heart never deserved the chance at it in the first place."

"That's very kind." And something a professional charmer would say. But, oh, to find a man who subscribed to such a platitude. "I broke off a relationship last year because the guy couldn't look up from his gaming console long enough to acknowledge I was there."

No matter what loud colors she had worn, she'd never broken through that man's wall. And she'd realized there was nothing she could do to her exterior to make herself pretty enough. A failure, certainly.

"I don't understand the preoccupation with those digital games," Asher said. "Some people literally live online. It's sad. And don't begin to compare getting lost in a painting to a computer screen, as one client insisted to me. They are not the same thing. Art is real. It lives and breathes. So much light there."

Maeve wanted to tilt her head against Asher's shoulder

and revel in their shared outlook on art, but she wasn't that irrational.

"But you must date more often than yearly?"

She sighed. "The most recent guy… We went on one date. I thought it went well. We shared common interests. He was an avid cyclist, and I looked forward to getting back into biking should we see more of each other. We'd exchanged info. He'd promised to text me. Days went by and he didn't, so I texted him. I finally figured out he was ghosting me."

"That's rough."

"Guess I wasn't good enough for him either. Maybe it's wise if I stick with the fake dating, eh? No commitment. All the fun?"

"Have we had any fun yet?"

"I thought our spying mission was daring and adventurous."

"That was beginner level. It'll only get more exciting. Promise."

"I look forward to it. We have couples' yoga today. What's more exciting than that?" She caught him rolling his eyes. "I know. But we're playing our roles, yes? We'll go on another spy mission this evening."

"Yoga it is. And wasn't there something about pottery later this week? Such adventure."

His sarcasm was not lost on her. "I can switch it out for container gardening, if you prefer."

"Let's stick with the pottery. Maybe I can try my hand at recreating a Grecian vase. What I wonder is, how do all these crazy classes improve one's relationship?"

"I think it's to do with working together. Sharing experiences. I guess we'll find out."

"I enjoy spending time with you."

"You…do?"

He nodded and stood, seemingly unaware of her startled reaction. He enjoyed spending time with her? Same. But what did that mean? Was there the possibility they might become something more than workmates faking it?

"Of course," he replied and gestured that they walk toward the resort. "You always bring along the best treats." With a wink, he wandered ahead.

Maeve's shoulders dropped. As did her heart. So she was a mere receptionist here on vacation as well? Organizing his life in the background? Of course, nothing more than a fake.

Best she remember her position and focus on what she came here to accomplish. Showing Asher she was worthy of a promotion by helping him secure a new artist.

An individual class, divided by women and men, was scheduled before yoga. Maeve had been initially uncomfortable sitting amongst the dozen women in a circle, each with a notebook on their laps. The moderator had guided them through questions to ask about themselves, and they quietly scrawled notes.

Thinking this was going to be about her relationship with Asher—make that *fake* relationship—Maeve had decided she'd have to fake write as well. Until the questions came.

Are you proud of yourself?

Have you accomplished what you want to achieve?

What does your future look like?

With or without your partner?

Do you feel as though you rely on your partner for happiness?

Heavy stuff. But also, it did make her think. For a flicker in time, she had been proud of herself. She had accomplished what she'd set out to achieve. Opening the shop, along with Lucy, blocks down from where she lived. She'd had the rent paid for a year, the shelves had been stocked, the sign hung on the window. And then the pandemic had settled like a dark cloud over small businesses. That accomplishment had quickly turned to a failure that hung around her shoulders like a boulder on a chain.

Her mum had only echoed her failure.

You're my daughter. Where's the Pemberton ambition?
In there for sure, Mum.

But while Maeve was forward-thinking and focused like her mother, she didn't have the same energetic, almost maniacal drive to put herself into any situation that might see her advancing. She was more subtle, quieter. An introvert who could exist amongst the extroverts, but never truly peel away her colorful mask. Her inner world was nothing like the colors she wore on her body. This afternoon's soft heather yoga pants and mint paisley top echoed her eagerness to learn but also to not be seen. To blend into the foliage that surrounded the resort.

When the moderator instructed the women to look up from their notebooks, straighten and breathe, Maeve realized how hunched over she'd been. Literally curled upon herself as she'd scribbled *failure* and *try again* on the paper. She did need to breathe. To try again. As weird as it seemed, this vacation was a chance for her to prove to The Art Guys that she could take on fieldwork. Which would provide the financial means to getting her one step closer to her dream.

But was she ready for field work? Only once, she'd held a paddle at an art auction. She hadn't won; she suspected her boss had known that before even allowing her the task but had wanted to give her the experience. She'd been a receptionist cum gallery attendant at that place. Hosting gallery showings had taught her how to interact with clients and to allow her art knowledge to shine. She had only a year of art school under her belt. However, she was capable. But she'd not had the opportunity to put that knowledge to real world use at her current job.

She and Asher needed to find and convince Tony Kichu to sell his art. And—she had the sudden thought—if *she* could be the person to do that convincing it would go a long way in showing her bosses she deserved a promotion.

In a manner, she was using this trip, and the fake relationship with Asher, to get ahead. Her mum would be so proud. Yet it didn't sit quite right in a part of her.

Asher was using her as well. He needed to be in a couple to attend this event and suss out the elusive Tony Kichu. The man needed this win. It would be selfish to take it from him.

As if she even could.

Oh, Maeve, you are capable.

It's balancing that capability with the desire to see the one man she looked up to shine.

"That's a wrap, ladies! The couples' session begins in half an hour. Help yourself to refreshments at the back of the room."

The women swarmed to the fresh-squeezed juices and fruit jelly mooncakes, while Maeve wandered to the window that overlooked the moss and lava field that Asher had deemed worthy of a fantasy story. She wondered if he'd had to answer the same questions in his session. Now, there was a man who was proud of himself and his accomplishments. He'd never been shot down and forced to start from scratch. The Art Guys was a billion-dollar enterprise. She'd seen their balance sheet.

Though she was aware he'd had to leave the brokerage for a few years before they'd hired her. The office guys were hush-hush on the details behind that. It couldn't have been due to a failure. Asher had easily stepped back into the lime-light and had taken on the role as The Face.

Asher deserved all the fame, accolades and social media likes that came his way, but she wondered if he ever felt as though something were missing. Had he accomplished what he desired? Was he fulfilled? Did he want a *real* relationship?

"I'll bring that to Tony," a voice sounded from across the room, alerting Maeve.

The moderator took an envelope from someone and left the room. Sparked by her desire to prove herself, and a hefty helping of intrigue, Maeve tucked her notebook into her backpack. Peeking out into the hallway, she spied the moder-ator and waited until she turned at the end of the long stretch of windowed hallway. Then she slipped quickly down the way and repeated her action, waiting for the woman to turn. She followed for a few seconds, when finally she heard an elevator ding. Rushing to spy the elevator doors closing, she saw that there were no floor numbers on the outer keypad.

"This has to be the way to the mystery man," she whis-pered with a smile. "Score."

He was not dressed for stretching out on a yoga mat. Suit coat abandoned and shoes removed, Asher sat cross-legged, fac-ing Maeve, who also looked uncomfortable, but not because of her clothing. She could move with ease. Her dusty purple leggings and paisley green cropped top emphasized every slight curve on her petite body. The light in the window-walled two-story room was delicious, made even more inter-esting as it landed on Maeve. Her thick raven hair gleamed with traces of garnet and was pulled into a high ponytail. Those severe black bangs and lush long lashes seemed to glint in the light as if touched by fairy dust. And—mercy, those lips of hers. Bow-shaped, deep cherry smoothing to a darker crimson. Hugged by apostrophes. They were quickly becoming an obsession of his.

The last thing he'd obsessed over was winning a bid on an oil painting by Pre-Raphaelite artist John Everett Millais. *Ferdinand Lured by Ariel* had been part of a private collection suddenly put up for auction. Asher had bid against museums, dealers and unrevealed collectors calling in across the globe. That day he'd spent more money than he had on any previous auction—his client's money, that is. He'd been given the opportunity to sit with the painting depicting a scene from Shakespeare's *The Tempest* for nearly an hour before the transfer team had arrived to box it up and ship it to Romania, the country it now called home.

Maeve's lips were more compelling than that painting's mysterious green sylph whispering in Ferdinand's ear. Whatever she whispered? He would listen.

This class was called Heart Chakra Trust. And while they waited for everyone to get into position, he leaned forward and asked Maeve, "What's a heart chakra?"

"It's right here." She placed a palm over her breasts at the center of her chest.

"And what does it do?"

She smiled. "It's the place where love resides."

"I knew that." He sat back, upright, wrists on his bent knees. "Good, then. Let's get on with this."

The sooner they finished this obnoxious exercise, the faster he could remove himself from this strange situation and go in search of Kichu's private apartments. He didn't mind the fake relationship, but he'd not expected classes where he had to examine his emotions and inner pride, like the all-male class he'd been in earlier. That sort of stuff was safely locked and sealed. Though, he had stalled on the *Are you proud of yourself?* question. Proud of using his good looks to move ahead in the world? Hardly.

Yet, how to step away from the mask and be the real Asher Dane? Some days he wasn't even sure who that man was.

"Class, we're going to engage in an exercise in trust and quiet acceptance this morning. Everyone move closer, bracketing your legs to the sides of your partner's hips."

Shuffling on the mats and a few hisses of annoyance accompanied Asher's hesitation. He looked to Maeve, who appeared flustered and unsure. The move would place them in a position he rarely even assumed with a lover.

He playfully nudged her calf. "For the fake, yes?"

She nodded. "Of course."

They gently moved toward one another until they had about a foot of space between their chests. Maeve's legs draped over his, and he relaxed his to either side of her hips. To say he could feel the sexual charge between them was not a lie. How could a man, any man, position himself so close to a woman and not feel some desire? And that he already found himself passionately obsessed with her lips did not make the situation any less awkward.

There was something so otherworldly about Maeve. And yet, not? She was…earthy. But also beyond.

The thought flashed Asher's memory back to an art history professor who had insisted Asher would never succeed in the art world because he was too surface level. He needed to get earthy and ugly. To dig his fingers into art and let it subsume him.

Earthy and ugly disturbed him. Unless it was packed in cherry red lips and mismatched patterns and colors. Maeve was the furthest from ugly. And her beyond-comprehension earthiness was irresistible.

"Now," the instructor said in a soothing voice as she

walked amongst the couples positioned on mats around the sun-drenched room, "place a palm on your partner's heart chakra."

Maeve lifted her hand and asked, "May I?"

"Of course." She could touch him whenever she liked. Though he sensed her nervousness. Out of his peripheral vision, Asher could see the other couples doing so, some reluctantly.

When Maeve's hand landed softly on his chest it felt as though he'd been blasted by a magical force that surged through his body and electrified every part of his being. He'd been zapped by an earth witch who wore secrets on her lips.

And he liked it.

"You can put your hand on me," she suggested shyly.

Shaken out of his wonder, he lifted his hand and held it near Maeve's chest. The top she wore was cut to just above her breasts. Not overly large or too small. Just the right size. He'd have to rest the heel of his hand on them... It felt intrusive, and he didn't want to force the touch on her simply because they were playing at being a couple.

All of a sudden she took his wrist and pressed his palm to her chest. "It's okay," she said. "I'm a big girl. I know what we're doing here."

Right. Just faking it. But...really? This touch did not preach removed observation to him.

The instructor called, "Now, rest your foreheads against one another, and close your eyes. Simply feel your partner's breath. Their heartbeats. Their beingness."

A hush fell over the room. Asher looked to Maeve, who smiled sweetly then bowed her head forward, which he reciprocated. With his forehead touching hers in another zap of bright energy, he closed his eyes and whispered, "We can do this."

"No talking!" the instructor called. "This is a silent communion of your souls."

Justly admonished, he took some solace from Maeve's suppressed giggle. It was silly, their position, palms to each other's chests and foreheads touching. But also...

Maeve's warmth and softness permeated his skin. The faintest scent of vanilla was not like perfume, but rather as if it exuded from a plant in a wild jungle. Raw and dark and a little like Maeve herself. Her breaths moved his hand against her breasts. A strand of her hair tickled his chin. Their noses almost touched, but he tried not to let that happen. Because there were too many sensory alarms going off in him. Touching Maeve was anything but calm inducing.

Yet, the longer they sat there, the subtle throat clearings and bodies shifting around them faded, and it grew into an intimate moment of just the two of them. Maeve's heartbeat thrummed against his palm. It slowed, growing calmer. Relaxing.

Did she trust him? She could. He would never do anything to harm Maeve. How did she feel sitting so close and touching him? Could she possibly move beyond the fakeness of all of it and step into the role of...?

His lover? A girlfriend?

Asher wasn't sure why that thought had arisen. He didn't want an involvement with Maeve.

Did he?

Oh, we know.

Maybe he did desire something more with Maeve. *Our* Maeve?

His Maeve.

Sensing she sat still with eyes closed, breaths measured, Asher had to suppress the intriguing thrill of whispering, "What are you feeling right now?"

Did she feel the electrical surge that seemed to move from her fingers through his chest and down his wrists, rocketing up his arms and to his chest? His entire body warmed, and it wasn't from exertion. He knew this feeling. The instant shock of attraction and—desire.

Maeve was not his type of woman. She was not tall and curvaceous. She did not style her hair and primp her face with cosmetics designed to draw the eye. Though her red lipstick always hit him right in the—well, *that* erogenous zone. She was dark and mysterious. Quiet on the inside. Yet she bathed herself in color. Beautiful but strange. She wasn't compelled by trends, or even matching colors. She was simply different. And so compelling.

Suddenly a whistle blew, and the instructor announced, "Kiss alert!"

The couples all looked to one another for explanation, and the moderator, with a laugh, explained that occasionally throughout the week a whistle would be blown. That indicated the couples should kiss. An effective means to re-establishing connection. There was no right or wrong, just that they made an attempt, even if they were angry with one another.

Asher looked to Maeve, whose expression bordered on horror. "We don't have to," he said. "It's…"

It was what? Crazy to want to kiss a woman he was attracted to? Not at all. Though, to do so in front of others, and for the first time, did feel uncomfortable.

And Maeve's look screamed *Get me out of here!*

"This is weird," she muttered. Their hands were still pressed against one another's chests, their heads still close. "I mean, I like weird things."

"Is that so?" He'd suspected as much about her. "I can make it weirder."

With that assumed permission, Asher kissed her quickly. A smack to her lips. He barely had a second to register the connection. To wonder if she'd closed her eyes. To decide whether the apostrophes crimped even deeper or smoothed away.

Maeve sat back and touched her mouth. Her wide eyes were...not smiling.

Asher swore under his breath. "I'm so sorry. I shouldn't have..."

"Please don't apologize for a kiss," she pled, and gripped one of his hands. "That'll make it even weirder." She looked around. One couple was still engaged in a kiss. The others were gathering their mats to return to the cubbies.

"It's what needed to happen. Sorry—" He caught his mistake. "I mean... Right. It's part of the fake. Uh... Let me help you up." He took her hand and together they gathered and rolled up the mats.

What had he done? He shouldn't have—and yet, he couldn't regret it because that wasn't his style. He'd done it. He hadn't even taken a moment to feel it, to really enjoy her mouth...

He should have paid more attention!

On their way out of the gymnasium, Maeve shouldered up beside him but didn't say anything. What to say to a surprise kiss that hadn't been asked for? That she might have construed as an affront? Might she have liked it?

Asher raked his fingers through his hair and blew out a breath. "Whew! That was unexpected."

So intense. And not even in a sexual way. With his hand over her heart, he had connected with Maeve. Until that stupid whistle spoiled the moment.

"It was weird," she said, "but I'm not upset about it. In case you thought you did something wrong."

With that, she walked ahead of him, heading toward the dining room.

Not upset? Whew! He'd taken a chance. It had been for show. But really? He'd wanted to kiss her. And while it had been no more than a second of physical contact, he had felt the electricity between them.

Next time—and he hoped for that next time—it wouldn't be but a flash.

CHAPTER FIVE

"It's up ahead around the corner." Maeve was distracted by Asher's violet, rainy scent as they slinked down the darkened hallway. It was deep and lush and made her want to lick him in inappropriate places on his body. And she wasn't even standing that close to him. His scent had literally infused itself into her pores during the chakra class, and she now carried him on her.

What that session had inspired in her libido!

She had felt Asher to her very core. Yet that feeling had gone beyond mere sexual desire to wanting to reach in and see if she could touch his soul. To push aside his outer shell and breathe in the inner wonder that she knew resided within. A wonder she'd witnessed as he'd gotten lost in a painting. One that was burgeoning as she got to know him better here at the retreat.

But she mustn't read too much into that intimate ten minutes in which they'd been so close some religions might insist they immediately marry.

And then that silly whistle! She wasn't offended that he'd kissed her quickly. It was the apology for the kiss that still bothered her. Sure, he was being a gentleman and trying to go along with the instructions while also not intruding on her too intimately. They had been playacting, after all.

She mustn't allow her heart—which had been touched

by Asher—to forget that. Because her focus was on getting ahead and gaining notice from her bosses. But not *that* kind of notice.

"Good job on the spying," he said as he pressed his back to the wall and then dared a look around the corner. "Clear."

The elevator dinged, and he suddenly grabbed her hand and skirted her back down the hallway in the direction they had come. They just made the corner as someone walked right by the spot where they had been standing.

Maeve's heart thundered. Asher still held her hand. Did he realize that? She clutched it, not wanting to let go. Hoping to restart that intense chemistry that had ignited between them on the yoga mat. Who cared about a spy mission? She was holding The Face's hand!

"Must be housekeeping. They're pushing a cart. Let's abandon this mission for now." He let go of her hand and directed her toward the main hallway that would lead to their room. "I'll take a look tomorrow morning."

"We've got more classes in the morning."

"Please, no more chakra touching."

"You didn't enjoy that session?"

"I…" He paused and took her in. If a look could feel like a hand over her heart, his did so. Falling into his eyes was not a hardship. And she didn't care anymore if she did blush. "I did enjoy it. It was intense. But as you can see from my outfit, I didn't pack for extracurricular floor activities. And what was up with that kiss whistle?"

She was glad he'd brought it up. That apology! Way to spoil the moment!

"It'll happen again," she said. "It took us by surprise. We should have planned for something like that."

"Who plans to be suddenly forced into intimacy with another person at the shrill peal of a whistle?"

"We were already deep into intimacy before that whistle."

"True. It was different, yes?" He moved along to walk slightly in front of her, turning to walk backward. "I mean it was so… I don't know how to describe it. It felt… You know."

Was he implying that he'd felt the same as she had? That it had gone beyond a sexual touch and into that soul-touching moment the instructor had implied could happen?

"I know," she agreed, hoping they were talking about the same experience. Maeve chuckled as they neared their room door. "It's okay. It was part of the fake. I didn't mind the kiss." Quick as it had been. Could next time be a little longer? Pretty please?

He paused before the door with the key card in hand, his eyes searching hers. "You sure?"

She nodded. "We can kiss again the next time the whistle blows."

"Like trained seals?"

She hadn't thought of it that way. Was he really put off by having to kiss her?

"Sorry." He slashed the card and pushed the door open to allow her to wander inside. "I generally don't kiss a woman without permission. It was awkward. Felt intrusive."

"So you want to fake it next time? Put our heads close and…? Nothing?" She shrugged. "Weird."

"You said you liked weird."

"I do, but I'm getting the feeling it's too weird for you. If you have something against kissing me—"

She turned to find he stood right there. She had to adjust her position a few inches backward. Tall, imposing, yet smelling like earth and rain. She couldn't read his mood. Was he angry, confused, bordering a dull mossy green? Unwilling to kiss her again? She hadn't expected a relationship out of this adventure, and they had agreed to fake it. However, most couples *did* kiss.

"I don't want you to think that I kiss like that all the time," he finally said. "It was a reaction. But if I have your permission, in the future I promise that any whistle alert will see that you get properly kissed."

Maeve's jaw dropped open.

Asher touched her under the chin and pushed her mouth closed. His patented charm twinkled in his eyes. "I'll take that as permission."

"It is," she said quickly, then inwardly kicked herself for unloosing her silly desperation. "I mean, of course, we're just trying to make things look good. A proper kiss is what is required to show them we're a couple."

"Good, then." He walked around her to his makeshift bed on the floor and grabbed some things from his suitcase. "My turn at the bathroom first. I did think to bring along swim trunks."

They had plans to soak in one of the geothermal pools. A delicious reward for an awkward yet fulfilling session of touch, sudden kisses and intrigue.

CHAPTER SIX

THERE WERE STRICT rules for entering the natural hot springs located behind the resort. A thorough shower and scrub—naked—in the shower rooms. Maeve slipped on her one-piece, which was a bright mixture of primary colors, and wandered out to claim one of the half dozen small pools unoccupied by another couple.

The pool, formed by seismic activity, was about three feet deep, lusciously warm and fringed with the scruffy turf that coated the manicured grounds. Sulphur tinged the air, but it had to compete with the verdant foliage and the fresh air unhampered by city fumes and pollution. Flat stones were placed here and there around the edge, obviously to set things on. Sinking into the hot springs defined bliss. The water was a fusion of shades from sky blue to dusted turquoise and a deeper fir green. The steam rising would give her a good facial, that was for sure.

After settling deep into the warm water, she was startled by Asher's approach. He ran toward the pool, looking ready to dive in. She put up a palm to stop him—

He froze at the pool's edge. Flashed her a charming grin. Then slowly lowered himself into the pool. Mercy, the man... Had. A. Physique. Those workouts she scheduled for him certainly paid off. Indulging in the eye candy of abs and pecs—how those muscles strapped his body and moved as if choreography with every step he took.

He closed his eyes and tilted his head against the smooth-edged stone. "Now, this is how a man takes advantage of a work trip. You like?"

Oh, did she like.

"I plan to come out here every day," Maeve said. "Twice if possible. I don't think I've taken a vacation."

Asher settled across from her in the pool. Their legs paralleled one another. The eight-foot-wide pool was as cozy as a hot tub.

"Ever?" he asked.

She shrugged. "Not since I was a kid. We would pack up the caravan every summer and visit our relatives and any national park we could find."

"I do love your Irish brogue. Faint, but it's colorful. What made you decide to move to London permanently? Why not Ireland?"

Because Ireland, while steeped with childhood memories, was merely a birthplace to her. She had no friends or close family there now.

"Our last vacation was right before my graduation. It was the trip that Mum and my da decided to tell me they were getting a divorce. Mum is a go-getter, and she had turned Da's expectations of what a wife should be on its head. He wanted her to wear an apron, cook, clean and greet him with a smile when he got home from work. She felt trapped and held back. And had begun to make a splash in the investing world. So they split."

"I'm sorry. Divorce must be rough for a kid."

"If I had been younger, I think it would have gutted me. Even at eighteen the experience was rough. But I've come to realize they do still love one another in their own ways, yet living together wasn't possible for them. Da loves his slightly bohemian, devil-may-care lifestyle. And Mum loves the challenge of obliterating the corporate ladder. Also, she moved to New York City that autumn. She loves the US."

"And you? What location do you prefer?"

Maeve shrugged. "I'm easy. London is lovely but expensive. But so are cities in the States. And Ireland doesn't call to me in any meaningful manner. I guess I prefer the place where I can put down roots and build my own business."

"And what sort of business do you intend to build?"

"I had a business. Opened it exactly one month before the pandemic. I don't have to tell you how difficult it was for small businesses, especially new ones without a lot of marketing and buzz, to survive at that time."

Asher shook his head. "Didn't last?"

"Two months in we had to close up shop."

"We?"

"My flatmate, Lucy, and me. And we were never able to come back from that. I had to liquidate and sell everything to pay my mother back for the loan she gave me."

The failed shop had sucked up all her savings. She'd immediately handed over the money from what she'd been able to sell to her mum to cover the loan. And had received a warning that she must succeed. All Pemberton women succeeded at their endeavors.

Not all Pemberton women had lived through an economically devastating pandemic when trying to start a business.

Still, it was difficult to brush off her mother's disappointment. And she didn't intend to. She would rise again.

"That's rough. I'm sorry," Asher offered. "And then you found The Art Guys? I want to say I'm happy that your business closed because had it not, you'd never have landed with us, but that doesn't sound so positive as it should."

"I'll take it. I needed the work, and I did study mixed arts at Westminster, along with night classes for business. The Art Guys is a good place for me. For now."

"You still have dreams of owning a business? What sort of business was it you had?"

"A color shop. We called it Fuchsia."

"And what does a color shop sell?"

"Color! We sold paints, pens, markers, paper, decorative items, everything a person could utilize to add color to their home. My goal was to eventually start a consulting service where I, acting as a color therapist, could redo a person's home or specific room by adding color to it. It's my thing."

"Apparently it is. I don't think I've ever seen you in sub-dued grays or blacks."

"I know my clothing isn't to your taste."

Asher made show of gaping at her.

"I've seen the way you look at me, a little confused, some-times shocked. My fashion sense isn't for everyone. I tend to express myself through color." Unlike her mother, who wore the subdued grays and blacks like a religion.

"Your fashion is strange to me. But it's also intriguing. Like you're a puzzle that needs to be solved."

Maeve had never heard herself described that way. She liked it. Not quite readable on the surface, but if a person spent a little time sorting through her pieces…?

She slyly turned to look over Asher's relaxed face. His hair was a masterpiece of tease, the curly brown locks de-manding a woman run her fingers through it. So handsome. And kind, even if he was a bit self-centered. It was because he was so focused on his work. And maybe some entitle-ment too. He had worked hard for his money and deserved every cent. The money didn't appear to corrupt him. He didn't own a splashy sportscar that she was aware of, and nor did he own a castle or flash bling on his wrist. He kept a small apartment in London—she knew; she authorized the monthly pricey rent payments for him—because he traveled all the time and hadn't the need for a real home. His focus was on art and putting it out there for the world to appreciate.

"So have you always lived in London?" she asked. She recalled their briefing on the flight here. "Did you say your parents moved to Bath?"

"Yes. My parents…they have been ill for a good portion of my life."

"Oh, I'm sorry."

"But they're doing better now. The move was what they needed."

He didn't seem to want to expound. Was that the reason he'd been forced to leave The Art Guys? She knew he'd taken extended time off before she'd been hired, but she didn't know why.

Teasing her lower lip with a tooth, Maeve vacillated on asking him.

"What?" Asher prompted. "I know you've got something burning in there, Marsha."

She didn't mind the stupid name. It was starting to feel like an endearment. Their own pet names for one another. Marsha and Windfield. Happily ever after.

Oh, Maeve. Get your head in the game!

Because this was just a game.

"I was pondering whether it would be okay to ask about your parents' illnesses?"

"It's…" He tilted his head against the turfed edge of the pool. His hair glistened with water droplets, and his muscled shoulders rose like tiny islands from the water. "It sounds crazy to most people, so I generally keep it private."

"Oh. I don't want to intrude."

"Let's talk about you." He leaned forward, floating his

arms before him. "That swimsuit you're wearing is totally Maeve with the bright colors. Though it does echo shades of Mondrian."

She laughed. "I know! Not your favorite artist. I like the color blocking. The green gives me energy, and the blue is grounding."

"That's interesting. I've heard you refer to the colors as an emotion. What is it with you and color?"

If the man could see her London flat he would understand. Or go mad from the utter craziness of it.

"Let's say," she said, "I have a ridiculous obsession with color."

"Ah!" He assumed a dramatic tone and quoted, "'Thank you for curing me of my ridiculous obsession with love.'"

"You love *Moulin Rouge* too?"

"One of the best musical movies I've seen. And it is certainly color drenched. So have you always been into color?"

That he shared her favorite movie was exciting. And intriguing. He wasn't the sort she'd expect to enjoy such a wild, bohemian movie, and a musical at that. If she could have pinned a favorite movie to him she may have guessed something a little more action intense.

"I'd say so," she said. "As a kid I was always coloring and painting my things. I'd get teased in school because my trousers didn't match my shirt. I didn't care. It's how I express myself. Over the years that obsession turned into the desire to share my fascination with others."

"Thus, the color shop."

"Exactly."

"Well, I hope you can find that dream again. But as I've said, if that means losing you at The Art Guys then I won't hope too hard."

"I was thankful to find this job at the height of the pandemic madness." She recalled the guys mentioning that their previous receptionist had quit for fear of catching something—anything—and had become a literal hermit. "Though, you must know I've spoken with Krew. I'm looking to move up and possibly earn a raise from you guys."

"Anything can happen."

"You think?"

"Yes, but I mean, we are known as the Art *Guys*."

Maeve nodded. Had she expected to be included in such an exclusive club? Perhaps. She simply needed a means to make more money so the dream Asher half hoped could come true for her could be accomplished.

"I get it." She fanned her steam-moistened face. "I've no field experience with The Art Guys to prove myself."

"You have to start somewhere. If the art business is really what you are interested in, I'm sure we can figure something out. But I sense your color shop is more in your wheelhouse."

"It is. But I'm losing Lucy as a flatmate next month, and I'm beginning to feel a little desperate—oh. I shouldn't have said that."

"I understand, Maeve. If we're not compensating you properly for your much appreciated work, I'll have a talk with Krew."

"The pay is fair. For a receptionist. But my dreams will never come true unless I start earning more. I've considered trying my hand at influencing, like Lucy does. She does makeup tutorials and—you wouldn't believe the cash she earns from that."

"Perhaps you could do color tutorials?"

"I've considered that. But I'm not a camera girl. There's a reason I avoid the camera crew on filming days. I don't possess the charm and unabashed ease that you do. It's necessary to be an influencer."

"I like you as you are. Though I've wondered if your quiet manner was because I've done something wrong."

"What?"

He shrugged. "You never meet my gaze when I'm in the office. And your smiles are so rarely directed toward me."

"Oh. I..." Was only ever trying not to swoon over the man! And here she'd thought him a bit standoffish as well, never trying to make conversation with her! "I'm not offended by anything you've done. Trust me."

"Good to know. We make a great team, eh? That spur-of-the-moment save we did this morning when we were discovered was spot-on."

"For someone who favors honesty, I did find lying along with you a bit too easy. This whole trip is a big lie."

"It's an adventure, Maeve. Look at it that way. And we may even learn something about ourselves along the way."

"Like how to connect with another person's heart chakra?"

"That was a weird session."

"It will get weirder. We have pottery hugging on the schedule."

"I can't imagine what that will entail."

"I can. And it sounds kinky."

Asher's laughter was throaty and deep. Joining in with him felt natural, and Maeve was able to brush aside the fact that she'd revealed her selfish desire to make more money by accompanying him here. Just enjoy the holiday? She could do that. Because she was learning more about the man who she'd crushed on for years.

Asher moved to the center of the pool and leaned in. "Don't look now but everyone is staring."

Maeve had to force herself not to scan the other pools where couples were bathing. "Do you think it's odd that we're laughing?"

"No, I don't—oh. Right. We're supposed to have issues. Hmm, good call, Marsha."

"Because you never get the directions right," she admonished, but playfully.

"Oh, yeah?" He splashed as he moved backward and pushed up to sit on the turf edge of the pool. "Well, you—" his voice raised with each word "—are always doing that—" he stood and then gestured to the sky "—that thing!"

Maeve caught his quick wink and realized this was another play. And she was in for the match.

"Oh, I'll give you a thing! That thing is—" she levered herself out of the pool and grabbed a towel "—something you will never understand!"

Out the corner of her eye she noticed a woman in one of the pools nod in solidarity. *Right, girl, you tell him.*

"I can't even look at you right now." Asher turned and marched away.

Realizing she would need to follow to get to the same door, Maeve did follow, stabbing her finger in his wake. "Maybe if you spent more time looking at me!"

Where that one had come from, she didn't know. A crazy thing to say. But she was acting right now.

Suddenly Asher turned at the edge of the grounds where the lawn met the back patio. His eyes were fiery. The water droplets on his body glistening. Who could ever be mad at such a fine specimen of man?

"I'm always looking at you," he said so quietly that only they two could hear. "But you never seem to notice."

With that, he marched inside the resort.

Maeve lowered the hand in which she held the towel. His words had entered her chest as if he'd forced them in with mere thought energy. She *did* notice him. Always.

But he'd always looked at her?

Was that a part of the act or had he been speaking a truth just now?

CHAPTER SEVEN

ONCE OUT OF a quick shower, Asher tugged on a plush robe and wandered past the small bed and onto the patio. The evening had provided focused classes for individuals on recognizing emotional signals in their partner and understanding love languages. It had been…more interesting than he'd expected. He'd had taken a quick meal in the dining hall with the other men and then they'd returned to another class on personal growth.

Maeve arrived in the room and veered immediately into the bathroom. He hadn't seen her since their soak in the hot spring. Had he inadvertently offended her during their impromptu argument? Hurt her?

Of course he had. He'd just taken a class that had taught him to recognize an upset woman.

He hadn't meant to yell at her. It had been part of the fake relationship. But that last statement—that he'd always noticed her—had been a truth that had slipped off his tongue.

The woman had scratched his surface. A surface that was clean and polished and made to charm others. The Face. How he hated that moniker at times. The Face wasn't concerned with how he made others feel, because he had developed a patented charm that generally left those in his wake smiling.

He'd certainly not been so shallow and egotistic when he'd started the brokerage with the guys. It had all seemed to explode out of him after he'd returned following the years away to care for his parents.

The Face would never yell at a woman, be it fake or otherwise. And The Face would most certainly never expose his real feelings to a woman.

Or have to wonder if he'd hurt her.

An apology to Maeve was necessary.

What a crazy trip this was turning out to be. He'd never expected the emotional aspects of it all. That he would struggle with his attraction to their receptionist as much as he was. But, yes, he was attracted to her. And with the two of them sleeping in a room together, it seemed like a perfect time to explore that attraction.

But what would Maeve think about such exploration? Was he merely reacting to his own libido? His pattern was always the same. See a pretty woman. Discover if she was interested. Kiss. Sex. So long. On to the next one. Was this the same thing again?

Something told him this was different.

And that awful kiss! It had been so quick. Forced. Unpracticed. And though she'd said she hadn't minded, he did. Never would he kiss a woman like that. He truly did want to show her what a proper kiss from Asher Dane was like. Which led him right back to his consternation that he was attracted to his receptionist.

Had he always been so? Sure, it annoyed him that she'd not paid him the proper attention whenever he stopped into the office. Was that because…?

"You really are interested in her," he muttered.

Startled by a commotion behind him, Asher turned to find Maeve standing in the open patio doorway, one foot dangling over the doorjamb. She'd changed into summery green striped pajama shorts and top that were speckled with bold red flowers. A crime against any artistic aesthetic, but apparently her means of expressing herself. What did the stripes and roses say about her mood right now?

"You can take the bed tonight," she offered.

"I won't think of it. It's yours. The floor is good for my back, as I've said."

"I don't believe one word of that. But… I'm done arguing with you for the night."

"Maeve, please." He rushed to her. "You know that was a fake argument back at the pool?"

She nodded. "I know. We're playacting. I'm just…" She faked a yawn against the back of her hand and turned. "It's been a long day. Those evening classes fried my brain."

"It's been a lot to take in."

Asher caught her hand and stepped across the threshold. He wanted to pull her into his arms, but it felt intrusive, too possessive. Despite the class, he couldn't read her emotions right now. She could be tired. Yet he intuited part of her had been offended by their argument, nonsensical and as fake as it had been.

"Some of what I said wasn't fake," he said softly. "About always looking at you." He winced. "Does that sound creepy?"

She chuckled softly and sat on the bed. "A little."

"I mean, I see you, Maeve. You're…beautiful." And a little strange. "You're smart and you have your finger on the office operations. We couldn't run as smoothly without you on our team. But me as well. I seek your approval, a glance, a smile, when I'm in the office, because…"

How to put this when he was just working all this out for himself?

"I like you?" he finally said.

She tilted a doubtful look at him. "Are you asking me or telling yourself?"

"I mean…well, yes. I like you. In a completely non-receptionist way."

"Oh." She nodded. It didn't seem apparent that she would respond in kind. Did he need her to? Probably.

But sometimes they want the acknowledgment.

Something he'd only learned today.

What was going on with his thudding heart right now?

"Good, then."

Now that he'd confessed that crazy, surprise desire, he was suddenly more nervous than he'd ever been around a woman. Asher fled for the patio and leaned on the railing. Behind him he heard Maeve climb between the sheets, punch her pillow a few times and settle.

He liked her?

That was the truest thing he'd spoken since arriving here at the resort. Stupid emotion classes! The woman had indeed scratched his surface. And he liked what had been revealed beneath.

CHAPTER EIGHT

ASHER WASN'T SURE how hugging was going to be incorporated into this pottery class. He and Maeve stood before a pottery wheel working cool wet clay into what they hoped would resemble a vase. Their creation was no small mantel tchotchke. This vase would hold volumes. Why had they been given so much clay?

Couples shared a wheel, and the instructor had specifically stated that unless they'd been spinning clay for decades, they shouldn't try any maneuvers related to the movie *Ghost*. That never worked, and they didn't need the mess.

He agreed that standing behind Maeve and manipulating the clay by moving her hands would feel awkward. Not that he wouldn't mind nuzzling his face into her hair. Romantic thoughts about Maeve came easily. It was the way her fingers slid through the wet clay and artfully worked to shape the vase. She was so intent, thoughtful. And when she caught his glance, her smile would brighten. She hadn't smiled at him so much in the entire two years she'd been working for him. His entire body warmed and the world felt right.

Hell, he needed to focus. But something distracted him when he heard a couple off near the back of the room muttering about Kichu's art.

Taking his hands from the vase and leaving Maeve to work her magic, Asher dipped his fingers in some water and took his time wiping them on the thick canvas apron he'd been provided while he focused on the conversation behind him spoken in whispers. The man speaking seemed to be aware that Kichu made art—and he was here to see it?

Daring a look over his shoulder, a sudden stab of recognition struck Asher painfully in his gut.

He turned back to the spinning vase. Maeve cast him a clay-smudged smile. But his focus remained behind him on the man talking about Kichu's art. What was *he* doing here?

Another glance confirmed to Asher the man was Heinrich Hammerstill. He owned a gallery that focused on modern art. Last year the man had been featured in an episode of The Art Guys and had made a mockery of Asher before the cameras. Called him just a pretty face and subpar. The producers had kept that clip in, despite Krew asking them to take it out.

The emotional residue from that experience still clung to Asher's bones. Because in the moment, he'd believed Hammerstill's accusations. Of course he was using his looks to get by. Of course he was lacking in real talent, selling only subpar works and—hell, he didn't even have a stable of artists that he represented. He was merely decoration for the brokerage, the pretty face who attracted clients to the real brokers, Krew and Joss.

Exhaling heavily, Asher winced at the tightening in his chest. He didn't want to believe any of it. Yet now his nemesis was here to remind him that he would never rise above the exterior and gain his own place in the art world.

Did he have competition to see who could get to Tony Kichu first and convince the man to sell his art? It was possible the man knew he was here, but Asher couldn't be sure. Keeping his back to Hammerstill, Asher smiled through his frustration and faked looking interested in Maeve's handiwork. One thing was certain: he needed to up his game and find Kichu. Fast.

"All right, class!" The instructor's voice brought the pottery wheels to a stone-grinding halt. "Looks like you've all created some lovely, if a few slightly crooked, vases. Now for the fun part!"

Asher looked to Maeve, who waggled her brows. She was in a particularly light mood today. Her peach sundress was sashed with a bright pink scarf with black skulls dotting it. It worked on her. A visual cue to her bright and open mood? Tinged with the mysterious skulls. Hmm...

He shouldn't be distracted by German gallery owners, and instead needed to focus entirely on his good fortune to spend time with Maeve, but...he did need to prove to Krew and Joss that he could bring in an artist, not just schmooze at gallery parties and blow up their socials.

"Time for the hugs!" The instructor explained that the couples would stand on either side of the vase and...hug one another, with the vase in between.

"Things just got weird," Asher muttered.

"We do like weird." Maeve gave a tug to the protective vinyl apron she wore, adjusting it to cover the front of her dress. "You ready for this?"

Approving of her jovial reply, he nodded. "I'm in."

With a glance across the room—Hammerstill's back was to him—Asher spread his arms around the vase and leaned toward Maeve. It was going to get messy. But at least this time he wouldn't be forced to perform an intimate act commanded by a shrill whistle.

When Maeve's arms slid along his torso, he did the same with her. Carefully. Testing. The object was to gently press the vase between them, leaving impressions. This was certainly a style of art he'd never experienced. Maeve laughed as her hair dipped across the top of the vase. He brushed it with his fingers then realized they were still covered with clay. And now her hair was. And so was the front of his shirt where the apron didn't cover. Giggles filled the room. Along with a few choice oaths.

"I'm going to need a shower after this," Maeve tittered, "or maybe a dip in the hot springs."

"I'll race you to the springs."

Her eyes twinkled and the apostrophes at the corners of her mouth teased. This was the most awkward yet intense hug he'd been privy to. Cold, squishy clay seeping through his shirtsleeves didn't dissuade him from enjoying the moment. He didn't want to let go of her warmth, her giddy lightness. Where was that kiss whistle when he needed it?

"I suppose," she said on a whisper, "if we were really a couple in a terrible emotional tangle, I would be feeling a little closer to you right now. Thanks for enduring such a silly class."

"Did I have a choice?"

"Probably not." Her sigh was followed by a smirk, and he sensed she'd taken that the wrong way.

"There's no one else I'd rather hug pottery with than you," he said.

"Yeah?"

"Swear to it. The light…" He tilted his head, allowing more of the light from the nearby window to beam across her face. It glittered on her mouth.

"The light?"

"It always seems to dance with you."

Her glittery mouth formed a surprised O.

"Like that. I appreciate how light changes art." And she was art.

"Everyone part carefully," the instructor called, "and then admire your work!"

Letting go of Maeve was more difficult than forcing himself to start an argument with her. Asher slowly stepped away from the vase, yet found himself snapping to Maeve's side like a magnet. There he felt like he wasn't being judged. Not expected to put on a show and be The Face. He could get messy and squish pottery with her.

"It's brilliant," she said of the crumpled clay. The tall vase was compressed and bent slightly to the left. The impression of Asher's shirt buttons lined one side. And indents from the bow tied in front of Maeve's apron decorated the other side. Along with a few fine lines from her hair strafing the rim.

"I like it."

"And we made it with our own hands." She nudged his shoulder with hers. "We work well together."

Yes, they did. Asher cast a glance around the room. Most couples were also admiring their work, but one set was arguing over something. Par for the course considering the reason for the getaway. "How are we going to get that thing home with us?"

"Now smash them!" the instructor called.

Maeve gaped at Asher. They'd both fallen in love with something they had created and now... Her jaw closed and a sparkle glinted in her eye. He felt that mischievous glint dance in his chest. With a nod, he confirmed that he knew what she was thinking. They both plunged their fists against the hug-crushed clay and pounded it down to a lump.

After many vigorous punches, they stood back from their destruction. Maeve exhaled. "Now, *that* was good."

Asher lifted his clay-covered fist, and she met him with the obligatory fist bump.

"First one to the room gets the shower." Maeve grinned.

"I'm going to hang back and…" Follow Hammerstill to see what the man was up to. She didn't need to know that he was still bothered by the incident, or that he was worried. "…ask the instructor about her art education. I suspect some Basquiat influence."

"I'll meet you for dinner in an hour."

"It's a date."

She glanced back to him, her chin lifting. The summer light glinted in her irises. In that moment, Asher read her acceptance, and it blasted him with a feeling that lifted him and made him float.

"Yes, a date," she offered, then shyly nodded.

He watched her leave her soiled apron at the door, then walk out. They hadn't gotten the kiss whistle. But he had gotten a sort of hug. And for some reason that meant more to him than all the hugs, kisses and intimate contact he'd gotten from any other woman. Because Maeve wasn't in The Face's life as a prop to use in a social media post. She was just Maeve participating in—

She *was* just faking it for him. How quickly he forgot this week was all play. Was it too much to hope that he might tilt the tables and interest Maeve in seeing him as more than a boss and perhaps even a man who was interested in her?

Did he want that?

You need to get earthy and ugly.

Yes, yes, he did.

CHAPTER NINE

A SELF-GUIDED SOUND experience currently immersed them. Maeve had noted the class, which was about healing sound frequency, and told Asher they should at least give it a try before heading off to their dinner date. It was only twenty minutes. They sat on the patio and closed their eyes, allowing the orchestral music to—do whatever it was supposed to do.

Maeve felt certain she should not allow her mind to wonder, but…really? While she knew this week was a scam, she would be dishonest with herself if she didn't admit to her desire that this fake could become real.

Holding her hand against Asher's heart during yoga and hugging him during that wacky pottery session had gone beyond a friendly touch. She'd felt every molecule of him on her skin. And she couldn't easily brush him off like lint or wet clay. The man was a royal earthy violet in her color index. And violet paired well with the crisp emerald she so often identified with herself.

Dare she push this further and see if he might have a real interest in her?

But how foolish. She worked for the man. And really, a man of his status would never date *the receptionist*. It was beneath him. While Maeve believed everyone was equal in soul and value, it was difficult not to equate riches with status and power. She'd never had dreams of landing a rich man and living the high life. It wasn't in her nature to go after someone because of what he could give her or how comfortable he could make her life. There had to be something inside…

What a crazy session pottery hugging had been. Destruction had never felt so satisfying. And if a girl were to get metaphorical, it could relate to her building her own business, carefully crafting the clay and guiding it into shape—and then standing back as the world smashed it to bits.

Except *she* had done the smashing. And it felt much better to control a failure than to stand back and allow it to happen. Perhaps if she viewed the failed shop as a learning experience instead of the drastically terrible event? But how to do so with her mother's voice sternly reminding her that she had failed? And really, wasn't it time to come to her senses and look for a real job? Not a silly receptionist who was expected to make coffee and appointments. That took little brain power. And it did not offer much potential of moving up the corporate ladder.

Maeve sighed. Ladders scared her. They seemed too unstable. And she much preferred soaring as opposed to climbing.

Smirking at her thoughts, she reminded herself that she'd never been a metaphor girl, and—that session with Asher hadn't been about failure at all. Rather, it had led her farther down the lust path. It was getting harder to convince herself that she must stick to business. Pleasure nudged itself firmly into her being, and along with it came the enticing offering of holding hands, hugging and kissing Asher Dane.

"There's been a twist to our adventure," Asher announced conversationally.

Maeve turned her head to land in his soft stare. She was reminded of *The Awakening of Adonis*. Waterhouse may have been painting *her* clothed in pink satin and leaning over the luscious Adonis reclined amongst the poppies. But in that painting Aphrodite kissed Adonis awake. And that kiss surely hadn't been so quick as the one they'd shared yesterday.

"A twist?" She shook away her fantasies and reached to adjust the volume on her phone so the music played quietly. "More strange than the fact that we are faking being a couple and also faking being at odds?" she whispered.

"I admit, it's difficult to imagine being at odds with you. We can't do the fake fight anymore. Been there, done that."

"I think we solved the *thing* anyway," she said of their fight yesterday. "We'll just have to sulk side by side, give the illusion we're displeased with one another."

"Sulking. It could work."

"But what's this new twist?"

Asher propped an elbow on the patio table. Maeve turned to face him directly. "Remember Hammerstill?"

She ran the odd name over in her thoughts but didn't immediately come to an answer.

"From the television show?" he prompted.

And then she remembered. Heinrich Hammerstill, an art broker to the stars who was also The Art Guys' biggest competition. During season one, episode three, when Asher had still been finding his place after rejoining the company, Hammerstill had won an auction, and afterward, when Asher had gone to shake his hand and offer congratulations, the bullish broker had accused him of having no talent whatsoever. Asher's humiliation had shown on his face, in his curved shoulders and in his softened voice. Krew had tried to get the film crew to cut that segment, but of course, they'd kept that salacious bit. Viewers devoured conflict and drama.

"He's here?" she asked.

Asher nodded. "Noticed him in the pottery class at the back of the room. I think he's with his wife. Maybe. The woman was young. He's an old man. I know he's been married a decade, at least."

"You think he's having an affair? Wait." The real issue stabbed her. "Why is he here? Do you think...?"

"There can be no other reason. He's after Kichu."

"We've still got a chance," she encouraged. "We'll find Kichu before Hammerstill does. Did you speak to him?"

"I had intended to follow him after the pottery class but had a change of heart. I can't believe I didn't notice him until now."

"The classes have been intense and focused. I haven't chatted with anyone besides you."

"Yes, and we have been focused on the fake. After that dressing down, for millions of viewers to see, I'm not up for another encounter. Though..." He exhaled and tilted his head back. "Perhaps I should charge the vanguard, eh? Show him who his competition really is and that I will not be defeated this time?"

"You're very talented and an excellent art broker, Asher. At the time, Hammerstill had the clout. Now? You've surpassed him immeasurably."

He sighed. "Yet I haven't brought in an artist to the brokerage. This is my chance, Maeve. I have to prove myself to the guys. I'm glad we're not filming this."

The idea of their shenanigans being filmed horrified her. "You know I don't like being filmed."

"If you would allow it, you'd gain so many fans. You'd have tons of followers."

"My ego is not stroked by followers and likes. Oh." She winced.

"You think that's what I'm all about?" He sat up and propped his elbows on his knees.

"No, I—"

"I get it. I'm the Face. The one who wins approval and success because of what's on the surface. As Hammerstill clearly stated, there's nothing of substance beneath. And woe to anyone who scratches that surface and sees what spills out."

"It's not like that," Maeve said. Yet she stopped herself from an apology.

He stood and wandered across the threshold into the room, calling back softly, "I'm going to dress for dinner."

Truthfully, Asher did have his egocentric moments.

But he wasn't a man of little substance. He was a genuine art lover, and the moments when he fell into a painting were the most exquisite. They took her breath away. If she should scratch his surface she would be dazzled by what seeped out. Dare she tell him that? It wouldn't mean anything to him coming from a mere receptionist.

Maeve realized she and Asher had had their first *real* argument.

The fake relationship was going well.

So why did her heart feel as though it had just taken a punch?

Asher leaned his shoulders against the bathroom door. He should not have wandered off like that. How thoughtless of him. Maeve had only stated the truth. A harsh truth. He did get off on an increase in followers and likes. He knew that was terribly egotistic. He'd never been a man to seek attention such as he had over these past few years.

His life had been a series of emergencies and recovery and devotion to his parents. They'd both been very sick, and Asher had spent much of his late teenage years tending to them. He'd been devoted to their care and wouldn't change a thing about it. And then, when he'd gotten away to university and had started his career with the brokerage, his mum and dad had needed him again. He had left The Art Guys because he loved his parents.

Three years ago Avery and Alice Dane had moved to Bath to be near a functional medicine doctor who was dialed into their sickness. He'd treated them with careful attention and knowledge and suggested they move to the country. They'd found a sweet little cottage in a rural area and their health had changed remarkably. And for the first time Asher had felt set loose, free to live his own life. And he'd done so, but at the cost of gobbling any attention he could get and feeding off it. It was something he'd not had those years caring for his parents. He'd always made sure they were the ones who got the attention, because they'd required it.

And now? He had become The Face. When the film studio had told them their new monikers for the show—*Promotion, fellas, it'll grab the viewers!*—Asher had laughed and shrugged and went along with it. He wasn't lacking in self-awareness. Not that he'd ever been vain about his looks. Though, vanity had crept into his veins as he'd begun to capture the attention he'd so desperately needed when playing caregiver to his parents. He'd discerned how to use his looks and charm to get what he desired. And it was useful in his profession. But no one could know it was a mask for the real guy beneath.

Asher Dane loved art. He knew it well. And it moved him. It told him stories, as Maeve had suggested. It spoke to him. It expanded his world beyond his pretty boundaries and invited him in, no expectations required.

The Face, on the other hand, dated beautiful women. Rich women. Models and celebrities. The Face could stand at the center of a party and command attention. The Face was listened to when he talked art. The Face won auctions merely by entering the bid room, wielding a bid paddle and flashing a grin to the competing woman across the aisle. The Face…

Was a sham.

Asher bowed his head. He didn't want to be a stupid moniker to Maeve. For the first time he was feeling a real connection with a woman. This let's-try-new-things-to-make-the-fake-relationship-succeed friendship they'd slipped into could lead to something more. Though, obviously, she looked to him as her boss, a man she'd agreed to help by being his fake girlfriend.

What kind of man asked a woman to do such a thing? How had he thought this was a good idea? He didn't want her to buy into the surface illusion of The Face.

He wanted Maeve to know the man inside.

"Asher?"

He pushed the door open and turned to lean against the vanity as Maeve looked inside. "Listen, Maeve. I'm sorry."

"There's no need to apologize."

"Yes, there is. I overreacted out there. And I think that was a real fight, not a fake one. It won't happen again. Promise." He gestured toward the main door. "Can we go to the dining room for a nice meal?"

"Of course. We should make a game plan for what to do about Hammerstill."

"No, I mean, to relax. Work is over for the day. I need—" to find himself in her eyes and not as a reflection of The Face "—some quiet conversation. I heard a rumor that Kichu has a gallery on-site. Maybe after a meal we can go find it?"

"Yes, I'd like that."

Asher followed her from the room, and as he did so, he inhaled the ineffable scent of Maeve. It was like a salty spring and fresh summer air. Tinged with the vanilla surprise of an indeterminate something he wanted to learn more about.

Could she see beyond The Face? Dare he let her in? Was he falling into this playacting and beginning to feel, well... *feel*?

CHAPTER TEN

THE DINING ROOM handed guests a picnic basket and suggested they wander outside and enjoy the sunset. Maeve had asked for a blanket, and now they sat at the edge of the forest in a quiet knoll that was manicured for such a scenario. Wildflowers bloomed to either side of them, and the air smelled verdant to match the green and violet sky.

No arguments echoed out from the patio behind the resort, Maeve noted. She wished everyone could have a good, healthy relationship and feel loved. So she'd had a few bad relationships. She'd also experienced good ones. A person had to stay in the game to find their match. She hoped it would happen for her sooner or later, but this weird playacting with Asher tilted her from that hope to fear that he could not see her as anything more than a means to an end. And she wasn't getting any closer to proving to him that she was a valuable asset that deserved a promotion at The Art Guys.

With that discouraging thought she looked across the blanket to where Asher sat with his legs spread out before him, arms crossed, then quickly uncrossed. He hadn't packed suitable reclining clothes, so she granted him the awkwardness he obviously exhibited. He'd foregone a suit coat and had rolled up his white shirtsleeves to below his elbows. His hair was always run-your-fingers-through-it messy but styled. And his glacier eyes looked much warmer with glints of gold twinkling from the candlelight, which flickered from the center of the emptied picnic basket. No color in his wardrobe. On occasion he might go with a pale blue shirt under his gray or black suit. She preferred that shirt. It danced with his eyes. Spoke softly, yet also with a tease she could not ignore.

This evening, she wore her tangerine sundress with a pink and black skull belt. Tangerine always felt slightly anxious yet with a tinge of giddy excitement. She could never decide if the color was happy or urgent. So the belt grounded that conflicting feeling. Yes, skulls were grounding to her. They represented life, in all its stages. Whew! The day had been an interesting one with pottery hugs and an unexpected argument. And it had all left her utterly unsure, to be truthful. About everything.

Thankfully, the food was excellent. They'd finished an amazing spring pea and asparagus salad. The bottle of wine was almost empty.

"The local wine here is incredible," he said. "Has a deep fruity tone to it that I wouldn't have expected."

"I'm not much of a connoisseur. I drink whatever I can afford."

She sat up straight as the dining room waiter stepped off the path and delivered a plate between the two of them along with smaller plates. A tower of chocolate, cream and fresh blueberries challenged them silently. Asher thanked him as he left with their used plates.

Maeve lifted her fork. "Think we can do this?"

"I'm up for the challenge."

They both forked portions onto their plates, then enjoyed the treat as the solar lamps set around the property suddenly lit up with the darkening sky.

"You're taking in that bright pink in the sky, aren't you?" Asher asked.

"It's mauve. And yes, it's startling. Clear and bright. Like a lingering remnant of a disco party after everyone has gone home. Tired yet exhilarated."

"You do have a way with color. That dress."

She smoothed a hand over her lap, ensuring the napkin was still there. If she dropped food on this fabric it would never come out. "Yes, my dress?"

"It's your color…but…"

"But?"

"I'm not sure. Everything you wear looks great on you, but that color seems a little…tense?"

He'd nailed it. Interesting.

"Tangerine is…apprehensive, I guess you could say. At least, it is to me. I tend to dress emotionally."

"I wonder if you've a bit of color synesthesia?"

She'd never thought about it like that. Synesthesia was a confusion of the senses that some people experienced. They might taste colors or smell shapes. The letters in their alphabets could all be a different color. Sometimes they even heard textures. It was a fascinating thing.

"I surround myself with color as a replacement for…"

For having to step forward and speak out. To put the real, bared Maeve Pemberton out there. Because that Maeve only ever seemed to fail.

"You are an artist who wears her canvas," Asher declared.

Maeve laughed abruptly, then quickly caught herself. "I've never been called an artist."

"I don't see why not. Art is everywhere. It doesn't have to be on a canvas or carved into marble. It's that sky out there that caught your attention. I could see you reading the story of it."

She loved that he'd caught on to her admiration of things in the form of stories. "What's life without a great story? Art is everywhere. We just need to pay attention and let it happen to us."

"Let the story life wants you to have…happen. That's poetic. I see art in this cake," he said with a lift of his fork. Sweet cream dripped to the plate. "The chef gathered ingredients and shaped them into something that others could admire and experience with their senses. And what about that crystal goblet? It's handblown. More artwork."

"Your shoes are art." Maeve joined in on the game. "The pounded leather with the tiny arabesques on the toes was lovingly crafted by a cobbler."

"I do love my Venetian cobbler. Now let's talk about more personal art. Like your eyes." He set down his fork and leaned forward. The flames dancing in his eyes lured her to look at him even as she self-consciously wanted to look away. "You know at one time in history they used to read irises to better one's health?"

"I think some people still do. Iridology?"

"I believe so. Your irises tell a story."

"And what story is that?"

"There's honesty and truth in there but also…something not quite right?"

Maeve set down her fork and pressed her fingers over her mouth as she chewed, looking aside. She'd already confessed to him that she was a failure. Why did he have to state it like that?

"Oh, yes, it's in there. But it's not just your eyes."

Her shyness emerged as he leaned forward more and stared lower.

"Your mouth," he said. "The dark cherry that stains your lips is unexpected, so daring against your pale skin. But the best part of the story is those apostrophes on either side."

"The what?"

"Each side of your mouth, there, indenting your skin like dimples, curls into little apostrophes. Striking," he said on a hush that flickered the candle flame between them.

Falling into his glittering gaze, Maeve melted into the compliments as they formed new images of herself and straightened her spine. She'd never been able to accept compliments without an excuse or an *Oh, it's just...* reaction, but she did not feel compelled to protest this time. Asher's regard held her enchanted.

Or rather, charmed. The Face certainly did know how to work his magic. Whew!

With that realization, she sat back and shook her head. "You're incorrigible."

"What did I do?"

"You've an innate way of enchanting people. When we finally do locate Tony Kichu, deploy that charm so we don't lose him."

"I wasn't deploying anything on you, Maeve." He sat back and rubbed his brow. "Did it feel false?"

No, it hadn't. But this entire trip was all about faking it. How could it have been anything but?

She set her napkin aside. Nothing with Asher felt false. That was what made this all so frustrating. Her body reacted to him as if this were real. Only her brain knew otherwise. "Maybe it's that thing that feels not right, as you mentioned."

She set her plate inside the picnic basket and blew out the candle. The landscape glittered with solar lighting. The mauve in the sky had disappeared. And she suddenly shivered. "It chills so quickly here at night."

"That's why you're feeling not right. Let's head inside."

Maeve stood and handed him the basket. Her phone pinged with a text. She wouldn't normally pay attention to it, but the bright glow from her phone distracted so she tugged it from her pocket and looked at the screen.

"Krew need help?" Asher guessed as he folded the blanket.

"No, it's my mum."

"Anything wrong?"

Her mum had sent a note and a link for a job in Dublin. Marketing intern at a paint company. That was interesting. Also surprising. Her mum wanted her to find a *real* job, but she had never gone so far as to send her a lead like this.

"It's all good. She checks in on occasion." To see if Maeve had come to her senses.

"You said your mum lives in New York?"

"Yes, she's the CEO of LilithTech. Created the business from scratch. But don't ask me to explain it beyond that it's about stocks, investing and focused on helping female clients. She's accomplished so much."

"She must be proud of her daughter."

"What for?" Maeve asked all of a sudden, and then realized her dismissive reaction might not make sense to him. "I mean, well…"

"I'm sorry, I shouldn't have assumed. You've got a fine job at a prestigious brokerage. That must impress her?"

Maeve took the blanket from him and walked up to the pathway, waiting for him to follow. "It takes a lot to impress Mariane Pemberton. A woman who has never had time for anything but moving up the corporate ladder, taking no prisoners and shoving aside any man who gets in her way. I'm not sure that sort of status is something I can or want to achieve. At least, not in the manner my mum expects it to happen."

Asher stepped up beside her. The growing darkness made it necessary to stand close to see one another's faces. Everything felt right about his closeness.

"I get the whole thing about wanting to be whatever your parents expect, Maeve. But don't let it stop you from seeking what your soul desires. I suspect, for you, that's a very colorful desire."

Oh, how he understood her. "Thank you. Sometimes it's nice to hear what I should be telling myself."

He took her hand, and they strolled toward the resort. Asher left the basket and blanket with a staff member, and they wandered inside. A class across the hall from the dining room was finishing. Something about dream reading, if Maeve recalled correctly. The whole rehab week was interspersed with a lot of woo-woo stuff, but she supposed the eclectic mixture was what drew all sorts to Kichu as a relationship coach.

"How about we find that gallery?" He tugged her toward a curving wood staircase, a work of art in itself.

The gallery was tucked above the dining room on the second floor. Seeing they were the only two in it scurried an effusive joy through Maeve's veins. Enjoying art without the hindrance of a crowd was always the best.

Asher strolled ahead, hands in his trouser pockets, checking out the room's structure. The floor-to-ceiling windows that overlooked the back courtyard and geothermal pools were portioned off with a wall that rose almost as high as the three-story ceiling. To keep daylight from shining across the artwork, obviously. Though now it was dark, and the glow of small spotlights near each painting beckoned.

The first was a Renoir. Asher stopped before it and gave her a glance as if to say "nice," but he didn't speak. His stance told her he was impressed. Head slightly forward, eyes taking in the canvas. Hands in his pockets slipping out and splaying before him as if he wanted to touch but would not. A subtle yearning in that pose. One she knew well.

"If the entire collection is this elegant," he said on a reverent tone, "Kichu's taste alone has me itchy to rep him."

Maeve wandered to the next painting, attracted by the soft colors in the reclined woman's dress. Pre-Raphaelite—Asher's favorite period for painters. She recognized the painting but not the artist. She should know this one!

"Hughes," he said as he shouldered up beside her. This time

his glance was more of a lingering summation of her expression. He didn't so much look at her as seem to breathe her in.

Mouth falling open in wonder, Maeve nodded in agreement. Or was it desire? The intimacy between them was growing. They'd gone from office associates who barely knew one another and rarely made contact to walking hand in hand, sharing snippets of their dreams and desires. A stolen kiss. A weird hug.

"Yes," he said on a whisper. "I agree."

Maeve smiled. She didn't even have to ask. He took her hand and they strolled to the next painting. Another from the Romantic era, featuring a besuited man wandering at the edge of a blurry forest, where strange creatures popped out to dance in his wake. Or perhaps to lure him across the thin place he straddled and forever into their clutches?

"The lighting in here is perfect," she said. "Whoever designed this gallery got it right."

"Like candlelight," Asher agreed. "No harsh fluorescents or spotlights. One should always have the pleasure of viewing the masters' works as they had worked on them."

"To consider how light affects paintings I always think of the Sistine Chapel."

"Yes?" He walked around behind her. He stood so close they were almost touching. Almost. But not quite. Yet he leaned in near enough to nudge her hair with his nose as he asked, "Tell me."

Just a little closer, she thought. *Kiss me there.* On the neck. It would undo her.

Maeve couldn't recall the last time she had been undone by a man. Had she ever? Was it already happening and she didn't label it that because it was so new to her?

"Oh." Maeve caught her wandering thoughts. "Well, I've not been to the Sistine Chapel, but I have read that the natural light is beautiful."

"It is." He winked at her.

Undone was a whisper away…

She cleared her throat. "Yes. Uh…and visitors stand below and admire the frescos that took Michelangelo years to create. At great pains. The man stood on scaffolding and painted, head tilted back." She mimicked the position. "Can you imagine?"

"I certainly hope he had a good chiropractor."

"Right? But what most don't think about is that he had to have needed an artificial light source for when the sun set or the days were cloudy. Candlelight being the only option."

She sighed and felt the warmth of Asher's breath against her neck. "Yes, like that," she decided, of both her story and what was happening right now. "The soft warm light of the candle. So close. Perhaps elevated near to his work. The quiet strokes of the sable brush against the plaster ceiling. The squish of oil paints being placed to form images. He'd perhaps have the Old Testament strewn open nearby. A reference for his work. A random bird may have flown in, perched to nest. And the quiet flicker of the candle flame, illuminating the bold colors he must have had to use for the minimal light."

Asher walked backward, taking her by the hand. "You see art the way I do. You experience the moment paint was laid to canvas. That excites me."

"The painting part?"

"No, the Maeve and her ridiculous obsession with color part." They strolled toward the exit. "What's your favorite scene in the Sistine Chapel? Mine's *The Flood*. I've been fascinated by the animals since I could name them as a child. My mum used to have a big picture book that featured the paintings in the chapel."

"Phemonoe is my favorite," she said. "*The Libyan Sibyl*.

I love the exquisite gold-orange-peach gown she wears. The aquamarine table spread. And that book. It's so lush."

"The prophetess in bright robes. Perfect for you."

He understood her obsession with color? This was…better than undone, this was…a success she'd never realized she needed.

Turning down the hallway that was lined with a wall of windows overlooking the twinkling landscape, the twosome walked hand in hand, but Maeve startled as a whistle blew over the intercom.

"Kiss alert," a voice announced. "You know the drill, people. Set your differences aside and kiss. We're moving toward the halfway mark. You're all doing so well."

When Asher turned and stopped her so her back pressed against the wall, Maeve's heart fluttered. But what he asked next gave her a delicious thrill.

"May I give you a proper kiss?"

"Yes, please," came out breathlessly. Her lungs panted as giddily as her heart.

Asher stroked the hair along her cheek and followed his movement down to her chin, where he glided his fingers along her jaw. Softly. Burnishing his subtle heat into her skin. He then slid a finger over her mouth.

"Art here," he whispered. "A story I want to learn."

Their mouths met. Yellow and mauve burst behind Maeve's closed eyelids, colors so joyous and happy and sensual that her lips curled to a smile as she tasted Asher's kiss. This wasn't a quick peck designed to fulfill some preconceived expectation. This was a kiss. The kiss she had fantasized about since meeting Asher Dane. And it was much more spectacular than any imagined scenario she had concocted.

He was everywhere at once, his earth and rain scent filling her senses. His taste of berries and chocolate melding into deep royal colors. The heat of him stabbed into her aura and connected like two bubbles coalescing. And when he deepened the kiss and she felt her body grow heavy and her knees weaken, his arm swept around behind her and held her firmly against his chest.

Oh, mercy. What was happening?

She was falling. Not to the floor. Not in love. But rather, into the man's story. It wasn't clear or even obvious, but she trod the edges of it, even walked over into the foyer where she felt his strength introduce her to a certain hidden weakness. She accepted and threaded her fingers up through his hair, tugging gently, wanting him always at her mouth. Passionate and needy.

And when he pulled back and caught his breath, she did so as well. He'd stolen her very breath and she didn't need it back. Yet, movement over Asher's shoulder prodded her to focus and—it was Tony Kichu, standing by the window, scrolling on his phone.

In that moment, Maeve's body, still under Asher's spell, reacted. It was fight or flight. And while logic insisted she stay and fight to keep him close and win another kiss, flight argued that this was the chance they'd been waiting for.

The chance that Asher needed.

She shoved Asher away from her and dashed down the hallway, calling, "You got this!"

"What?" he called after her.

What a silly exit! Maeve hoped she'd done the right thing. She'd left Asher alone in the hallway with the man they'd come to find. Fingers crossed he could charm him.

And then quickly return to her for another kiss.

CHAPTER ELEVEN

WHAT THE HELL? Just when he'd felt it was safe to give Maeve a real kiss—wham!

Asher touched his mouth. She'd shoved him away from their kiss. Had it been so terrible? He hadn't thought so. In the moment, her body had fallen against his. He'd caught her, thinking she might even buckle at the knees. Their mouths had melded, her fingers exploring hair and skin. Her breasts had crushed against his chest. It had been a perfect moment.

"Oh, sorry, didn't see you there."

Asher turned to find a tall, solemn man with long straight black hair standing before the window, a phone in hand. He'd seen a photo of him in the research material Krew had sent him for this trip.

"Mr. Kichu." Asher moved over to shake the man's hand. "It's a pleasure to meet you in person."

Where was Maeve? What she was missing! Had she seen Kichu? Well, he wasn't going to lose this opportunity, despite the nagging inner voice that insisted he'd blown it with Maeve.

"Asher Dane," he offered. "I'm here with, uh…my girl-friend." A would-be girlfriend? Too much to hope for. He wasn't on his game with Maeve. What was he doing wrong?

Kichu was tall and lean, clad in loose white clothing that was probably environmentally, ecologically and whatever else friendly. He wore his hair in a high ponytail that tugged his face smooth. A ski-run nose punctuated his face.

"You are enjoying the experience?" the guru asked in a soft voice tinged with a Japanese inflection.

"It's very interesting. I feel it's…helping. Yes, it's been good for us."

In ways he hadn't expected. Yet had he negated all that good with a kiss? Women did not usually run from him following a kiss.

"I am pleased." The man looked to his phone again. Obviously, not at ease with the conversation. What sort of self-help guru wasn't comfortable with speaking directly to those he sought to help?

No time to wonder. If Asher didn't act quickly…

"I've had opportunity to explore the gallery," Asher said. "I see you enjoy the Romantics."

Kichu nodded, focused on his phone.

"I understand *you* also dabble?"

"Hmm? Yes. Uh…"

"I'd like to see your work," Asher said. "I'm an art broker. My firm represents artists worldwide. We have a stellar—"

Kichu held up a finger. "I have a call I must attend to."

"Of course." Asher strolled about ten feet away from the man, turning his attention out the window as Kichu chatted in another language with someone.

Narrowing his gaze on the solar lamps dotting the back landscape, his heart clenched. Why had she shoved him like that? If she hadn't liked the kiss, she could have politely—well, what?

Maeve baffled him. If it wasn't wondering how to take in her colorful yet boldly clashing exterior, it was turning inward and realizing that he was starting to think she meant more to him than just a receptionist.

When someone beside him said, "Excuse me," Asher stepped aside. An employee pushed a laundry cart past him. After she had passed, Asher turned to Kichu and—the man was gone.

Swearing under his breath, Asher dashed down the hallway to where it met another hall and looked both ways. The man had slipped away without even saying a thing to him? Purposefully? The man was evasive, protecting his privacy at all means. Had he played his hand too quickly? What had happened to The Face's charm?

He hadn't been focused. His thoughts had been split between work and…

"Maeve."

Grass green for her sleepwear. Always. The color made her feel grounded and energetic. All shades of green, but emerald and mint were truly her colors. Maeve brushed her teeth and wandered out to the bedroom just as Asher walked in. With a heavy sigh, he nodded to her and went into the bathroom.

She was eager to learn how it had gone with Tony Kichu, but his sigh did not bode well. Stepping out onto the patio, she tapped both the solar lamps and a soft glow bubbled the two comfy chairs. Glass bottles of water sat on a wood tray, along with a basket of ginger nut biscuits, thanks to the staff who sneakily reset the patios while they were in sessions. She munched a cookie, enjoying the ginger tingle.

Ten minutes later, Asher strolled out in his pajama bottoms and no shirt. Why he did that to her—well, she couldn't request he wear a shirt to protect her eyes from all that fabulous brawn. And really, she enjoyed the view.

"Judging from your sigh when you entered, I'm guessing it did not go well."

He plopped onto the chair, grabbing one of the water bottles. Tilting back a good swallow, he then leaned his head back and took in the vast constellations in the dark sky.

"I did speak to him. But I wasn't on top of my game. He took a phone call, and while I was standing aside, trying to politely not listen, he made his escape. Just vanished."

"What?"

"I didn't get a chance to do more than introduce myself and let him know I was interested in looking at his work."

So he hadn't deployed his charm? Wasn't that The Face's talent? He should have wrapped Kichu around his little finger.

"I was distracted," Asher confessed.

"By what?"

He turned on the chair and set the bottle on the table between them. Lamplight glowed over his face, gifting his skin a golden sheen. Maeve caught a breath at the back of her throat. He was so beautiful. More compelling than any artwork she had seen.

"By the most unique artwork in my world."

His face was sincere and his eyes sought her like an arrow to the target. Struck, she whispered, "What artwork is that?"

"You."

She didn't know how to respond. That arrow detoured from her eyes and soared directly to her heart. He thought she was…? *She* had distracted him?

Well, she had literally just considered how he distracted her.

"But." He leaned back in the chair, his averted attention drawing out the arrow from her chest along with it. "You pushed me away after that kiss. Rejected me."

"No, I—"

"I don't know what I did wrong, Maeve. I did ask your permission."

"Asher." She reached across the table and touched his thigh. "I pushed you away because I saw Tony Kichu. I knew it would be your chance to speak to him. I didn't want you to lose it."

"You could have said something. I was sure you had rejected me."

"There was no time. It was a gut reaction. I didn't want to speak and scare Kichu away. And it worked, yes? You got to introduce yourself to him."

He nodded, but his dreamy stare had resumed. And now he clutched her hand. "I don't care about Kichu right now. I'm glad to learn you weren't shoving me away because my kiss offended you."

"Far from it. In fact…"

Dare she? This was, after all, a fake relationship. Yet they hadn't needed to put on a show for anyone when they'd been alone outside the gallery and the kiss whistle had sounded. Though, it had been a good show for Kichu, obviously.

"In fact?" he prompted.

"It was good that we were kissing when Kichu wandered by, wasn't it? Playing the role of a couple."

"Oh. Of course. We are playing a role. I forgot myself."

"You did?" Was it possible he could have *wanted* to kiss her? She slipped from his grasp.

"Yes. I promise it won't happen again. And when the whistle blows, I will always ask permission." He stood and rubbed at his back. "See you in the morning."

He'd dismissed what she'd hoped was a real connection forming between them. The man was all work and no play. And the way he eased at his lower back with his fingers.

"You can take the bed tonight. That floor is not good for your back, and don't argue about it."

"What if we share? I mean, we've spent the past few

nights sleeping in the same room. We know each other well enough… Hell, Maeve, the floor is uncomfortable. And it's only for a few more days. Surely we can share the bed like two adults and not…"

"Oh, of course. Not." Not get close enough to do any of the wild and sexy things she had imagined over and over. "We could…try?"

He nodded. "It's settled then. Which side do you want?"

She followed him into the room, leaving the patio door open, for the night was sultry and warm and there were no insects to worry about fluttering inside.

"Uh…left?"

"Ah, the sinister side. An appropriate choice for my devilishly colorful Marsha."

Smiling at the moniker, she sat on the left side while Asher sat down on the right. He tapped the lamp to darken the room. Moonlight beamed pale luminescence across the bed and his hands. Elegant yet strong hands. Capable of touching her gently. And also commanding her.

Together, they lay on top of the sheets, heads to each of the pillows. While their bodies did not touch, Maeve could feel Asher's body heat waver toward her, tickling its way inside her pores. His royal violet and earthy scent grew heady, the only thing in the room. His presence induced in her a crazy maelstrom of want, desire and caution. If she were to move even slightly, her shoulder or leg would touch his. Would he construe it as an advance on her part? Did she want him to take it that way?

Yes, please. And…

Her mother's voice announced that she would never find her way to success by pleasing a man.

Maeve had no intention of doing such a thing. But how to sort out what was business and what could become pleasure? Her intention had been to not allow her heart into this fake relationship.

"This is weird," she finally said.

"Super weird."

She laughed at that agreement.

He added, "We're adults. We can do this."

"Right. We can share a bed. No problem. Just two business associates away on a work vacation."

"Right. Business associates." His tone sounded tight. Unsure. Or perhaps nervous, as she was.

Maeve turned onto her side, putting her back to him. About the only way she could possibly get through the night. How to sleep with the one man she lusted over so close to her?

"Just an advance warning," he said. "I'm a snuggler. It's something that happens when I sleep. So if you wake up and find my arm around you, please don't freak out."

Maeve's entire system went into overdrive when she imagined waking with his arms around her. "Thanks for the warning. Good night, Windfield."

"Good night, Marsha."

Smiling at their shared joke, Maeve closed her eyes and knew the only way she was going to sleep tonight was if the sandman poured out his entire sack.

CHAPTER TWELVE

MAEVE'S COLOR CHOICE this morning was certainly interesting. Asher took in her violet-striped chinos, the bright yellow T-shirt and the dash of brick-red scarf around her neck. It was a good thing he was attracted to her or he'd have to wear sunglasses to be in the same room.

Fortunately, they were outdoors, surrounded by lush forest and the chitter of insects. A strange bird call fascinated him; he had no clue what kind of bird it belonged to. Captivated by the light pouring through the tree canopy, and also distracted by Maeve's colors, he had to caution himself to keep one eye on the trail.

Maeve walked ahead on the unpaved hiking trail formed by smoothed earth and the occasional stone or log embedded in the path. She paused often to inspect an interesting plant or mushroom. Today's assignment was a hike. They had been emailed a list of questions to discuss at various spots along the trail.

He was thankful he'd brought along a pair of running shoes because the terrain was rough. And after deciding a white dress shirt wouldn't quite go with the knee-length shorts he'd packed, he'd made a trip to the gift shop and now wore a heather T-shirt with a rainbow-colored logo depicting a circle and clasped hands. It still smelled of the lavender incense that had been burning in the shop. He may have beat Maeve on the weird clothing scale today.

The things he did for his job.

But smelly fashion aside, the day was cloudy yet warm, and the forest they trampled through smelled amazingly verdant and wild, and even a little musty. None of the sensory information was processed too intensely because it had to compete with his thoughts about Maeve.

He had woken this morning with an arm draped over her waist. Still sleeping, she hadn't been aware of his closeness. He'd lingered, taking in her warmth. He could have snuggled closer, buried his face in her hair to inhale her vanilla scent, but he'd caught himself. He wasn't a creep. Though he had closed his eyes and...breathed her in.

Then he'd carefully slid away his arm and sneaked out of bed, leaving Sleeping Beauty to wake on her own. He'd brought back pastries while she had showered.

Whatever was happening between the two of them, it involved a push and pull. He still wasn't sure if she was going along with the fake or if she saw him as something more than a boss who needed her help. It had only been a few days. He mustn't expect her to fall madly in love with him.

But the thought that she may put a smile on his face. He and Maeve Pemberton? What a unique pair. It was like hanging a Michelangelo beside a Pollock. The two didn't go together at all. And yet, they did warrant attention.

"There's a rest stop ahead," Maeve called over her shoulder. "Did you bring along water?"

"And two pastries."

"You are an excellent packer," she declared as she set aside her hiking pole and leaned on a wood railing that overlooked a narrow creek. "It's so beautiful out here!"

Yes, she was. Er, right. She was talking about nature. Eh. Same thing.

"Does an excellent packer forget to bring along casual

wear?" He handed her a bottle of water from the backpack the resort had issued them. "Pastry?"

"Not yet. You couldn't have known this retreat would require all this outdoor exercise and yoga and such. I like the purple shirt on you. It's a tint of your real color."

"My real color?"

"Yes, your scent is like a royal violet, mixed with rain and earth. I see you as that violet color. Like something a king would wear, only a little dusty around the edges."

"I've never been described in such a manner. Usually the media leads with cocky, charming and self-important."

"You believe everything the media writes, don't you? I mean, it is all true."

He cast her a surprised gape and playfully punched her upper arm. "Thanks a lot, Marsha."

"Don't worry. I know the arrogant charm is a facade."

"Do you? Because some days I'm not sure myself who Asher Dane really is."

"There's a kind and caring man under The Face," she said. And then she dared to add, "The Face is a bit of a fake, like we are this week."

"Maybe." He leaned forward on his elbows and peered down over the bubbling creek. She was spot-on. "The Face does get The Art Guys the media buzz required to be a success."

"I can understand the need to hold your own alongside Joss and Krew. You three are remarkable."

"If you say so." If he was so remarkable, then why didn't he have a stable of artists like the other guys? "This has been an interesting few days. I thought it would be a bunch of dull classes inside an auditorium."

"Same."

"So what's the question for this stop?"

She pulled out her cell phone and scrolled. "Hmm, we tell each other what we want for our future. An easy one. I've already told you I have plans to someday own a color consulting business."

"And I hope that dream becomes your reality. My future?"

He turned to rest his elbows on the railing and studied her face. Those long black lashes looked as though they had mascara on them, but he knew she wore little to no makeup beyond the deep red lip stain. A heady tease to his libido. And after waking beside her this morning? His future suddenly seemed so unimportant.

And yet… "Beyond wanting to win over Kichu and prove to the guys I'm the entire package. As well, I've been feeling the call to become…less."

"Less?"

"Yes, less… The Face. More real. Not so out there. Honestly? Maeve, I want to start a family. To know what love is like and to share that with another person."

"Doesn't everyone?"

He glanced to her. "You want a family?"

"Oh, yes, it's an important part of life. Learning to share and love and teach."

"Yes, teach." His kids would appreciate the arts, but they would develop their own likes and dislikes independent of their parents' desires. "And limits on the social media stuff for the kids," he added.

"You don't want your children to have as many followers as you do?"

"That's The Face, Maeve. Not me."

She compressed her mouth and the apostrophes deepened. He reached to touch one of them, which startled her.

"Sorry." He shrugged. "Those apostrophes are so cute."

She touched the edge of her mouth.

He'd stymied her. But he liked seeing her undone. A little off. An unsteady flicker brightened her green eyes. How the light did love her. There was never a moment Maeve Pemberton's light did not attract him.

"The Face was created by the show producers," she stated.

"You get it."

"I do." She tucked her phone away and leaned against the railing beside him. "Why did you leave The Art Guys for those few years? You mentioned something about your parents? I know you also said it was personal…"

Asher crossed his arms, leaning against the railing. It was personal, but Maeve had inserted herself into that private space, and he wanted her to know she was safe there. As he felt safe telling her about it.

"My parents have been sick for a good part of my life. It started when I was a teen. None of the many dozens of GPs they saw could determine why. They prescribed medications that never worked. Some even seemed to make them worse. One time my mother had a severe reaction to a medication that saw her in hospital for weeks."

"I'm so sorry. What is it they have? And both the same thing?"

"We didn't learn what it was until a few months before I returned to the brokerage. They suffered malaise and dizziness and general fatigue. So much so that some days they could barely walk. They needed me to get groceries and cook meals for them most days. General household upkeep was my job, as well as taking care of the lawn. And forget about them being able to drive. I would take them to the GP. Caring for them occupied my teenage years. I was able to go to university and start the brokerage, but it became apparent they needed full-time care, so that's why I left for those years."

"Asher, I'm so sorry. That must have been difficult for you growing up. Did you have friends?"

"Not many who would understand I couldn't go to the cinema because I needed to watch my parents. And dating was a bust. Well, I did take out a few girls. But I could never get beyond worrying about my parents to really enjoy myself. It wasn't until I was on a flight headed to an auction and read an article online that I began to piece things together.

"A massive cell phone tower had been installed very near where we lived months before my parents began to show symptoms. It was possible they had developed EMF sickness."

"I've heard of that. Some people can't endure the radiation and frequencies put out by electronics like mobile phones and Wi-Fi."

Wow, she understood! He didn't have to face off against disbelief or accusations that it was all in his head. Something that occurred all the time as he'd been navigating his parents' sickness with them. Such experience had formed a hardened shell on his exterior. Perhaps even had planted the seeds to The Face. Given him a mask to wear to fend off those who thought he was ridiculous.

"Exactly, and sometimes even the electricity wiring a home," he continued. "Our lives are flooded with electromagnetic frequencies that are not aligned with our body's natural frequencies. We are electrical beings. We're not meant to swim in a literal electronic soup. It's a difficult diagnosis and most doctors dismiss it as all in the patient's head."

"But you weren't affected by it?"

"Not everyone will be affected as severely as my parents. Though I do take precautions. I don't carry my phone unless it's necessary. Keep it on airplane mode whenever possible.

And most of my suit coat pockets are lined with a faraday fabric that blocks electromagnetic frequencies, keeping the radiation away from my body. It's also why you can never contact me in the middle of the day. I don't turn my phone on unless I need it. And have you ever seen me use a laptop or tablet? I don't, unless it's a client's and I need to show them something."

"I'm glad you explained that to me. I would have never guessed. And your parents? How are they doing now?"

"All my research led me to a GP who knew exactly what the issue was. He suggested mum and dad relocate to the country, get as far from London and the digital world as possible. Which wasn't an easy task. Eventually they found a place just outside Bath. An old cottage that was still wired from the early nineteen hundreds and used bells and rope to signal the staff and has a chicken roost outside and—well, it does have modern plumbing. It's the perfect home for them. And they've improved ninety percent."

"That's so good to hear. And that's when you were able to return to the brokerage?"

"Absolutely. My parents have always harbored tremendous guilt over my having to care for them. I could have hired in-home care, but believe me, I would have never wanted to be anywhere else."

"I'm so glad they found a place to live that allows them to be healthy. You are a good son."

"I can't imagine treating them any differently than they treat me. I'm blessed to have been raised in a loving family." And to have found a woman who truly seemed to understand him. Remarkable.

"So that makes me curious about how The Face works into all this?"

"What do you mean?"

"How should I put this without offending you…?"

Asher crossed his arms over his chest, sensing what was coming. "Go for it, Marsha."

She smirked. "The Face is charismatic and charming. Out there. He knows how to work a room *and* a person to get what he wants. Doesn't really jive with the kindhearted son who sacrificed years of his work at The Art Guys to care for his parents."

She got him. She really got him.

"I think The Face burst out of me following that stint caring for them. Part of me…" He winced. He'd thought about this after that class on emotions. And it was so true it hurt. "I craved the attention. And I saw what a charming smile and some complimentary words could do to a person as I was navigating the health care system with my parents. I learned I could get through any situation with body language and, yes, even some manipulative words. I'm not proud of it, but I quickly learned that one must have an advocate, a voice, when they are struggling through the health care system. I had that voice. And I softened it and gave it a flirtatious tone because it got me to where I needed to land."

"I can understand that. Please don't feel guilty. You did what you had to do for your parents. You gave your life to them, sacrificing a social life and friendships. It makes sense you'd want to grab it all now."

"Just because it makes sense doesn't mean it's right. That arrogant charm you mentioned has outgrown its stay. I don't like that label. I mean, I work it. I know what The Face brings to the brokerage. Sure, I'll take the credit for bringing in the media interest. But I'm so glad you can see the real me."

"I have always seen that man." She collected her water bottle and stood to turn toward the path. "And I like what I see."

She marched onward, into the sweet piney forest. And Asher's heart followed before his footsteps did.

"She likes me," he whispered. And it felt as wondrous and exciting as if a younger version of himself had discovered love for the first time.

Later Maeve munched a chocolate macaron as she wandered along the rocks edging the same stream they'd crossed earlier. She sat on a large rock, kicked off her shoes and dipped her bare feet in the water. So nice after walking for hours.

They'd discussed a few more questions.

Reveal something you've never told your partner.

She had kept it light by telling him she was afraid of the color puce. *Come on! Who names a color that?* And he'd played along to reveal he couldn't brush his teeth without mentally singing "Twinkle, Twinkle Little Star."

A few deeper questions remained on her list. But she was enjoying herself too much to wander into those. The day was perfect. And with no one else but Asher beside her, she could relax. Forget about making the future a success. Leave her mother's chastising words in a dark corner. Be in the present.

Settling beside her, Asher peeled off his socks and plunged his feet into the water. "Cold!" He cringed, but then placed his feet back in the water. "But invigorating. A nice pick-me-up after hiking for so long, eh?"

His wink hit her right where all that soft mushy swoony stuff had been collecting over the years. Right now, a kiss would make that stuff explode from her like a volcano spewing lava. Probably best to contain herself. Or maybe not? They were alone…

"I think the resort is beyond that thick of trees," she said.

Asher reached for her mouth. "May I? You've macaron crumbs…"

"Oh. Uh…sure."

He wiped off the crumbs. Taking his time. Eyes focusing intently on her mouth. And if that wasn't an invitation…

Maeve leaned forward and pressed her lips to his. Kissing Asher was a dream come true. They were having some fun learning about one another. And the bonus was the growing intimacy.

His fingers threaded through her hair at her nape, tickling an erotic shiver along her spine. Leaning into him, she deepened the kiss. This was a moment she would never forget. And yet, she did work for him, and—how would Krew and Joss take this?

Breaking the kiss and touching her lips, she whispered, "I shouldn't have done that."

"Why is that?"

"Asher, you're my boss."

"Believe me, Maeve, when we kiss it has nothing to do with the fake relationship. Well, that first one in the yoga class might have been. But since then? I kiss you because I want to. And you kissing me?"

"I couldn't not kiss you," she hastily confessed. "And… I don't want it to be fake, yet…"

"Yet?"

"I don't know. It doesn't feel right, no matter how often I think about—"

She caught herself. Tugged in her lower lip with her teeth. How often she thought about kissing him? How *not* winning him would only notch another failure for her tally?

"Please don't let me being your boss bother you," he said with a quick kiss to seal that statement. The way he looked at her always stole her breath. As though there was no one else in this world. She was his focus. "There are no rules saying we have to keep it business only."

"Sounds good. In theory. But what about when the week is over and the goal is accomplished? Do I return to my desk, leery of making eye contact with you and regretful that this, whatever it is, didn't become something more?"

"Do you...want something more?"

"You see? You think this is just for the week. And when we return to London it's back to the status quo again. I can't risk the heartache."

"But that's what life is for, Maeve. You're supposed to let it happen. I promise I won't ghost you."

She stood, grabbed her shoes and stepped up the mossy bank to the hiking trail. "I don't know. This feels...suddenly dangerous." Stuffing her wet feet into her running shoes, she twisted until they slid in. "I should have never said anything. Should have played along with the fake relationship. But it's never been fake to me. I...need to be alone for a bit. Give me a five-minute head start."

She dashed off, double-time.

She felt like a fool. The kiss had been perfect. Yet she had allowed a ridiculous misgiving to nudge into that perfection. She'd failed. But not in a manner her mother would scoff at. Mariane Pemberton would approve of Maeve avoiding utilizing a man on her climb to the top.

If she pleased her mum, then ultimately Maeve felt she would never win. At least not when it came to her heart.

CHAPTER THIRTEEN

ASHER FOLLOWED MAEVE'S retreat until she turned toward a curved trail amongst the trees.

It's never been fake to me.

Really? She'd *always* had feelings for him? That was re-markable to learn. And it wasn't as shocking as he expected. Because he may have felt the same only never realized it. Until this trip.

Until he'd kissed the girl and she'd run away. Again.

He took a different path around back of the shower build-ing toward the far end of the resort. He wasn't sure if that door would open from the outside. He and Maeve hadn't yet ventured that way. Worth a try.

Walking up the wood-paved aisle toward the door, he spied a man coming out from the building and his mood rose in anticipation—until he saw who it was.

"Hammerstill," he muttered tightly.

The gruff representation of a living tree stump recognized him and shook his head. "If it isn't The Face. My partner thought she saw you here, but I couldn't imagine a man like you being in a relationship long enough to have trouble."

"Same," Asher said. "I thought you were married, Ham-merstill? And not to the woman I've seen you here with. Got a little something on the side going on?"

The man winced. Asher had guessed correctly.

"None of your concern."

"You're right. Your private life isn't of interest to me. What is, is that you seem to be here for ulterior motives. Not necessarily interested in rehabbing whatever it is you're tagging as a relationship?"

"I could imagine the same of you. You after Kichu?"

"Maybe. Spoke to him last night, in fact."

"Is that so?" The man crossed beefy arms over his barrel chest. "How did that go? Wait. Let me guess. You charmed him with your million-dollar smile and dazzled with that easy camaraderie. And then when it came time to seal the deal? You choked."

The bastard was so presumptuous! Asher didn't choke. He'd never lost a client or failed to obtain the best deal and art those clients expected of him. One time—unfortunately, on film—he'd lost an auction. And that thought switched his brain to Maeve telling him how her mother told her she was a failure. He knew exactly how Maeve felt!

"You choked again, Dane?" Hammerstill prompted.

"Kichu had a meeting." Asher set aside his thought about Maeve. "We plan to talk. Soon."

"We'll see about that." Hammerstill lifted his burly chest and pointed in the air defiantly. "The race is on!"

He barged past Asher and made his way toward the geo-thermal pools.

Yes, the race was on. And Asher had a leg up because he'd already made contact with the elusive artist. Now to get a look at the artwork everyone wanted to own.

He tried the door and found it locked. Exit only? Figures. Tracking along the building so Hammerstill didn't notice his defeat, he rounded the resort and veered toward the reception area. But the thought of Maeve failing in her mother's eyes bothered him.

She needed support. He knew that feeling.

* * *

Maeve had managed to avoid Asher for a few hours by slipping into a "girls only" session on Making Time for Yourself. The trouble was, she had too much time to herself. And she wasn't in a real relationship. The class information had wafted around her ears, slipping in and out while her thoughts were preoccupied with the tiff she and Asher had earlier. For a pair who were not even a couple in real life, they seemed to be meeting plenty of challenges. The fake relationship had become reality.

And that confused the bloody heck out of her.

The class ended, and Maeve slipped out with a quick "thanks" to the instructor. It was evening, and hunger nudged her stomach, so she headed toward the dining room.

It hadn't been a tiff. Well. She had allowed herself to admit to him that she wished what was going on between them might be more. But she knew it wasn't to him. Those kisses? He was playing a role.

Or maybe he wasn't?

Again, the confusion would end her. What was real and what was fake?

She, unfortunately, had *not* been role-playing. It was impossible not to allow her heart into the act when the man she desired touched her and kissed her and had slept beside her all night. She'd woken in the pale morning hours to feel Asher's arm draped across her waist. It was as if her body wanted her to be alert, to note the touch, so she'd woken in a sort of reverie.

His arm across her waist had been an unconscious act. But for those minutes when she'd lain there like a statue, because she hadn't wanted to wake him and lose the touch, she had experienced some heady emotions. Romance and passion. Excitement and desire. Bliss, comfort, even satisfaction. As if they were a real couple and it had been just another morning wrapped in one another's arms.

Then she had cautioned her fantasies. Everything she knew about Asher Dane was being turned on its head. He wasn't an egotistic spotlight seeker. His need for attention had been a result of years of selfless attention to his sick parents. He deserved the notice he got now!

She wanted to reach into him and make him understand that she cared about him. That she was on his side.

It felt risky. And premature. And yet, he had indicated that his kisses were because he *wanted* to kiss her and not in a fake way—but for real.

Her phone pinged and she tugged it from her dress pocket. While stalking back to the resort from the hiking trail, she'd opened the link to the application her mum had sent for the Dublin job. In that moment she'd felt, at the very least, she should apply and see what the job might offer her. A backup may be wise should her prospects with The Art Guys fall flat. The text confirmed her application had been received. They would notify her soon if they wished to set up a video interview.

"It's being smart," she said to her unsure thoughts. "I have to keep my options open."

Especially since she wasn't expecting this trip to advance her at The Art Guys anymore. All she was learning from Asher was how to sneak around.

Entering the dining room, she immediately saw Asher at the back near the window. He gestured her over. A good sign he wasn't angry with her. Not that he should be. Hell, *she'd* stormed away from *him*. She was not a drama queen. Yet she'd not been prepared for the roller coaster of emotions soaring through her this week!

"I wasn't sure you'd come," he said as she seated herself

across the small table from him. Candlelight glinted in his hair and pale irises. "Bold red and a dusty turquoise," he said of the colors she'd chosen with great care before heading off to the Making Time for Yourself class. "What does that mean?"

To Maeve, red meant putting up a shield to keep others back. She'd been apprehensive while dressing. Now she felt more like the blue scarf that indicated a cool yet cautious eagerness.

"Just a dress I pulled out from the closet." She picked up the goblet and sniffed the deep red wine. "Fruity."

"It's delicious. But I don't for one moment believe that you just threw on that dress."

She quirked a brow. "You think I'm lying?"

"I would never accuse, but…" He nodded while he shrugged.

Caught. "Doesn't matter what it means. What's for dinner?"

"Four courses. Filet mignon. Tiny potatoes. Fussy foamy stuff. You know the deal. I suspect that red…"

He wasn't going to let it go!

"Is…" He rolled his thoughts over so long she could see the process dance in his eyes. "It means stop," he decided.

Maeve couldn't prevent a chuckle. "That's a no-brainer. But no."

"No?"

"I'm not so obvious with my colors." She decided to throw him a bone. "It's caution. Maybe a bit of exterior armor. I feel like we went the wrong way out on the hiking trail. Or I did. I shouldn't have said the things I did."

"About wanting this to be more?"

Wow, he grabbed right for the arrow lodged firmly in her heart. Maeve nodded, thankful when the waiter arrived with their plates, which featured a miniscule chunk of what she hoped was red meat surrounded by pink drizzle and some truly Lilliputian carrots, with the greens barely fraying to the plate edge.

"This is one bite for me," Asher said.

"I hope the dessert is an entire pie." Maeve lifted her fork. "Thank goodness for the monster pastries they serve at breakfast."

"When this is over I promise to take you out and treat you to a real meal." He lifted his goblet to toast and Maeve met it in a *ting*. "We both need real food."

"Hear! Hear!"

"For every tiny carrot you eat," he suddenly said, pausing her with a fork tine speared with a marble-sized carrot, "I want some truth."

Maeve lowered her fork. "About what?"

"Do you really want this to be a thing? Us?"

She stared at the carrot, pearled with butter sauce. If she didn't confess her truth they would leave and go back to the same old, same old. She may or may not earn a raise or chance to prove herself worthy of a promotion. It was what she desired.

And yet. Advancement was only a step toward her goal. She wasn't going to erase her mother's voice from her brain after a few days at a couples' spa. So why not reach for something that she desired in equal amounts? Like the handsome man waiting for her to speak.

Maeve ate the carrot. One chew. Time for the truth.

"I do," she finally said.

Asher nodded appreciatively and tilted back a long swallow that emptied his glass. He signaled to the waiter, who brought over another bottle and refilled his.

"I know it's silly," Maeve started.

"I certainly hope not," he said defensively. "Else I might

think you're playing another kind of game. And I'm not sure how to play that one."

"You see?" She set her napkin on the table and sat back, feeling frustration swell and chase away her appetite. "That's the problem. We're playing games. *Are* they a couple? *Are* they having trouble? Can they sleuth out the elusive artist? Will they win him over? Can she earn a raise? Can she ever fulfill her dream?"

Asher reached across the table and placed his hand over hers. He nudged her, and she turned her hand up so he could clasp it properly. "I could make that dream of yours come true right now. How much do you need to open the consulting business?"

Maeve slid quickly from his grasp. "I don't want your charity."

"I know. And though it was a genuine offer, please don't think I was trying to buy you for— I know you need to do this on your own. That's what makes a dream a dream. It's something a person accomplishes. It isn't handed to them."

Maeve felt a tear threaten in her eye. He understood.

"I ran into Hammerstill earlier," he said. "He's my nemesis. Makes me feel like… You saw the footage. And he made me think about what you said about your mother calling you a failure. You are not a failure. You are one of the most put-together, smart, amazing women I know. You'll have another chance at that shop. I know you will."

That tear was almost ready to spill…

"I care about you, Maeve."

He pulled her hand up and kissed it.

"Thank you. That means a lot. You're not a failure either. Hammerstill is a bloody pompous jerk who saw an opportunity to bring someone down to his level and jumped at it. You shouldn't let it continue to bother you."

"I thought I was the one encouraging you? You're so caring toward others. That's not being a failure. That's a special quality not many possess."

"You're the same. After hearing about how you cared for your parents for years? Asher, you are a strong man. You don't need to prove yourself to anyone."

"That said, I do genuinely want to develop my own stable of artists."

"This could be your chance. It will happen."

She sipped her wine and her shoulders relaxed.

"Now back to the real topic of conversation." He laid his palms on the table before him and met her gaze. "I'm not sure what is happening between us right now, but I don't want to run away from it. And I don't want it to be a game we're playing. We're mixing business with pleasure here. And while that has sometimes been a norm for me, it feels off. Just as you said. This is…different. And you deserve more attention than I can offer when I should be focused on the goal."

She didn't like hearing what he seemed to not want to clearly state. That he had to focus on work. And she was a distraction. Never had she felt like a distraction to a man. And truthfully? It was more exciting than it should be. Especially since she knew the one rule of this game: it's all fake.

"We are workmates," she stated to remind herself. "Not something we should risk destroying because of some silly game we decided might win us an artist."

"Maeve, the whole boss/employee thing doesn't bother me. That shouldn't affect our work in any manner. You make me feel…" He searched his thoughts. "*Feel*, Maeve. Things I haven't felt before. It's like I don't have to work for your interest. The Face means nothing to you. You give me your attention freely. That means so much. And I don't want to stop kissing you. And I don't want to stop waking in the morning with my arm draped across your body."

So he'd known they had touched, slept so close? And he'd not said anything. Kept it to himself. As she had chosen to do the same. A silent passion. Of course she'd given him her attention frccly. It wasn't difficult. But keeping it was the challenge. One that they both needed to face.

"But I do need to catch the client before Hammerstill does," he said. "And so…"

"I understand. I do."

"I don't think you do understand how much…"

The waiter arrived to take away their plates. A few bites had not satisfied Maeve. How could she eat when her relationship was the topic? They both wanted to go that direction. There was only the distraction of still playing the fake in the way.

She didn't understand how much *what*? He cared about her?

Another waiter arrived with dessert, sweeping it grandly before them before placing it precisely at the table center. It wasn't miniscule. It was a tower of vanilla cake smothered in red sauce and fresh cut fruit, served on a massive plate with two dainty forks placed to either side. This place was certainly focused on satisfaction via sweets!

As her gaze met Asher's wide eyes, the two of them laughed at the silliness of the meal. And it released some of the tension she felt over what was happening between them. He'd kind of, sort of confirmed he might feel the same about her. But he didn't want to focus on her right now.

Of course, this was a business trip. And she was determined to make advances, no matter how little they may ultimately serve her goal. Time to get her head back in work mode.

CHAPTER FOURTEEN

THE EVENING WORKSHOP was in the gymnasium. The couples sat on yoga mats but were promised they wouldn't be flexing any body parts tonight. Candles flickering everywhere gave the room the aura of a cathedral, one of peace and safety.

Maeve noticed the couples who had been arguing most virulently at the beginning of the retreat had seemed to settle, sat a bit closer, some even held hands.

The instructor thanked them for their participation in the hike that one couple had gotten lost on. They'd had to send in a rescue team to find them; they were recovering in their room this evening.

"Those questions we sent along with you weren't that difficult, were they?" the instructor joked. "Sorry. We have one final question that requires your discussion this evening. And that is, now that you've shared your dreams and goals for the future, how will your partner help you to achieve that goal? Okay? Discuss!"

Asher's shoulder hugged against hers, and he leaned in to whisper, "We've got this one, Marsha."

"Do we?" While comfortable snuggling against him, she wasn't as confident as some of the couples who had found new reason to reconnect with their partners. Asher wasn't her partner. Much as she wanted him to be. "I can't help you with your goal."

"Wrong. You are helping me. You were the one who ditched my kiss so I'd have the opportunity to talk to Kichu. It was my fault I failed the task."

"Don't call yourself a failure."

"Oh, yeah? I won't if you don't."

"But I am…"

He slid his hand into hers and tilted his head against hers. "Maeve, not many women succeed in opening a shop in a large city at such a young age. You are remarkable. You had a vision. You fulfilled it. It wasn't your fault some nasty virus decided it wasn't time for something so innovative as a color shop."

"I've never thought of it that way."

"You should. You succeeded. Now you'll try again. And you will accomplish your goal."

"But I don't see you having a hand in that. I don't need anyone's help."

He bowed to meet her gaze. "It's okay to ask for help. Support. And I'm not talking financially. I want to be there for you."

A warmth swirled in her chest. The words felt like kindness come to color in soft violet. "Why?"

"Because you matter to me. I care about you."

Hearing him relabel her failure as something akin to an accomplishment twisted all the beliefs her mother had implanted in her over the years and forced them to the surface.

"I'm not sure I can succeed again," she said softly. "I got a loan from my mum the first time. I won't ask her again."

"Then you'll go to a bank. You'll bring along the best references from me, and I'm sure Krew and Joss will offer theirs as well."

"That's very kind of you."

"I'm not offering to bankroll your project because I understand that you like to do things on your own. But know, the offer still stands."

"I appreciate that, and… I won't forget."

"Hey, you file all my tax forms and banking information. You know what I make. I can afford to support a woman-owned color therapy business."

Maeve laughed softly. "I have seen your bank statement. It's obscene. But…"

"But?"

"It's not who you are. You are not defined by your bank account or by what your millions of followers think of you. I know that. But do you know that?"

"I thought we were talking about you?"

"You have a tendency to deflect the topic of conversation when it veers toward you."

"Guilty. Fine. I believe my worth is not based on the opinions of others. But The Face does love to play the game."

"The Face is a part of you that you should never abandon. But don't you realize it's not about The Face? You need to let the real Asher Dane out more often. I like him."

"You like me?" He nudged her playfully with his shoulder and sing-songed, "Marsha likes me."

"There's a lot to like."

"Now you're being sappy." He touched the corner of her mouth. An apostrophe? She'd always thought those crinkles were superfluous and annoying, but when he touched them, she was thankful for her uniqueness.

"Class," the instructor called, "your homework for tonight will be intense."

Gazes darted around the room. Maeve straightened next to Asher, who winked at her. Intense for a fake couple pretending to fight who had decided in real life to chill everything? But then again, maybe not? Could her life be more confusing right now?

"That mirror in your room is there for a purpose," the instructor announced.

Maeve's heart dropped. She could feel Asher's body tense beside her.

"Tonight you'll sit or stand before the mirror, fully clothed, and touch one another. Really feel your partner's very being. Go inward and see how that makes you feel. Can you connect on a level beyond sex? You can give instructions where you are comfortable being touched. Touch but no sex! All right, good night, everyone. See you all in the morning."

Asher stood and held out his hand to Maeve as she rose beside him. "I think that red you're wearing fits the moment," he said. "Caution."

He hit that one right on the mark.

Maeve stood before the mirror studying the wrinkle in her tomato-red dress. The fabric never stayed smooth. But she wasn't an ironing kind of girl. For some reason, staring at the wrinkle distracted her from looking at the woman standing before a floor-to-ceiling mirror anticipating what must come next.

Asher was in the bathroom brushing his teeth. They'd laughed as they'd returned to the room, suggesting they try the mirror assignment. Just for kicks.

Just for kicks. And the highest stress level she may have ever registered. Because she wanted Asher to touch her. Everywhere. But not because someone assigned them to do so.

"Why are you doing this to yourself?" she whispered.

"What was that?"

The scent of mint preceded Asher as he swung around the corner and into the main room.

His reflection showed freshly tousled hair.

That she could lose herself in.

A charming smile.

That she could surrender to.

Crisp business shirt unbuttoned two buttons down.

That she wanted to remove.

And a curious tilt of his head as he discerned her inner thoughts.

Maeve caught herself and checked her stance. No drool. No leaning toward the man she wanted to inhale, devour and consume. "Wondering if this assignment is too silly to attempt?"

"Nonsense." He stepped up behind her, and placing his hands on her shoulders as if a gentle teacher set to guide her, he smiled at her in the mirror. "It'll be interesting. That is…are you okay with me touching you? I'm okay with you touching me."

"Oh, yes," she said, a little too quickly. "I mean, we've kissed. We are…"

He leaned closer and said near her ear, "We've started something, Maeve."

Oh, yes, they had.

"And this assignment isn't so much about the touch as the connection. At least, that's how I understand it."

True. Which promised to be much more intense. If they did it correctly.

"Can I—" he stepped closer so she could feel his chest against her back "—hold your hands?"

She nodded.

He clasped her hands from behind, and the move pressed him even closer to her backside. They weren't body to body, but their distance would not allow the sneakiest of warm summer breezes to slip between them. Thinking of which, she'd opened the patio doors to allow in the night air. Somewhere in the background a bird cooed, perhaps luring his or her mate to snuggle for the evening.

"Remember," he said on a teasing tone, "no sex…"

Maeve let out a nervous chitter. "Of course not. That would be breaking the rules."

But not her rules. Not in a million years would she ever push away Asher Dane and refuse to make love with him. She wanted him. And…was this too dangerous a task to attempt? To allow him to touch her. To touch him. And to *not* have sex?

"Certainly, we must have our rules," he whispered.

She glanced at his reflection in the mirror and spied his smirk. What was she getting into?

"I understand what this assignment is supposed to do," he said. His fingers loosened within hers, and his hands began a slow glide to her wrists and up her bare arms.

"What's that?" she asked as calmly as possible. Her skin began to electrify and her body to sing. He paused at her elbows, and the soft trace of his fingertips along the insides of them insisted she close her eyes to keep from looking into his delving gaze.

"It's a trust thing," he said. "But also, how many couples really touch?"

"I think that's a thing when you're a couple," she said. "I mean, you can't be one and not touch."

"Sure, but hear me out." He glided his fingertips up to her shoulders bared but for the narrow straps. "Okay, if I keep moving?"

"Yes, of course." Stop him? Never!

"Good." His glide moved along the tops of her shoulders and to the base of her neck, where he toyed with her hair and earlobes. "I know couples connect, but do they really… simply…touch? We have sex with our lovers and that's…sex.

How often do we slow down and linger on the curve of our partner's earlobe?"

Maeve wanted to sigh but she held it back. The caress of her earlobe was weirdly erotic and—she had never had a man do such a thing to her. Sex truly was a strange act that two people seemed to fall into and perform as if by rote.

Hello, I'm horny, let's satisfy one another but not really look into one another's eyes.

"Taking the time to explore should be first and foremost," she whispered.

"Exactly." He nuzzled his nose into her hair, burnishing along her neck. "You smell good. Like spring and vanilla."

"You smell like royal violet and the earth."

He smiled against her neck, and his fingers pulled back her hair to fully expose her neck. "Right. My color. I would expect nothing less from one so ridiculously obsessed with color. But your dress…"

"My dress?"

"You said earlier it was a cautionary color."

"My mood has changed since I put it on. Now the color has blossomed into a lush, juicy…" Now she did meet his gaze in the mirror. The room light was as low as candlelight, but his smile over the top of her shoulder warmed her to her bones. "Desire. Keep touching me?"

"I couldn't stop now if I wanted to."

Allowing herself to relax, to take in every molecule of the man's presence, Maeve dropped her shoulders as his hands moved down her spine and to her waist. While he did so, his head remained near hers, and…the kiss to her neck was utterly soul spinning. Asher's mouth opened against the tender rise along her vein and his tongue crept out to tickle, taste. Linger. Gasping, she bowed her head, curling into the sweet sensation that coiled in her core.

Every part of her body focused on that one spot on her neck. Her fingers curled and her thighs squeezed together. Her belly softened as she felt a tingle swirl lower. Deep violet kisses punctuated her neck. Each one shoving in that arrow lodged in her heart deeper and deeper.

One of his hands slid around her waist. A certain claiming. Maeve threaded her fingers through his. She wanted to turn around and touch him, to run her fingers through his hair, to…relax even more into the sure climax that teased at her. But it was too soon. Too presumptuous. And—what about the rule?

"My turn?" she said on a gasp.

"Of course."

Damn the no-sex rule.

She turned and, the intense connection breaking, took a moment to meet his gaze. There was nothing whatsoever The Face about Asher Dane at this moment. No false charm. He wasn't faking anything. The compassion and desire in his glacier-blue eyes enticed like geothermal pools. Warm and inviting. A heavenly retreat.

Maeve slid her hands up his shirt front and…unbuttoned a few more buttons. Smoothing her palms over his skin, she marveled at the hard muscle beneath and the warmth that burnished skin against skin. Asher sucked in a breath. The sound of his pleasure lured her closer, and while marveling over his hard pecs, she leaned up and kissed him.

Violet kisses warmed her soul. And ignited her craving to a heady blaze. This kiss quickly grew urgent. Not at all polite. She wouldn't want it any other way. The man's soft groan as she deepened the kiss worked like a call to her inner sex goddess. Satisfaction was required to appease that deity.

She pulled off his shirt and tossed it to the floor. He slipped down one of her dress straps. The only way more clothing was going to be removed was to take off the whole dress.

"We may be exceeding the boundaries of the assignment," she noted while she drew her fingernails lightly down his torso. The man's muscles contracted and he hissed softly. Her goddess arched her back and smiled wickedly.

"Screw the assignment." He lifted her and set her on the bed, leaning over her as he did so that she fell back against the bed. "I want you, Maeve. And this is not fake. This is real. We are…"

"Real," she finished. "Yes, I want you too. But we'll fail the assignment."

"Figured you for a studious sort."

"I've failed here and there."

"Want to fail again? With me?"

She pulled him down onto her, and he rolled her so she was on top of him. "It'll be my best failure ever."

CHAPTER FIFTEEN

A GLINT OF pale sunlight twinkled Maeve awake. It was too early by mere mortal standards. Before six. Her body protested rising so she rolled over to find Asher smiling at her.

"Morning," he said in a sleepy tone.

"Not yet. Roosters don't even rise this early. I want to cling to sleep a little longer."

"Would a kiss be too invigorating?"

She snuggled against his body, hugging her breasts to his chest and—quickly learned a part of him was very awake. She kissed his jaw and nuzzled against his neck. "It would be." But only because she didn't want her morning breath to scare him off. "Although…" She glided her hand downward. "A slow, deep hug wouldn't wake me too much."

He moved closer and they joined slowly, sweetly. "Feels right here."

"It does."

"Never fake, Maeve. I promise."

And as they moved rhythmically, she closed her eyes to the bliss of being wrapped in Asher's arms.

Asher wandered the room in his boxer briefs and out to the patio. He didn't worry that other guests would see him; each patio was screened on one side. And if someone did? Let 'em look!

Maeve, who had risen to shower after they'd made love, had then left to collect pastries for breakfast while he'd showered.

The sun had burst on the horizon. The light permeated his skin and seemed to dance with his molecules. The day felt more promising than a recently discovered lost Picasso that could net millions at auction. He had made love to Maeve, and it had felt more right than anything. Not like a fling or a hookup in a city in which he was spending a few nights to attend an auction. What he had with Maeve was mature and real, and it baffled him because—*was* this the real thing? Could he have what he desired from her? His crazy goal about family and children and happiness with a lifelong partner. He'd not initially thought of her as someone who could be a part of his life. And now he couldn't imagine making another step without her by his side.

Every clue he got from her echoed the same feeling. That she was in this for whatever came next. Would it be fair to her to attempt a relationship while he remained her boss? How would visits to the office be received by Krew and Joss if he kissed the receptionist upon arrival?

Asher shook his head. The guys wouldn't care. And he didn't care if they did care.

We know.

But the long-distance part would be difficult. Challenging. He liked what he had started with Maeve. He didn't want to rush into scenarios that made it wrong.

But there was still the reason he'd come here in the first place. Krew and Joss would not be pleased if he returned to the office kissing his receptionist sans a new artist.

He had to get on his A game today and track down Tony Kichu. But they had a day in town planned. The rehab classes were completed. A day of sightseeing offered a getaway to use their newly learned partnership skills in real life. Couples would report back later this evening and fill out questionnaires and rate the course. Then tomorrow morning was graduation, and following, the flight back to London.

As soon as he arrived at Heathrow Airport, Asher had to catch a flight to Bangladesh to attend an auction. That left him about a day to find Kichu and sign him on. He should not go into town today, but instead stay behind and stalk the guru… Though not spending the day with Maeve sounded like an even worse plan.

Might it be easier to locate Kichu while everyone was away? The man would let down his guard; maybe he'd wander about the grounds.

Asher turned to face the room. Inside, the rumpled bed-sheets gave him a smile. There was yet a lot of ground to cover at the resort. If he stayed behind, he still might not find Kichu, and then he'd have lost a day spent with Maeve for nothing.

"I'll track him down this evening. It will happen."

That was his story and he was sticking to it.

Maeve waited for the elevator, a box of pastries in hand. She loved the *pain au chocolat* that was made fresh every morning. It was always warm and flaky, and the right amount of dark chocolate oozed into every bite. Asher seemed to enjoy anything she brought him, so this morning it was a choice of croissant or cream-filled donut.

Bouncing on her heels, she realized her smile had not softened since she'd risen. After a shower, she'd spun into the room to model her yellow sundress splattered with pink polka dots for Asher. Yellow for creativity and the sky was the limit. She'd bounced into a kiss with him and had promised to return as quickly as possible.

Leaving him standing there in nothing but a sheet wrapped about his hips had been difficult. They'd broken the rules last night.

Did that mean this was a real relationship? She wanted to rush ahead into that status but didn't want to make a fool of herself. It could have been a natural reaction to the touch exercise. It may not have meant as much to Asher as it did to her. In her experience, men were more physical than women. They could have sex without emotion. But herself? Sex meant something to her.

And so did Asher.

They needed to get straight about what that tousle in the sheets—twice, including this morning—had meant. Was it being too controlling on her part to want to know? She didn't want to ruin what she had with him by asking questions and making it weird.

I can make it weirder.

He seemed to understand her. So she decided to ride the moment and try not to overthink it too much. It had been sex. She needed to…go with it. Not expect a marriage proposal or lifelong commitment over one night together.

When the elevator door opened, she felt the presence of another person rush to enter behind her as she got in. Turning, she aimed to press the floor button but someone she recognized beat her to it.

"First floor?" Tony Kichu asked.

"Yes, uh… Mr. Kichu. It's so nice to finally meet you. My…partner and I have really enjoyed the retreat."

"That's a lovely shade of yellow," he commented on her dress. "Creative."

Enamored that he intuited the golden color's exact meaning, she effused, "I was feeling a creative surge this morning. It also invites opportunity."

He looked at her anew. "You navigate by color?"

"Color is a big part of my life. I tend to dress emotionally."

The door opened, and he pressed the hold button, seeming interested. "I tend to wear white because it is neutral and allows me to embrace whatever the world wishes me to notice."

"And this morning you noticed me," she said, and didn't even show the inward wince at such a presumptive statement.

"Indeed. You are here with Mr. Dane? The art broker?"

"Yes, he's my…" Lover! "Partner. Well, you know that. It's why we're here, isn't it?"

Stop being so idiotic, Maeve. Use this opportunity!

"Asher mentioned he spoke to you briefly the other day. He's very interested in seeing your art."

"I don't show it to anyone."

"I'd like to see it. I mean… I love art. All art. And I'm not a dealer or someone looking to buy art. You shouldn't feel uncomfortable showing it to me."

"My work is very…particular. But it does incorporate a lot of color."

Sensing an opening, she stepped up to block the doors and matched his stance. "I do like color."

He took a while to look her over, his soft gaze taking in her hair and face and clothing. Nothing sexual, more like seeing a like soul.

"Perhaps," he said. "But you are on your way to breakfast? Or in the middle of it?" He looked to the box she held.

"It'll keep. If you have a moment right now, I'd love to see your work."

With a nod, he started to walk. "Come with me."

Having forgotten about their plans to spend the day in town, Maeve sped down the hallway toward their room. She was too excited, filled with a visceral joy at having seen Kichu's work. She'd been in his studio a mere ten minutes, but in that time she had fallen in love with his paintings. And she was the only person who had seen them? It was too amazing to comprehend!

She couldn't wait to tell Asher all about it. He was going to—

Maeve stopped abruptly in the center of the hallway, box of pastries in hand. She'd begun to think Asher would love Tony Kichu's art. But she knew better. She knew Asher's taste. He wasn't going to love the wild, busy, colorful style. It would likely be the ugliest thing he'd ever viewed.

And Asher Dane did not do ugly.

While looking over the canvases, she had briefly considered trying to win Kichu herself and bringing him to The Art Guys to show her worth. His artwork had captivated her. She would love to represent him.

Could she?

No, Maeve, you agreed to this fake relationship to help Asher nab the artist. You can't do that to him.

Only someone like…her mother would be so cruel.

It could be her means to getting what she desired.

Maeve tugged in her lower lip. What to do?

CHAPTER SIXTEEN

ASHER TEXTED THE waiting driver to give him another five minutes. Where had Maeve gotten to? She could have picked up pastries, distributed them to the entire resort and eaten her own—and his—in the time she'd been gone. He'd showered, dressed and readied for their venture into Reykjavík this morning. One final group event was scheduled for dinnertime, but otherwise all couples were heading out for a day away from classes, pottery hugging and kiss whistles.

When the door to the room opened, his anxiety fled. Maeve's bright smile summoned his return smile. But...

"We should head out," he said. "Where have you been?"

She held a box. Asher handed her the bag she'd packed earlier and reopened the door. "I was talking to someone..."

"Tell me about it in the car? The driver is waiting."

"Right, sorry. Yes, I'm excited to do some exploring. Let's go!"

Once in the back of the car, Asher gave the driver instructions to take them to the Blue Lagoon just outside Reykjavík. They planned to start the day there and then move into town for some sightseeing. He wanted it to be a romantic excursion. A way to show Maeve he really was into developing this relationship.

As the landscape sped by and they passed areas that had been recently covered by fresh lava flow from a surprisingly active volcano, he raked his fingers through his hair and then had to laugh as he finally looked at Maeve. She sat there in her cheery yellow dress, her lips pursed and her attention fixed on the scenery that swished by, holding the pastry box carefully.

She tilted a dark cherry smirk at him. "What?"

"Are you going to share those or do you want to hold them on your lap the entire day? What's got you distracted?"

"Uh, well…" She offered the box, and he took a flaky croissant. "It's nothing. For now."

"For now? Sounds ominous."

"Let's enjoy our breakfast and the day. We've been doing heavy-duty couple bonding and soul revealing all week. I want today to be light. Promising."

"Same. You said you were talking to someone? That's why you were late?"

"Yes, just…another woman in the retreat. She's found the event very helpful. Brought her much closer to her husband."

"I've noticed a general sigh amongst the participants. Hands are being held. Voices are calmer and more respectful. Do you think…?"

Maeve gave him a *go on* look as she chewed.

"Well." He set his half-eaten croissant on the box cover she'd set between them. "We've grown closer."

She nodded, still chewing.

"Confession? I hadn't expected to get so close to you. What started as a…" He glanced to the driver, who wore dark sunglasses and could hear everything even though the radio played some weird flute music at a low volume. "You know," he said.

"A fake?"

"Yes. But, Maeve, it's not anymore. Is it?"

"Something has certainly…begun?"

"You don't sound very sure."

"I don't want to step over any lines."

"Please step, crush, shuffle, obliterate any lines you feel still exist. Maeve…" He took her hand and bowed his head to kiss it. "We've become…"

How to say it? To blurt out that he was her boyfriend and she his girlfriend was making a large assumption. That they were a couple? Were they? He felt as though they were. But that implied so much. And it had occurred in only four days? Yes, it had happened quickly, but it felt so real, so true.

"I know what you can't say. I'm not sure I dare say it either. It could work," he said softly. "Do you want it to work?"

She nodded. "With all my heart."

"But something is still holding you back?"

"I…"

The car slowed to park as the driver cheerily announced they had arrived at the Blue Lagoon. Outside, a family toting beach bags wandered by. Asher surveyed the full parking lot, realizing this would probably not be the romantic getaway he had intended.

"It's always busy in the mornings," the driver said. "You want me to stick around for an hour or two?"

"Yes, please, if that's all right with you," Asher said.

"It's your money." The driver tapped the clock on his dashboard.

"Not a problem. Shall we?"

Maeve nodded, and with what seemed almost a regretful smile, she pushed open the door, leaving the plate with their half-eaten pastries on the seat. She bent to peer in at him.

"I do," she said. "I really do."

She closed the door and went to the trunk, which the driver popped open, to grab the bag she'd packed for them.

Asher gripped the door handle. "She does? What does she…?"

Ah. He'd asked if this relationship was something she wanted to do.

"Nice."

After a shower, Maeve met Asher in the crowded lagoon, the hot spot to visit in Iceland. The creamy blue springs steamed from the volcanic magma in the earth. It was a massive lagoon that sported stairs leading into the springs in many spots and cooling pools, saunas, a steam cave, massage waterfall, a bar that served juice, alcohol and smoothies, and even a mud mask bar where you could smear the silica-and-algae-rich mud over face and body. Hundreds of people dotted the waters.

She and Asher waded into the lukewarm water, wandering hand in hand, and eventually found a nook where one other woman floated serenely.

"This was a bad idea," Asher said.

It was. Now she was here, she could only think about what she needed to tell him about meeting Tony Kichu.

"I should have rented us a private suite. There are too many people to relax. Not very romantic either."

She swung a look toward him. "Is it supposed to be romantic?"

"I wanted it to be." The emotion in that statement grabbed her by the heart. The Face had left the building. Only Asher remained, and man, did she adore him.

No way could she ever steal an artist from him.

She winked at him. "It is what we make it."

His smile returned. "Very well, Miss Colorful. Tell me about the color of this water. How does it affect you emotionally?"

"It's serene and yet full of mysterious energy," she said of the pale, creamy blue water. "The color makes me feel like relaxing yet at the same time as if I could run a marathon."

"Interesting." He pulled her closer to him.

Snuggling to sit on his lap, she tilted back her head and he met her with a lingering kiss. Were there people around them? She didn't notice. In Asher's arms, the rest of the world disappeared.

"What's the most interesting place you've visited on your trips to buy and sell art?" she asked.

"I love Romania. Visited Dracula's castle."

"Really? Did you suffer a bout of anemia while there?"

"No bites. But the landscape is gorgeous. And deadly. The Carpathian Mountains are jagged and dangerous, set against thick forests that a man could surely get lost in and never be discovered, except maybe by a pack of wolves. If vampires did exist, you'd find them there."

"Joss has some work there next month. A lost manuscript or something intriguing."

"Sounds right up his Indiana Jones alley. I like adventure, but when it comes to art, I prefer it dry, clean and under the best lighting. Do you think I should expand my interests? I do have a narrow field of interest when it comes to the Romantics and lush masters."

Yes, please, Maeve thought. Could he expand his interests within the next few hours so when he finally saw Tony Kichu's art he wouldn't freak out? Because one of them certainly had to sign him on with The Art Guys. She had to tell him about her meeting with him. Yet Kichu hadn't wanted to see Asher until tomorrow.

"I need to prove myself to the guys, Maeve. I've put this evening aside to locate Kichu and work my charm on him.

And frankly, I've been questioning the whole power of The Face lately."

"You do know it's not your good looks that get you by, don't you?" She understood that he did indeed think that. Ingrained in him after being released from a compassionate caring mission for his parents. He'd not taken anything for himself. And now The Face wanted whatever he could grasp. "Asher, you have so much care and concern for others that it permeates everything you do."

"I don't know about that."

"You sacrificed years of your life caring for your parents. And it's not something that you utilized just for them. I see it in you all the time. Sure, you're a handsome guy. But it's what's in here—" she pressed her palm over his heart "—that other people feel when they are around you. They sense your compassion. Your intense love for the art, which is a language you speak so well. The Face is not Asher Dane. And Asher Dane is the guy who ultimately wins the auctions and appeals to his followers."

He smirked and shook his head. "You have a ridiculous obsession with me, Marsha."

"Maybe I do."

An obsession that she'd gotten to indulge in this week. An obsession that prodded her to cheer him on and do what she could to ensure he got what he came here for. This trip had been for Asher, and she wanted to see him succeed.

"I have something to tell you. I thought it could wait, but it's too remarkable not to spill. I wasn't talking to someone from the retreat when I was late."

"Oh?"

"It's amazing news, and I would have told you right away, but you were in a hurry to leave and I didn't want to tell you with the driver listening… And it's not going to happen until tomorrow anyway…"

"What *were* you doing while on the hunt for pastries?"

"I met Tony Kichu in the elevator."

"Maeve," he breathed. His eyes brightened.

"I told him I was there with you and that I loved art and—he took me to see his artwork."

Asher gripped her by the upper arms. "He did?" A variety of emotions played over his face, from surprise to excitement to concern. He swiped a hand over his hair, which was beaded with moisture from the steaming water. "What went down? What did it look like? Tell me everything!"

"He wants to meet with you tomorrow morning after the closing ceremony."

"He does?"

She nodded. "I said you could be the only one to represent him." She had to believe that for herself as well. This was Asher's win, not hers. "What with your eye for detail and color, he could trust you."

"That's so generous of you."

"It's the truth. I mean, his art is amazing. He showed me five canvases. They are so colorful! And—they are modern art, for sure. Lots of spatters and geometrics, but also, some incredible freestyle networks that run through the backgrounds. It's hard to describe. Oh, Asher, I felt so much looking at them. They spoke to me. You have to represent Kichu."

"I will. I mean, I'll have to assess the art, but judging by your enthusiasm I'm sure I'll like the work."

"Well." With a wince, she spread her arms across the surface of the water to put a little distance between them. "There is a problem."

"What's that?"

"It's not your thing. Not…beautiful."

He screwed on a disbelieving face. "Come on, Maeve, my taste doesn't always tend toward beauty."

She recounted some of the masters he loved. "Waterhouse, Millais, Rossetti, Woolner. And that's just the Pre-Raphaelite Brotherhood. Don't get me started on the entire sixteenth century. You love those artists."

"Because they are beautiful—oh." He looked aside. Realizing what he'd said? Trying to conjure one artist who wasn't considered aesthetically beautiful? "Well, there's…"

While he considered which artists he favored who were not renowned for their beauty and lushness, Maeve sank up to her chin in the blue water. She could tell that his meeting with Kichu was not going to go well.

"Don't you think I've got an open enough mind to embrace all styles?" he asked. Maeve felt the accusation in his tone. A touch of challenge, even. "Do you agree with Hammerstill? That I'm all surface and no substance?"

His defenses had gone up. And she was to blame.

"Oh, Asher, not at all. I shouldn't have made it sound as if you wouldn't be interested. You are going to love Kichu's work as much as I do, I'm sure. You've got this." She took his hand and squeezed it. "I know you do."

He nodded. Let out a reluctant exhale. Not entirely a believer in what she'd said?

Once again, she was handling his life in the background. And she wasn't sure if she'd made it better or worse with that interference.

In town they stopped in a quaint shopping area, and Maeve dragged Asher through a few Nordic clothing shops. She purchased a paisley scarf dyed a bright turquoise, violet and yellow. And when she spied a pair of expensive bright pink heels, he bought them for her. She'd initially said no.

It had taken but a kiss for her to concede. He liked earning her smile as he'd handed her the bag. Something so simple as a pair of shoes brightened her entire face. He wouldn't mind having her face in his life all the time. Truly. She was the most beautiful piece of artwork in his life.

Leading him out of the shop, she pulled him down the sidewalk. They passed a gallery with a closed sign on it. No paintings inside, only a sculpture or two.

His tastes went beyond the beautiful. Didn't they? Did she think he might not have a chance at winning Kichu as a client? He couldn't help feeling offended by that. Was this how it felt to let someone in? It annoyed him. But also, it was a strange sort of ache that niggled at his armor and punctured a hole in it, allowing that kindness she saw in him to leak out. Maeve was teaching him to recognize that earthy ugliness his professor had once insisted he get in touch with.

And honestly? He liked it.

Inside a souvenir shop, Maeve floated toward the back, drawn by kitschy colorful items. Asher spun a rack of postcards, browsing photos of the town, handmade dolls, tables set with traditional food. When finally one with a colorful rock outside a parked RV popped up. The rock wasn't painted, but rather it looked as though someone had crocheted a riot of colored yarn about it. The caravan was plastered with various logos for rock bands. Before it stood a lanky man in overalls holding a wooden staff.

"Ugly," Asher muttered. With a smile, he selected the postcard.

Then, he gave the rack another spin and a card with a swirl of pastel colors that looked like AI art stood out. He plucked it out and went to pay for them.

Maeve met him at the doorway.

"You got postcards?" she asked, seeming surprised that he would.

"One for you." He tucked the ugly postcard inside his suit coat pocket then gave the other to her. "It screams Maeve Pemberton, don't you think?"

She studied the wild colors and laughed. "There may be hope for you, after all, Mr. Dane."

Back at the resort, the evening meal was delivered to their rooms. They dined on the patio, watching the sun set in vivid violet, pink and orange above the mossy volcanic field.

"I'm going to remember this sky," Maeve said, sipping the dregs of her wine. "I might have to paint a wall those colors."

"Heaven forbid." Asher, noticing her gape, quickly added, "I mean…what wall?"

Maeve laughed. If the man ever saw her flat, he might have a heart attack. An art attack? It would disturb him, for sure.

She shrugged. "With Lucy moving out, I feel the urge to try something new in the bathroom. The sunrise colors are similar to the ones on this postcard." She'd set the postcard he'd given her on the table. "You never showed me yours."

He tugged out the card and handed it to her with a churlish smile on his face. It was…

"Seriously?" she asked.

"Pretty ugly, eh?"

"I'm impressed. Asher Dane does have an eye for ugly art. Though, I wouldn't call this art."

"Certainly not. But it makes me think. Maybe I've spent too much time coasting through art and not allowing myself to really breathe it."

"You breathe art, Asher. I've watched you."

"Yes, but only the stuff I deign to be worthy. Time to expand my horizons?"

"Oh, I hope so." She tilted her glass toward him, and they met in a *ting*.

"I'm excited for tomorrow's meeting with Kichu. You did this for me, Maeve. You were the one who got his attention and convinced him to show me his art. I've failed you as a teacher. But you have achieved the task on your own. Bravo!"

"You are not a failure, and I will take that bravo. I'm excited as well. I really love his work. It speaks to me in the color language I know. So. Who's sleeping on the floor tonight?"

"Are you teasing me?"

"Yes. I'll take the floor."

His jaw dropped open.

Maeve's laughter increased to shrieks of joy as he lunged for her, grabbed her by the waist and hefted her over his shoulder to carry her inside. "We'll see about that," he announced, and then tossed her on the bed.

CHAPTER SEVENTEEN

THE FINAL CEREMONY was silly to Asher. The couples were called to the front of the room, embraced one another and received red roses from the lead instructor. Kichu watched from a video screen. Was it really that difficult for the man to make an appearance for his own event? Since when could a recluse even make a living, let alone a fortune, as a renowned relationship coach?

Well, he supposed this week had improved his relationship with Maeve. Hell, it had *given* him a relationship with Maeve. Sex again this morning had been so right. Like he didn't have to perform to impress a woman, nor did he need to cater to her unknown needs. Maeve was very vocal, and she'd even directed his hand here and there. He loved that. The communication between them was instinctual. At least between the sheets.

As for when they were fully clothed and preparing to leave the resort in a few hours? Both of them were quiet as they prepped for the meeting with Kichu. Maeve was packing and making the bed, despite him reminding her that was a job for the maid. She tended to neaten everything behind the scenes. Even his life.

Maeve had been responsible for this meeting with Kichu. He owed her. And yet, the only thing she needed, she wouldn't take from him. What was money? A loan that she could use to start her business? To him, it would barely make a dent on his ledger. And really, if she would accept a loan, there was no way he would ask for repayment.

Did she feel as though he were trying to buy his way into her life? Maeve was independent. And he knew if she had the opportunity to reopen the shop she'd dreamed about she would be a success. And her mother would be...

Well, that was the kicker. Maeve wanted to please a domineering mother. Asher couldn't relate to that. But then again, he had dropped everything in his life to care for his parents. He believed children should honor, respect and care for their parents. And Maeve was obviously trying to honor hers by showing her she could be a success.

"She won't fail," he said to his reflection in the bathroom mirror. He swiped the razor along his jaw to remove some missed stubble.

Now, as he adjusted his tie and hair, Maeve fluttered in to touch up her lipstick, her hair, her dress. The big event was happening in less than an hour. And she looked...

"Stunning." He turned and caught her hand before she could flit back into the other room. "Maeve, you are beautiful." But the announcement made him frown. He released her hand. "That color..."

"Green is my happy color," she said and floated out into the main room, leaving him to turn and face the mirror again.

Beauty was his thing? She'd been adamant about that. Listing all his favorite artists, who, indeed, had produced some of the most beautiful works over the centuries.

Of course, beauty was his thing. It had served him well through the years. There was nothing wrong with admiring a beautiful artwork. But that wasn't all he admired. Though, to think on it, there were no masters he could name that produced anything but beauty.

And he did know ugly when he saw it. Matsys, Goya, Chagall, just to consider a few of the masters. And don't even get him started on the modern artists. Leave those works to others who could understand the horrible dysfunction immortalized on the canvas.

He glanced to the postcard he'd propped against the mirror. What of all the things that were not beautiful? That were weird and strange and intriguing?

You must become open to the earthy and ugly.

Maeve was not ugly. Maeve was a unique beauty. She was…earthy and colorful and studious and simple and complicated. He'd never quite been able to look at her and figure her out for her eclectic color scheme, but she had grown on him this week. Because he now understood what made her tick. And she wouldn't be Maeve Pemberton if she were not a wild riot of mismatched colors and patterns. He wouldn't have her any other way.

Could his taste in art alter in such a manner? Be opened to looking beyond the surface beauty? To accept that which he deemed ugly?

His ego loomed behind it all. An ego that had escaped its chains after years of tending his sick parents. A part of him that had wanted to be seen and recognized had taken control. Had successfully brought the media and masses to The Art Guys and made them a name. Yes, he'd take credit for that.

Honestly? He didn't need that credit any longer. He could do with less. No fame. Maybe a little. The fame and notice he received did transfer to the brokerage. What Maeve said about it not always being about him was true. Through the years he'd sucked it all up, shining in the attention. Was that why he'd never taken on an artist? Because to do so meant allowing that artist to shine, to step aside and allow the spotlight a new muse.

Wow. He suddenly got it.

The Face must be set aside. He simply wanted to be Asher Dane, a man who loved art—and was open to seeing all kinds in a new light—and who adored a woman with multitudes of color in her eyes and punctuation marks at her mouth.

"I've developed a ridiculous obsession with Maeve," he whispered.

"What's that? Are you ready?" She popped her head back into the bathroom. "That tie is perfect. The violet is your color."

"It is?" He touched the tie but was lost in her strange beauty. Maeve was the key to escape his self-imposed artificial world of beauty and expectations.

"It is. It's the color I see when I smell your delicious youness."

"My youness? You mean my cologne? It's…specially made for me."

"Of course, it wouldn't be anything you could buy off the shelf. I love it."

She kissed him, and all he could think was that he wished she'd said she loved him.

Ending the kiss with a quick one to his nose, she grabbed his hand. "Let's go snag you a new artist."

As they strolled hand in hand toward the elevator, Maeve checked her texts. She'd received a confirmation from the job application, and it indicated the date for their online interview. Next Monday! That was three days from now. And… she wasn't prepared.

Had she really thought it a good idea to look for another job?

What was a good reason to not confirm? She'd changed her mind? She didn't want to move away from a man she had begun to have a relationship with? Dublin held no interest for her? She had decided to tough it out for a few more years to see if she could rise in the ranks at The Art Guys?

"Your mum?" Asher asked as the elevator doors slid open.

"No, just…"

She couldn't tell him she'd applied for a job. It had been a spur of the moment decision to create some means of backup, a place to fall should she find herself back at the reception desk without a raise or a future that indicated she could accomplish her dream.

"It's to the right," she directed as Asher stepped out of the elevator.

Tucking away her phone, she thought about how he kept his turned off most of the time. She should have left hers in the room today. Now she would be even more nervous about this meeting. Because a yay or a nay from Kichu might decide her future.

CHAPTER EIGHTEEN

ASHER SHOOK HANDS with the elusive Tony Kichu and took in his simple white kimono, loose slacks and long obsidian hair, a portion of which was pulled into a topknot at the back of his skull. Behind him were displayed a Japanese gold Satsuma vase and other collectibles situated prominently in his main living area. Maeve, after shaking his hand, wandered to inspect the tall vase, leaning forward but keeping her hands behind her back.

Green was her happy color? And violet for him? Those colors were complimentary.

When he realized Kichu had spoken but he'd not caught what he said, Asher had to yank himself from his thoughts about Maeve—*his ridiculous obsession*—and focus.

"So, shall we take a look at your work?" Asher asked.

"Of course. This way." Kichu strolled on bare feet down a long white hallway that featured what Asher guessed were Ming vases set into the walls and lighted perfectly. He wasn't an expert on ancient pottery. "The two of you work together?"

"Yes," Maeve said. "As I told you, Asher is my boss."

"We've been dating four or five months," Asher added with a look to her for reassurance. Best to keep up the cover. He didn't want to reveal their fake relationship when he was so close to finally seeing the art.

"About that," Maeve agreed.

"An excellent program you have here," Asher said to Kichu's back. "I'll be recommending it to my friends."

Kichu paused before an open doorway and gestured inside. "My studio."

Asher waited for Maeve to enter first, then took in the vast room. One side was all windows looking out over the steaming geothermal pools and the periwinkle sky. Canvases lined one wall, some propped on the floor, others set on wooden easels. A blank canvas sat at the center of the room, stretches of paint-spattered clothes covering the marble floor. But the most shocking sight was the vast array of paint. Everywhere. In every color. Splattered and splotched and smeared and stroked.

Asher blinked. It was as if he had to mentally guide himself to breathe a lower amount of oxygen. There was so much color it sucked away his breath. At first glance he didn't realize the splotches and splatters were canvases. Finished works?

Veins tightening, his fingers clenched. The sanctity of art itself had been trampled, graffitied and blown up. Splattered like a runny egg thrust at the wall. Crushed from a tube of oil paint and drizzled indiscriminately. Blocks of color showed thick brush strokes, blending olive and yellow and crimson and—

This was not art! This was…a mess. A child's tantrum. A—

Swallowing back the oath that climbed up his throat, Asher noticed Maeve's hopeful smile and the bounce on her toes as she awaited his summation. She in her happy summer green and cherry lips. Of course she would find this chaos beautiful. It emulated her mind!

Forcing a smile, Asher approached the paintings. If one could call them that. There were similarities to Pollock's splatter paintings, but not so ordered or even intentional. Influences of Shimamoto were also evident. Yet what the man had done with color was an aberration. How could Maeve actually…? No, he didn't have to wonder. This must be her Xanadu.

Kichu joined him to stand side by side. The man's quiet presence felt too soft and gentle for this crazy explosion and utter waste of paint.

"I know my style is not for everyone," Kichu said. "It is why I rarely show my work."

"But so many would love to own your work," Maeve stated from the other side of Asher. "The use of color is… arrogant."

Asher flashed her a stunned look. She'd got that one right.

"Yet," she continued, "inviting. It speaks in whispers and screams. And takes the viewer to such intense places. Don't you think, Asher?"

No, he did not think!

But, hell. He sensed she was offering him a means to ingratiate himself to Kichu. She had warned him he wouldn't like the works. And he did not. She knew him so well. That fortified his heart and very soul. And he didn't want to lose her regard.

And yet, he could feel Maeve's insistent hope in the tone of her voice. She needed him to like Kichu's art for reasons… Well, she might return to London having helped him to gain an artist. That would show well to the other guys. They may agree it was time to allow her to move beyond the reception desk.

On the other hand, if her taste was so terrible, Asher wasn't sure he could agree on that promotion at the brokerage.

And really, did she harbor notions that he hadn't the constitution to represent such an utter blemish on modern art itself?

He swore inwardly. This retreat had opened his heart and shifted his perspective. He needn't rely on beauty and surface looks to succeed. To get others to like him. To exist. As well, he'd fallen for Maeve. His strange yet beautiful Maeve. He didn't want to let her down.

And yet…

He had also learned to be truthful on this retreat, for perhaps the first time in his life. And he if lied now he may regret it forever.

"It's ugly," he announced.

Maeve's inhale alerted him. But he couldn't represent art he could not connect to.

"Thank you for your honesty," Kichu said. "You are the first person who has had the courage to tell me the truth. I appreciate that."

"It's not without artistic value," Asher found himself saying. "But it's…not something I can represent. I'm sorry." He shook Kichu's hand. "I won't take up any more of your time. Thank you for this week. It's taught me a lot."

Kichu nodded silently.

"But maybe if you thought about it a few days," Maeve said even as Asher turned to exit. "It is a wild riot of unexpected color, but you've learned to appreciate…"

He paused at the door, knowing the word she did not say was *me*. Yes, he'd learned to appreciate her. He'd gone beyond appreciation. And now, as her mouth dropped and she blinked, he couldn't find the path to that easy acceptance she'd offered him.

She shook Kichu's hand. "I'm so sorry. I do love your work. I'd love to… Well, you'll find someone who can represent it, I'm sure of it."

I'd love to...

She'd love to represent Kichu's work? Asher felt surely if anyone could manage to look at the work any longer than a glance it would be Maeve. Yet, she had no experience whatsoever in representing an artist. And he certainly wasn't the man to teach her. Because what experience had he? He was still zero for zero when it came to acquiring artists. And perhaps even she had led him here knowing the outcome? What was she playing at?

Pity they'd wasted all this time for this disastrous result.

Asher held out his hand for Maeve and called another thanks to Kichu as she approached him. She didn't take his hand. Instead, she rushed past him. He had to step rapidly to keep up with her. When they landed in the hallway outside Kichu's private apartment, she started to run.

"Maeve! Let's talk about this!"

"Our car arrives in half an hour."

Yes, they had a flight this afternoon. Back to London for Maeve. But for him it was only a layover as he headed to Bangladesh.

She was upset he'd not liked Kichu's work. And...he didn't know how to make this situation better.

CHAPTER NINETEEN

ON THE DRIVE to the airport, Maeve scrolled through her emails. A means to look busy and not talk. She told Asher that Joss had an issue with a reservation—which he did—and that took some time to work out.

Once seated in first class and with a glass of wine in hand, she wanted to close her eyes and try not to inhale Asher's royal violet essence. Impossible. The man had permeated her bones. She felt sure she'd smell him, feel him on her skin, at her lips, even when she was home and he had arrived in Bangladesh.

One thing to be thankful for, this exit would be swift after they arrived home, not drawn out with them sharing a cab from the airport to their respective homes. And then having to wonder if they dared to suggest one might go home with the other?

The relationship felt…not completely true. Unsustainable. Perhaps as false as it had begun.

By rejecting Kichu's artwork, Asher had rejected *her*. In that moment, when Asher had said the word *ugly*, and she'd watched Kichu bow his head and nod in reluctant acceptance, Maeve had felt that exchange as a knife in her heart. Gone were the Cupid-drawn love arrows. Asher's verbal blade had stabbed deep and sure.

Of course, she had known he wouldn't like the art. It

wasn't his style. It was weird. It was too colorful. It challenged the aesthetic beauty he worshipped.

Tony Kichu's art…was *her*.

And once again she had failed.

She had failed to help Asher procure an artist. She had failed to show him that viewing the artwork in a new light could result in an appreciation for it. She had failed to prove that she was of value to the team and deserved a raise, a new position that would see her thriving and achieving her dream.

Might *she* have offered to represent Kichu? No, she wasn't in a position to do so. And Asher may have taken that as a direct assault against their work relationship. The last thing she'd wanted to do was hurt him. Or ruin his chances at proving himself to his coworkers.

As she glanced at the text on her phone, her heart dropped even lower. Of all the people to contact her when she was feeling lowest. Her mother. Asking about the Dublin job.

"Listen, Maeve, I'm sorry."

She swiped to ignore the text and tilted her head against the airplane headrest. "You don't need to apologize to me, Asher. It's been a long week. I'm tired."

"Is that your way of saying you don't want to discuss it? We need to. We…"

His heavy sigh echoed in her bones. Because he lived there, and she felt every part of him, every emotion, every movement, every sound, smell and sigh. She wanted to grip him by the shoulders and yell at him.

See me! Accept me! I am that weird colorful woman who baffles you still.

He had been so close to seeing her.

"Tell me what I've done wrong," he said in a soft but desperate tone.

Maeve winced. If he didn't know, that was half the problem.

She could play the spurned lover and sit there silently ignoring him—but that didn't play well with her soul.

"It was…" She thought it through. "I knew you wouldn't like Kichu's work. Perhaps I should have prepared you better."

"Maeve, you are not responsible for my work or the clients I represent. Sure, I failed to snag Kichu as an artist. There will be other opportunities for me to show the guys I can bring in artists."

"I loved his work. It spoke to me."

"All those colors. I know it did. And in that moment when I was looking at it, I wondered if I should lie and say I loved it. That I'd represent him. I knew that would make you happy. But… I've learned some things about myself this week. And being honest with the way I present myself to others is a big part of it. I had to tell the truth."

She appreciated his honesty, but it still hurt.

"You make me feel…" He rubbed the back of his head in frustration. "Honestly? I felt like you've had my back this whole time, and then in Kichu's workshop you were trying to force his art on me. Like you didn't trust I could form my own opinion. It felt a little…underhanded."

Maeve swallowed. She hadn't meant to convey that at all. But if he'd felt that way she had to honor that feeling. She had only tried to encourage him to view the art in…in the manner she viewed it.

"I'm sorry," she said. And she really was. "I was trying to subtly influence you."

He turned his head on the headrest to eye her, their faces but inches apart. If he didn't smell so deliciously violet this would be much easier for her. But fact was, she'd lost her heart to him this week. And then he'd crushed it. And now he was acting as though that trampling couldn't possibly matter as much as it did.

And very likely she had done some trampling herself.

"When does your connecting flight leave from London?" she asked.

She knew that he had to hop on a plane to Bangladesh for an auction tomorrow morning.

"If we land on time, I'll have about twenty minutes to dash to the next gate."

Her phone pinged again, and she tugged it out to check the screen. She knew that was rude, but the distraction was very needed. It was a confirmation for the interview time.

"Joss again?"

"No, I ironed things out for him. It's… Asher, I sent in an application yesterday for a marketing job in Dublin. This is a confirmation for an online interview."

His gasp hurt her heart. She didn't want it to go like this. But she wasn't sure they had a future anymore. Most especially, her future at The Art Guys felt stagnant.

"I'll talk to the guys," he said. "We'll give you a raise."

"I don't want it handed to me because you think that's a way to…" Please her? Keep her at the brokerage? If only he did want to keep her! "I'm not sure we can work. We're so different."

"Maeve, differences make for a vibrant relationship. Is it me?"

She inhaled and bowed her head. Of course, it was him! She desired everything about him. Was she being too harsh? Too judgmental? Perhaps he might come around? Really. It had been one artist. An artist she'd known he wouldn't like. Why her need to stick to this one point?

Because it felt like rejection.

"I need to sort this all out," she said. "Maybe you leaving so quickly is a good thing. To give me space to get my head straight."

"Straight about us? Because, Maeve, I…"

He couldn't say it. Because he wasn't so sure about their relationship anymore.

Asher Dane didn't understand her, after all. He could never handle the colorful and weird Maeve Pemberton.

"You are strange and beautiful," he said.

She lifted her gaze to meet his. "What?"

"You are a little strange. Not in a bad way. Just in that supernatural, colorful, beaming out green and fuchsia and orange in your special way kind of strange. I get that. I understand how you navigate the world. And I want to embrace it. I've tried to…"

He pressed a hand over her heart chakra. Maeve lifted her chin to stop the tears that threatened. It was too late. Wasn't it?

Their differences might never coalesce.

The moment the plane hit the tarmac Asher's heart dropped lower than the airplane had. Maeve immediately busied herself with the luggage. Was she avoiding him? He sensed she was angry over his rejection of Kichu. Not at *him*.

He hoped that was the case.

And yet, she had a job interview? Something she'd applied for while at the retreat? Had she been plotting behind his back the whole time? Setting up a means for backup should the ploy to recruit Kichu not come to fruition? He should have asked her more about it, but he didn't know how to deal with upset Maeve.

He wondered what color represented her current mood. Certainly not the green dress she wore, and which she'd said was the color she most identified with.

As they disembarked and walked through the Jetway, he

wanted to pull Maeve into his arms and tell her he loved her. But did he love her?

He felt as though he did. This weird tiff over Kichu was messing with his mind. Making him question the entire week. *Had* it all been fake, after all? If she intended to interview for another job and leave him…

His phone pinged, alerting him that his next flight was boarding.

Maeve paused with her rolling suitcase and met his gaze. "You need to run," she said.

"I can't walk away from you like this. I… I'll miss my flight. We need to talk."

"You need to be at that auction tomorrow morning. The client depends on you. I'll be fine to catch a cab on my own."

"It's not that…" His phone pinged again. Asher swore. He did need to run.

Leaning in to kiss her, he winced as Maeve turned her head so his mouth landed on her cheek. "I'll text you."

"Thanks for the week," she said softly. Then she grabbed her suitcase and walked away.

And with another ping from his phone, Asher began to walk backward, unable to tear his sight from the woman who had stolen a part of him with her apostrophe smiles. And she was taking that part with her now. He didn't want it back. But he wasn't sure how to make things right. Should he fall before Kichu and apologize and offer to represent him? That wouldn't sit well with his heart.

Nor Maeve's. She'd know he was only doing it to please her, and that was unacceptable.

Turning, he began to run toward his next gate.

Maeve hailed a cab and gave the driver an address to a location she'd been meaning to visit. It was around nine in the evening, but she didn't want to go home yet. Lucy was on a weekend getaway with her fiancé so the flat would be dark, lonely and too quiet.

Hugging herself, she tilted her head back and zoned out on the flashes of city lights zipping by. Asher's flight was probably already in the air. They hadn't time to say a proper goodbye.

The real goodbye had been said in Tony Kichu's studio when Asher had called the artist's work ugly. Maeve had felt that in her being. Everything Kichu had created resembled a piece of her life, a colorful burst of her very soul.

So this was the end? A quick kiss in the airport and a promise to text? It felt dismissive. Not hopeful. Not as if she could claim him as anything more than a man with whom she'd had a good time and... Now back to their roles as boss and receptionist. And she couldn't abide a friends-with-benefits relationship with anyone, most of all Asher Dane. It was all or nothing.

She felt as though she had fallen hard and splattered across the ground in all the colors of Kichu's brilliant canvases.

Wiping away a tear, she inhaled and composed herself. She could come up with a new plan to a better future. To continue to work at The Art Guys. But how to do so and be around Asher? Krew and Joss had been so kind to her. Truly, she did feel like *our Maeve*. Like they were a family apart from her broken real family.

But Asher didn't fit properly into that weird and makeshift family. She knew how she wanted him to fit. But it seemed he wasn't ready for such an adjustment.

Was the job interview more of an excuse to exit grace-fully from Asher's life than a real goal? She didn't want to move back to Dublin. Her home was... Well, she wouldn't call London home. Sure, her da lived here. They got together a few times a year. New York was where her mum lived when she wasn't traveling. Again, she never saw her more than a few times a year.

You've failed again!

She had failed to help Asher get the artist. Failed to move up at work. And she had failed to get the guy who made her heart dance and glow purple and green.

"This is the place."

Alerted by the cabbie's voice, Maeve glanced outside. A streetlight shone over the vacant shop front sandwiched between a record shop and a plant emporium. It had come on the market two weeks ago. It wouldn't remain available for long. The storefront was pristine and painted a sallow mint, which she would refresh with pink and ochre stripes.

"Do you want to get out?"

"Uh, no. Can you take me to another place? I've a list that I want to check out." She gave him the next address on her running list of dream shop locations. And she didn't arrive home until after two in the morning.

Stepping into her dark flat, Maeve let her suitcase drop as she closed the door. No one to greet her and welcome her home. She wanted that. A place where she felt welcome, loved. A family.

But more than anything she wanted to feel the warm acceptance she'd felt standing in Asher's arms. A place she'd thought her colorful world fit.

CHAPTER TWENTY

AFTER ASHER WON the auction, his client had asked if he'd stay for a few days to catch another private sale, which he was happy to do. It wasn't the commission that attracted him, but rather the mutual taste in art and the pints they shared at a local pub later. As well, the client knew a local artist who was looking for representation. Asher had an appointment to meet with him in an hour.

Joss and Krew had taken the news that he'd refused to represent Tony Kichu with their standard accepting, "You'll find one sooner or later." Passing over Kichu hadn't felt so much like a failure as a letdown. Asher was not holding up his part of the partnership. He'd been so close. But to be truthful with himself, he was good with not taking on Kichu. He'd been honest in a moment when a simple lie could have gained him prestige with the brokerage and...won the girl.

Maeve would have seen through him if he'd taken on Kichu. She knew him better than he knew himself some days. She saw Asher Dane, not The Face. He wanted to make Maeve proud. Had he lost that chance? In the three days since they'd parted, he'd been so busy he'd only managed to text her regarding some client paperwork.

Now, as he sat in his hotel room nursing a chilled whiskey, he could tap out a few words to her. But he let his phone sit in a suit coat pocket across the room. She had asked for time to think. About them? About leaving the brokerage? Hell, he shouldn't have blurted out that he'd give her more money to keep her at The Art Guys. That had been an act of desperation. Maeve was too smart to fall for that.

And he was too smart to treat her heart so poorly. He had to be true to his newly opened heart. A heart Maeve had been successful in brushing off, polishing up and hugging—around pottery—until he knew that nothing else mattered but what she thought of him. His self-esteem had gotten a new polish as well. He didn't have to be The Face around Maeve. And he felt sure Asher Dane could be present more often than The Face as he moved forward in his work.

Why hadn't he immediately realized that by rejecting Tony Kichu's art he was also rejecting Maeve? It had not hit him until they'd been sitting on the plane and she had confessed to trying to influence him. Maeve had adored the crazy splattered work that Asher couldn't even begin to understand. But that was the thing, wasn't it? He hadn't understood Maeve Pemberton either, until he'd spent time with her. Learned her.

What *did* she think of him? Could she see that he was gaining self-esteem? That he no longer felt the need to wear The Face as a mask? He'd rejected Kichu's work and had survived. No false charm necessary.

But that rejection had hurt Maeve. He'd thought of her every moment since he'd had to dash away from her. He abhorred the distance between him and the one thing that made his heart sing.

A woman of many colors. All he desired was to become her favorite color.

He must make things right between them. And he knew how to do that. Lunging for his phone, he dialed the resort and, after utilizing The Face's charm, was put through to

Tony Kichu. The man defensively announced that he'd refused Hammerstill's offer of representation and wouldn't
consider Asher again. Although, he did know who he would
like to represent him.

It made sense. And it made Asher happy. With that initial discomfiting bit of business out of the way, he spent the
next half hour convincing Kichu to create a commissioned
work for him.

Maeve signed off from the video interview and headed in
to work. The interview had gone well. Maybe?

Didn't matter. She didn't want the Dublin job. Yet she
felt as though she needed it as backup. The interviewer had
sounded interested and fascinated by her love for color. She
said she'd get back in a week; there was a list of potential
applicants she had to interview.

Fair enough.

The office was dark when she arrived after 10:00 a.m.
Joss was away on a job and Krew had auctions in town all
week. She flicked on the lights and eyed her half-circle desk.
She loved that desk. It was curvy and highlighted by gentle
overhead lights. The command center from which she ran
the office. And she did it well.

With a sigh, she set her purse under the desk and pulled
up a project on the computer. Krew had received a list of
paintings to bid on at auction for a wealthy client who was
recently divorced. The vindictive wife had sold all their artwork while he had been waiting to win the right to keep
the home and the art. Now he wanted it back, at all costs. It
would prove an art scavenger hunt. Exactly the sort of assignment the analytical yet competitive Krew would enjoy.

Looking aside from the spreadsheet she was creating for
the art hunt, Maeve caught her chin in hand and stared out

the window at the gray sky. Rain was due within a few hours. Fitting, because life felt colorless since landing in London days earlier.

She hadn't spoken to Asher, though she had answered two of his texts regarding a hotel snafu and had sent paperwork to him to have his client sign. He hadn't mentioned anything about...them.

Why should he?

Maeve sighed. She'd lost him. And she wasn't sure how to get him back. Could she run away from it all and focus on her dreams instead of the hole in her heart that seemed to widen daily?

She had fallen in love with Asher Dane. And it wasn't fake. Or some silly crush fantasy. But he was not a color that seemed to fit into her world. A rich dusty violet. The color of royalty, midnight gardens, bejeweled insects and...the man who had pulled a gray cloud over her heart.

Four days later, Maeve was offered the job as marketing director for the Dublin office. To start in two weeks. Would she accept?

Leaning back in her chair, with Krew's voice muted in the background as he spoke behind the closed door with a client, she stared at the email that had new-hire paperwork attached for her to fill out and sign. The pay was nearly double what she was making right now. A few years there would allow her to save enough to open another shop. It was the path to her dream.

At the expense of walking away from something she loved. It wasn't this job that called to her heart. Though she did take pride in it, and adored Joss and Krew. They really were her family. A family she hadn't dared to tell that she was looking for other work. Had Asher mentioned it to them?

Krew hadn't said anything. And she hadn't seen Joss since returning to London.

"This failing stuff is exhausting," she muttered.

But then she sat up straighter and shook her head. If she had learned anything this week it was that she viewed the world differently than others. And that her perspective should not rely on the opinions of others. Yes, her mum considered her a failure. But Asher did not. In fact, he'd convinced her that she was merely learning, gliding in her own way toward what she desired.

She had been labeling her life incorrectly! And if her mum insisted on seeing her in one way, then so be it. Maeve didn't require her seal of approval. Because Mariane Pemberton's approval was only granted through her purview of what was success and what was failure.

"I will open another shop," she said with exacting determination. "It'll happen when it needs to happen."

She wanted to thank Asher for changing her perspective. He was due in town today. He didn't need to stop by the office. She wasn't sure if she wanted him to or not.

Yes, she did want to see him. But could her heart handle looking into his glacier-blue eyes and wondering if she had thrown away the best thing she had ever had?

They should talk. Maybe this could all be ironed out with a heartfelt conversation. Or maybe the man would simply never understand her. And that was fine. She shouldn't expect him to. She didn't completely understand him. He had his ineffable parts. As did her mum. And as did Maeve Pemberton.

Clicking open the attached file on the email, she glanced through the new-hire forms, and then shook her head. She'd save it for when she got home. As long as she was in this office, her attention would be devoted to this work.

CHAPTER TWENTY-ONE

THE NEXT MORNING, Maeve adjusted the bouquet of yellow daisies she'd set on her bedroom chest of drawers. Last night after work she'd pick them up, along with a takeaway. She'd been in need of some cheer, but the daisies had not played their part. They had wilted overnight and the stems were bent. There was no saving them.

"Figures," she muttered. "Seems to be how my life is going right now."

A glance to the pink heels she'd set on the floor at the end of her bed took away her breath. Asher had insisted she have the strappy stunners. They'd go perfectly with a summery dress. And a walk with the one man who had stolen her heart.

Asher had not stopped into the office yesterday even though he'd landed at the airport midafternoon. Was he trying to avoid her? If so, she didn't want to participate in a mutual avoidance scheme for the rest of her days at The Art Guys.

Grabbing her laptop, she crawled onto her bed and opened the new employee form. The atmosphere at the office had altered since she'd returned. Krew was apprehensive around her. Had Asher told him everything? That he'd had a fling with the receptionist and...

And what? The world felt off-kilter. And she wasn't sure

where she would land should a good shake occur. In Asher's arms should be the answer. But that they'd not had opportunity to talk, nor had he reached out to her since parting at Heathrow, did not bode well.

Time to refocus on her dream. A dream that suddenly felt less colorful knowing that a dusty shade of royal violet might be absent from it.

Out in the living room, Lucy called that she'd be back later. She had a dress fitting appointment. Yet before the front door closed, Lucy also called, "You've got a visitor!"

Maeve never got visitors unless it was her da, and he usually texted that he was in the neighborhood and was stopping by.

Pulling on a pink sweater over her orange and green paisley sundress, she wandered out to the living room, unsure who could possibly be there. She stopped abruptly, catching her breath at the sight of the man standing in the doorway.

The missing color.

Behind Asher, Lucy winked at her, then closed the door as she left.

"Asher."

He set aside what looked like a large wrapped canvas. Must be something he'd acquired for work?

"Maeve."

With a sudden lift of his head, he took in the living room, which was Maeve's finest creation. His eyes wandered from the bubblegum-pink cornice heading one wall, down the blue-and-silver-striped wallpaper, and landed on the purple velvet heart-backed chair. Beside it sat the yellow side table, which featured a bouquet of bright orange roses—silk—and a trio of tiny blue cats before the vase.

"What is this?"

He wandered into the room taking it all in as if he were

in a gallery of strange and assorted oddities. Maeve felt an initial humiliation that he had discovered the very core of her, and then it fluttered off to be replaced by a satisfied nod. This was her home. She had created it. It was *her*. And if he didn't like it, then that sealed it: he could never like her. And she would have to accept that. Because she'd almost come to accept that they couldn't be a couple.

Almost.

"This." He stroked his fingers over the curve of a white and pink plaid lampshade. The violet fringe circling the bottom jiggled. "And this." A turn placed him before a bookshelf she'd painted lavender, which featured her and Lucy's book collection in color-coded order. "This is…"

He turned to her, his mouth open in awe. Did his eyes glint? Of course, they did. Those glacier blues were The Face's secret weapon. And she could smell his earthy violet color. Oh, how she'd missed that. Missed standing close to him. Missed the stroke of his fingers exploring her skin. His quiet summation of her. His deep laughter and playful manner. Missed everything about him.

"I know it offends your taste, Windfield," she offered, "but it's me."

"Yes, you and your ridiculous obsession with color." He studied the room a bit longer.

While she rubbed a hand up her arm. It wasn't ridiculous, it was who she was. Take her or leave her.

Just when she expected him to say something, he pulled her to him and kissed her.

Nothing could prepare her for the joy that melted across her skin and seeped into her veins. She'd been so worried she'd lost him. And now he was kissing her. Holding her against his body. Speaking to her with his lips, his tongue, his breath. She never wanted this to end. Could they stop time and exist without the world missing them?

"I've been thinking about your kiss for over a week," he said. "Your dark cherry kisses. I dreamed about your riotous colors. They were the craziest and most exciting dreams I've ever had. And, well…" He gestured to take in the entire room. "This explains everything."

"Asher, I…"

He kissed her again. "I'm sorry. I realized that by rejecting Kichu as a client you took that as a rejection of you."

"You…you figured that out?"

"Yes, but in the moment, I was thinking that perhaps you had wanted me to fail—"

"I would never! Oh…" She winced when he met her gaze. "I mean, I may have considered that I could possibly represent Tony Kichu, but I knew it couldn't happen. And I genuinely wanted him as an artist for you. But I think I pushed too hard to get you to see beauty in something that was, truthfully, ugly."

"Kichu's artwork isn't for everyone, that's for certain. You really thought about representing him?"

She shrugged. "I have no experience. It was a wild dream."

"Dreams are supposed to be wild. Maeve, I don't want to push you out of my life. I love you."

Her mouth dropped open. Heartbeats thundered. And she couldn't stop herself from saying, "I do too. I love you. But…"

"But nothing. I'm learning, Maeve. It's a slow process, and I will get there."

"You're there. Trust me. You have my heart."

He placed a hand over her heart chakra, and she did the same to him. Then they laughed and kissed. "That woo-woo stuff is silly," he said. "We'll keep that our little secret."

"Trust me, I don't want anyone else touching your heart chakra."

"Same. But… I still believe I made the right call with Kichu. I could never be the best representative of his work. But I know who can be."

"Who? You didn't hand him over to Hammerstill?"

"Funny thing is, Kichu didn't want to work with that bombastic asshole either. He also made it clear he would never be comfortable working with me."

"You spoke to him again?"

Asher nodded. "I called him and stopped back into the resort yesterday on my way home. There was something I had to do. But first." He took his phone from his suit pocket and pressed the call button. "I've Krew and Joss waiting for a conference call. If you'll indulge me?"

Maeve shrugged. She wasn't sure what was going on. And she was still floating on his confession to being in love with her. Yes, oh, yes! Had she been thinking to apply for another job to put herself away from the only man she'd ever loved? Fool! His timing could not have been better. And yes, she truly believed this relationship had happened for a reason.

Krew answered and Joss called a hello. "You're at our Maeve's place?" Krew asked.

"Yes, well, er. Yes." Asher winked at her. "*My* Maeve is standing right here. I've told her that Kichu didn't want to work with either me or Hammerstill. I haven't told her who he does want to work with."

"Go ahead," Joss said. "Don't keep her in suspense."

"I don't understand," Maeve said. "What's the big secret?"

Holding the phone between them, Asher took her hand and said, "Tony Kichu asked if you would represent him as an artist for The Art Guys."

Maeve gaped. Her heartbeat doubled. This was incredible. But…

"Is she happy?" Krew asked.

"I'm not sure." Asher narrowed his gaze on her. "*Is* she happy?"

Maeve nodded. "Yes, but… I don't know what to say. It's very exciting. But can I do it? I mean, I've never represented an artist. And I'm only the receptionist."

"Maeve," Krew said, "we discussed this last night. The three of us would like to promote you. Rather, create a new position for you. Here's the deal. We need you as the receptionist. You keep our office and our lives in order. You are a wonder. But maybe you could be the receptionist slash broker-in-training? We'd have you shadow each of us in turn to learn the ropes. And eventually we'll replace you at the front desk. Of course, your salary will increase. We don't want to lose you, Maeve. Joss and I have been worried since you returned from Iceland that something was up. That you weren't happy here."

"Oh, I am. I mean…" There was still her dream of someday opening her consulting shop. She had to be honest with them. "Did Asher tell you guys about my dream to open a shop?"

"I did." Asher took her hand. "They understand that you've a goal."

"And we're behind you one hundred percent," Joss said. "With the clout you'll gain working with our network, that could transfer to you gaining a bigger clientele."

That was all the encouragement she needed. "Yes, I'd love to take on the new receptionist slash broker-in-training position."

With a bounce she nodded to Asher, and he thanked the guys and told them they'd stop in tomorrow and the four of them could go over Maeve's new role at The Art Guys. He hung up, and she plunged into his arms for a hug.

"You did that for me?"

"Honestly? It was Kichu's request. He felt the two of you bonded over his art. That you got him."

"I do get him."

"I understand that now that I stand here in your amazing home. This place, Maeve. It's a work of art."

"That drives you bonkers? Be honest."

"It's like I'm standing inside your brain. And I think Kichu created a great vision of it."

"Of what? My brain? I don't understand."

He picked up the wrapped canvas and handed it to her to unwrap. "I called him right after I arrived in Bangladesh. Asked him to create something that represented the two of us. I think he mastered it, yes?"

Maeve let the brown paper fall from the canvas and gasped at the sight of the colorful abstract. The black background held an explosion of colors, mainly greens, emeralds, blues and hints of the tangerine that she did adore. And yellow, her happy color! But there at the center was a dizzy spin of dusty violet. The very color she equated with Asher.

"Is that…" She pointed to the center.

"It's me. And you. Kichu said you were such a riot of mystery and color that you could not be contained on the canvas. But that purple splotch in the middle is me, fitted into your heart. I asked him to do it like that. Do you like it? You'll be the first to own an official Kichu."

"Oh, Asher, it's perfect. This is incredible."

Setting aside the canvas, she spun and landed in his arms for a thankful hug. No pottery separating them this time. And no misunderstandings or faking. This was real.

"I love it here," he said. "With you. I can't imagine holding anyone else's hand. Hugging anyone else. Kissing anyone else. Maeve, you anchor me. I've been floating through life, getting by on a moniker that appeals in an aesthetic way, but those days I spent with you? I felt tethered. Grounded. You opened my eyes to discover the earthy and ugly."

"Yes, well, you didn't particularly care for the ugly."

"No, but I saw it. And I know it needs to be a part of my life to be fully whole. More rounded. Open. It's an amazing feeling. And I could think of but one thing this week I've been away. I want less The Face and more realness. Maeve, what I'm saying is that I'm in love with you and I want what started as a fake to be real."

She kissed him. "It is real. It really is."

EPILOGUE

SIX MONTHS LATER Maeve had introduced Tony Kichu's art to a select clientele. Maeve worked closely with Krew, who represented many clients who adored modern art, to match the perfect client to a specific canvas. But when the guys had suggested she add more artists to her list, she had politely declined. She was still finding her feet, accompanying Asher to auctions when he was in town and learning the ropes.

And honestly? She'd taken a new business plan for Fuchsia into The Art Guys and had shown it to the guys. Joss had already turned her on to one of his clients, who was looking for a colorful edit to her home.

"Do you think they're upset that I didn't want to take on more clients?" Maeve asked as Asher parked down the street from the rental space she'd been eyeing for Fuchsia.

"No, they knew this was your goal. Perhaps they're a little disappointed, because you're so good at what you do. They'll get over it. They know you're *our Maeve* and will always be a part of the family. But finding a new receptionist will be a challenge. You are irreplaceable."

"I'm not gone yet. And I do want to continue working with Kichu. I'm so glad you guys agreed to my suggestion for one day a week at the brokerage, and, well…it'll be a while before I switch to that schedule. I still need to qualify for a loan. That building is not cheap."

He turned off the car engine and leaned across to kiss her, then tipped up her chin. "I thought we'd discussed this?"

Asher had offered her a loan, zero percent interest. She would be a fool not to take it. They had been lovers for half a year. Boyfriend and girlfriend. Partners. They had kind of, sort of moved in together. After Lucy had left, Asher had offered to pick up the rent if he could use it as his landing place. An easy offer to accept. But still, he was only in the city four or five days a month. And yes, he did fly her in on the weekends to wherever in the world he was working. Two days of sightseeing, dining and lots of sex. And those three activities were not evenly divided. Maeve felt sure that visit to Morocco had been spent entirely in the room! Still, on the weekdays, she missed him desperately.

However, if she accepted money from him it would bind her to him in ways beyond the physical and even emotional. If anything did happen to their relationship it could become a sticking point that might destroy them both.

"You know I like to have control over my life," she said to his insistent stare.

"I do know that. But you also know when I say loan I mean a gift. Maeve, please let me do this for you? Let me give you a place where your dream can come alive in vivid color?"

She looked down the street where the shop sat. The Realtor had said he'd open it for an hour so she could stop in and make plans. It was the perfect place. And mentally, she had already painted the front in pink and violet stripes and the interior walls in pastel mint and peach and...

"Say yes?" Asher prompted.

Before logic could argue, she vigorously nodded. "Let's do this."

She rushed ahead to the shop and walked inside the dark

room. The electricity had yet to be connected. Afternoon light beamed through the front plate glass window. The Realtor had left a flashlight across the room on a dusty counter that had once displayed handmade paper and ink pens.

The door jingled as Asher walked in, and she spun to find him going down on one knee before her. That charming smile caught her by surprise as he lifted a ring box before him.

"Maeve, the most strange yet beautiful color in my world. My favorite color. My heart chakra's soulmate. Would you marry me?"

Taken utterly by surprise, she clasped her hands against her chest. Her fantasy man had become her friend and lover. And now he wanted to be her husband? Overwhelmed and thrilled, she nodded as tears burst from her eyes.

Asher stood and slipped a beautiful ring on her finger. "The main stone is garnet," he said. "Because that is the color of you." He stroked her lips, then kissed her. "And the smaller stones circling it are amethyst."

"The color of you," she whispered. "Oh, Asher, I love you."

"Let's make a family together. Beautiful and lush and earthy and even a little ugly." He laughed, and she bowed her head to his. "To a colorful future."

* * * * *

ANOTHER SHOT
AT FOREVER

HANA SHEIK

MILLS & BOON

Every writer knows writing is tough sometimes.

So, this one is for me.

CHAPTER ONE

ZAYNAB SIRAD NEVER intended to divorce her husband at his sister's engagement party, and yet that was exactly what she planned to do when she showed up and proverbially darkened his doorstep with the impending news.

If there was ever a time for her to rethink her plan to serve him the papers, now was it.

It wasn't helping her resolve that the pleasant sounds of the party on the roof terrace drifted down to where she stood at the front entrance. She hadn't known there was a party happening until the guards at the front gate had informed her. Behind her the taxi she'd taken idled on the front drive alongside a number of other vehicles—her first indication that she'd have an audience for what she was about to do.

While one part of Zaynab squawked that she should come back at a later date when she could end this quietly, the part of her that had been waiting and dreading this moment for a little over a year now kept her feet rooted and straightened her shoulders.

I have to do this now. I've waited long enough. We both have...

Ignoring the wobble to her legs and the swooshing upheaval of her stomach, she stepped forward and grasped one of the polished silver handles of the large two-door entrance. Without delay Zaynab pulled open the door, passed hurriedly inside, and hadn't realized she'd been holding her breath until she released it when the front door clicked closed loudly behind her. "There's no going back now," she muttered under her breath.

Despite knowing that the hardest part still awaited her, taking this first step was a small victory of its own. And right now she needed to reward the small wins to steel her courage and banish her growing anxiety.

Swallowing past the anxious knot lodged in her throat, Zaynab turned to face the home that had never felt like hers in spite of being married to its owner and technically being the house's mistress.

Everything in the foyer looked the same bar the addition of the glittery ribbon and bright sweet-smelling flowers festooning the gleaming black banister of the staircase. Two dour-faced guards, hands poised behind their backs, stood fixed to their positions, one near the base of the stairs and the other at the top, their eyes tracking her as she walked toward the stairs. As always her gaze briefly dipped to the guns holstered at their waist belts, a new kind of nervous flutter working up her esophagus at the sight of the weaponry.

But aside from staring her down, the guards made no moves to deter her advance forward. Relieved, Zaynab surmised that they must have been informed of her arrival and clearance by the security personnel standing guard outdoors. It was one less thing she had to worry herself about.

I already have enough on my plate.

"You can do this," she quietly rallied herself.

Gathering her long black skirt and abaya up in one hand, she clutched the handrail and climbed the staircase to meet her fate.

She needn't have asked the guards for directions as she passed a few more on her way up the second flight of stairs to the third floor. String music, chatter and laughter from the party carried louder now. With this many people in one place, security had to be a top priority to the homeowner—her husband.

The man she'd come to divorce.

"You got this. Just walk right up to him, look him in the eyes and say, 'I want a divorce.'" It sounded simple enough to her as she repeated the course of action, but as boldly as Zaynab entered the house initially, her trembling hand betrayed her when she opened the door to the terrace far more cautiously. Because now there was only this last obstacle she had to pass. And it wasn't much of a deterrent as the door easily unlatched and opened.

The first thing to greet her besides the now unfiltered noises of the party was the stunningly bright light of day as she crossed the threshold and closed the terrace door behind her, her eyes having adjusted to the darker interior of the house. Then after blinking several times and growing used to the daylight, she took in the sight before her with a slackened jaw.

Though she'd been up on the terrace before, it might as well have been her first visit because it looked like a whole different place.

Strung with a canopy of fairy lights and silky silver drapes, the whitewashed posts formed a long overhead trellis that led from the door to the far edge of the roof. Zaynab tilted her head up and surveyed the transformed setting, her awe multiplying as she walked into the party and took in all the beautiful changes to the scenery. Gone were the wraparound teak sofa with its colorful cushions, the large potted palms and the fire table, all replaced by long, shining white oak tables, sturdy cushioned benches and a large dais where a band was playing live music, the fluted notes of a wind instrument blending with the brisk keystrokes from the piano as a lively song matched the general mood of the party.

Each table was adorned by simple but elegant greenery, more string lights and candle votives. The table settings were untouched, a clue that the party must have only just begun since the guests hadn't dined yet. That knowledge gave her hope that maybe she could complete what she'd come to do without garnering too much attention. Still, her stomach churned when she walked a little farther onto the terrace and deeper into the party. Guests milled around the tables, some seated, everyone spread out and clustered into groups. From the looks of it, no one had come alone.

Except for me.

It dawned on her that she stood out like a sore thumb.

And she wasn't alone in noticing that she was an out-lier. A few guests caught her eye, their curiosity clear in their lingering stares and furrowed brows. Was it her imagination or did their lips move faster as they watched her? Were they talking about her, wondering what she was possibly doing there?

Or perhaps they could sense that unlike them, she had no official invite. Not from the bride-to-be, or her groom, and not even from the party's host—her husband.

Well, *her husband* until she handed him the folded papers inside of her shoulder purse.

Thinking of the divorce she'd come for slowed her racing heart rate and calmed her mind a little. She had a reason to be here, though for a different reason than everyone else. And even though it wasn't the most opportune of settings, she would try very hard not to ruin the party for anyone. Zaynab was determined as ever, despite being in the company of strangers, to meet with her husband and do what she should have done a year ago.

Divorce him.

End their farce of a marriage and move past this stage of her life finally.

Zaynab searched the faces in the crowd, certain he'd be there. Somewhere. He was throwing the party for his sister's engagement after all. She grew frustrated when she didn't spot him. Walking and scouring the crush of guests, she smiled awkwardly a few times when she snagged more curious looks from these strangers. One of them was a pale-haired white woman, her chin-length bob a blond so icy it bordered on colorless. Despite her frosty coloring, her eyes were shining pools of hazel warmth and her smile invited Zaynab to slow and stop beside her.

"Hello, newcomer," the woman greeted her cheerfully, peeling herself out from under the arm of a lanky dark-haired young man who flashed Zaynab a grin. "If you're worried that you missed anything, don't be. Lunch hasn't begun, and no one's given speeches yet." The woman raised a champagne flute to her with a widening smile. "Are you with the bride-to-be or the groom-to-be?"

"Um, neither actually." Zaynab watched as the woman's smile flipped downward and confusion pinched the space between fine ash-blond brows. "I'm looking for…the host."

My husband was on the tip of her tongue, but that would require a long-winded explanation and she wasn't in the mood to divulge.

"Ara?"

Zaynab tensed up, her body freezing at the sound of his name as it always seemed to do these days. She forced herself to nod and watched as the woman tapped a long manicured nail at her chin thoughtfully.

"I arrived a lot earlier than everyone, and I definitely saw him then, but not since."

"Oh… I was hoping to speak with him."

Smiling, the woman held up a finger to her and turned to regard her companion. "Lucas, did you see where Ara went?"

"Who?" the dark-haired young man said, his head swiveling to them from the conversation he'd been having with another couple.

"Ara. You know, Anisa's older brother."

Anisa. Another name Zaynab hadn't heard in a while. She hadn't met Anisa officially yet, and given her reason for being there, she hoped to avoid a run-in with the bride-to-be at all costs.

"Well, why didn't you just say that, Darya?" Lucas scratched the scruffy beard at his cheek, hemming and hawing comically before he finally shook his head. "Nah, I don't remember. He's probably around though."

Zaynab could only pray that he was. Seeing as they couldn't help her, she thanked Darya and Lucas and walked away.

She didn't get far before she heard someone calling for Anisa.

It wasn't hard to tell who the bride-to-be was, as she was dressed in a white, gold-threaded guuntino, the traditional body-hugging outfit a favorite among Somali brides. And if her lovely dress wasn't a giveaway, Anisa's smile radiated an effulgent glow that spoke of her upcoming nuptials and future bliss.

Zaynab immediately recognized it because *she* had glowed just like that with the brilliant hope of what her married life would be like. Sadly, that spark in her was quickly snuffed out by the coldly cruel reality of her unhappy marriage.

Shaking away her depressive thoughts, she moved back into the crowd and studied Anisa from a safe distance.

Trailing behind her in a tan suit, with his gaze firmly glued to Anisa was a man Zaynab recognized more readily. Nasser, though she hadn't seen him for some time. Nasser worked in the private security sector where he ran his own company, and Ara had hired his services some time before Zaynab and he had married. She'd only met him once but that didn't stop her from being surprised that he was Anisa's chosen life partner. From her recollection, Nasser was similar to Ara in that he was frigidly taciturn and not at all easily approachable. But she wouldn't have been able to tell, not by the way he stared at Anisa. All she saw now was an unmasked abundance of love for his intended bride.

Impressive. I guess love does have some wonders, Zaynab mused.

Nasser palmed his clean-shaven jaw sheepishly as he joined Anisa in standing before an elderly couple. Judging by the way Anisa and Nasser shared similar embarrassed expressions, it seemed that they had been caught doing something they shouldn't have been doing together. They were quickly forgiven, as the older woman and man embraced them both.

Zaynab presumed they had to be Nasser's parents. They couldn't be Anisa's. She might not have been able to get Ara to open up about himself much, but it was common knowledge that both he and his younger sister had lost their parents in a tragic boating accident.

Though her marriage to him might be ending very soon,

it didn't stop Zaynab's heart from panging in sorrow for Ara's loss. She couldn't fathom what it was like to lose one's parents so very young. She'd hoped secretly that she could fill that void and be his family once they married, but now all Zaynab desired was for their divorce to be filed and eventually finalized.

It was why she kept an eye on Anisa and Nasser. Surely Ara wouldn't be too far from his sister and future brother-in-law.

Where are you?

Biding her time wasn't working well. Anisa and Nasser mingled with his family some more before chatting with their guests and doing the circuit. Zaynab found a corner to avoid a meeting with them and pulled out her phone, resorting to messaging Ara since she couldn't track him down.

I'm here, at the house. I was hoping we could talk…

She thumbed the send button before she wimped out.

Staring up from her phone and looking around, she felt a fresh wave of exasperation and dread when Anisa and Nasser stopped to talk to the blond-haired Darya. Their chat was animated, laughter and gesturing relaxed as if the trio knew each other well. Worried that she would be mentioned, Zaynab backed toward the exit, pasting on a smile and praying she would make it without a confrontation.

As she did, she sent another message to Ara.

Leaving. Meet me at my hotel.

Sharing the pinned location of her hotel and feeling like she was far enough to safely turn her back on the party and make her hasty exit, Zaynab whipped around only to slam into a hard, warm wall. A wall that expelled an indignant huff upon contact and had big hands that quickly and firmly locked around her shoulders.

"Zaynab," the wall said her name in a huskily deep, familiar voice that had her heart thundering from one breath to another and her head swirling with a number of emotions from apprehension to breathless anticipation.

She'd been looking for Ara all this time and now that he was in front of her, she didn't know what to say. Didn't even think she could move out of his grasp.

"Security informed me that you had arrived," he said as way of explanation.

"I…" She struggled to speak and realized it wasn't helping that his hands were still on her. Shrugging his touch off, she continued, "Yes, I didn't want to pull you away and decided to come up and look for you, but I couldn't find you."

"We must have missed each other then."

Zaynab couldn't understand how she could've missed him, but now that her eyes alighted on his figure, she knew why he hadn't jumped out to her immediately. First, he wasn't dressed in his usual business attire, and his choice of a polo shirt, chinos and high-top sneakers threw her for a loop. But more disconcerting than his atypical outfit was the warm smile he cast to a guest that called his name. Raising his hand in greeting, he gripped her wrist lightly with the other hand and tugged her after him.

"We need to talk," Zaynab told him.

"Not here," was his curt reply before Ara drew her after him gently, away from the merriment that was his sister's engagement party.

* * *

Running into his estranged wife at Anisa and Nasser's engagement party was a security measure Ara hadn't even thought to consider.

And why would he? They technically hadn't seen each other face-to-face for a year. Any communication they'd had since Zaynab left him to return to her home in London was short and infrequent. He counted a total of three brief calls with her. The first call had been shortly after she left, and he'd inquired about her safe landing, while the second call came from her a few days later. When he'd answered her call, she'd quickly explained that she hadn't meant to call him at all but that she'd made a mistake.

Admittedly that had stung him far more than he anticipated.

But as fragile as his ego was after that, it was the third call that lingered in his mind. The last one before they went a year's stretch without speaking.

When she called and asked for a divorce.

His jaw clenched at the memory.

Though it shouldn't have surprised him when she asked. After all, they had been married for a couple months at that point but they were virtual strangers. More than anything the fault was his. He hadn't known how to be a husband to her, to love and value her the way she deserved. She might believe otherwise, but their estrangement wasn't anything he'd planned.

Like their marriage, it just happened.

And Ara neither knew how to fix whatever had broken them—nor did he think it was worth fixing. Zaynab shouldn't have ever been with him, and since he couldn't undo time and make it so that she never had met him, he figured the least he could do now was hear her out. Because she hadn't flown thousands of miles from the UK to coastal Somaliland for Anisa's engagement party.

So he should have been prepared when after ushering her out of the house and into his car, she opened her purse, pulled out papers, thrust them at him and said, "I want a divorce."

That word again.

Ara lifted a heavy hand and thumbed the ignition button, the steady hum of the engine not enough to drown out the pressingly dull sound of his heart beating in his eardrums. A sudden heat wrapped its hot, clammy fist around him and held him in its thrall, squeezing at his airway and forcing him to breathe more carefully through his nose—lest Zaynab realize what was happening to him.

Besides, once he breathed enough times and calmed his body's instinctual reaction, their divorce wasn't truly shocking news. More unwelcome as it added another task to his overflowing work schedule.

Convincing himself it was the additional unwanted workload she'd now dropped in his lap that was causing his startling physical reaction, Ara sat back, grasped the wheel and drove them away from the house and any prying eyes that might see them together. More than not wanting attention drawn from Anisa and Nasser announcing their engagement to their friends and family, he quietly admitted that he wasn't ready for his divorce to be made public yet.

They didn't speak again during the drive to her hotel.

And then only when they entered her modest hotel room.

"How did you know where I was staying?" she blurted as soon as the door to her room closed behind him.

He arched a brow. "You messaged me the location."

"Right. I forgot that I did that…" Zaynab turned her

back on him, but not before Ara caught her anxiously sinking her teeth into her bottom lip. She dropped her purse and the papers she'd been holding onto her bed—the ones he hadn't taken from her yet—and she walked over to slide open her balcony door and let in a cool breeze.

Stepping closer to her, he tasted the ocean in the fresh mid-October air as it fluttered through her hijab and flooded the room. She must have an even better view of the Indian Ocean and Batalaale Beach from her balcony than he did from his hilltop house. If nothing else calmed him, it was looking out over the white sands of the beach and the sparkling blue waters that had been his home all his life. He would've hoped that the vista offered her the same serenity, but judging by the way her shoulders practically touched her ears and her arms caged her middle, Ara didn't think Zaynab cared much for the view.

He couldn't blame her. They were, after all, about to end their marriage.

Curbing a sigh, he asked, "If you planned to meet here, why did you come to the house?"

"I didn't mean to do that either. I just… I didn't want to wait anymore." A stronger breeze whipped at her headscarf, the black chiffon wrapped tightly to her head, a reminder that she hadn't removed it. It was the first time she'd done that. When they'd lived together, just the two of them, Zaynab never wore her headscarf around him. As husband and wife, she hadn't had to be modest with him.

He supposed that too would change once the divorce was official.

It was an odd thing to fixate on given the heavy subject they had to face.

Zaynab turned from the open balcony and looked at

him, concern creasing her brow and a frown curling across her pursed lips.

"I hadn't planned to come to the house," she said softly, her arms banding around her tighter, "and I certainly wouldn't have come had I known about Anisa's engagement."

Ara frowned. *Yes*, he thought guiltily, that was his fault. Though in his defense, they rarely spoke and he assumed a call from him wouldn't be welcomed by her.

"I would've called with the news, but I figured you might be busy."

By the way Zaynab worried her bottom lip, he knew what they were both thinking about. Or rather, *who*.

Her mother.

Part of the reason he hadn't disturbed her was for her mother's sake. It would've been unfair to distract Zaynab when her mother required her undivided attention, and understandably so. They hadn't spoken about it, and Ara had only heard the news from one of Zaynab's distant relatives, but he couldn't imagine what she'd been going through after learning of her mother's cancer diagnosis.

It was one thing to lose family—he knew that all too well, unfortunately. And yet another to watch them suffer and not be able to do anything to help.

"How is your mother?"

If he hadn't known what to look for he'd have missed the slightest tremble to her chin.

"She's fine," she replied. "In remission now, alhamdulillah."

"Alhamdulillah," he echoed, with a lot more relief than he'd expected to be feeling. He had first met her mother, Fadumo, at his and Zaynab's nikah. Being that her only child was getting married, Fadumo had flown to Berbera from London for the special occasion. Though she had been there to support her daughter, Zaynab's mother hadn't treated Ara with anything but maternal kindness, and in that way she'd reminded him of his own late mother... So, naturally, he was relieved to hear that her health hadn't only improved but been restored.

Ara didn't fault Zaynab for not telling him that her mother had been sick during their marital separation. Not when they both must have known that this day would come.

That their divorce was imminent.

The awkward silence that followed had him shifting his weight from foot to foot. And the restlessness was compounded when Zaynab glanced at the papers on the bed.

Seeing that he couldn't avoid it any longer, he picked them up, tension priming his muscles as he perused the small sheaf of papers. It didn't take him very long to relax. And then to grow confused.

"This is an application form for a khula." He directed his scowl from the papers to her stubborn expression.

She jerked her head in short affirmation, a look of determination staring back at him.

A khula was the only way a wife could initiate divorce proceedings.

"I went ahead and spoke to my local Muslim law council," Zaynab explained when he didn't speak. "We'd have to go through the application process, and I'd have to pay back your mahr—"

"No." The word slipped easily from his lips as he set the papers down on the bed. Fighting the urge to rip up the divorce application forms, he narrowed his eyes at her. "This isn't how we'll do this. Your dowry is not up for discussion." Although he knew without paying him back her bridal dowry, she wouldn't even be able to start the process of khula.

He would give her the divorce, but he'd do it in a way where she wouldn't have to be deprived of the dowry he'd promised her.

"A khula is unacceptable."

"But I want this done now. I don't want to wait three months until it's official."

She was talking about iddah, the three-month waiting period. If *he* divorced her, Zaynab and he would still technically be married for three of her regular menstrual cycles. That meant she wouldn't be officially separated from him until after those three months.

"Did you intend to remarry?" He hadn't even considered that possibility, and he didn't care to, not when his thoughts veered toward a blistering anger and...jealousy. Denying it was pointless; he was jealous of what her impatience insinuated. Was there another man waiting in the wings, biding his time for Ara to be out of the picture fully? It would make sense why she seemed so disinclined to perform iddah. And it wouldn't shock him if there was a lover awaiting her eagerly.

Zaynab was a beautiful woman. It couldn't be hard for her to find someone to replace him.

"Is that why you're rushing to perform khula rather than a talaq?" The talaq was the more accepted practice of divorce, where the husband would initiate the divorce proceedings. It was far less complicated, and it wouldn't require her to return any part of her dowry. "I can't see why else you'd be impatient."

If looks could kill...

Well, he wouldn't be standing in front of her.

"After this I think I might not ever remarry," she said,

seething, her words stabbing into him and fueling his bitterness more.

"Still, the iddah period serves a purpose," he argued.

"It's not even like pregnancy is an issue. Doing iddah would be a waste of time."

She had a point, of course. They hadn't ever consummated their marriage. And since the chance of immaculate conception was impossible, the three-month waiting period was unnecessary.

"That may be so, and yet I don't want to rob you of the dowry."

Zaynab rolled her eyes and kissed her teeth. "You wouldn't be robbing me—I'm *choosing* to give it back. Just sign your half of the papers...please, Ara."

His name came out as a softly exasperated plea, and it nearly weakened him into agreement.

"Pregnancy isn't the only reason the iddah exists," he heard himself say, his voice gruffer. "It's there as a measure to ensure a couple truly want a divorce, and that there's no path to a reconciliation." Sealing the distance between them, he stopped in front of her, the space between them vibrating with the heat of their bodies and the tension of their situation. "Divorce is hard enough without regrets."

Zaynab sniffed at his words. Being a few inches shorter than him, she lifted her chin to stare him down and it made him feel small.

Though not small enough to stop him from saying, "Are you so certain that we're beyond a possible reconciliation and any regrets?"

It was as though his brain and his mouth were disconnected. Ara couldn't explain why else he was pushing against the divorce so suddenly, especially since he wouldn't force Zaynab to remain with him. He told himself a year ago when she left him that it didn't matter what happened to their marriage and that it was for her to decide what she wanted. *That I would go along with whatever she desired.*

And she was clearly telling him that she wished for their relationship to end.

So why couldn't he just shut up, and do as she asked and sign the papers? It would be the rational course of action.

But apparently he was feeling irrational, because he cupped her cheek and stroked her soft skin, the simple touch unlocking an ancient primal part of him.

"Wh-what are you doing?" she stammered, her eyes widening but her body remaining still. She could've stopped him from touching her. Stepped back and ended the contact.

But when she didn't, Ara touched her a little more boldly. His hand slid down and framed her lower jaw, felt the tension buried beneath the smooth brown skin and deep in her jawbone. He tipped her chin back further, and with his thumb indenting the soft flesh of her bottom lip, Ara inhaled sharply when her mouth parted open, her tongue swiping out suddenly and wetting the tip of his digit. He could tell by the way her eyes widened that she hadn't meant to lick him. And yet that knowledge didn't douse the heat firing through his body.

They had come here to begin to finalize the end of their marriage.

And somehow he was now holding her, his arm secured around her back and their bodies pressed close. He turned them and walked her back toward the large, comfortable bed a few feet away.

Zaynab gasped when the back of her legs made contact

with the bed and gave way, bending, bowing and sending her reeling backward onto the cushioned support of the bed comforter and mattress. Ara followed her, his hands pressed by the sides of her head, their chests no longer touching and yet both matched in their heaving breathlessness.

Her eyes rounded with shocked confusion, sparked with a newer emotion. Desire, he recognized quickly, feeling the same yearning pumping molten heat through his own body.

"I'm just making sure that we're both certain this is what we want." Ara took her chin in his hand again, his face lowering closer to hers until he could feel her sweet, warm breath stirring over his lips. "I can't walk away with any doubts. Can you?"

For a second she did nothing but swallow audibly, but then she shook her head, the motion causing her hijab to slide a little back off her forehead, the baby curls she'd smoothed at her hairline peeping out. Teasing him. Firing up his need to see more of her.

She didn't object or stop him as he revealed her. As he drew back the hijab with a gentle hand, she lifted her head to help him and he settled the material at the base of her neck, which only fueled the fire for his lust. He couldn't have worked fast enough, but the result was well worth his patient endurance.

"Braids," he breathed, pulling her hair free of the hijab that had restrained them and carding his fingers through the long, silky golden-brown lengths of her microbraids.

Ara lifted a palmful to his mouth, brushing their softness over his lips and groaning when he caught a tantalizingly sweet whiff of her hair. It wasn't enough for him to bury his nose into the hair he had trapped in his hand;

he desired the source and moved to tunnel his face into the side of her neck, her braids tickling his face and the scent of her oud perfume, fruity shampoo and whatever was naturally *her*. Dazed by passion, he ended up with his lips pressed to the pulse beating right above her clavicle.

Her soft little gasp wasn't what drew his head up.

No, it was her hands at the back of his head, digging in suggestively until he rose up over her again, their lips in perfect alignment were he to descend to her.

Before Ara could decide whether he wanted to go as far as kiss her, Zaynab pulled him down to her and made the decision for him.

He groaned as her lips moved hesitantly against his, her soft exploration of him causing his arms to nearly buckle and testing the limits of his self-restraint to do anything more. But as he told himself that this was all it could be, he felt Zaynab's legs brushing his thighs, her ankles pressing into his backside with an urgency that matched the now-confident slide of her mouth against his.

It was counterproductive for them to be doing this—torturous even, considering why they had come together.

And as if to remind them again, the loud distinct crinkle of paper reached his ears.

She didn't break from his mouth, tipping her hip to the side while he ripped the offensive papers for the divorce application free from under her. Flinging them away haphazardly, not caring where they ended up or if they blasted to oblivion, he pushed her deeper into the bed and kissed her to breathlessness. And she returned the favor, driving him onto his back at one point and moving away from his mouth to nip and trail her lips along his jawline to a sensitive earlobe.

He knew he should've stopped them.

But it was when Zaynab lifted up the bottom of his shirt that Ara realized that even if he desired to, there was no ending what they had started, not without any hurt feelings. He hadn't been a good husband to her, but this one time he wished to give her what she wanted.

First this moment together, and then the divorce she asked of him.

CHAPTER TWO

ZAYNAB DIDN'T KNOW what made her angrier at Ara: that he'd abandoned her with a signed divorce application after their one-time passionate mistake, or that after refusing to give him any more thought, she was now fully reminded of him at her doctor's checkup.

She stared in horror as her family doctor confirmed what she'd suspected and dreaded.

"You're pregnant, Zaynab."

Pregnant? She was *pregnant*?

Whatever else her doctor said was slowly overtaken by her harsh, grating breaths as she barely held together her composure when all she wished to do was scream.

"Your HCG levels… It's a lot later in the first trimester…"

"I'm pregnant." She hoped that saying it would settle her thundering heart, but she only grew more faint sitting upright on the exam bed when her doctor smiled and nodded patiently. Zaynab didn't even bother asking her if she was certain. She had the result of her blood test in her hands, not to mention a pregnancy test currently occupying the dustbin in her flat's bathroom. She'd done the home screening when her usually regular cycle hadn't arrived not for one but two months. It hadn't taken her long to do the math after and then drop everything to visit the nearest chemist to her flat.

The home test had told her exactly what her doctor had: that in less than nine months she'd be a mother.

"It can be overwhelming even when it's anticipated, but especially when it's not. Know that there are options," her doctor told her with a meaningful look. "I have brochures explaining those details. I'll let reception know to pass them to you once we're done here."

Zaynab pressed her hand to her swooping belly and croaked, "Are we not done yet?" Because she'd heard plenty enough. Now all she wanted to do was leave the doctor's office, stop by the corner shop for ice cream and go home and pretend like none of this was happening. Like her life hadn't been irrevocably changed in what felt like a blink of an eye.

And all for what? One ignorantly blissful moment of pleasure, that was what. Had she known the bliss was a ticking time bomb, she might have reassessed allowing the reptilian portion of her brain to have its fun.

It physically pained her to listen to the doctor's next instructions, the sterility of the information feeling both unreal and upsettingly her new reality.

"Since you're nearly at twelve weeks, we can begin certain genetic and blood testing. I'd also like to book you for your first ultrasound scan, if that's all right with you?"

Zaynab bobbed her head weakly.

And that was how the rest of her doctor's appointment went, and she left the office with brochures burrowed discreetly in her purse along with the times and dates for the next string of appointments for her prenatal care. The sun beamed warmly overhead as she stepped out into the chilly January morning, the snowfall from last night already mostly melted off the footpath except where it clung stubbornly in brown-topped patches to the curb. She couldn't believe that a little over a week ago, she was ringing in the New Year with the resolution that this year she'd focus on self-discovery and reclaiming joy for herself.

Though she had avoided thinking about him, Ara had been half the reason she'd made the resolution. The other half was inspired by watching her mother battle her cancer diagnosis and come out the victor.

Pride for her mother shone through her as brightly as the afternoon sun washing down over the gray rows of buildings in this part of the city. She turned her face up to the warmth, saddened that it couldn't melt the solid fear sitting heavily in her stomach the way it had the snow.

She groaned, remembering that her next chat with her mother would be interesting now that she was expecting.

And she wasn't the only person Zaynab would have to tell.

Despite how he'd cowardly sneaked away on her after taking her to bed, Ara had the right to know he was going to be a father. As daunting as it would be to send him the news, she would have to brave through it because the alternative of not telling him wasn't an option. But it didn't mean that she had to do it immediately. She'd just found out and needed her own time to process and sort through her feelings before she added any of his emotions to the mix.

Later, she promised. When she had her head on straighter and the timing was right. And likely over a voice message because she couldn't handle seeing his handsome face while she delivered the bombshell of an announcement.

She was nearly halfway to the bus stop when her phone thrummed several times in succession with incoming texts before her ringtone nagged at her. The impatient caller turned out to be her childhood friend Salma reminding her they had a standing lunch date.

"You forgot, didn't you?" Salma clucked loudly.

Zaynab had forgotten, but she had a good reason. And she must have been quiet enough that Salma sensed it and asked more soberly, "Are you all right, love?"

"No, I'm pregnant," she said, the sob choking out of her surprising her. Because as wildly upsetting to her world as the news of her pregnancy was, she hadn't once felt the urge to cry until then when a familiar voice asked after her well-being.

Salma comforted her over the phone until they met face-to-face, their lunch plans at their favorite restaurant canceled for takeout at Zaynab's flat on her well-worn but comfortable leather sofa and a sitcom playing on the TV. Much later when she'd calmed down, Zaynab followed Salma's gaze to the open and half-packed luggage in the corner of the sitting room.

"I almost forgot about that…" Zaynab trailed off with a sigh. In a few days she was due to leave for a work-related trip to Mauritius. She'd been looking forward to the trip until this morning when her world had been upended. But as much as she'd like to call in sick, her agency wouldn't be able to send a replacement so easily. Working as a personal support care worker was fulfilling, and her current position of two years was with a client she'd grown to care deeply for. Opaline was a sprightly octogenarian in spite of her knee replacement, double hip replacement and recent cataracts surgeries. It hadn't stopped the elderly woman from accepting an invitation to attend a family member's wedding in the beautiful East African islands.

She'd not only invited Zaynab, but Opaline had also

seen to it that her grandnephew and attorney-in-fact, Remi, had paid for Zaynab's ticket and accommodations as well as her meals. Remi was counting on Zaynab to care for his great-aunt during their travels. Their generosity meant a lot to her, and it was why she wouldn't cancel on them.

"Come on. I'll help you pack," Salma said, her smile sympathetic. Being a nurse, her friend understood the grueling hours of the workload in their chosen fields.

It was hard carving out time for herself when it was in her nature to care for others.

Her mother when she'd been battling her cancer.

Opaline and Remi.

And now a child that would rely solely on her. She touched a trembling hand to her abdomen.

So much for my New Year's resolution...

Later when Salma had helped her finish packing and called it a night, Zaynab sat in her flat alone. She stared at the phone gripped in her hand and the message she had hastily thumbed out before her nerves got the better of her.

I'm pregnant, and it's yours.

The last part seemed redundant and it had churned her gut to even type it, but she didn't want him mistaking or doubting who was responsible. Not that she believed that Ara was the type to shirk his duties, and yet he hadn't been a real husband to her, or even much of a friend.

"You never really trusted me," she murmured.

But that wasn't her problem right now.

She hovered an aching thumb over her screen, rallying her courage to send the message before finally doing it. As soon as the text started a new chat with him, Zaynab shut her phone off and dropped it on the cushion beside her, knowing that whatever response it generated from him would be a worry for her tomorrow.

Ara hadn't worried much about how his tomorrows would look, mostly because he planned so far in advance that not much took him by surprise.

Not his sister Anisa's engagement announcement—he'd seen the attraction between her and Nasser long before they had acted on it. And not anything else related to his life, professionally or personally.

In fact, not since his parents' deaths had he felt the groundless sensation of true, utter shock.

But Zaynab's message was a close second.

I'm pregnant, and it's yours.

Those five words had circled his brain—taken over dominion of every thought, and stymied most of his action for days after Ara had received her news. His distraction was poorly timed as he'd traveled from home for important business. Business that required his full and undivided attention, not that he blamed Zaynab. It wasn't news that he would've wanted her to hide from him, even though she could have concealed her pregnancy and the truth of him being an expectant father.

With how Ara had treated her, he would have expected her to never contact him again.

Beyond feeling relieved that she hadn't hidden it from him, he couldn't specify exactly how he felt besides this hollowness. It wasn't all that helpful that he didn't have much time to himself to sift through his feelings about becoming a father.

Between back-to-back meetings, he barely found the time to sleep or sit for a meal.

But if his sleep deprivation and slight malnourishment

was what it took to seal this latest business deal, then he would gladly suffer it.

As the owner of Africa's largest shipping company, Titancore Transport, his shoulders carried a tremendous weight of responsibility for the thousands employed by him and his clients, but now Ara was looking to do more for his country too.

A total of three days elapsed before he finally deigned that the business proceedings were going smoothly enough and could be handled by some of his trusted executive staff. No sooner had Ara made the declaration did he begin to board a privately chartered flight for Mauritius.

Although he'd been tied up, he had looked into Zaynab's whereabouts, not knowing if she was still in her London flat or residing with her mother in the English countryside.

It was surprising when he discovered that she was in far closer reach to him. In less than five hours his plane was touching down and taxiing toward the one passenger terminal at the Sir Seewoosagur Ramgoolam International Airport, Mauritius's primary airport.

He had a car awaiting him on arrival. By the time the car stopped in front of the resort's main entrance and he stepped out to be greeted by staff, he willed patience that he wasn't wholeheartedly feeling and sought details of Zaynab's room.

Ara clenched his jaw at the memory of falling on Zaynab like an animal. It had been over two months ago since she'd come with her divorce application, but it might as well have been yesterday with how vivid the memories playing in his mind were. And with those memories came the awakening of a familiar hunger to take her in his arms again and repeat what they'd done step by step, as though his slip in judgment hadn't caused the situation they were now in. Instead of entertaining his powerfully magnetic attraction to her, he should've been ashamed of his sense-less and unalterable mistake. Should have been prepar-ing to grovel at Zaynab's feet for burdening her. But each step that carried him closer to her eroded his shame and, in its place, a heady anticipation to reunite with her arose.

An anticipation that hadn't existed a few days earlier. Before she'd messaged him with the announcement of her pregnancy, he'd been certain she wouldn't contact him ever again once he had done as she desired and signed her di-vorce application. Their lives were different enough that they'd likely never cross paths, and if for some reason they did, Ara didn't torture himself into hoping that she'd speak to him. *That she'd forgive me.* After all, it would only be fair that she treated him with the same indifference he'd shown her in their short marriage.

At least that was what he envisioned would come next. Only now that had changed…

Because of their whirlwind passion, fate had forced them together.

In a matter of a briefly worded text he'd gone from ex-pecting never to see her again to figuring out how to keep her in his life for as long as he breathed, and the absurdity of it had Ara indulging the smile lifting his mouth.

Slashing a hand down his face a moment later, he schooled his features into neutrality as he spied her suite up ahead, the number on the door like a beacon. But as eager as he'd been to be near her again, Ara found him-self shifting on restless feet as reluctance gripped him in front of her door.

He couldn't be sure what lay on the other side, but he only hoped that she would hear him out once she opened the door.

With that he raised his hand to knock—

Only for the door to swing open, his fist breezing through midair before he drew his hand back, his scowl immediate.

The man blocking his path had at least a couple inches or three on Ara, and though his lanky limbs looked weaker in his well-tailored suit, he compensated with an unspoken air of authority that rivaled his own.

Authority that threaded his demanding tone when he asked, "Who are you?"

Before Ara could tell him that he'd taken those words right out of his mouth, a sweet voice Ara would have recognized anywhere called out, "Remi? You haven't left yet—"

Rounding the corner of the entrance hall, Zaynab cut herself off and stopped in her tracks as Ara's eyes locked on her.

He'd envisioned their reunion so many different ways over the course of the past few days, yet he hadn't considered the surge of emotions seeing her would unleash in him. Desire blended with satisfaction and intrigue as Ara trailed his gaze over her. Like this stranger she'd called Remi, she was dressed as though she were heading to an event. Threaded with a bevy of sequins, the pale gray floor-length maxi dress whispered over the polished white floor tiles as she walked a couple steps toward him, the surprise that had seized her beautiful round face framed by a white lightweight hijab.

"Ara?" she whispered his name in a way that shouldn't have stirred him below the belt but did. "What are you doing here?"

"You know him," this Remi asked her, ignoring Ara completely now and irritating him in doing so. But what annoyed him even more was Zaynab shifting her stare to Remi and nodding.

Jealousy surged through Ara and sat over his chest like a weight as she bit her lip and gave Remi an embarrassed smile. Whoever this man was to her, he clearly mattered enough to warrant not only her shy feelings, but an explanation.

"He's my—*was* my husband."

Her deliberate use of the past tense hadn't gone missed, and if he weren't in their company, Ara might have clutched the spot above his heart that panged the hardest at the blow of her words. Instead, he stared hard at her and said, "We need to talk."

Not that it mattered to Ara, but Remi's frown flicked between them. "Would you like me to stay?"

Ara had to check the urge to grab him by the collar, heave him out of the room and slam the door closed behind him. But he refused to devolve into a beast, even though an animalistic anger pulsed through him and tensed and primed every tendon and muscle in his body.

Zaynab calmed him a bit when she shook her head. "No, that's all right." Then with another of her smiles, she said, "I already held you from the party long enough. Please, tell Opaline that I'm fine and I just need a little rest."

Remi hesitated, but in the end he nodded curtly at her, leveled a glare on Ara that clearly was a parting warning and then stalked off in his highly polished leather shoes after Ara cleared out of his path.

Ara entered the resort suite and closed the door after him. As his hand released the door handle he suddenly had a flash from the past, when he'd done the same thing back in Berbera, and how their conversation in her hotel room had led to them sprawled in a sweaty tangle of limbs in her hotel bed.

Closing his eyes and balling his fists at his side, he took

a moment to strengthen himself before he opened his eyes and turned to Zaynab.

She had moved back from him, her arms crossed and her wary look telling him everything she didn't need to. She was worried by his presence, and that was the last thing he wanted to make her, and not only because she was carrying his child.

It was as if everything clicked into place right then, seeing her, knowing that she was now bound to him in a way that was above law.

He hadn't known what to feel when she told him of her pregnancy, but now—*now* Ara reflected on how he'd nearly lost his life a year ago. How empty and purposeless he'd felt when he had first lost his parents sixteen years before that, how he had focused so hard to be all the family his sister needed, and how he'd poured his whole being into expanding on the business he had inherited from his mother and father. As accomplished as it might have looked on the outside, he could no longer ignore that it hadn't filled the ever-present, ever-hungering void deep within him.

But he had his answer finally, his eyes resting on her stomach.

Their child might not have been planned by either of them, but it was exactly the purpose Ara had been waiting for. And like every true purpose, a plan needed to follow. His idea was not only self-admittedly ludicrous; there was also the added pressure and extra hurdle of getting the child's mother on board.

And judging by the way Zaynab's eyes began to narrow in suspicion, Ara didn't believe for a second convincing her would be easy.

CHAPTER THREE

"YOU STILL HAVEN'T told me what you're doing here." Zaynab heard the nervousness trembling through her voice, despite having quietly and fervently hoped that she wouldn't sound as weak with shock as she felt in seeing Ara again. And of all the places she wouldn't have thought to ever see him.

Mauritius was supposed to be the place for her to reset her emotions and get a grip on her new and reeling reality of pregnancy. She knew that she would eventually have to speak to him, but she had chosen to ignore the text she'd sent him until she returned home. It would have given her the time to figure out how to handle his feelings about their new shared responsibility.

That's assuming he even wants to be in our child's life.

But now it was apparent that fate had another plan in store for her.

And there was no point in her hoping that he hadn't received her text and just shown up for some other unexplained reason. She curled her fingers under her elbows and wrapped her arms around herself tighter, feeling safer under the lasering power of his hard, assessing stare. The coldly blank set to his handsome face was typical for him. She could count on one hand how many times he'd smiled around her, and none of those few times had ever been directed at her. Sometimes she wondered if the issue of their marriage—the true reason why they couldn't make it last was because of her.

Was it that he didn't want to be with me?

They hadn't married for love, she had known and accepted that. And if it hadn't been for Sharmarke...

Zaynab didn't think of her father too often, and when she did, she never really thought of him as her *dad*. He hadn't been in her life past the first ten years, choosing his political career as a statesman over his family. Then her parents divorced and she moved from Somaliland to the UK with her mother. Now at thirty-seven, she hadn't cared to renew a relationship with him, but when he'd called her out of the blue a little more than a year ago, she hadn't been able to shut him out of her life. Mostly because her mother had been so thrilled that they were bonding. Zaynab would do anything to make her happy.

But if she were being honest with herself, she had also been curious to know more about her father. She'd spent the better part of her childhood and a bit of her adulthood starved of his attention and now, suddenly, not only had he popped up, he'd also shown *interest* in her.

At first Zaynab had maintained her firm and thorny defenses, keeping their discussions brief and only ever over texts. Slowly those texts became phone calls, then video chats before finally Sharmarke surprised her with a visit, and naturally she'd forgotten to keep her guard up and seemingly forgiven him of his past absenteeism. The hope she hadn't bothered with then made her *believe* that she could trust Sharmarke. Made her think that he wanted to be a proper parent to her.

That he loved her...

And pathetically she'd thrown open the doors to her

heart and her life and let him in, never once imagining an ulterior motive.

For a while everything had been perfect. She had both her mum and dad in her world, and they felt like a real, normal, *happy* family doing real, normal, everyday things together. So normal and happy in fact that sometimes she wondered whether she'd dreamed up the whole thing. That in some delirious, desperate state that she had fantasized the perfect family scenario. And that any moment she would wake up and realize that none of it had been reality. Even then she'd known it had been too good to last.

So when Sharmarke had suddenly asked her to consider an arranged marriage that would be good for his business connections and revealed his true intentions for seeking her out and nurturing a relationship with her, she'd known her wake-up call had come. Zaynab keenly remembered alternating between wanting to burst into tears and screaming out her bitterness and devastation at him. In the end she'd been left chilled to the bone by her so-called father's cold betrayal. Spurred on by vengeance, she had agreed to meet this man Sharmarke was trying to get her married to. Then the plan had been for her to ruin the meeting, chase her would-be suitor away and embarrass her father before cutting off all contact with him for good.

But that hadn't happened, she thought sadly. Because despite being certain that any marriage Sharmarke had a hand in wasn't for her, she had fallen instantly and incomprehensibly in love with Ara the moment she laid eyes on him. The instant that his darkly magnetic stare locked its intensity on her and made her feel like no one else existed in his world.

She should be ashamed of herself but recalling that

first meeting always put a silly smile on her face to her utter frustration.

Zaynab quietly sighed, looking warily at him as he closed the door and turned to face her. She flinched at the way his dark brows slashed over even darker eyes that narrowed as he walked forward and closed the short distance to her.

He stopped just as she began wondering and worrying if he meant to embrace her. It was fanciful thinking, of course, because aside from that one blip a couple months ago, Ara hadn't ever shown her physical interest. Most of their conversations had to do with impersonal subjects like their respective careers. They barely even spoke about their families; Ara seemed to avoid mentioning his sister and his late parents, which led Zaynab to believe there was not much point of speaking about her mother and her own childhood when it appeared he didn't care about her enough to ask or wonder.

Only now, in a twist of irony they were compelled to speak about family.

Their own. Because it was growing inside of her, and in a little over half a year, they would be parents.

Six months.

She wished he'd given her more time. Heck, it would've been nice if he'd let her know that he was going to drop in on her unceremoniously.

Which reminded her that he still hadn't answered her and explained why he'd shown up unannounced and how he'd known to look for her in Mauritius of all places.

Annoyed and curious now, she felt her brows puckering as she asked, "How did you know I was going to be here?"

"I have my methods," he said with a jerk of his chin

over his shoulder. "Who was that man to you, and what was he doing in your room?"

Zaynab had a hard time picking her jaw up off the floor at his very plain insinuation and sheer audacity, otherwise she would have lashed him with her tongue sooner.

"Not that it's your business, but he's my employer, because I just happen to be working." She bristled, unfolding her arms and holding them stiffly at her sides despite wanting to throttle him. "And he was in my room because I wasn't feeling well and he walked me from the wedding party his family are all attending."

Ara's expression changed in a flash, his coldly impassive face flickering with concern. "What's wrong?"

Zaynab could hardly believe her eyes and was stunned into silence. *He cares...* But then she watched his focus sail down to her stomach, and her heart sank, dropping down to the very spot where his eyes were trained. *The baby*, she mused. Of course it was their baby he was worried about, not her at all.

Biting back down her annoyance, she snapped, "I was a little queasy. Considering my current state, I've been told it's normal enough." She passed a hand over her lower stomach and watched in fascination as his own hands curled into fists at his side. Almost as though he wanted to touch the proof, feel the new tautness to her belly and set aside any doubts that he might still hold that they were expectant parents.

"How?" he rasped and caught her off guard when he flipped topics.

Zaynab arched a brow and sniped, "'How' what? How did I get pregnant? Or how does pregnancy occur?" Goading him was probably not her brightest idea, but he had asked the annoyingly obvious question, and in doing so made her feel somehow like it was her fault. Meanwhile in all likelihood he wasn't blaming her at all.

"You're upset," he observed silkily.

Clutching onto her anger and refusing to be weakened by the sound of his voice, she rolled her eyes at him. "I'm tired and my stomach still feels a little upset, so excuse me if I seem inhospitable right now." Then because she couldn't handle not squirming under his quiet assessment, she spun on her heels and padded barefoot back to where she'd been lounging on the patio. Ara followed her outdoors, his stare all that much more powerful when he was standing over her lounge chair.

Again, fighting the urge to wriggle like prey under his predatorial gaze, she waved to the chair beside her with a quiet invite.

He was here now. They might as well talk about their future, even if she was still getting used to the idea that Ara would now be in her life forever, although it wasn't in the way that she had once thought it would be. Their marriage might have ended, the paperwork filed and submitted and only waiting to be approved, but now they were going to be parents, whether they liked it or not. Or at least she would be because she hadn't considered any of the other viable options.

As shockingly unexpected and upsetting as it first was, over the past few days she knew in every fiber of her being that she wanted this child, just as deeply and madly as she'd wanted its father once.

Unlike Ara though, their baby would be a part of her life.

She wouldn't ever force him to be a father, knowing that he had to want to do it on his own and with no compulsion from her, no matter how much she would've liked for him to be in their baby's life. Besides, it wouldn't be the first man in her life who hadn't wanted Zaynab. For the better part of her existence, her own father hadn't wanted anything to do with her.

It was a truth that was still hard to swallow sometimes.

Although mostly her mother had been more than enough for her, it hadn't stopped Zaynab from picturing what her upbringing might have been like with Sharmarke around. Would they have had regular father-daughter outings? Would he have proudly placed her photo on his desk and humblebragged to his friends about her whenever he had the chance?

Zaynab would never know.

If she could prevent her child from feeling the same painful thoughts and doubting their self-worth, then she would try. But it would help if Ara made it easier to read him. As always, he made it hard to tell what he was feeling or thinking. And without some direction, Zaynab didn't know how to begin to untie her tangled thoughts.

"What do you want to do?" Much like his last question, he surprised her.

"Honestly, I haven't given it too much thought. I only found out recently. I'm still processing what it means for me now." Zaynab chewed the inside of her cheek before continuing, "All I know is that I want to keep the baby."

She wanted the baby. Ara's relief sagged him forward where he sat on the lounge chair across from her.

He hadn't even considered that she might not desire the pregnancy, but now that she'd said it, it eliminated a fear that hadn't had the time to fully manifest. Ticking that off the mental checklist he had running, he asked her, "What else?" However he could make this easier on Zaynab, he would. After all it wasn't him that had to do the heavy lifting, at least not initially. He wanted this to go as smoothly for her as possible.

"I want to remain in London," she said, her tone firming and letting him know that there was no further discussion to be had. "Also, a forewarning—once the baby's born, I might move to live with my mother initially. In case I need help for the first month or two."

Okay. That was something he *had* thought of and was a huge part of the plan he began brewing quietly.

"I'm not going to force you to move to be in their life," Zaynab said this with a hand resting over her belly, "but it would be nice for you to be. That is, if you want to."

She sucked in her bottom lip and looked away from him making Ara understand that this was something she'd thought of, his possibly not wanting to be in their baby's life. Suddenly he had to wonder if she meant what she said. If she wasn't trying to push him away and hadn't made future plans of her own, that is. Plans that didn't include him being in the picture. On some buried rational level Ara knew that he shouldn't, but his mind veered back to the encounter with her employer, Remi, or whatever she'd called him. She had smiled familiarly at the man, and there was obviously some bond between them that had made Remi care for her.

Perhaps she had moved on.

Perhaps their relationship was more than boss and employee.

He wouldn't be shocked if it were true. Remi would be a fool if he couldn't see that Zaynab was a catch of a woman. Both beautiful and with brains that had drawn Ara to her in the first place. From their first meeting, he'd been taken with the way she handled topics from politics to sciences with an earnestness that had them talking for many hours. She had engaged his mind in a way no woman before her had.

And he was certain no woman after her would either.

Now that he'd lost his chance with her, fiery envy at the lucky man who would woo and win her over ate away at him.

Maybe that was why Ara tossed caution out and, rather than gently guide her toward the idea he'd had, he came right out and told her.

"We should move in together."

Zaynab goggled at him. "Move in together?" She repeated his words back barely above a whisper. She blinked owlishly, her hands then tensing over her stomach right before she shot up to a seat…and swayed in place, her eyes squeezing shut—

He reached forward, his hands securing around her shoulders while his heart seemed to have launched up into his throat. Breathing harshly, he looked her over, her closed eyes having snapped wide open as soon as he touched her. The last time he'd been that close to her it had led to them kissing and then creating the life that now grew in her.

"Are you all right?" He gritted his teeth, fear for her well-being still gripping him.

"It's just a little dizziness when I sat up too quickly."

She brushed his hands off her with a frown, not seeming to feel the same spark of heat he'd felt when they came into brief contact.

Her confusion having vanished quickly, she said, "Did you just propose that we move in together?"

"I did."

"Why?"

"I want us to properly raise our child."

He thought his response more than sufficient, yet Zaynab gawked at him. Speaking slowly and carefully enunciating every syllable as she might with a young child, she said, "And how does us moving in together have anything to do with that?" And then before he could answer, she raised a hand, palm up to show that she wasn't finished speaking.

"Actually, you don't need to answer that because my answer is no."

"No?"

"No," she stressed. "We don't need to raise our child under one roof. I'm happy that you would like to be in their life—thrilled to bits, really, *but* I don't see why we can't co-parent separately."

"It would be easier for one," he drawled, "less demanding for a child to be ferried between separate homes and less taxing on us."

Zaynab only huffed and turned her nose up at him, appearing nowhere close to warming to his proposition. "That's not a good enough reason to live together."

"Then we do it because we're married."

Now she eyed him like he'd grown an extra head right in front of her. "No-o-o," Zaynab stretched the syllable, "we aren't. I filed the paperwork already."

"That might be true, but if my calculation is correct, you haven't finished your iddah period."

"So? I know how iddah works. We'd have to be intimate for our divorce application to be null and void, and we haven't been since I filed."

"Again, you're correct. However your new...*condition* changes that." Ara looked pointedly at her stomach, an edge of possessiveness clanging in him every time her hands touched the area. He flexed his fingers open and closed as discreetly as possible, knowing that any contact with him would likely not be welcomed by her just then, not when her eyes narrowed in an accusatory glare.

"Explain," she demanded.

He obliged her. "Your pregnancy stretches the iddah period to until your due date."

"That's barbaric!" Her brown cheeks were rosier, anger seeming to brand onto her glowing skin.

"Not barbaric, logical. It reduces the…*question* of parentage."

Fire and frost flashed in her eyes. "Is that what this is? Are you doubting me?"

"I'm not," he said quickly and sharply, his flared nostrils an indication that his temper was rising now too. But how could it not when she was being so difficult? He locked his jaw and calmed much of the gruffness from his tone before he replied, "I hold zero doubts that is my child in there. It's why I only want what's best."

Ara rose slowly, fighting against the instinct to stay by her side but knowing that she needed time to absorb what he'd told her. "Since I've said my part, I'll leave you to gather your thoughts and contact you later."

She glowered at him and pruned her lips in defiance, refusing to speak to him.

That was fine by him. There wasn't a point in forcing her to agree. Zaynab had to want to do this with him or it wouldn't work.

Though Zaynab was in Mauritius to work, it wasn't hard to enjoy the sunny island when her employers were determined that she not spend every moment working. Between a litany of pre-and post-wedding parties, Remi had lined up a list of activities for her to do with him and, if his great-aunt's health allowed her, Opaline occasionally joined them too.

Her guilt that she wasn't more grateful to Remi's thoughtfulness was only amplified when he took her on a picnic and hike, just the two of them, and he'd been careful to keep her on an easier trail. The picnic was delicious, the hike through the jungle trail thrilling, but it was the surprise of a scenic waterfall at the end that had her feeling rotten that she wasn't as present in mind as she would've liked to be. All Zaynab could think of was the inevitable answer she'd have to give to Ara soon.

The answer she was sure he'd come hunt for himself if she took too long.

But then Remi got a call that pulled him away, and since he couldn't take it right beside the roaring waterfall, he hurried back up the trail that had gotten them there, one ear pressed to his phone while he covered his hand with the other ear.

Zaynab watched him go before she sighed and faced the natural curtain of water and its shallow pool. She pulled her sneakers and socks off, suddenly wanting to feel the cool chill of the stiller pool, her skin itching from the rise of humidity. The rainfall from earlier only added to the cloying heat in the jungle's atmosphere and made her wish that she'd brought a swimsuit. Not that she'd have gone swimming with Remi watching.

Sighing again, she settled with gathering up her long skirt and treading through the water until she waded up to her knees. Then she tipped her head back and closed her eyes to the spray of water now sprinkling her face like the wings of a moth, an easy smile pulling at her lips.

If only she could remain this relaxed, maybe she could

find the strength to face the so many unknown variables of her future.

Would she be a good mother? Could she be enough for her child if things didn't work with Ara? And now that she was thinking of him, why was he really pushing for them to move in together?

What's his agenda?

Zaynab didn't know how long she stood there, but her calves cramping was an indication. Just as she was in the middle of bidding the waterfall a quiet farewell, she heard a stone rustle and crack against another stone behind her on the embankment to the pool. Remi had to be back.

She glanced over her shoulder, the greeting on her tongue vanishing as she saw it wasn't Remi at all, but Ara.

Zaynab watched him silently as he left his shoes by hers and treaded through the water to her. She waited until he was beside her to peer up at him. "Did you follow me here too?" she asked sullenly. "What happened to giving me time to think?"

"It's been nearly two days, and my patience has its limits."

"Well, I don't have an answer for you."

Rolling up the sleeves of his dress shirt, he stared back at her quietly. Meanwhile the powerful spray and misting waters around them steadily soaked his shirt into clinging to and shaping the thick, corded muscles typically hidden beneath his business suits. Muscles she'd gotten a feel of just once and admittedly still secretly lusted for.

Gulping now, Zaynab looked away from the temptation he posed her. "I wasn't living with you during most of my iddah, so why does it have to be different now?"

"That was my mistake. I shouldn't have let you go then."

"You walked away," she corrected bitterly, the sting of waking up to a bed all alone forever imprinted in her mind.

"I did, and I shouldn't have done that."

She wanted to ask why he had, but the truth frightened her, the possibility that maybe she wasn't enough for him or their marriage. And Ara didn't offer an explanation, his low, gruff voice filling her ears as she turned her head off to the side where he wouldn't see how she furiously blinked back tears.

"Six months," he declared, piquing her interest. "If in that time we can't live together...peacefully, then we figure out how to co-parent separately."

"And our marriage?" she wondered. She wasn't rushing to hope that he would be reasonable, though if he really meant what he said, maybe they could figure this out together as a united front. Not married anymore, but happily raising their child.

"At the end of the six months, the end of your iddah, if you still wish for a divorce, I will give it to you."

His face was still unreadable, but she couldn't detect deception. Intuition told her that she could trust him to uphold his word.

As if reading her mind and sensing that she'd become more amenable to his outlandish suggestion to play house together, Ara shifted to face her and raised a hand between them, his thick brown fingers hovering, waiting—waiting on her permission to touch her stomach, she realized.

Nodding quietly, she clamped her teeth into her bottom lip and held still as he slowly reached for her.

She freed the breath she'd been holding when his warm palm skated over her belly lightly before settling with his fingers outstretched. Zaynab looked down where he held her and then slowly drew her eyes up to him, finding that he was far closer, his face much nearer than it had been. If she didn't know that all he'd wanted to do was connect with their baby, she would've believed he wanted to kiss her.

"Six months?" Ara asked her again.

"Six months," she heard herself agreeing.

CHAPTER FOUR

SIX MONTHS!

Zaynab could still hardly believe that she'd agreed to living with Ara for six *long* months, or roughly what remained of her pregnancy. After she had been so adamant that his suggestion was an awful idea, and she was certain she wouldn't ever agree to it, it hadn't taken long for her to fold.

She blamed the beautiful waterfall and her softness for him.

If she closed her eyes, Zaynab could see Ara staring at her heatedly, his shirt soaking wet from the misty spray of the fall's gushing waters, and his hand warming her fluttering stomach—

She shook her head, annoyed by the blush now heating her face. If it had been his strategy to obliterate her resolve with desire, then he'd succeeded. Of course it only highlighted why she shouldn't have agreed. Why this idea of his posed a big problem. *I'm still weak for him.* Still hopelessly crushing on a man who hadn't taken their marital vows seriously and had pushed her from his life. Once she knew that he didn't love her, she had to escape. And she almost had until…

She crossed her arms to cover her belly and the baby they'd created together.

Despite her reservations—and the fact she was certain that this plan of his was still very much doomed—Zaynab grudgingly accepted that her pregnancy changed everything. It was why she was sitting beside Ara in his fancy white Porsche, speeding down a southbound motorway that cut through the sprawling metropolis of Mauritius's capital, Port Louis. If they were doing this, they'd have to talk seriously, and Zaynab knew they had to do it before she boarded her flight out of Mauritius that evening. So, as soon as she woke that morning, and with that clock ticking ominously in her head, she messaged Ara and asked to meet up after breakfast.

She anticipated that the conversation would be difficult.

What she hadn't expected was for him to propose they take a drive and have their serious discussion away from their luxury resort. She didn't think he had a specific destination in mind, but was a little curious when they seemed to be headed away from the northern part of the island.

Not curious enough to allow it to distract her, however.

"We should still divorce," she said, turning her head away from her passenger window and the panoramic sights of Port Louis.

Ara's side profile was hard to read even with her being close enough to breathe in the heady, knee-weakening scent of his fresh, citrus-bright cologne. She stiffened against the instinct to lean over the center console and sniff him. Sniffing him would send the wrong message, especially given she'd just told him that her mind wasn't changed where their divorce was concerned. Besides, mixed signals were the kind of thing that would complicate their already overcomplicated situation.

"Did you hear me?"

"I heard you," he said, his gaze briefly flickering off the road to her.

"Just because I agreed to live with you again doesn't mean our separation shouldn't still happen."

"If that's what you wish," was his rumbling response, as unemotional as his expression.

Zaynab stuffed down her rising frustration. Ara was telling her exactly what she wanted to hear, and yet his easy agreement chafed her and she couldn't quite place her finger on why it bothered her. And not wanting to really analyze what she was feeling in depth, she continued on as if she weren't perturbed.

"I'm still not convinced that moving in together is a good idea." Pressing her hands to her still-flat stomach, she said, "I want what's best for the baby."

"Then wouldn't that be having us both in their life?"

"That would be nice," she conceded. In a perfect world, she and Ara would be able to co-parent while cohabiting in peace. No hormones driving her wild, tempting her every time those dark eyes of his zeroed in on her and made her want to silence any warning bells going off in her head and indulge every passionate thought Ara inspired in her...

And no heartbreak.

Because that was what she risked most if she was to live with him again. The first two months of their marriage had taught her not to entrust Ara with her heart. Instead of receiving the same love and attention that she was giving him, she'd ended up lonely and starved of the affection Ara should have given her. Surviving that isolation once took most of her willpower; doing it again might destroy any shred of strength she had left.

Zaynab's bottom lip trembled, and she blinked away the watery heat from her eyes and looked back out the car window and the passing cityscape. Breathtaking as Port Louis was with its position being picturesquely sheltered between the semicircle of verdant Moka mountains and the dark aquamarine waters of the Indian Ocean, she struggled to admire its beauty.

Silence reigned in the car, and it only made the noise in her head that much jarringly louder. Doubts clamoring to be heard one over the other.

What if he hurts me again? Can I trust him?

Do I want to trust him?

Zaynab didn't have the answers. She only hoped she wasn't making a mistake by allowing Ara into her life once again.

Ara was no stranger to tense situations.

He'd dealt with them a number of times in his boardroom during tough meetings, and certainly whenever he angered his little sister, Anisa—which these days with her being stressed about her wedding plans was more often than not.

Yet all of his past experience abandoned him right then with Zaynab.

The awkward silence that started once they left the city limits of Port Louis lasted the hour-long drive from one end of the island of Mauritius to the other. Ara struggled to figure out how to break it. Every time he rustled up a bit of courage, he'd cast a quick glance at Zaynab and lose his grip on his bravery. Unlike him she didn't seem pressed by the quiet or look to be in a hurry to end it as she stared at her phone.

And why would she?

She'd restated that she wished for the divorce, making it clear that her agreement to live with him again had no bearing on their relationship…or the absence of it in this case.

Ara tightened his hands on the steering wheel, wringing the smooth leather until his fingers ached and the threat of callouses on his palms compelled him to ease his grip. It was one way to relieve the frustration choking him. Frustration born from the fact that he had only himself to blame for the tension between him and Zaynab. He hadn't been a good husband to her, and it had pushed her into leaving him.

And then he'd slept with her, not once considering their impassioned union would result in a consequence.

He couldn't change what had transpired in the past, but he could do something about their future together. At least so long as he didn't give Zaynab a reason to change her mind. That was why the silence in the car was worrying.

Hearing their GPS indicate they were closing in on their destination gave him some hope though.

A large colorful billboard advertising the tea estate up ahead was the first break in the stretch of green pastures that ran alongside the main road. Zaynab lifted her head up, her focus no longer fixed to her phone screen.

"'The Bois Cheri tea factory,'" she said, reading the sign. "Is that where we're headed?"

"It is." He tried not to preen when Zaynab's breath hitched a few minutes later, the gush of rain-scented air that blew in when she rolled down the window prompting him to look her direction.

Ara hid a smile when she closed the window and gasped, "Oh, wow, it's beautiful."

A sight to behold, the neat green rows of tea plants climbed the hill and seemed to point to the expansive structure at the hilltop. As he turned the Porsche off the main thoroughfare and down a smaller lane that led to the structure, Ara had more trouble concealing his amusement. His lips twitched when a smiling Zaynab barely waited for him to find a spot to park in the crowded lot outside the colonial building before she unbuckled her seatbelt and opened the car door. Meeting her outside, he resisted puffing up his chest and led her to the entrance.

There a staff member connected them with their prepaid tour of the tea factory housed within the estate.

As fascinated as Ara was to hear the long history of the grounds and building and the delicate, multistep process of tea cultivation, in truth he was more invested in Zaynab's reaction to it all. She smiled politely as their tour guide explained how the colonial rule of British, French and Dutch settlers had intermingled with the local Mauritian culture, and she beamed when they watched a demonstration of the factory workers sorting tea leaves and bagging them. Later, when they had taken a short break during their tour, Zaynab easily struck up conversations with some of the other tourists in their group.

He'd forgotten how friendly she could be.

When their tour guide finally announced the end of their walkabout of the estate building and its grounds and encouraged them to explore on their own, Zaynab ventured toward a footpath that led straight through the rows of tea plants and the lake beyond. She stopped and laughed a magical sound as a small curious boar strayed onto their footpath, blocking them from exploring the row of tea plants and the lake beyond.

Ara stepped in front of her instinctively the instant the wild pig snuffled closer, its snout raised up and its black eyes locking on Zaynab.

"It's not going to hurt us. It's just a piglet. Poor thing,

probably lost its mother." Zaynab tutted at Ara and pushed past his defenses, her hand outstretched palm first as she cooed at the snuffling creature. Emboldened by her stillness, the small wild pig snorted softly and approached her. After a thorough sniff of her hand, she was given the green light to stroke its head.

"Did you lose your mother?" she asked, her voice soft and sweet.

Though every nerve in his body wanted to put himself between her and any source of danger, Ara clenched his jaw and forced himself to stand back. After all, it was only a tiny little pig. *What harm could it do her?* And he was rewarded for his patience when Zaynab let out a peal of giggles. The piglet ran circles around her, seemingly chasing its own tail. At the delightful sound of her laughter, a pleasant shiver chased down his spine and loosened the tension wringing his muscles.

But his momentary peace didn't last long. A sharp squeal nearby ended it quickly.

The wild boar that tore around the corner skidded to a halt, zeroed in on the piglet wriggling its small body and gave another angry squeal before charging straight for them.

Adrenaline slammed into him and erased the smile that had begun to pull at his lips. Not thinking of anything but needing to protect Zaynab, Ara's arm shot out and wrapped around her waist, pulling her toward him and away from the piglet. In one fluid move, he tucked her behind him and shielded her from the oncoming danger.

By that point the larger boar had slowed its charge, bristled in place and squealed sharply at them.

The piglet responded with a shorter, weaker squeal.

Ara held his ground, knowing that turning his back

could open both himself and Zaynab to an attack from the unpredictable animal. Refusing to take his eyes off the angry boar that could only be the piglet's missing mother, he slowly and gently walked himself and Zaynab backward. The staring match ended when the piglet shot toward its furious parent. Giving them one last sharp-eyed look, the mother boar snorted and herded its youngling away.

Even after they were clear of the threat, Ara didn't budge until he registered Zaynab pulling free from him.

Standing beside him now, she laughed nervously. "Whew, that was a scary close call."

Scary didn't encompass the riot of emotion squeezing off his airways. He turned to face her, his hands locking around her elbows, eyes skimming over her. "Are you all right?"

"I'm fine," she reassured him.

Her words spoken gently weren't enough to convince him not to assess her for any injury. And he was silently grateful that she allowed him to do so. Once satisfied that she hadn't gotten hurt, Ara pried open his tightly clenched jaws and said, "The tea tasting should be beginning."

It was the perfect excuse to whisk her away back to the safety of the tea factory.

Again, he was thankful that Zaynab didn't struggle against him. Ara wished that was all it took to ease the disquiet fisting his heart. Like his mood, the clouds grew stormier, the pale gray churning darker.

They climbed to the second-floor covered balcony of the building where the restaurant operated when the rain started. Their small table, like the other tables all aligned in a row against the wooden railing, was set up for their private tea-tasting experience. Normally the stream of hot water from the teapot and the inviting steam curling up from his cup would have calmed him. Embedded in Somali culture, tea was a large part of his upbringing, and he'd always preferred it to a cup of coffee. Though right then he didn't think he could sample the assortment of herbal and black teas past the calcifying bile obstructing his throat.

He couldn't stop replaying the incident with the wild pig defending her piglet and how close Zaynab had been to bodily harm. And not just Zaynab, but their baby—

It would've been my fault. Because it had been *his* idea to bring her here.

Zaynab hadn't even seemed to care that she was nearly mowed over by an enraged boar.

"Are you okay?" Frowning at him, she lowered her teacup.

Ara forced his leg still and scowled, grumbling, "I'm fine."

"Really? Because you look ready to leap out of your skin," she remarked with raised brows. "Is this about the wild pig?"

She spoke as if the boar hadn't represented everything he feared happening to her without his protection. All he wanted to do was safeguard her and their child, and Zaynab wasn't helping him do that.

Why was she making this so difficult for him? And why was she fighting against their living together when it made the most sense to both be there for their baby?

Ara bit back his boiling frustration, knowing that unleashing it would have the opposite effect on Zaynab.

So, he attempted a different tactic. One he'd considered but had hoped he wouldn't need to use. Even thinking about his parents pained him as freshly as if they passed yesterday and not more than sixteen years ago. But it felt like a last resort now to get Zaynab on board with his plan.

"It is and isn't about the boar," Ara replied gruffly.

Blowing a sharp breath out his nose then, he continued, "Losing my parents changed my life. I wouldn't wish that loss on my worst enemy, and it's why I'm trying to do everything I can to keep our child from...from experiencing that too."

He hadn't been able to save his hooyo and aabo—hadn't even gotten to say goodbye and it haunted him still. If he could trade all his wealth to guarantee their baby never had to feel the pain he'd been dealt, he would do it in a heartbeat. But he didn't have that power alone. Zaynab had to want the same thing too.

"That's why I want us to be on the same page. It's why I think we should live together."

Zaynab looked down into her teacup, her fingertip circling the rim slowly. Waiting for her to speak her thoughts was torturous, but eventually she said, "I still don't think it's a good idea."

"Tell me why."

She sighed and met his stare. "I understand where you're coming from, and I want the same thing, but..."

"But..." he urged.

"*But* we've tried this already." Zaynab looked away, though not before he spied the pained expression flickering over her pretty face. "And we failed at that, didn't we? I might not know what it's like to lose a loved one, but my parents' divorce was ugly, and I—well, I just don't want that for our child either."

"I didn't ask for the divorce."

She whipped her head back to him with a ready glare. "I might have asked for the divorce, but that's only because it felt like the only solution. And I'd rather a clean break than be reminded that my marriage is a product of my father not truly wanting me."

They rarely spoke about Sharmarke. Zaynab's father was a barrier between them even though he was no longer in their lives.

"If what happened with your father is something you can't overlook—"

"What happened with Sharmarke has nothing to do with us," she cut in. Then, her eyes softening, she sighed. "I can't speak for you, but our marriage wasn't happy for me. And regardless of what my father did or didn't do, things would have ended up the way they did for us anyway."

Hearing that their divorce would've been inevitable for her stabbed into his chest. Worse, he couldn't do anything to assuage the pain as Zaynab was watching him carefully, her teeth locking onto and worrying her bottom lip.

"It's all right if you lay the fault at my feet."

"Why would I blame you for something *he* did?" she asked skeptically.

"Because I helped send him to prison."

It wasn't a secret that Ara had gathered the evidence against her father that had locked him away forever.

One of the hardest choices he'd had to make, but Sharmarke had allowed his political clout to get to his head and committed unspeakable, evil crimes against innocent people. It had fallen on Ara to either be his accomplice or to stand up against the injustice. He'd chosen the latter, and though he knew it had been the right decision—the morally good one, it hadn't made living with it any easier.

"It would be perfectly understandable if you blamed me."

"But I don't," she said firmly. "Sharmarke deserved the several life sentences for his crimes. If I'd known what he was doing, I would've locked him up myself. I should thank you."

"Thank me?"

She jerked her head in a nod. "I'm glad someone saw through his lies. Saw him for who he truly was."

Ara gazed at her in wonder, shocked to see no condemnation staring back at him. *She's not angry with me.* He had always thought that she secretly accused him of imprisoning her father. It was why he avoided the subject around her, and partly why he had spent their marriage avoiding her. At first he had wanted to protect her from who her father was, but after witnessing the harm Sharmarke had caused, Ara worried whether loving her would only bring him pain.

The kind of pain he'd felt after losing his parents.

They lapsed into their own little worlds after that, drinking their tea in a silence that was thicker than the misting rain falling outside.

"You know, six months isn't that long," Zaynab said, breaking the silence.

Then she smiled prettily and the sight of it delivered a bolt of crackling heat through him.

Ara wanted to agree, but with the way his heart was juddering, six months was already feeling like it would be a lot longer than he bargained for. He was doing this to protect her and their child, but now he had to wonder who would protect *him* from the heart-racing, chest-tightening, flushed skin feelings that Zaynab awoke in him every time he was close to her.

Feelings he highly suspected would only grow stronger if they moved in together.

CHAPTER FIVE

"DON'T FALL IN LOVE."

Sitting cross-legged on her sofa in her cozy little London flat, Zaynab lifted the pen off her small notebook and read over what she wrote.

It was the only rule she made for herself.

The only one that could wreck everything before it even started.

If she and Ara were going to make living together work, this one rule needed to be observed strictly. Because the last thing she needed was to forget that they weren't playing at pretend house, but rather trialing a co-parental existence that would provide the best environment for their baby.

Although Zaynab still thought living with him was a bad decision, she at least now understood why he was pushing for it so hard.

"Losing my parents changed my life."

Not once had Ara ever been that open about his feelings and thoughts. He could discuss business practices, politics and social ideologies all day, and that had attracted her when they had first dated, but she had imagined he would grow more comfortable around her after they married. She never knew what he was thinking and it made living with him difficult.

Yet for the first time ever, glimpsing his emotions had given her a wealth of information. One, he wasn't as coldly unemotional as she thought, and two, under his seemingly impenetrable exterior there was a beating heart that mourned his late parents.

"It's why I'm trying to do everything I can to keep our child from experiencing that too."

He'd spoken those words painfully and, now as they played back in her head, her chest tightened with her sorrow for him.

She could appreciate why family was important to him, and why he would want to be close to their baby, yet it didn't make moving in together any less nerve-racking. They had tried this before. It hadn't worked out for them then, and expecting a baby only exacerbated her apprehension. What if they argued? What if living with him stressed out her and the baby?

What if this is a mistake?

Either way Zaynab wouldn't know what it would be like until he finally arrived in London.

Their time in Mauritius was two weeks ago. Two weeks since she last saw him, but Ara had begun messaging her regularly. He'd even sometimes call, and though never longer than a few minutes, she liked that he asked after her and the baby's health. It felt like they had talked more in those couple weeks than they had in all of their marriage. The promising change in him almost had her anticipating seeing him again.

Almost.

Seeing him meant having those dark eyes of his piercing her, his smoky, spiced cologne swimming through her space, and all the memories of his arms around her. And

Zaynab just didn't know whether she was ready for that yet. "Or if I'll ever be ready for it," she whispered.

The doorbell ringing interrupted her musing.

In her hurry to answer her caller, she stubbed her toe on the small boxes she had piled right by the sofa. She had started packing slowly and hoped that she would be prepared when Ara arrived. With her apartment being so small, they'd decided that it was better to find a new place.

"Coming!" she called when the doorbell buzzed a second time.

She tugged down on the hem of her oversized hoodie over her leggings. Figuring it could just be a neighbor asking her for a cup of sugar, Zaynab went to the door.

A peek through the peephole told her it was not a neighbor calling.

Breathless, she opened the door with a shaky hand and faced Ara.

"Zaynab," he greeted. No "hello" or "how are you," just her name rumbled in that deep, deliciously sultry voice. She clamped down the urge to shiver in response, her clammy hand tightening on the door handle and pulling the door open wider.

In the short time apart, Ara hadn't changed except for one way: his beard was thicker and darker, and it only drew her eyes to his blade-sharp nose, sculpted cheekbones and dusky brown lips. His long overcoat was drawn open allowing her to a good look at the finely tailored three-piece suit he had on.

Somewhere out there she just knew some magazine was missing its cover model.

"May I?" he asked, pointing past her with the handle of his umbrella.

She blushed at having been caught ogling him, stepping

aside and turning to watch him enter her home. Closing the door and sealing out the wintry air creeping in from the outside, Ara turned his back to her temporarily, leaving his umbrella against the door and his shiny leather shoes on the mat before facing her.

It gave her just enough time to get a grip on her swooning when his familiar fragrance wafted over to her.

"Tea?" she offered with a meek smile.

He nodded and she flitted away into the open kitchen plan.

Feeling him shadow her, she busied herself gathering the teacups while the kettle warmed to a slow boil on the stove. She'd always thought her kitchen as a restful place, but that was before she had six feet of lean muscle looming behind her, reaching up over her head to help her pull down plates from the cupboards for the biscuits she'd planned to set up as a quick snack. It didn't matter that she could have reached for the plates perfectly fine herself. Her foolish heart thumped harder.

"The ultrasound."

Ara moved away from her to the fridge and plucked off the magnets holding their baby's first ultrasound.

It had been a few days ago since Zaynab had gone in for her scan. Ara had joined her over a video call, and although she'd appreciated that he had made some effort to be there for that special moment, she would have liked for him to have been there in person instead. Holding her hand when the sonographer had talked her through the process. Marveling with her as their baby made their first appearance on the technician's computer screen, the soft lub-dub of the heart filling the sterile exam room. And hugging her when she'd sat up and held the first ultrasound in her hands.

But she didn't want them to argue about it, not now that they were trying to be on the same page. So, she swallowed her disappointment.

"I have your copy of Button in my wallet. Remind me to give it to you later, all right?"

"Button?" he echoed.

Zaynab smiled, abashed that she'd have to explain. "Yeah, um, well it kind of looks like they've got a button nose."

Wrinkling his brow, Ara held the ultrasound at different angles. Zaynab could see him struggling to envision what she meant, and before she realized it, she was at his side, leaning in and pointing it out for him.

"Right there. It's just like a button, don't you think? Well, that and we can't keep calling him or her 'the baby.'"

"I see what you mean," he said, his warm, mint-scented breath stirring over her face as he turned his head to her. She'd been in such a rush to explain their baby's nickname that Zaynab hadn't considered personal boundaries. Now having infiltrated his space, she was even more susceptible to his magnetic aura.

With one look he made her feel like the only person in the world.

The only person in his world.

She gulped, her face heating up under his scrutiny, and needing his attention off her again, she nervously gestured to the grayscale image. "See, those are the arms, the little face, and the legs flung up over their head, like Button's doing yoga in there." She was babbling now, and Ara had to have known. Everything she was telling him he'd already seen for himself when he had joined her virtually for the ultrasound.

Worried about what she'd say next, Zaynab closed her mouth and retreated back to unpacking biscuits for them.

"When did you arrive?" she asked, using the excuse of plating their store-bought crisp biscuits to keep her back to him.

"Around noon."

Zaynab was glad she wasn't looking at him, otherwise he would've clocked her shock. It was past four now, so he'd been in the city for hours and he hadn't bothered calling her. Her confusion and irritation didn't last for long though as Ara explained himself.

"I would have come earlier, but I had an errand to oversee," he said.

"Errand? I didn't think you were familiar with London." She knew that though Ara's company was big, and he had investors and clients all throughout the world, he preferred staying near his home in Berbera.

It was why Zaynab had worried he would change his mind about living in London and try to talk her into moving back to Somalia.

But seeing him now, in her tiny kitchen, allayed that fear.

At least it did until he said, "I had to see a woman about something."

"A woman? What woman?" She hadn't meant to blurt out her curiosity, or to whirl around to him and gawk, but the thought that he hadn't contacted her because he'd first gone to see another woman hurt more than she was expecting. Not that she was expecting him to be seeing other women. *And not that I should care...*

Ara's easy, handsome smile disarmed her suspicion though. "The estate agent," he said. "We need a home, don't we?"

* * *

Getting Zaynab out of her flat wasn't as difficult as Ara imagined it would be. As soon as he'd told her about the home he purchased, she was eager to see the place for herself.

Well, "eager" was a stretch.

Nervous was probably a better description. Throughout the hour-long drive from her neighborhood to West London she gripped onto the worn brown leather handle of her purse and sat silently beside him. He'd been ready for her to pelt questions at him, but he knew that she was more likely still processing his sudden appearance at her doorstep. The only reason he hadn't called beforehand and forewarned her of his arrival was because he'd wanted to see their new home first and ensure that the estate agent he had hired had done their job properly. It had to be perfect for Zaynab...

Perfect for their growing family.

Family. That word was sitting better in his mind with each passing day. Whether they divorced or not, they would be a family now, and if Ara couldn't have Zaynab as his wife, then he still wanted to provide for her and their baby. As long as he breathed, they wouldn't go without anything. He silently swore the oath again, as he'd done almost every day since he had last seen Zaynab.

Now that he was with her, he was just ready for them to truly begin this journey together as soon-to-be parents.

And it started with showing her their home.

Zaynab's breath hitched, the brisk but soft sound clapping like thunder in the silence of the car. He glanced at her and fought a smile when he glimpsed her wide-eyed awe.

After gearing the car into Park, he exited and circled around to grab her door before she did. She was still gawking out the windshield and whipped her head to him when he opened the door.

"This is it?" she squeaked the words out, stepping out of the car and straightening her baggy hoodie. In a hurry to see the new home, she hadn't changed out of her adorable outfit.

"This is it," Ara repeated.

Besides wrapping up his business affairs in Mogadishu, he'd spent the past couple weeks apart from Zaynab searching tirelessly for a home that would suit her. The staff at the estate company that he'd worked with had just about nearly reached their wits' ends when Ara had finally seen it; the ideal house for Zaynab. Ironically it was the antithesis of what he'd have chosen for himself. But one look at the pastel-hued stucco exteriors of the terraced houses in Notting Hill, the lush, private communal gardens, and tranquil atmosphere away from the busier central heart of London, and he knew he'd found the perfect home that complemented both him and Zaynab.

She pressed her hands to her stomach and softly wondered, "Which one?"

He opened a charming wrought iron fence, walked her beneath a dormant flowering tree covering their front property, and up a short flight of stone steps to their terraced house with a seafoam green door. Ara unlocked it and swung it wide open, gesturing for her to enter before him. He'd gotten a thorough tour from the estate agent and inspected every inch of the four-thousand-square-foot, three-story town house, which would now work to his advantage because he'd have nothing to disturb him from watching Zaynab's every single reaction.

Of course he wouldn't be able to do that if Zaynab remained rooted in the entrance hall, her lightly glossed mouth parted open and her head swiveling as she assessed her surroundings.

"Would you like me to give you a tour?"

She nodded slowly, closing her mouth but mesmerizing him with those large bewildered eyes of hers.

He couldn't blame her for being overwhelmed. The town house dripped with the kind of excessive wealth that surprised even him. Although with its hefty price tag, he expected nothing less.

Ara followed her facial cues as he guided her along the three separate flats that made up the grand town house. From the foyer to the sitting room, through the kitchen and dining area, and into each of the six bedrooms and five bathrooms plus the cloakroom on the ground floor, he highlighted the prime features of the home that was theirs—but only if she wanted it to be. And it was hard to tell what she was thinking when her features remained fixed in surprise.

Nothing changed that until they came to the end of the tour.

Then Zaynab asked, "Isn't it a bit...overly done?"

Ara swept his gaze over the glamorous townhome's primary bedroom, but unable to pinpoint what the trouble was, he shrugged. "Feel free to redesign the decor to your tastes."

"It's not about taste," Zaynab stressed and threw open her arms. "It's far too much space, isn't it? It'll only be the two of us until I give birth, and even then all of this is excessive. Three families could live here."

"We're not letting any of the floors." Though they technically could and keep one of the separate flats for themselves, Ara scowled at the idea of having strangers in close proximity. No amount of background checks would offer him the peace of mind to allow that to happen. He'd always known that people were unreliable. Zaynab's father came to mind. Sharmarke had been like a mentor to Ara, tutoring him in his university-level business courses, and when his parents died, he'd become a surrogate father figure.

That was why it had felt like a betrayal to learn of the atrocities that Sharmarke had committed. Knowing that he'd willingly allowed that evil into his life was a reminder that Ara couldn't ever be too careful around others.

Even Zaynab could hurt him if he wasn't careful, if he allowed himself to give in to the fanciful thinking that this was about saving their marriage rather than providing the best life for their child. And in order to do that, Ara needed Zaynab to be content.

"If this house doesn't suit you, we can look at other available properties together," he suggested, frowning when she shook her head.

"No, it's not that. I just... I'm overwhelmed."

"So, the house is all right."

"It's perfect," she said with a snort and a roll of her eyes. "Are you kidding me? My mum wouldn't believe it if I showed her."

"We can have a guest room reserved especially for her for when she visits."

Naturally he would've thought Zaynab would be pleased by his suggestion, but her expression grew panicked.

Before he could wonder if he'd misspoken, she paced in front of him and said, "I haven't told you yet, but my mum, well she doesn't know that we're doing *this thing* that we're doing."

"Living together," he clarified.

"Yes, that. She doesn't know, and I'm not ready to tell her, so..."

"And you wish for me not to tell her either." Ara filled in what she was obviously struggling to ask of him.

"Please," she said with a nod, her hopeful little smile and beautiful brown eyes melting some of the ice that had seeped into him when he realized that he'd become some sort of dirty secret to her. Though nowhere nearly enough to keep him from clenching his jaw and jerking his chin in affirmation.

But he couldn't entirely let it go.

"Why hide it?" he asked.

Zaynab's smile slipped and she stopped pacing, looking away from him at the doors leading out from the bedroom to the balcony. "My mum doesn't know about the divorce. And I'm not ready to tell her about that either, especially now that it isn't final. At least not yet."

It wasn't the first time Ara heard her sounding adamant about dissolving their marriage. She was set on making it happen, and these six months were only a stumbling block to her. A part of him had hoped that she would be more open to reconsider their relationship. Not for the sake of love or anything so romantic, but because it would be easier on their child. Although his parents hadn't lived to see him today, they had given him a happy, stable family life prior to his leaving for college. He didn't know the type of man he'd be without knowing that kind of love and dedication.

He wanted the same for his son or daughter. And when he pictured that, he couldn't see a life without Zaynab by his side.

Telling her all of this would probably just push her further along the path of divorce. If he wanted this, he'd have to approach the subject carefully, and not right then when she was smiling again and beautifully if not a little sadly.

"I know you might not understand, but it would break her heart to know that we're planning to end things." Zaynab opened the balcony doors and walked out, gripping the iron railing, and heaved a sigh that wasn't entirely despondent. "This place *is* really like a palace. I would be so lucky to call it my home."

"Good, because it is yours."

"What?" Zaynab rounded sharply on him, the pretty view of this affluent neighborhood forgotten. "What do you mean 'it's mine'?"

"The transfer of ownership isn't official until you sign off and have a solicitor notarize it, which I could help you seek out."

She stared at him speechlessly.

Unnerved by her quietness, Ara curled his fingers through his beard. Had he displeased her?

"I can't accept this," she said with a slow shake of her head.

"Why not?"

Her eyes widened, and she looked at him as though he'd asked the obvious. "Because I just can't, Ara. It's too much."

"It's a gift," he intoned.

"It's a *house*. A very big, very expensive house."

He could tell there was more to her reason for not accepting the transfer of ownership than what she was saying, but since he couldn't pry the whole truth out of her, Ara settled on appealing to her senses.

"It's also a part of your mahr." As part of the marriage contract they'd both signed, he and Zaynab had agreed to a contractual dowry that he'd pay if they were to ever divorce. And now that that was looking like more of a reality, Ara had zero intention of depriving her of what he'd promised her. "It's my obligation to you, and the house should satisfy it."

When she still didn't budge, he moved in closer to her— as close as he dared to risk a whiff of her honeyed oud fragrance, then after lowering the hand lazily combing through his beard, he fished the house key from inside of his coat pocket.

The key itself wouldn't be needed to enter the house. Not when he would soon have the home equipped with state-of-the-art biometric locks. But for now the key was symbolic of the house's true owner.

"Take the key, Zaynab." He held it out to her.

"I don't know what to say," she murmured, the indecisiveness still playing out over her beautiful face.

Taking her hand gently, he turned her palm up and settled the key in her grip and closed her fingers around it.

"There's nothing more to say," he told her.

He let her go, not expecting her to raise her other hand and touch his cheek—

Ara jerked back from her.

Zaynab pulled away too. "The scar…"

"What about it?" he heard how gruff he sounded and hated that he'd revealed more emotion in that moment than every other time with her. And considering the way the last time he let his feelings out to play had resulted in her pregnant, Ara rather preferred not being emotional.

"It's healed well, that's all." A beat of silence throbbed between them and then she quietly wondered, "Does it hurt you?"

"No."

"May I?" She lifted her hand again, and damn it, but he couldn't deny her.

He wasn't too bothered by the scar before, but lately,

ever since he'd returned from Mauritius and knew that she awaited him in London to start a life with him, Ara had grown obsessed with the physical disfigurement. It represented a time when he'd been at his second most vulnerable, when the explosion that had rocked the hotel he had booked in Mogadishu was bombed randomly. The first time was when his university administrators had pulled him aside and informed him that he had lost his parents.

Growing the beard hadn't been purposeful, but once he looked in the mirror and saw less of the scar, he liked it.

She traced her finger over the old wound gently, following the puckered lighter line from where it started at the top of his cheekbone, right below his eye, and slashing down to just above his lower jawbone. He expected her to stop where his beard concealed that larger, lower portion of the scar, but Zaynab kept moving down, her fingertip softly tickling him and raising goose bumps over his arms.

"You're growing your beard?"

Hearing the question in her voice, he grunted affirmatively, unable to do more than that.

"It looks good," she praised.

She slid her finger up and then cupped his cheek, her thumb smoothing over the scar gently. He closed his eyes and swallowed down the growl rumbling through his chest. God, was she doing this to drive him to madness and beyond? As strong-willed as he could be, it was taking a Herculean effort not to give in to the sheer sinful temptation she posed him right then. But he *couldn't* kiss her. He couldn't lower his head and remind himself of how she tasted. He. Just. Couldn't.

"Ara." She spoke his name on a breathy little whisper before leaning closer.

Gritting his teeth from the sheer force of self-restraint, he had a flash of déjà vu when they were in such a position.

Maybe it was a good thing then that a dog began barking loudly and sharply from one of the nearby terraced houses.

"If you ever need to talk to someone," she said, and drew her hand away and stole the chance of kissing her from him.

Ara tightened his lips but nodded. He probably never would, and yet knowing her offer was available made him hotter for her. That certainly wasn't the way he should feel about the wife that was determined to divorce him.

The wife who was carrying his precious baby.

And the wife who might have almost just kissed him, and whom he certainly would've kissed back.

CHAPTER SIX

A FEW WEEKS ago Ara wouldn't have pictured himself idling in his car in the middle of London while waiting on Zaynab to finish up working and meet him outside.

And yet also a few weeks ago he hadn't thought he'd be a father.

Hadn't ever imagined that he would be excited to meet his son or daughter.

But here he was, looking at his copy of the ultrasound that Zaynab had gifted him and stroking the small pale face in utter awe at the life he'd helped create. A life that would rely on him to protect it.

Ara gritted his teeth as fear prickled his scalp.

Every day brought him boundless joy but also a creeping doubt that he wouldn't be able to keep his family together. And what happened when the doubt eclipsed the happy moments he had thus far shared with Zaynab on this journey of parenthood?

She pushes me out of her and the baby's lives.

Ara tucked the ultrasound back into his wallet, his mind stormier now. A knock on his car window made him realize he had zoned out and missed Zaynab's arrival. Quickly unlocking the car door for her, he braced himself as a rush of wintry air flooded in with her. She dropped back into the passenger seat and heaved a long drawn-out but contented sigh, reaching out and hovering her hands over the car heater.

"That feels so good. It's nearly the end of February and it's still freezing," she groused, shivering and rubbing her hands up and down her arms. "I hope you weren't waiting too long."

He shook his head. "I only just got here." It was a lie; he'd left early to avoid any traffic. He didn't want her waiting in the cold for him, not when he volunteered to give her the rides to and from her workplace.

"And you're still good to go shopping? Because the fridge is dangerously close to empty, and the pantry's getting near there too."

Ara started the engine and pulled out before replying, "Of course, we can't have Button going hungry."

Zaynab snorted. "Forget Button. Mama's hungry," she joked.

"Let's eat dinner first then. The groceries can wait."

Just as he began interpreting the stretch of silence from her to mean she wasn't interested in his offer of dinner, she said, "Are you sure? Because I'd rather not take up more of your time. I feel bad enough when you pick me up. You know I could just take a couple of buses and the tube."

"It's no bother for me to drive you around, and I might as well familiarize myself with the city."

"Okay, but you'll let me know if you ever change your mind."

He wouldn't be doing that ever, and yet seeing that she wanted confirmation for her peace of mind, Ara dipped his chin. "You'll be the first to know if that happens. Now, how about you tell me how your day went."

The remainder of the drive was filled with Zaynab giving him a play-by-play of her eventful day working with her elderly client, Opaline. He listened while she told him about the salacious gossip at the high tea party that she helped host with Opaline for a gaggle of the older woman's friends. She drew rumbling laughter from him a couple of times, and he carried the easygoing mood into a busy East London fast-food eatery.

"We might not find a seat," Zaynab warned, turning to look at him over her shoulder when she was pushed back against him by a couple rowdy teenagers play-fighting in line in front of them.

Settling his hands over her shoulders to steady her against him, Ara made eye contact with the teens and glared menacingly enough for them to straighten up after a quick apology. Satisfied that they wouldn't continue their horseplay, he looked down at where his hands still gripped her. She had her back pressed to his front, the soft dip between her waist and wide hips temptingly within reach, and her body heat seeping through his button-down shirt and awakening his ever-present desire for her.

Being attracted to his wife wasn't a problem, but it would complicate their arrangement. Reminding himself that Zaynab wanted their divorce to still happen was a good way to cool his overheated blood.

Once he was able to do that, taking his hands off her and putting some fraction of space between them was easier.

"Let's go someplace else," she suggested.

He quietly obliged, and they strolled back out onto the high street where they had a wide and varied selection of restaurants and cafés to choose from. Zaynab picked for them again, and he didn't argue.

Unfortunately, this restaurant was just as overpacked as the other one had been.

"We're not having much luck, are we?" she said with a soft groan.

"We don't have to wait to eat. There's always the option of food delivery," he said after seeing the way she rubbed her stomach. He didn't want her going hungry on his watch.

"All right, I guess we can do takeout," Zaynab agreed. "It might be a long while before we're seated."

Ara shadowed her as she turned to leave the restaurant, his hand instinctively settling over the small of her back. She'd already nearly been toppled over by unruly kids in the other restaurant; he didn't want a repeat performance of that as the dinner rush seemed to be striking every eating establishment within walking distance.

Zaynab had almost reached the exit with him by her side when her name being called stopped them both.

A smiling woman in a hot-pink hijab and mustard-yellow blazer and trousers was beelining their way. "Zaynab! It is you!" she exclaimed and threw her arms around her before Ara could react. He would've assessed the woman as a threat if Zaynab hadn't gasped and hugged her back tightly.

"Oh, my goodness, Neelima," Zaynab said, pulling back and grabbing her friend's hands. "How long has it been? And when did you get back from working in America?"

Grinning, Neelima pulled her left hand out of Zaynab's grasp and flashed it so that the diamond ring was hard to miss.

Zaynab's loud, exalted gasp drew heads their direction.

Squealing together, the two women hugged again.

"We've been married six months now, but my husband's job brought him here about a month ago. We still haven't found a place of our own, so we're living nearby at my parents' place."

Ara gave up following the conversation after that, instead waiting for Zaynab to finish catching up with her friend. He looked around to ensure no other surprises sprang up on them. When he looked at Zaynab, he smiled at seeing her glowing expression of happiness. And he was caught staring at her by both Zaynab and her friend.

"Who's this?" her friend asked, the smile she gave him more restrained and polite.

"My husband, Ara." Zaynab said it so easily it surprised him, especially given their divorce was still very much the elephant in the room with them.

"You're married too!" Neelima clapped her hands happily, and both she and Zaynab giggled together. Then came the shower of questions from her friend. How long had they been married? How did they meet? Was it love at first sight?

Zaynab answered most but that last query. Her friend Neelima didn't notice, her curiosity about his and Zaynab's relationship seemingly sated, but Ara wondered what it meant that Zaynab hadn't responded.

And now that he was thinking about it, had it been love at first glance for him?

Meeting Zaynab wasn't anything he'd planned. Her father orchestrated it, first approaching Ara about a possible marriage match. Of course Sharmarke hadn't disclosed that the match was with his daughter and only child from his first marriage. Not until Zaynab was standing before Ara on their first date aboard his yacht. He'd taken one look at her on his ship's deck, the blue ocean as her backdrop and her pretty face and white abaya awash in the orange glow of sunset, and he'd been as close to smitten as he could be...

He could pretend that he'd been searching for love, but the truth was Ara hadn't cared about any of that. In the beginning his sole motivation in agreeing to a blind date with Zaynab was to lower Sharmarke's guard and get closer to his dark secrets. It had been around that time that Ara had started digging into his father-in-law, and he'd been getting nowhere until Sharmarke started trying to matchmake him.

He still had no clue what her father's motivation had been for playing matchmaker, though if he had to guess Sharmarke had been thinking the same thing and had wanted to spy on him. Not just spy but ensure that he wasn't getting closer to unearthing the truth about his criminal activities. And if that was true, Ara was to blame as he'd provoked her father's suspicion when he had first tried to ask Sharmarke about the heinous crimes he had committed and tried to cover up.

All of it dredged up ugly memories that he had worked to put behind him over the course of the past year. Still, Ara often pondered what Zaynab's life might have been like had he not endeavored to unmask Sharmarke's misdeeds.

We might not have ever met.

And their baby certainly wouldn't exist.

His throat worked around the hard knot that manifested at the awful thought. He swallowed it down when Zaynab's friend walked away and she turned to him with a bright smile.

"Looks like our table might be ready." Zaynab pointed to the host beckoning them to the back of the bistro.

* * *

"So, this is where you grew up."

Zaynab masked her smile at Ara's terribly concealed curiosity. Since he'd discovered this was her old neighborhood, he hadn't stopped looking around with a gleam of intrigue in his eyes. He had barely touched his dinner, his spoon suspended over his red lentil soup, his food taking a back seat to his interest in her.

A familiar skitter of thrill electrified her as his dark eyes bore into her.

Once she would have loved to have this attentive version of him all to herself, and though she appreciated that he was trying now, a part of her remained vigilant and suspicious. It wouldn't be the first time someone in her life had lulled her into believing that they had turned over a new leaf for the better. It had happened with Sharmarke—and it could be happening with Ara right now. Still, even as she considered that possibility, she couldn't help but hope that she was wrong.

That Ara wasn't tricking her like her father had done, and that he actually cared for her more than he was letting on.

Pushing aside her muddled thoughts, she munched on a fermented cauliflower, the comfort from the sour and salty burst of flavor settling her nerves.

And she was glad for it when Ara tipped his head slightly to the side and asked, "Will you tell me about your upbringing?"

Zaynab nodded, wariness creeping over her, the amusement she'd felt earlier at his curiosity now gone.

"What would you like to know?"

"Whatever you're comfortable sharing with me," he

said and set down the spoon he had drifting over his still untouched soup.

Surprisingly that calmed her far greater than she would've thought, mostly because one glimpse into those dark pools of his eyes and she knew that he hadn't said it merely as comfort. He was allowing her to take full control of the narrative. Besides her father, she couldn't name another man who was as self-possessed as Ara, and so utterly in charge of not only every aspect of his life but that of the people around him.

After all, he'd talked her into living with him again. But he also hadn't given her a reason to regret that decision so far.

Zaynab smiled at that.

Ara's kissable full lips lifted in response, the corners of his mouth curling up ever so subtly, the warmth of the gesture touching the lightless depths of his eyes. As great as it was to have his attention exclusively to herself, even more than that Zaynab decided she liked his smile.

"Okay," she said slowly, "but, fair warning, I might end up rambling on."

With the way Ara continued to look at her, riveted on her every word, she surmised that he hadn't changed his mind about hearing her tell of her childhood.

She started from the beginning, when she and her mother had first moved from their big, manor-like home in Hargeisa to London, the culture shock alone had almost been too much.

"I hadn't wanted to leave my friends, my home..." *I didn't even want to leave Sharmarke.* Because there had been a time when she'd loved her father so very dearly and couldn't understand how she could live apart from him. "I was ten, so it just felt like my whole world fell apart overnight, and I was powerless to do anything about fixing it."

She paused to savor another pickled vegetable, a carrot this time.

"For the first few months, all I remember was begging my mum to take us home, and when that didn't work, I asked her to send me back alone. Back to Sharmarke because I was sure that he was missing us too. That he was missing me.

"But when those months had passed, and I heard nothing from my father, I started to accept that my mother might have been protecting me from the harsh truth: that Sharmarke wasn't missing us at all, and that he had wanted us out of his life."

She hurtled into the painful memories of her mother scrimping and saving her pay from a number of low-wage jobs to make ends meet, the disrepair of their low-cost housing, and the awkward readjustment to a new life that was especially hard on her when she'd been so young.

"I felt so out of touch with my classmates who were so far ahead in their English studies, and everything around me was so alien," Zaynab recalled.

"Sharmarke sent us money, but it was never enough. Not for the rent, for the groceries, my schoolbooks and supplies and the English tutoring I needed on the side."

Across the table, Ara's brow grooved with deeply disapproving lines, his scowl darkening as her story unfolded. He interlaced his fingers together and, with his elbows on the table, he steepled his hands under his bearded chin. His look urged her to continue.

She didn't think she had it in her, not around the bile curdling in her throat at the mention of how her so-called father had treated her and her mother, but she pushed on.

"The only thing that made it better was our next-door neighbors. My best friend, Salma, her parents and her five siblings."

If it hadn't been for Salma and her family, Zaynab didn't know how her life might have ended up.

"Besides helping us settle in and navigate our new life in the UK, Salma's parents would help my mum translate documents from Somali to English for the immigration offices. They would look after me while my mum would go off to work one of her night shifts, and they'd never treat me any differently than one of their own children. And Salma helped me a lot through school."

She couldn't ever repay them for their kindness to her and her mother. More than that, while Zaynab had lost her father, she had ended up gaining a whole bunch of new family members in Salma's family. She wished that it was completely enough for her; that Sharmarke's abandonment wasn't a sore subject for her, that she felt nothing but indifference.

But she'd never fully understand why her own father hadn't wanted her.

Not that that was Ara's problem. Figuring she'd probably spoiled his mood for dinner, Zaynab looked up and startled at the menacing scowl on his face.

She gulped and stammered, "W-well, I didn't expect for that to get so serious. I'm sorry if I ruined our dinner."

"You have nothing to be sorry for." His fingers flexed and tightened under his chin. "If I possessed the power to punish your father for those specific crimes against you, I would."

And in that moment, in the face of the pure anger storming over his handsome features, Zaynab truly believed he would have. She even suspected that he was playing out exactly how he'd inflict the punishment on Sharmarke. Her stomach turned over and, shaking her head clear of unpleasant images of torture, she smiled weakly.

"As much as I appreciate that offer, I think he's already been punished enough." Multiple life sentences in prison in return for all the damage his political greed caused his victims seemed a fair enough sanction. And she hoped that her father was taking his criminal charges seriously and reflecting on his moral failings.

She bit her lip thoughtfully, not sure if she should ask the question in her head, but then gave in to the drilling need to know. "Was Sharmarke like that with you? I know that he was a friend of your parents."

"No, he never showed that cruel side of himself to us."

The fact that Ara had answered quickly and with no hesitation only proved what she'd always suspected: that her father cared more about her husband than he ever had her. Zaynab knew that Sharmarke was proud of Ara and his many professional achievements. From the moment he'd first mentioned arranging a marriage for her, Sharmarke had spoken highly of Ara.

And though his almost father-like pride for Ara was obvious, so was Sharmarke's fear of him. It became particularly apparent when they had flown to Mogadishu in a hurry when news of Ara's accident there had reached them in Berbera. While she'd been worried that Ara would never recover from his traumatic brain injury or wake from his medically induced coma, Sharmarke had wrung his hands outside Ara's hospital room and had fretted about what secrets Ara had uncovered about him.

"I don't know who got into his ear, but now he believes I'm capable of evil. He wants to ruin me—shame me!" Sharmarke had griped to her, the memory of him pacing

back and forth across Ara's private hospital room, sweat glistening on his brown brow and his white teeth bared at the very real threat Ara posed him still very sharp in her mind.

It wasn't the first time she was hearing of Ara spying on him.

"I need to know what he knows, and I need you to tell me," her father had instructed her after pulling her away from some of her mother's relatives at her and Ara's nikah. Using the pretense of taking special father-daughter photos, he'd found a secluded spot to grasp her shoulders tightly and make the request of her. *No, not a request,* she corrected. He had basically demanded for her to spy on her new husband. *"You're my daughter. My flesh and blood despite what poison your hooyo might have leaked into your ears. I'm the reason you've even married, so you owe me this."*

Zaynab hadn't known what to think, or who to believe was the wrong party—Ara or Sharmarke. She could've asked Ara about it now, but she didn't know what Pandora's box that line of questioning would open, especially when they'd been doing so well living together.

She wouldn't allow Sharmarke to wreck that for her. He'd caused her enough emotional harm to last her a lifetime and more.

Sadness clanged in her at that truth, and on impulse, she reached for her plate of pickled vegetables to soothe the ache in her soul, at least until her fingers scraped over the empty plate.

Before she could sulk too much, Ara placed his side of pickled vegetables by her.

"I'll likely not touch them," he said when she tried refusing.

"Oh, okay. Thanks." Popping fermented cabbage into her mouth, Zaynab squeezed her eyes shut and moaned in sheer culinary delight. When her eyes landed back on Ara, she blushed, realizing she'd allowed her pleasure to run away with her. "Sorry, I've been craving pickles more than usual. I think it's the pregnancy cravings because I could probably just eat heaps of the fermented vegetables alone and call it a night."

After that, their dinner resumed more quietly but peacefully. Other than a few comments about their delicious Middle Eastern dishes, Zaynab didn't mind that Ara was mostly silent.

In fact the next time he spoke was when their bill was delivered and Ara refused for her to pay.

"I ate way more than you did," she argued.

"And that's because you're carrying my baby," he said.

He made a good point, but she still conceded with a little huff.

Adding an extremely generous tip, and with a half-crooked smirk smacking of his victory, Ara stood and walked away to deliver their fully paid bill in person.

Unable to help herself, Zaynab followed him with her eyes. The tailored cut of his blazer molded to those broad shoulders of his, and his trousers hugged his backside perfectly and had her grateful that she was seated when her legs weakened on her.

Needing a distraction before she melted into a goopy puddle, she whipped out her phone and scrolled her apps aimlessly until a text from Salma popped up.

"Ready to leave?"

At the sound of his voice, Zaynab snapped her head up to Ara and then fixed her sights on the large jar of pickled vegetables in his hands. Not giving her a chance to ask, he explained, "I figured it would save some time rather than calling in and ordering when you had a craving."

She couldn't deny that the sight of the jar already had her drooling.

Ara then looked pointedly at her phone. "Did you want to finish writing your message?"

"Yes, if you don't mind. Salma just texted to ask if I'd still want to have our first iftar together. It's sort of a tradition for us." It started after she and Salma both moved together to enroll at the University of Edinburgh. Between Salma's nursing courses and her work placements in the Health in Social Science program, going home for all of Ramadan hadn't been a viable option for either of them. Like her, Zaynab knew that Salma looked forward to iftar together every year.

But she was stuck on a response. With Ramadan less than a week away, and Ara being with her this year, it naturally made sense for her to spend that time with him.

He seemed to understand her dilemma. "Why not invite her over?" he proposed.

Concealing her surprise, Zaynab hedged, "You wouldn't mind?"

Ara frowned down at her, looking adorably baffled. "Why would I mind? She's a close friend of yours, and it's Ramadan. Spending quality time with family, friends and community is a hallmark of the holiday."

Huh. She didn't take him for someone who really cared. When she'd first lived with him, she hadn't met any of Ara's friends. As for his family, though Sharmarke had already told her of the sad fate of Ara's parents, Zaynab had heard he had a sister and expected to meet her. But at their nikah, he had informed her his little sister, Anisa, lived abroad in Canada and was too indisposed to attend their nuptials.

"And anyway, your friend will be around our baby. I should meet her."

Zaynab grinned. *That* was more like the excessively cautious man she married.

Now she just had to wonder whether Ara would carry that suspicion with him when Salma came over for dinner, and if he even understood what he'd gotten himself into by giving Zaynab permission to officially introduce him to her outspoken best friend.

CHAPTER SEVEN

WHEN ARA AGREED to meeting Zaynab's friend Salma, he had seen the opportunity for what it was: a chance to get to know his wife and the mother of his child better. Living with Zaynab this past month had been enlightening, but that short time couldn't give him the same insight that her best friend of over twenty years could, and so he was looking forward to their iftar meal with Salma tonight.

And this was despite Zaynab teasing, "Are you sure you're ready for this?"

"Only if you are," he said with confidence. How hard could sitting through a few questions from her friend be?

"Famous last words," she whispered, snickering. Her snicker cut short when he came up behind her while she set up their tableware for the evening. With his chest nearly touching her back, he held out the soup spoons she'd forgotten, and watched her transform into the portrait of shyness as she accepted the spoons from him and avoided his eyes.

Amused by this swift change in her, Ara cleared his throat and once she braved looking at him, he said, "We're going to have a good dinner."

"I'm sure you'll win her over with your food. I still can't believe you didn't tell me you could cook."

His chuckle only gained him a swat on the arm from her.

"Seriously, where did you learn how to make all this?" Zaynab swept her hand toward the kitchen where varied dishes rested on plate warmers for their first iftar meal.

It wasn't that Ara kept that part of him secret, but before this night there was little time in his scheduling to cook as much as he'd like. Since moving in with Zaynab, he'd adopted more of a work-life balance, and that freed him up to not only spend time with her, but to help prepare dinner for her good friend.

And he should thank her. He'd forgotten how rewarding it could be to cook for someone else and watch as they delighted in his culinary talents. There weren't a lot of people in his life now that cared about that part of him. His parents certainly hadn't, not when he'd told them that he was considering taking a year off from his business program to apprentice with a well-renowned Somali chef who he'd admired. They'd nurtured his abilities in the kitchen up until that point. Then suddenly, almost overnight, his mother and father threatened to retract their financial support.

"Someone has to run our business someday," his mother had urged.

"You're our son. Naturally, it has to be you," insisted his father.

Ara stiffened his limbs as their voices echoed down the chambers of his long memory. He didn't like to think of them in that light. Didn't like the way that version of his parents made him forget how much he missed them.

Unlike his mother and father, Zaynab clearly was interested, given the way she'd happily volunteered to taste test all of his dishes. Now she was looking at him and waiting patiently for his explanation.

Just as he opened his mouth to answer her, the doorbell rang.

"Well, that's her," Zaynab announced with a sigh and a smile. "Too late to back out now."

He had the sense that she wasn't just taunting him anymore. This dinner had to be far more important than she'd let on.

Ara didn't have any friends that were close enough for their opinions to matter to him, at least he didn't any longer. He sympathized with her because he imagined it was how he'd feel with Anisa and Zaynab meeting—an event that had yet to happen. And when that happened, he knew he'd be sweating bullets worrying about whether his sister and wife would get along. Put like that then, it was fair that Zaynab was anxious about him meeting her friend.

Ignoring the doorbell chiming a second time, Ara reached for her arm and stopped Zaynab on her way to the door.

"Everything will be all right." He moved from gripping her arm to taking her hand and giving her a squeeze he hoped communicated comfort.

Smiling and appearing more relaxed, she squeezed his hand back.

Then she slipped free of him and went to answer the door at the chirp of the third and final doorbell.

"About time, babes," he heard Salma drawl before she stepped in and pulled Zaynab down to hug her. He couldn't get much of an impression of her until Zaynab ushered Salma in from the cold and closed the front door.

Side by side, the two women couldn't be more different.

Though Zaynab had been in the kitchen with him for a long while now, she had just pulled off her apron and set it aside. Now he could fully appreciate her lush curves in a café au lait–colored tunic and trouser set, her feet shod in fuzzy black slippers, her hair free of her hijab and drawn up into a high sleek ponytail, and her makeup enhancing the naturally alluring glow of her rich brown skin. Salma was shorter by half a foot, though she wore knee-high boots with the tallest heels he'd ever seen. She was also slender and her big dark curly hair puffed around a small heart-shaped face. Shrugging out of her coat and letting Zaynab take it and walk away to hang it up, her friend stood in a long sweater dress and a fuzzy faux fur vest, looking approachable enough outwardly until she turned up her nose and pinned him with a frosty look.

Waiting in awkward silence for Zaynab to return, Ara witnessed Salma blink and resume a neutral expression. As though she hadn't just been glaring daggers at him.

"Have you two met yet?" Zaynab asked sweetly and looked between them.

Ara reminded himself that this meant a lot to her, and that it didn't matter how many dark looks Salma slung his way, they were both there because they cared for Zaynab. If he had to be the bigger person, then he would take that high road proudly and quietly.

It wasn't that Zaynab had believed dinner with Salma would be quiet, uneventful—peaceful even. She'd just *prayed* that it would be. But from the minute her friend walked in and met Ara, any semblance of hope escaped Zaynab.

Salma had sharpened her long nail extensions to do battle and defend her, whether Zaynab wanted it or not. And her choice of weapon? Silent treatment. She ignored Ara, first giving him the cold shoulder while he and Zaynab gave her a tour of their home and then again when they were seated in the living room to wait out the final few minutes until their first day of fasting ended. Not knowing if Ara had sensed Salma's passive-aggressive attitude toward him, and whether that was why he deferred to her to do the talking, Zaynab sat between them and carried the conversation as cheerfully as she could given their awkward situation.

She was glad then when the call to Maghreb prayer sounded from her phone. She had set the reminder so that they wouldn't miss breaking their fast, but first she passed dates around for them to eat and poured them glasses of water.

After Ara led her and Salma in prayer, they gathered for iftar in the dining room.

Although Zaynab was famished, with the stifling atmosphere hanging over them, she found it difficult to enjoy the delicious dinner that Ara had worked hard to make them.

Salma continued to ignore him for the most part, except when she was forced to interact with him. Once because he was closest to the small bowl of basbaas, a green hot sauce, a staple in Somali cuisine, and another time when she complimented Zaynab on the shami kebab after doling out seconds onto her dinner plate.

"I would love to take the praise, but I'm not the chef," Zaynab said to her with a smile and nod at Ara.

"I see," was all she said to that, her lips thinned in displeasure for a long time after. Zaynab even noticed Salma didn't go back for thirds either.

Once they were finished with their dinner, and looking far more exhausted than he should have, Ara offered to clear the table and fetch their dessert. That left Zaynab to usher Salma back toward the sitting room. Once she was certain that Ara couldn't hear them, she rounded on her friend with a glare.

"You promised you'd be nice," she reminded her. Worried that Salma might act like this, Zaynab had called and warned her earlier to bring an open mind with her to their intimate dinner party.

Salma huffed, "But I *am* being nice..."

Not believing that for a second, Zaynab arched a brow, and Salma groaned and flopped back onto the sofa cushions, arms crossed in petulant rebellion.

"Okay! Fine, I'm not being nice at all." Salma scowled. "Why should I be though? He's the reason I didn't even get to take time off work and celebrate your nikah in Berbera."

Zaynab smiled as Salma pouted childishly. "You know that I agreed to the fast deadline for our marriage." When Ara had proposed, she hadn't seen a reason for them to be engaged for long. She was so sure she loved him—so very certain in her choice to be his bride that she hadn't ever thought their marriage would be at risk of falling apart...

And it was hard not to be reminded of it when Salma argued, "All right, but when you first came back a year ago, you were so unhappy. I hated that he made you sad. Give me one good reason why I should play nice after that."

"Because Ara spent all day slaving away in the kitchen, making our dinner. I told him about our iftar tradition, and I think he wanted to make this first day memorable for us both. Also, he's been looking forward to meeting you." Zaynab rattled off the long list of good deeds, surprised at how quickly heated she'd become on Ara's behalf.

She told herself that it was because he didn't deserve Salma's poor treatment when he'd been nothing but polite in return.

And maybe I want Salma to see this version of him that I'm seeing... This sweet, thoughtful, and highly attentive version of Ara who Zaynab could see herself living with, not just for the remaining five months of their six-month agreement, but maybe, *possibly* maybe forever.

She startled at that thought.

Was that what she wanted now instead of the divorce? To live with Ara permanently, raise their baby in this home they were building together, and even try at saving their marriage?

Zaynab shook her head, bewildered at where her thinking had gone.

And she wasn't alone in the confusion.

Eyes as wide as saucers, Salma unfolded her arms and sat up ramrod straight.

"Zaynab, you… You really sound like you care about him."

It was Zaynab's turn to frown. Still confused, she shrugged her shoulders and pressed both her hands over the fluttering in her lower belly. "Well, I have to, don't I? He's the father of my child."

"No, not like that," Salma interjected, leaning in and studying her with narrowed eyes. "I mean, you *care* for him."

"I said I did."

"You like him!" goaded Salma.

Blushing to the tips of her ears, Zaynab snapped her head to the entrance of the sitting room in case Salma's voice had carried.

"Yes, I like him, but not in the way you're thinking. Now, hush, I hear him coming back."

But not letting it go completely, Salma winked at her, mimed zipping her lips and grinned impishly. "Uh-huh. Okay. Whatever you say. My lips are sealed."

"Oh, just be nice, all right?" Salma could wind her up

all she wanted, but Zaynab was drawing the line with her attitude when it came to Ara.

And Salma seemed to take her warning to heart. Seemingly oblivious to being the subject of their conversation, Ara carried in a tray of frozen chocolate dessert he'd baked himself and cups of tea, and Salma accepted her slice of cake and tea from him with a smile and a friendly enough "Ta!"

He looked visibly taken aback for a moment before his usual brooding mask fell into place.

Zaynab ducked her head to hide her smile, relieved when the conversation flowed more naturally after that. It wasn't perfect by any standard, but at least Salma was attempting to be polite this time. She asked Ara about his business and culinary skills and how he liked his stay in London, and though her questions and his answers weren't indicative of them ever becoming friends, the evening ended on a far more hopeful note than it had begun.

All except for a small speed bump that happened when Salma was heading out.

Zaynab walked her to the front door, with Ara trailing behind them closely.

Salma confirmed her rideshare was there and, insisting that they didn't walk her outside, she crushed Zaynab in a hug. When she let her go, Salma narrowed her eyes sharply and suddenly to where Ara stood and pointed a finger at him.

"You make sure you don't do anything to hurt her or the baby, otherwise you'll have me to answer to, mister."

"I would hurt myself first rather than hurt her."

Zaynab's heart thudded at the darkly stern conviction in his words.

Apparently having seen something in his expression

that made her believe his words, Salma bobbed her head firmly and then, blowing an air kiss at Zaynab, she opened the door and left.

Zaynab stood frozen in shock, surprised at what had transpired around her, and she didn't move until Ara passed her to lock the front door and secure the house alarm.

"Why do I get the sense you two are conspiring against me?"

He smiled. "I don't think *conspiring* is the right word. We both merely share a vested interest in your and Button's safety."

She followed him to the kitchen and jumped in when he started loading the dishwasher. After they'd done that, he turned to wash the remaining overflow of dishes in the double sink.

"I'm sorry if Salma came off as, well, *forceful*." Zaynab peeked over at him but found his facial expression offered her no hint of what he was thinking. "Dinner wasn't so bad though... Right?"

"No, it wasn't awful," he said with a shrug.

"Wait. What was that?"

Ara flicked her a quick glance. "What was what?"

"That little shrug." She mimicked it for him, her heart thumping as she wondered, "Did you not like Salma?"

He set down the sudsy plate he'd been cleaning, washed his hands and twisted the tap closed before he looked at her.

"I know why it matters to you that I like her, but at the end of the day she's your friend. My liking her or not shouldn't change your opinion of her."

"That doesn't answer my question."

Sighing, Ara rubbed a hand over his beard.

"It's okay. I won't get upset, promise. I just want to know what you think of her."

"Very well. She's rude," he said, surprising her with his abruptness.

Even though that was a fair summarization of how Salma acted, Zaynab opened her mouth, ready to defend her friend.

But Ara continued, "I also now know that she cares deeply for your well-being, and it eases my mind to know that you have her by your side. Between Salma and your mother, you'll have plenty of support for when the baby comes. At least after you tell your mother of the pregnancy. You might not even need me…"

He said the last part quietly, almost resignedly, before he lowered his hand from combing through his beard and turned back to wash the dishes.

Zaynab clamped her lips together, not knowing what to say after his statement.

All she knew was that the need to embrace Ara was so overwhelming, she wrapped her arms around her middle to avoid the instinct to hug and pour comfort into him.

Why would he think that she wouldn't need him?

She remained puzzled as to where he'd gotten that idea until she wiped the last of the dishes he'd finished washing, then it struck her swiftly.

It's my fault!

When she looked at it from his perspective, it was easy to understand where his sudden irrelevancy sprang from. First, she had initiated their talk of divorce. Though she didn't regret asking to end their marriage, knowing that she needed a clean break at the time, Zaynab had never considered how Ara might have felt and always just assumed he couldn't have cared if she left him because he hadn't seemed to care when they were married.

And more recently she'd requested that her pregnancy and their moving in together be kept a secret from her mother.

If he had done that to her, she would've felt pretty irrelevant too.

She couldn't do anything about the divorce, at least not when she wasn't sure how she felt about their marriage anymore.

But her mother not knowing? That was something she could remedy right then.

They had no sooner finished cleaning up from their dinner when Zaynab picked up her phone.

Ara had no clue what she was up to until she pressed her mobile to her ear, smiled cheerfully and said, "Salaams, Mum!"

She had rung her mother. He was gleaning an idea of where she was going with this, but he didn't expect her to turn on her phone's speaker and set it down on the kitchen peninsula between them.

Her mother jumped into immediately wondering why Zaynab had called so late, the anxiety plain in her voice when she asked in Somali, "Are you okay?"

"Yes, Mum, I'm all right. I've only rung to tell you something," she answered, flashing him a quick smile that just as rapidly flipped over into a frown when he reached over and pressed the mute button on the call.

"You don't have to do this," he said firmly.

"Did you just mute me?" She waved him away and glared when he pulled the phone back as she reached out to unmute the call.

"Hello?" her mother called. "Zaynab, hooyo macaan, are you there?"

"Listen, if you're doing this because you feel pressured to make this announcement, don't."

He didn't want her making a hasty decision to fulfill some obligation to him. *It's my fault though.* If Zaynab felt guilty, it was because he'd gone and opened his mouth and let slip a fear that he'd only begun feeling as of late. A fear that he wasn't needed by her, and not certainly when she was surrounded by the love and support of her mother and friends who were like family to her.

But that was his problem, *his* concern, and Ara hadn't wanted any of it touching Zaynab and their baby.

Of course he'd ended up slipping up and now she possibly felt responsible for his fears and doubts.

Zaynab appeared to understand what he was thinking though.

She wasn't glaring at him anymore, her eyes far softer on him now. "As sweet as that is, I've already made up my mind. Now, my mobile, if you please."

And before her mother hung up, Ara sighed, unmuted the call and handed Zaynab her phone.

"Still here, Mum," she reassured her worried mother. "Like I said, I have something to tell you. Well, *we* have something to tell you. Ara is here with me."

That was his cue to lean in and greet his mother-in-law. She sounded elated, her worry melting into loud, overenthusiastic effusions of maternal care. Ara blushed at all the lavish praise she showered on him.

"Mum, you're giving Ara way more attention than you normally do me. Should I be jealous?" Zaynab teased.

"Why didn't you tell me he was there with you?" her mother lightly scolded her. "I know you missed him, but I hope you didn't ask him to come over just because of that. That poor boy, I can only imagine the amount of work his business requires of him— "

Visibly flustered, Zaynab groaned, "Mum, stop!" She avoided his eyes and switched her mother off speaker and pressed the phone back to her ear.

Ara stared at her in surprise. Zaynab had… She'd missed him. Why hadn't she ever told him?

Because I never gave her the impression that I cared, and never gave her the attention she deserved.

He had trouble swallowing that truth down as he listened to Zaynab begging her mother to stop embarrassing her. Eventually she turned back to him and, still looking shyly at him, placed the phone down, the speaker back on.

"Okay, Mum, let's try this again," Zaynab said calmly. "The reason Ara is here and the reason we're calling now is because we were waiting to tell you that… That I'm pregnant."

He was wrong if he'd thought her mother had been gushingly loud earlier at discovering that he was with her daughter. The moment she'd learned she was a grandmother-to-be, Zaynab's mother screeched her happiness and threatened to rupture their eardrums in the process. When her mother began ululating like she would at a wedding, Zaynab laughed out loud and wiped tears from the corners of her sparkling eyes, her radiant smile pulling at something deep in him when she looked at him like no one and nothing else existed outside of that special moment. Not the ecstatic shouts of her mother congratulating them, not the memory of Salma warning him before she left and not even the worry that he could cause Zaynab to hurt again.

CHAPTER EIGHT

THOUGH A FULLY grown woman, Zaynab still loved waking up on Eid morning.

When she'd been young, it was the promise of getting money and gifts from the grown-ups in her life, but now, it was the nostalgia she lived for. Well, that and the promise of tearing into a fluffy yellow cambaabur. Served during Eid, the traditional Somali crepe-like pancake was the first thing Zaynab looked forward to on that special day. Her mother made the best cambaabur, though sadly she wouldn't get to glut herself on any this Eid.

Since clearing out their old home in the city seven months ago and moving to her cute little seaside town, Zaynab's mother hadn't returned to London for a visit.

She would have asked for her to come over, but she knew the nearly five-hour journey for her mother would be too exhausting. Despite conquering several rounds of chemo, and enduring plenty of hospital stays, her mother happily being on remission from cancer didn't completely scrub Zaynab's concern for her. So it was out of the question to put her through the kind of travel that might wear her down and undo all her mother's healing progress.

But when Zaynab had hoped to visit her with Ara instead, her mother had insisted over the phone that they not worry themselves with the journey. She cited Zaynab's pregnancy and chided her on traveling when she was in such a delicate state. Arguing with her hadn't worked, mostly because her mother had talked Ara into her line of thinking.

"I know you want to see her, but she could be right. A lengthy car ride won't be comfortable for you, or for Button," he'd said to her after they had gotten off the phone with her mother.

Petty of her, but Zaynab paused brushing her teeth and frowned at her reflection in the bathroom mirror, annoyed still that he hadn't taken her side on the matter. Wasn't he *her* husband? Sure, they might be headed for divorce, but shouldn't their bond count for a little more support?

She knew she was being silly, and that they both only wanted what was best for her and the baby, but it didn't stop her from grumbling about it while getting ready for the Eid activities in store for her and Ara that day.

It wasn't until she was fully dressed and opened her bedroom door that her irritation came to an abrupt halt.

Zaynab sniffed the air and closed her eyes, immediately placing the familiar scent. It was cambaabur, and its freshly baked aroma wafted through the halls and permeated the whole house as she climbed down the floating stairs to the ground floor. It had to be Ara. Since discovering he could seriously cook up a storm, he'd been treating her to scrumptious meals, day and night. Ramadan had always been special to her, but it was made only more so when she was rewarded after a long day of fasting with one of his culinary masterpieces.

And she really shouldn't have expected Eid to bring an end to him delighting her with his food.

Her mouth watering, she followed the divine smells to the kitchen and beamed when she saw Ara's back to her as he stood over the stovetop. Sleeves rolled up and an apron tied around him, he was moving steadily, pouring the yellow batter and working between two frying pans. And judging by the plate of towering, steaming fresh cambaabur behind him on the shiny marble countertop of the kitchen peninsula, he'd been cooking for a while. She would even guess that he'd gotten up at sunrise since it was only a little after seven in the morning.

Ara was so busy toiling at the stove, he hadn't yet noticed her presence.

Zaynab didn't rush to inform him. Seizing the moment to watch him instead, she leaned against the side of the arched entranceway to the kitchen and pressed a hand to her chest, her heart so full knowing that he was working hard to make this Eid meaningful for them.

If she thought about it, it already was pretty momentous. *Because it's our first Eid together.* And not just the two of them, but their baby was technically there too. Zaynab raised her free arm and wrapped it around her stomach, the smile splitting over her face lighting up her insides. She didn't think anything else could make her happier right then. Except she didn't count on Ara glancing over his shoulder at her as he finally realized she was there.

"Good morning," she said with a shy little wave and walked into the kitchen. After pulling out a stool at the peninsula, she sat facing him and tracked his movements as he lowered the dials on the stove and, covering both frying pans with lids, he turned to her.

"Good morning," he rumbled back, his smooth, deep voice rousing a thrilling little shiver from her. He then nudged his chin at the cambaabur and said, "Go ahead and eat without me. I'll join in once I finish up the rest of the batter. Can I get you anything to drink? Tea or yogurt?"

"Yogurt," she said quickly. "Definitely yogurt." She wrinkled her nose at the suggestion of pairing cambaabur with tea.

Like he had the Eid pancakes, Ara whipped up the yogurt drink for her, even stirring in the sugar before he passed the mug over.

"So good," she moaned at her first bite, her eyes nearly rolling back in pleasure. "It even tastes like my mum's."

"That's because it is your mum's."

Zaynab's eyes bulged at his comment, but when she went to open her mouth, the small bite of cambaabur jammed in her throat. She jerked forward and coughed violently and thumped her chest.

Ara was by her side in the blink of an eye, pushing away her cup and plate and patting her back. Together, their efforts dislodged the food and got her breathing easier.

One last thump of her chest and she croaked, "W-what did you just say?"

The smoke detector pealed before he could answer.

Calmly walking over to a security panel, just one of many scattered throughout the house, Ara pressed in an alphanumeric code, aligned his thumb to a biometric reader and finally silenced the fire alarm.

He then pulled the frying pans off the stove and, prying the lids off, fanned at the thick acrid smoke pluming out at him.

Zaynab was focused on him, and even rose up from her seat to lend a hand, when a new voice floated into the kitchen.

"Have the cambaabur burned?"

"Mum?" Forgetting to help Ara, Zaynab popped out of her stool and onto her feet and stared at her mother like she was seeing a ghost. As shocked as she was to see her, she rushed over and embraced her mother tightly. It was only once the welcoming scent of her mother's favorite bakhoor perfume filled her nose that she didn't think she could ever let go. "Mum, what are you doing here?" she said, still clutching her.

If her mother hadn't peeled her back by the shoulders and kissed her cheeks, Zaynab would have continued clinging to her.

"What do you mean? To celebrate Eid with my beautiful daughter and her handsome husband, of course."

Zaynab stifled her exasperated groan. "Okay, but *how* are you here?" Not that she didn't love the idea. No, she was fighting back happy tears.

Her mother gave her a secretive smile and then tipped her head over Zaynab's shoulder. At Ara.

Understanding slowly, Zaynab turned to him. "You did this?"

"Ara called me a few nights ago, after we had spoken and decided for you to both stay in the city. He told me how much it would mean to you to have me over for Eid."

"Well, he's right," Zaynab agreed, sniffling again and then flicking her watering eyes up to the ceiling with a laugh. "But I don't understand. How did you get here so fast?"

Her mother's eyes twinkled. "I flew on a private plane. A very big, very beautiful plane that my son-in-law sent to me."

"Is this true?" Zaynab spun around to Ara.

He nodded. "It seemed the safest and fastest method."

And now because of him she had her mother with her, and right on time to celebrate Eid.

"I love that you're here, Mum. I've missed seeing your face, and talking over video calls doesn't count."

This time her mother engulfed her in a hug, pulling Zaynab down to her height and rocking her from side to side.

Drawing back, her mother cupped Zaynab's cheeks and smiled, her own eyes glistening with unshed tears. "I missed you too. Now let's stop crying. It's Eid, and we all should be happy."

"But these are happy tears!" Zaynab laughed again and, pulling back from her mother, fanned at her face to stave off the waterworks. When she was positive her makeup wasn't running, she waved for her mother to sit and eat with her. And when her mother asked for some tea with her cambaabur, Zaynab used the excuse of popping on a kettle to sidle up to the stove beside Ara and whisper, "Why didn't you tell me?"

"Your mother made me promise to keep it a secret. In her defense, she wanted to surprise you."

She didn't know which filled her with joy more: that he was defending her mother's reasoning, or that he'd helped orchestrate bringing her mother to her so that they could celebrate Eid together. Never would she have ever imagined that Ara would have done something so sweet for her. At least, she wouldn't have thought him capable of it a couple months ago. But since they'd moved in together again, Zaynab recognized that he was making more room in his overflowing schedule for her. Beyond feeling less and less invisible to him every day, she also no longer felt like a task he could cross off his to-do list, and more like a partner in this marriage that once seemed so utterly doomed to her.

It's everything I wanted from the start.

Everything that was now making her question her previous, possibly hasty impression of him and their unhappy past attempt at living together.

* * *

Ara had been keeping a tally of things in his life that had changed since Zaynab reentered his world.

Right off the bat, there was a lot more laughter. Especially now that she was growing comfortable around him. And she'd have to be comfortable to be laughing at him in the background after some older aunties had stopped him outside the masjid following Eid prayer and practically tossed their daughters in front of him.

Extracting himself from them, Ara hurried over to where she stood, a hand clapped to her mouth but her eyes shining their mirth at his expense.

"You could have lent a hand," he grumbled at her, fighting his own smile when she guffawed at him.

"And shatter the hope of those poor aunties? I think not. Besides, I can't imagine you didn't soak up that attention. Come on, admit that you—"

Zaynab gasped as he snaked an arm around her shoulders and pulled in close to her. Ara hadn't meant to cut her off midsentence. It was simply that he'd noticed the aunties had been hovering in the wings, watching his interaction with Zaynab carefully and he hadn't wanted to give them any more hope.

Because even if he and Zaynab divorced, he'd already decided that marriage with anyone else wasn't for him.

From his peripheral vision he could see the brood of aunties collectively sigh in disappointment before scattering through the courtyard—he only presumed in search of eligible bachelors.

Following them with his eyes until he was certain the coast was clear, Ara looked down at Zaynab, the apology ready on his tongue evaporating.

Gawking up at him, her head slightly tipped back, eyes

wide and frozen on his face, and her soft-looking painted mouth rounded in astonishment, she had a hand to his chest and the other clutched at the simple gold necklace that echoed the gold threads in her lustrous pink dirac. He didn't normally care for the traditional Somali garb, but on Zaynab, Ara seemed to have unearthed a newfound appreciation.

Even though the dress hung over her loosely and she wore a blazer that covered most of her top half, the white belt cinched above her swelling belly had taunted him with the hint of womanly curves he knew she possessed. Curves that were now pressing into him and unlocking the desire he kept sealed away for both of their sakes. But wanting Zaynab? That was always simmering below the surface. And with each day that passed together, the temptation of giving in to his lustful urges grew more appealing.

No. I can't do that to her, at least not again.

She'd come to him for a divorce, and what had he done? Seduced her into bed and impregnated her.

Ara ground his teeth at the memory of his barbarism. Though he'd been intensely attracted to her from the very first moment they had met, he had done well to keep it under lock and key for a reason. He was damaged. His confidence broken ever since he'd lost his parents, and his trust was only further abused when Zaynab's father had then gone on to betray him with his crimes. Ara had married her to protect her from the threats her father's criminality might pose her.

So when that threat was locked up with Sharmarke, he'd hoped that he could repair what he might have broken with Zaynab.

But then she'd asked for a divorce, and though it destroyed that hope he had for their marriage, Ara knew that he'd be doing right by her if he gave her the clean break from him that she clearly yearned for.

It should have been a lesson to him this time around, and a reminder that they were only living together once more for their baby.

That's all that matters now. This baby, and the family the two of us will build around him or her.

But even as he thought this, he didn't make a move to drop his arm off her shoulders or pull away. Instead, he raked his eyes over her, taking in the swell of her breasts as her chest rose and fell rapidly under his stare, then over to where her henna-painted fingers curled into the front gold embroidery of his black thobe.

She appeared as entranced by him as he was spellbound by her.

And despite being in the center of the overly populated sahn outside the masjid, when she sucked in her bottom lip, he was transported back to several months ago, in that hotel room of hers in Berbera. A kiss was what had undone him then—and it was looking like a kiss would be doing it again.

Eyes glued to her mouth, he lowered his head, his heart sounding loudly in his ears and filtering out the Eid merriment filling the masjid's large central courtyard.

A little closer...

An inch or two more.

He could feel her sweet breath puff over his sparking lips, and then—

"Zaynab? Ara?"

Her mother calling out to them jolted him back from her and, simultaneously, saved plenty of unsuspecting witnesses from being scandalized.

Ara dropped his arm off Zaynab and she stepped away,

shyly bowing her head and keeping him from seeing her expression.

Zaynab nudged him then. "Come on. I don't want to miss the Eid festival."

As she dragged him along to the festival, her hand on his long, loose sleeve, Ara caught the amused grin stretching his cheeks up.

Zaynab saw it too as she smirked back at him and hauled him along with the Eid crowd spilling out from the masjid and onto the city streets.

Across from the masjid was a park, and though Ara hadn't paid it any mind when they'd arrived at the masjid for Eid prayer, he could now see that the expansive area of greenery hosted an abundance of tents and stalls, and a large central stage for the festival's musical entertainment.

"Hurry!" Zaynab urged, pulling him with her to the heart of the party. "I don't want us missing out on all the fun."

CHAPTER NINE

As THEY SQUEEZED their way through the crowded thoroughfare between stalls and tents, Ara calculated that there must have been hundreds if not thousands of people there. Normally he would've regarded that many people in one area as a viable hazard, and then he'd be expending all his energy on how to minimize said hazard, missing what was in front of him. But right then security risk assessment couldn't be further from his mind.

They took pictures together and then joined the dancing near the stage where a live band played catchy, chart-topping tunes for the crowds. When they'd started slowing down around noon, Zaynab lured him toward a food truck parked nearby, and they hauled fizzy drinks, cheesy chips and gravy and doner kebab to the first empty picnic table they spotted beneath a cluster of early blooming cherry blossoms.

"Having fun?" she asked him, her grin ever present.

He chuckled. "Fun isn't the word I'd use, but it's close." Exhilarating would be more like it. His humor slipped as he recalled when the last Eid he'd celebrated with his parents was, over sixteen years ago. Had he known that his parents would die a couple months later and that would be the final time he'd get to celebrate with them, he wouldn't have dared act the way he had to them.

Banishing the rest of where that memory would take him, Ara blinked free of the past and stared into the unease on Zaynab's pretty face.

"Ara? What's wrong?"

She lowered her fork and swiped her mouth with a napkin, and he hated that she was now frowning because of him.

He could lie to her. Pretend like he wasn't reminded of what he'd lost. But while sitting with her and partaking in the Eid festivities, one look at her knitted brows and the concern shining out of her eyes and he knew that he'd be telling her the truth.

"I was just thinking of my parents and the last Eid we spent together, that's all."

Her hand settled over his atop the picnic table, communicating quiet sympathy. "Do you mind if I ask about them?"

Ara hesitated, but then he shook his head, realizing that he wasn't as pained by the thought now that she proposed it.

"What were they like?"

Of all the questions, that one was the easiest for him to answer. Smiling, he said, "Thoughtful, generous, nurturing—though we didn't see eye to eye all the time, I counted myself lucky to have them as my parents."

"They started your family's shipping business, right?"

He nodded. "From the ground up. They'd often tell me and Anisa that it was the second most precious thing in their lives, with us being their first." He hung his head, smile vanishing as he swallowed thickly. This was the part he hated talking about, and though he'd never have considered saying anything, delving into the past had loosened his stiff tongue. "They'd always planned for me to take over once I came of age and they'd trained me on everything."

"Why not Anisa?" Zaynab asked the question he'd often wondered himself.

"She's nine years younger, and since I was the oldest and their only son, I became the natural choice of heir for them." And Ara hadn't minded at first, but then that was before he'd gone to board at his university and before he had started discovering his independence and his own dreams.

"You didn't want that," she said, intuiting his mind.

Astonished, Ara recovered and bobbed his head solemnly. "One night, I'd gone to a new restaurant with some friends. The chef and owner was an older local man who had spent many years traveling the globe, and all in the pursuit of his culinary calling. The food he made for us that night," he groaned softly at the memory, licking his lips.

Zaynab laughed. "So, that's who I have to thank for all the good food you've been making me."

"I'd say he was more the spark. After that night, and that experience, I started practicing in the kitchen on my own. My parents were proud especially. They'd often get me to cook when they had company over for dinner. At least they *were* proud until I announced that I wanted to take a year's break from my business program. Then, almost overnight, they retracted their support."

Zaynab squeezed his hand. "I'm sorry that happened to you."

There was more he could have said, but Ara left it at, "Even though I couldn't see it fully then, I now understand where they were coming from. They were just worried about what would happen to their business legacy.

"And after they died, it seemed the natural course for me to take up their mantle." More than that it had felt imperative to him. Like if he worked hard on the company's behalf, toiled in enough sweat and sacrificed enough of his personal life, that he'd make amends to them.

That they'd forgive him wherever they were.

That I'd be able to forgive myself...

"The first Eid without them, I tried for Anisa's sake to be cheery and normal."

"But you couldn't," Zaynab said, completing his thought. She rubbed her thumb over the back of his hand, leaning in. "It's okay. I'm not judging you. No one in their right mind would, Ara. You were young, you just lost your parents and now you had to step up and be your whole family to your sister. Honestly, I'd have fallen apart."

He nearly had too. The first few years were the worst. On top of being Anisa's primary caregiver, juggling his schooling while sitting in on company meetings and learning the ropes from some of his parents' most trusted executives, it was almost too much for an eighteen-year-old to handle.

"I didn't have time for my friends, barely had time to myself, and so with each year I found less of a reason for Eid." And when Anisa eventually learned to stop asking him to take her to the Eid festivities happening in town, and she'd slip away with friends instead, Ara had retired from celebrating.

Until now, he thought, looking at Zaynab and acknowledging that it was her who'd given him a new outlook on the holiday.

"Today has been...illuminating. I forgot how Eid could be." At least what Eid was like when one was surrounded by the love of family, friends and community.

Ara smiled at her, the weight that had been pressing down on him mysteriously lighter now. If he hadn't known better, he'd have said she cured him.

But he realized that he'd done that on his own. *By talking to her*, he surmised. Letting out some of his most consuming thoughts and easing his burden.

He looked down at Zaynab's hand on his, knowing in his heart that she was one of the people he cared most for.

Never had Zaynab imagined that she'd have a chance to spend Eid with Ara. Certainly not with their divorce looming over their heads. Then again, she also never dreamed that she would be twenty-two weeks pregnant and counting. So she supposed life had thrown her quite a few curveballs lately.

Living with him again had been a concern, but Zaynab could now see she'd worried in vain. Ara was nothing like the cold, distant version she'd gotten of him the first time they had moved in together. Now he was spending time with her, opening up to her about himself and his past, and being vulnerable in this sweetly trusting way that had her heart and mind all twisted up with thoughts of him.

Thoughts that were heating up her body and making her want to shrug off her blazer and flap a hand over her blushing cheeks.

She'd always been physically attracted to Ara. And though that was what first hooked her when she met him, she'd stuck around because she had seen glimpses of unbridled passion lurking inside him. Not the zeal that she had seen him direct at his business, but a hunger that he starved and kept caged away deep within.

Zaynab had known it was there, and it was also ultimately why she had married him, yet she hadn't gotten to feel its full brunt until he'd kissed her and consummated their marriage for the first time.

And now, besides carrying the consequence of that powerful ardor of his, there existed this hole in her brimming with longing.

When she wasn't tiptoeing around it, she was flat-out resisting her yearning for him.

Ara seemed clueless, and she mostly preferred it that way, except for when she wondered if he felt anything of what she was feeling.

Zaynab peeked under her lashes up at him, looking for any obvious signs that pointed to him wanting her.

They were standing on the footpath, beneath the blooming magnolia in front of their home, their car and driver having only just dropped them off. Ara's hand closed around her arm, stopping her from pushing through their front gate.

Turning very slowly to face him, and seeing how close he was to her now, she smiled nervously.

There was a charged current in the air, like a storm crackling warningly even though the sky was beautifully clear.

Her mother was staying with her and Ara, but she'd told them to head home without her and that Salma's parents, whom she'd bumped into at the festival, would be driving her home later.

Zaynab was glad for that now as Ara crowded her against the wrought iron gate, his hand moving up, long, agile fingers curling under her chin and tipping her head back. Oddly, despite the lovely early spring weather, they were alone out on the footpath. And so not a soul would have witnessed when Ara stroked his thumb along her bottom lip, his brown eyes never softer and warmer than right that instant.

"I had a good day," he said, his voice husky and low.

"Did you? I'm glad," she chirped, not knowing what else to say, his touch having apparently fried her brain.

"Thank you."

"For?" she squeaked.

"Today. For reminding me what Eid could feel like again."

She was still a little speechless, but she managed to whisper, "You're welcome," right before her brain actually shorted on her. Because Ara's thumb stilled on her lower lip as he pulled in and kissed her forehead, his warm mouth like a searing brand to remind her of this moment forever.

Zaynab hadn't even thought she'd closed her eyes until she opened them at the feel of Ara pulling back. But all he'd done was move his hand over to frame her cheek. Her disappointment didn't last too long as Ara flicked his powerful gaze to her lips, and a second later, he slowly inched his head lower. And unlike when they were at the masjid, and it seemed to her that he had intended to kiss her then, this time nothing and no one interrupted them. The only thing that stood between them was the short time it took for his mouth to seal hotly over hers.

He kissed her with that hidden hunger she'd married him for, and though she sensed he was holding back, there was nevertheless a passion in the way his lips and tongue stroked hers, and a longing from how his arms wrapped around her and hauled her against him.

She didn't think anything could pry her apart from him.

No, nothing could make her want to break away from the fierceness of his kiss.

Absolutely nothing—

Ara ripped back from her, breathing hard and touching his forehead to hers. "We shouldn't have done that. I shouldn't have…" He broke off and gnashed his teeth, drawing back from her and jerkily lowering his hands off her burning face, as though touching her had scalded him.

"I don't want to compromise your iddah, Zaynab. That kiss… *Any* intimacy would ruin it."

His rational explanation pressed pause on her humiliation. Now she understood why he was suddenly acting skittish.

"I understand," she said, still winded from their deep kiss.

"For now, let's just pretend it didn't happen." As he said that though, the heat from earlier crept back into his eyes.

Zaynab gazed back at him, and the butterflies trapped in her ribcage whirled about and smacked into her rabbiting heart. She tried to reconcile this man in front of her with the man who had driven her to ask for a divorce.

The same man who her criminal father had accused of spying on him.

She knew why she'd married Ara…

But is that why he married me? To use her to spy on her father.

A new ache manifested in her then. This one begging for her to ask Ara if any of that was true. Was their marriage ever real to him at any point?

Instead of voicing her doubt out loud, Zaynab shoved it back into the dark corner of her mind where it had a semi-permanent home and where it couldn't interfere with this happy little moment.

CHAPTER TEN

ZAYNAB WAS SURE she could name several positives of being pregnant, but not when she was getting up every other hour to go relieve herself.

Groaning loudly, she kicked out of her bedsheets and drew up to a seat, feeling blindly for her slippers and shuffling to the ensuite.

Of course when she slipped back into bed was when her stomach chose to grumble incessantly. Knowing there was no point in trying to go back to sleep, she left her bed again and walked zombie-like to her bedroom door. At one in the morning, she expected the house to be quiet. Even though Ara had been working more these past few weeks, and sometimes well into the night, he'd be in his office on the ground floor, and so any noises he might have made wouldn't bother her where she slept on the third and topmost floor of their home.

Naturally, Zaynab tensed as what sounded to her like a muffled moan broke the peaceful hush and froze her in her tracks.

But the hallway was empty, the wall sconces dimmed and casting shadows.

There were three other bedrooms on that floor. Two were empty, but the third one, at the front of the hall and closest to the stairs was Ara's bedroom. The door was always closed to his room, and she'd only ever been in there once since they had moved in together over three months ago. And though she wanted to respect his privacy, when she heard another faint noise coming from that vicinity, Zaynab walked slowly to his room.

As she did, two thoughts struck her. Either Ara had called it an early night, or it wasn't him at all and a burglar had broken in…

Ara wouldn't make it easy for any burglar.

Zaynab snorted softly, allaying her fears quickly. With all the measures he'd taken to safeguard the house for them, she couldn't help but feel a little bad for any thief who targeted them.

In front of his bedroom door, Zaynab hesitated and lowered the hand she had raised to knock. She didn't want to go barging in there and alarm him for no reason. Worse, he could be fast asleep, tired from all the work he was doing. Suddenly, it seemed silly to wake him simply because she'd heard a strange noise or two, especially since she now noticed whatever it was had stopped making the sound.

Just as she began chalking it up to her sleep-addled brain hallucinating the whole thing, Zaynab stilled as the noise rose up again. She pressed her ear to Ara's door, and holding her breath, she listened.

There! Another moan—or maybe it was a groan?— pressured her into deciding.

That's it. I'm going in there.

Because naked or not, his well-being was important to her. She wouldn't ever forgive herself if he had injured himself and she didn't check to see whether he needed help.

Grasping his door handle, Zaynab knew the door would open. He'd once told her that she could come fetch him at any time during the night if she required him. But right then it was Ara who needed her, and so she was relieved that he'd had the forethought of leaving his bedroom unlocked.

She squinted into the darkness, waiting for her eyes to adjust a little before she treaded inside.

The moaning was much louder now that she was in the room with him. Without the door muffling the noise, she could make out the distressed notes in his groans.

"Ara?" she called out softly. Emboldened by her own bravery as she crept closer to the bed, she raised her voice. "Ara? Wake up. You're having a bad dream."

At least that was what she supposed was happening.

She could see his shadowy form in the bed and moved closer, trying to see if he was facing her direction or not. Resisting the urge to turn back and flick on the bedroom lights, she gripped the edge of the bed, leaned in and called his name once more.

He grunted in answer and shifted in his sleep.

"Ara—" Zaynab's breath hitched when he suddenly flopped onto his back, his hand fisting his sheets, and even though she couldn't see his face, she could hear the contorted pain in his rasping breaths. Whatever demons were chasing him in his dreams, they appeared to be catching up and fast.

She didn't know what made her do it, but she reached out and touched his hand, caressing the tension from his knuckles.

It seemed to be working. In his sleep, Ara relaxed, his hand loosening over the bedsheets and his breathing evening out. She smiled, happy to have brought him some comfort. And for a while she was content to stand guard and protect him from the worst of his terrors. But once

Zaynab thought to slip away and let him get some rest, he turned his hand around and caught her wrist, startling her into almost screaming out.

When her heart rate returned to normal, she tried to gently pull away, and when that didn't work, she attempted to pry his fingers off her wrist.

About to just pinch the back of his hand and wake him when he started murmuring, she stopped trying to break free and listened as the incoherent mumbling turned into words.

"Stop... Don't... Not them... Hooyo... No, *no*, don't... No, aabo..."

Realizing he was dreaming of his parents gave the nightmare context. Zaynab went still, the fight to force his hand off her arm no longer a priority, and her heart twisting in her chest for him, knowing she could never rescue him from the terror of his past. Ara's hand squeezed tighter, his grasp moving into bone-crushing territory very quickly.

"Ara!" she cried out and slapped the back of his hand before digging in her nails and hoping that did the trick.

"Zaynab?"

Hearing him say her name in confusion didn't let up the pain he was unknowingly inflicting on her.

"You're crushing my hand!" she yelped through gritted teeth.

Immediately, his fingers went lax over her wrist in response. Slipping out of his hold and clutching her throbbing hand to her chest, she saw him move in the dark, his bulkier shadow shifting over to the side a few seconds before the room was bathed in soft, white light.

She blinked rapidly, wishing he'd have warned her first.

Once her eyes adjusted to the change in lighting, she

saw him leaning back against his headboard, shirtless, the remote controlling his room lights in his hands and a darkly questioning look lasered on her.

"What are you doing?"

"You were having a nightmare. I just came in to check on you, and then you started squeezing my hand really hard." She winced as she prodded her wrist, sensing a bruise in her near future. "Remind me not to try waking you again," she muttered, blushing and looking away when his piercing stare bored into her. Then in the silence, she shuffled a couple steps back to the open bedroom door, wondering if she could make a smooth exit.

Before she could try, Ara drew off his bedclothes in a flourish, revealing that he hadn't been sleeping in the nude.

Still his black silk pajama bottoms left little to the imagination. And hers was happily spinning out fantasies as he closed the distance to her in a few long strides.

He held out his hand to her.

Understanding what he wanted, Zaynab slowly pulled out her arm to him and allowed Ara to take her hand.

"Easy," she said with a grimace as his fingers gently brushed over the now tender underside of her wrist.

She had been annoyed with him until she saw his brows furrow and his lips thin in what looked to her to be a mix of regret and concern. And she certainly heard it smacking in his low tone as he observed, "I've hurt you."

"No, I'm fine, really. I just bruise easily is all."

"We have to ice this now," Ara said, not having shifted the blame off himself and taking immediate action to remedy his mistake.

"Hold the ice there, and I'll just grab the ointment."

After leaving her with those instructions, Ara moved

fast to the cloakroom, grabbed the first aid kit and headed back to where Zaynab was waiting for him in the kitchen.

Glad to see that she was listening and holding the ice pack to her wound, he moved to stand beside her rather than take the other stool at the kitchen peninsula. He didn't deserve comfort, not after what he'd done to her. Even before she'd revealed her unhappiness and asked for a divorce, Ara had suspected he could hurt her, but he never thought that threat to her could be physical.

But as he took a deep breath, and gently pulled the towel-wrapped ice pack off her hand, he came face-to-face with the pain he caused her.

Reddened flesh ringed her wrist and glared up at Ara accusingly.

I did that to her...

He forced his hands from clenching into fists, keeping them steady while he opened the first aid kit and pulled out the anti-inflammatory salve he needed from it.

"I can do that," Zaynab offered.

But he shook his head and lied, "It will be a lot quicker if I do it."

She gave him a look that said she didn't believe that for one bit. The truth was that he needed to atone for his mistake, and it would be easier for them both if she would let him have his way. Expecting Zaynab to argue, he was surprised when she simply slid her injured hand closer to him and waited patiently.

Though she was compliant, sitting through his swabbing the salve onto a cotton bud and massaging it lightly over the red imprints of his fingers on her, she asked, "I understand the ice pack, but isn't the ointment a little excessive?"

"The ice will keep the swelling from spreading, and the ointment with any inflammation."

"It's a bruise. I've had plenty and they usually mend themselves," she said before smiling and cocking her head to the side. "More importantly, where did you learn to be such a good nurse?"

"You'll have to thank Anisa. She was running around all the time and hurting herself as a kid." He rested her hand down on the towel and ice pack, capping the ointment and tossing the used cotton bud in the dustbin.

"Bumps, cuts, scrapes and loads of bruises. She even broke her arm once, and since I couldn't repair the fracture myself, we had to make a hospital trip."

Zaynab laughed. "Sounds like a typical enough childhood."

He supposed it was, but after losing their mother and father so suddenly and violently, Ara hadn't wanted Anisa to leave him too. Although as her older brother he'd always been fiercely protective of her, when half their family was gone overnight, his overprotectiveness of Anisa had only intensified multiple times over. When she was younger she hadn't minded it as much, clinging to him more in the absence of their parents. But as she grew older, Anisa would rebuff his helicoptering, until she finally told him she was moving abroad for her postsecondary studies and career.

"I might have cared for her a little too much," he admitted gruffly.

"You were her older brother. From what I've heard Salma tell me, it comes with the territory."

Ara wished he could take Zaynab's comfort, but he said, "I didn't approve of her leaving to study and work abroad, and so in my anger, I stopped talking to her and we didn't speak for four years."

Four long years that he'd wasted being angry with her. That was time he could never get back, but that he was trying to repair, starting by helping her with her upcoming wedding.

"I'm sure she's only happy that you're speaking again." Zaynab echoed what he hoped: that Anisa didn't hold a grudge against him for how childishly he'd acted.

Talking about his sister was reminding him of his parents and the nightmare he'd just had of them. If he closed his eyes and listened carefully, he swore the explosions of bombs reverberated in his mind, the screams for help from the injured, his mother's wails and his father's cries for help all mingling together into blaring white noise—

"Ara?" Zaynab was leaning forward, her fingertips touching his over the cool marble counter. "You looked deep in thought there."

He frowned when she pulled her touch away, relying on the calm she brought him. Grateful that she stopped the nightmare from pushing into his reality, and clinging onto the distraction she presented, he asked, "Why are you awake so late anyway?"

"Well, first, I needed to go to the washroom," she said while a shyness tinged her smile, "and then I was too hungry to go back to sleep."

Realizing that he could help her there, Ara headed for the fridge. "Let me fix you something."

"No need! I was craving pickles again."

Standing before the open fridge doors, he smiled despite the dark mood still clinging to him. He grabbed the pickles she requested and two plates and forks.

He wasn't smiling though when, spearing a pickle, Zaynab glanced at him and wondered, "So, what were you dreaming about? It sounded terrifying."

"It was," he agreed.

"Maybe you'd feel better if you talked about it."

Ara highly doubted that it would do him any good, and he was opening his mouth to tell her that, only Zaynab then said, "In your sleep, you called to your mother and father. That's why I thought, perhaps, you would want to talk about it."

Hearing that he'd been crying out for them poured ice through his veins. He didn't know what made him colder, that Zaynab knew it was his parents he'd dreamed of, or that he was opening his mouth to explain.

"I was dreaming of them."

"Does that happen often?"

Shaking his head, his thoughts all jumbled, he answered, "No. Not anymore. But, at first, yes." Sighing, he tried again and with the hope he sounded more articulate. "The dreams were worse right after their deaths."

"Have you tried talking to someone?"

She meant a therapist. As much as there were things he loved about Somalia and Somaliland, the progress toward mental health was still slow going there, the stigma and superstition far stronger around it than in the UK.

"No, I haven't seen a professional. Though I imagine it could help, I've mostly outgrown the terrors."

Zaynab's frown told him she thought otherwise, but she wisely didn't push the subject, not when he was barely getting through their conversation.

"My work in Mogadishu must have me thinking of them more lately. They always wanted to expand their business there.

"Truthfully," he rasped, "I don't know why I'm dreaming of them."

Sometimes he wondered if it was because he would

soon be a parent himself. A part of him did worry that he wouldn't know what to do when it came time for him to hold his and Zaynab's baby in his arms. That he wouldn't be able to protect his family this time either, and that, just as he hadn't been there to save his mother and father from their cold-hearted killers and lost them forever, he'd lose Zaynab and their child too.

She didn't know that his parents had been murdered.

Ara had kept that fact hidden from not just Zaynab, but most people. It was an ugly but crucial detail that was left out of all of the media reports. A boating accident was the tragic story spun for the public, and he'd been happy to go along with it if it kept people from interfering with his grief.

But now, and most illogically, he wanted to tell her of all people.

So, he did.

"When I dream of them, they're always crying out to me, begging me to help them just before they sink under the ocean and drown." Ara's breaths sawed out faster, his heart pounding against his sternum. "But just now, in this dream, they were trapped under a building rocked by an explosion." It wasn't unlike what had happened to him in Mogadishu. If he hadn't been found by a group of volunteers searching the smoking rubble of the hotel that had been targeted, Ara accepted that he would've died that day.

He didn't know why his dream had diverged this one time. His only theory was that his brain had merged the two tragedies together, and in doing so, amplified the terror of both and tortured him.

"Like I said, I don't know why exactly it's happening now. But then again, I could be having the dreams because they were killed." He said it so casually, forcibly detaching himself from the powerful emotions violently churning inside of him. They wouldn't sink him under, not with the way Zaynab's eyes widened and she slid off her stool and approached him slowly.

Ara could see what she wanted to ask, so he said, "I didn't say anything because most people don't know it's the truth. And because their killers are long gone and will likely never be punished for their crime."

"Ara, I'm… I can't even…"

"It's fine," he said stiffly, excusing her from struggling to find words and turning away from the pity he worried was coming. He expected the awkward quiet that came with his confession.

What he wasn't ready for was Zaynab's arms to slip around his middle.

She hugged him from the side, her cheek pressed up against his shoulder and her eyes closed, a sniffle drifting up to his ears. It wasn't long after that he felt her tears wetting the T-shirt he'd tossed on before coming down to the kitchen with her.

He was stunned, and not only because of her embrace but that she was crying for him.

Tears that he hadn't allowed himself to cry.

And now with her soft, breathy sobs the only sound between them, Ara felt a strange heat burning his eyes and clawing at his throat. It would be a first, as he hadn't even cried when he'd laid his parents to rest. No, even then he had to hold strong for his sister and their family's business.

But he knew that if he let go of the part that held him from leaning into the warm support she offered, and if he hugged Zaynab back, that Ara would do what he'd always fought against doing…

I'll fall apart, he thought with gritted teeth and tears

filling up his eyes fast, knowing that he wouldn't be able to stop if that ever happened.

Afraid of the feelings she'd unlocked in him, Ara pulled away from her and cleared his throat of the hoarseness clogging it, his gaze purposefully avoiding hers.

"If you're done eating, you should head back upstairs and try to sleep… For the baby." He added the last part, hoping that she didn't think he was trying to control her.

When she didn't respond, he hazarded a glance at her and regretted it instantly. She was gazing at him with redness tinging her eyes, her lashes darkly wet from her tears and her chin trembling as though she was fighting to hold back a fresh display of waterworks on his behalf. Wildly, none of it robbed her of her beauty.

And all that observation made him want to do was bundle her up in his arms and hold her for as long as they both needed.

"You should come up and sleep too," she implored.

She was right. He should try and sleep, but with everything he'd experienced—the nightmare of his parents, bruising Zaynab accidentally, then revealing to her that his mother and father were murdered and making her cry—Ara didn't think he'd be resting peacefully anytime soon.

"Maybe," he said noncommittally, "but I'll be in my office until then, if you require me."

He sensed her lingering, hopeful look fixed on him for a while, but eventually Zaynab gave up. And it was only when she was slowly walking away from him that Ara looked longingly after her.

CHAPTER ELEVEN

ZAYNAB LIKED TO think of herself as being quite patient.

At least she *had* a lot of patience, but the next few days following her and Ara's late-night tête-à-tête featuring her craving for pickles and his nightmares had shown her that she couldn't wait around for him to make the first move. Not unless she wasn't willing for the awkward silence between them to ever get better again and go back to the way it was before it began feeling like he was drifting away from her intentionally.

And she had the sense it was purposeful. Like Ara was erecting the same unclimbable barriers at the start of their marriage, when they were first living with each other. Laying those bricks down, piece by piece, and concealing the secret parts of himself that he'd been showing her slowly but steadily since they'd moved back in together.

It was those hidden parts to him that she recognized had been the reason she'd fallen for him in the first place.

His honest thoughts and feelings, and his unbridled passion; all of it back behind those tall, thorny walls around him. That haunted her the most. All that progress… *Only for him to return to the way he was.* To the man that she'd wanted to divorce.

Zaynab had mulled over it for several days now. She'd already been quietly worrying about his work schedule creeping into the time that he used to spend with her. But she hadn't said anything, figuring that he wouldn't be preoccupied with his business affairs forever. And she knew that his work was important to him, and she wanted to support him because of it. If that meant that she stood by quietly and kept her unease to herself, then so be it.

But she questioned whether staying quiet was the right choice, or if she'd only been ignoring the warning signs dropping like breadcrumbs and pointing toward the frustrating changes in Ara. Now Zaynab was staring longingly outside his office door, her hand poised to knock but her courage wavering on her at the very last moment.

She was still undecided whether to go in when the double doors suddenly swung open, forcing her to startle back and stare wide-eyed at Ara as he stepped aside with a silent invitation for her to enter.

This wasn't the first time she had entered his workspace. Naturally well-lit by an array of long, narrow picture windows, anyone walking in would immediately be drawn to the focal point of the space: a massive L-shaped executive desk that oozed luxury with its gleaming darkstained wood surface, supple leather inlaid desktop and modesty panel, and exquisite craftsmanship that gave the desk its illusion of floating from where she stood at the office's entrance. The other furnishings were two high back leather accent armchairs, a glass coffee table and a credenza doubling as a coffee station.

The only difference in his office was that Ara wasn't alone.

A young black man was standing in the corner with a tablet grasped in his hands and a smile directed at her.

He looked familiar, though she couldn't place him in her memory right then, and she was more curious how Ara had known she was outside.

"How did you know I was…" She trailed off, seeing exactly how he'd known that she was skulking outside his office doors.

Framed by built-in shelves, a large flat screen show-cased several tinier monitors, twelve in total, and she immediately recognized they were locations through the house from the kitchen to the staircase, the front hall, and dining and sitting rooms and right outside their front and back property.

Ara had told her about the security measures, and though he'd pointed out the hidden cameras, it had never occurred to her to ask him to see the feeds.

But she now knew how he had detected her presence and known to open his office doors for her.

And at the same time it struck Zaynab that he must have seen her standing outside nervously.

Before she could slink off in embarrassment, Ara asked, "Is there something you needed, Zaynab?" and, with a jolt, reminded her why she had come seeking him in the first place.

"I thought we could have lunch together?" Zaynab eyed the familiar man whose face she still couldn't place, adding softly, "Unless you're busy."

"We were just about to take a break," the smiling man chimed in.

Ara's scowl said otherwise, but he nodded and his features appeared to soften the longer he regarded her.

"Let's reconvene in an hour or so." Ara inclined his head at the man before he turned the full power of his gaze on her. "Did you have anyplace in mind for our lunch?"

"Who was that man back in your office?" Zaynab asked as soon as the server left them with their lunch orders.

They were seated out in the open at her request, and though the security risk would've been lower inside the café, Ara had to admit that she was right about it being too beautiful a day to waste sitting indoors. That and there was a calming effect to watching people go about their lives on the popular, shop-lined street. Couple the pleasantly balmy spring weather with the rare sunshine beaming overhead, and it only seemed to lure more people than usual outdoors.

"Daniel. He works for the security company I've hired."

"I knew he looked familiar! And Daniel works for your sister's fiancé, Nasser, right?"

"That's correct." He'd been working with Daniel for a while now, and as the head of his security team Daniel had earned Ara's trust in shaping the safety measures around his business and also around the home and life he shared with Zaynab. But these days, he barely saw and spoke to her.

It was torturous to yearn so desperately to be with her, but to also know that it was safer for him to avoid her.

Because he was starting to give away too many of his secrets to her. Telling her about the real cause of his parents' deaths had made that obvious to him.

It's safer for her too.

He'd physically harmed her by bruising her during one of his night terrors. Then made her cry when she had learned about his parents' murder. And, if all that wasn't enough, Ara couldn't allow himself to forget that their divorce was still very real and possibly on the horizon as her delivery date quickly approached.

In a couple months, their six-month arrangement to live under one roof would come to an end. Zaynab would have to decide, once and for all, if a divorce was what she desired.

And though a part of him still wanted her to choose to stay with him, a new feeling began to stir inside of him, driving in deeper the wedge that had appeared between them over these past weeks, and this emergent emotion was pushing him toward letting her go.

Freeing her from any obligation to him.

Though he hadn't been willing to listen, it was as she said once: they never needed to be married to co-parent. *I just wasn't ready to let her leave yet*, he quietly admitted, if only to himself.

The sullen mood at their table was at odds with the bright, sunshine-filled day.

Head bowed and eyes glued to her plate, Zaynab was eating, but her heart didn't seem into it.

Feeling like a monster, he opened his mouth to apologize for his far from stellar company and was interrupted by his phone lighting up. He had set it on mute, but he left it facing up on the table by his plate, in case anything came up that required his urgent response. And seeing his little sister's name flash on his phone screen activated his brotherly worry for her.

"Anisa, what's the matter?"

Ara yanked the phone away from his ear at Anisa's sudden shriek, the sound more excited than terrified, but hearing it still ratcheted his heart rate through the roof.

"Happy birthday to you!" she sang loudly and out of tune.

Zaynab must have heard his sister's off-key singing because her curiosity flashed into surprise.

After her singing, Anisa chattered away and asked him about how he was spending his birthday.

Considering he'd completely forgotten what day it was, he grumbled, "I'm working."

Anisa sighed as loudly in his ears as she'd sung, then lectured him about needing to lighten his workload before finally revealing the reason she had called.

"Nasser and I are coming for a visit." She went on to explain that it was to do some shopping for her wedding later on that year—shopping she could have easily done where she was now in Canada. Which was why he sensed that the visit was also a good excuse for her to check in on him. Anisa had been texting him regularly since he'd come to London. She knew that he was living with Zaynab and that she was pregnant, and as excited as she was to be an aunt soon, he felt an undercurrent of worry from her. Though he didn't know if it was worry for him or Zaynab, or heck, even the baby, whatever Anisa's real reason for the sudden visit, he would always still welcome her.

So, instead of interrogating her, he asked, "When?"

"Four days from today. I know it's short notice, but we've already booked our flight."

Ara let her know that was fine, and after exchanging a few more pleasantries, they ended their call. He placed his phone down and acknowledged Zaynab's inquisitive look.

"My sister and Nasser are coming for a visit. She was also calling because... Well, I'm sure you heard her."

"I think half the café and street did," she remarked dryly on Anisa's screeching over his birthday, earning a small, amused smile from him.

"Anisa's always been *expressive*."

Zaynab laughed breezily. "Well, it will be nice to finally meet her. And, even better, they'll be here for the baby shower next week." Then after a noticeable pause, and looking far more solemn, she said, "I didn't know it was your birthday."

He stopped smiling and shrugged, knowing that her intrigue was warranted.

"It might sound like a lie, but I forgot what day it was." In the same way he hadn't celebrated Eid for years before this recent one with Zaynab, his birthday had become a nonevent since his parents' passing. Another reminder of a personal life event that was stolen from him with their deaths. "Anisa might be the only one who remembers what day it is," he said. And even then, for the four years he and his sister hadn't spoken, he'd gone without any birthday wishes.

Zaynab sat in contemplative silence, but then she smiled and said, "Happy birthday. I guess lunch is on me then."

Though he tried to argue, when the bill came and the server held out a payment terminal, Zaynab tapped her card faster than he could. Ara couldn't find it in himself to be annoyed, not with the way her triumphant grin made him smile. And she continued to smile even after his phone interrupted them again, the screen lighting up with Daniel's name this time.

"We're on our way," he said after seeing that nearly two hours had elapsed since he and Zaynab had left the house for their lunch. He rang up the driver next. Even though they had walked the fifteen minutes to the café, it was time he didn't want to lose walking back now.

"Actually, I'm going to stay behind and meet up with Salma soon anyway. She wants to do a little shopping."

Hearing the first of this, Ara frowned but nodded. He didn't like leaving her, but her friend would be keeping her company soon. "All right, but you have the driver's number. Call him when you're done shopping. I'll even let him know to give Salma a ride if she wishes it."

Zaynab thanked him, and in a few minutes, he was in the back of the car and pulling away from where she sat alone at their table, watching and waving to him.

Despite having a criminal for a father, deception and guile didn't come as naturally to Zaynab.

So lying to Ara about Salma meeting with her and sending him off back to the work that lately consumed his attention was hard on her. But the moment the car ferrying him away turned the corner, she sprang up and strode away from the café, determination setting her shoulders straight and holding her head up high.

She was on a secret mission to make this birthday as special for him as possible.

But as she walked into the cute, colorful little shops lined along Notting Hill's famous Portobello Road, Zaynab found this was a far easier task imagined than accomplished.

She had gotten to know more about Ara since living with him here in London then when she'd first married him and moved into his beautiful big home in Berbera. And yet shopping for the man was still a challenge. He seemed to have everything at his fingertips already, what with his tremendous fortune. What could he possibly want that she alone could give him?

Still, Zaynab managed to cobble together what she thought might work, and after shopping for a couple hours, she took up his offer and rang for the driver.

She swore the driver to secrecy as he helped haul her shopping bags into the car, and then from the car and inside the house. Giving him a tip and thanking him, Zaynab sneaked upstairs, praying that none of Ara's security cameras caught and ruined her surprise for him. She'd tried her best to disguise the presents with innocuous brown paper bags. He would only think she'd been shopping a lot, and that would keep him from guessing what she had in store.

Once alone in her room, Zaynab set to work wrapping his birthday gifts.

Her back ached by the time she sat back and admired her hard but loving effort to surprise him.

Now she wasn't deluding herself into thinking that her presents would, like magic, fix whatever had frayed between them. But she did hope that it would be a start to a conversation toward healing and that this hurdle before them would be only that, an obstacle they could surmount together.

With that positive mindset buoying her spirit, Zaynab went about her day as normally as possible and counted out the hours until dinner when she would see him next.

In spite of his workload, Ara still ate meals with her regularly enough. Yet the mood between them was decidedly different than what it used to be. Rather than the easy flowing conversation, he now spoke less frequently and getting him to talk more than a few words was like squeezing blood from a stone. She might as well be chatting with herself sometimes...

Or better yet, a wall.

Zaynab sighed, shaking off the sourness crowding in with her despairing thoughts and smiling until she felt hopeful again.

Because there was no way Ara wouldn't be knocked off his feet with this surprise. When the familiar decadent smells of a warm freshly cooked meal perfumed the entire house, Zaynab crept out of her room with the gift bag behind her back and hurried faster downstairs than she usually did.

Though he'd been working more, he still found time to cook for her. And just as every evening before, Ara had the table set and ready when she entered the dining room, and all she had to do was grab the seat beside him at the far end of the table.

He was already seated and waiting on her.

Normally they would eat, but Zaynab didn't sit immediately, instead standing by her chair and attempting to not squirm or fidget when Ara looked up at her raptly.

Blushing plenty though, she cleared her throat and pulled around the gift bag she hid behind her back. "For you," she said quickly and almost breathlessly.

She had a whole pretty speech prepared, but she forgot all of it the instant his eyes clapped on her.

He didn't keep her waiting, taking the silver straps of the gift bag and pushing away his table setting to open his present.

One by one, he silently pulled out the gifts. A self-heating mug for all the tea he drank, a silly book full of dad jokes that he could use when their baby was older and a photo album he opened to the first page and where she'd tucked into the photo sleeve the first and more recently second ultrasound of Button, side by side.

Zaynab sucked in her lips, the gifts self-explanatory, but still wanting to explain what each gift meant to her and, hopefully, what it could mean to him.

Eventually Ara stood and walked up to her.

She held perfectly still, waiting to see what he would do and finally hoping to understand how he felt.

"Thank you," he said simply, his voice deeper and

gruffer with indiscernible emotion. Even now his eyes were guarded and his expression closed off to her.

But when he took hold of her shoulders, Zaynab's rising concern eased off. He kissed her forehead, the imprint of when he'd done it first at Eid still emblazoned in her mind and heart. She expected it to feel the same but it didn't. Desperate to recreate that feeling from before, she closed her eyes and leaned in, her nose tickled by his beard and her rounder, tauter baby bump pressed up against the hard, flat planes of his abs beneath his soft dress shirt.

She only opened her eyes when he lifted his mouth away and held her back at arm's length.

Looking at him was torture afterward, seeing the emptiness staring back at her when her lungs were constricted so tightly it hurt to breathe. Hurt to speak up as he sat back down, returned her gifts into the larger gift bag and placed it aside at the foot of the dining table like all of it was an afterthought now to whatever came next. In this case, their dinner. And then later, she knew, it would be his work that took precedence over everything else. Including being with her.

And although Ara had shown his gratitude, it had felt empty. *Forced*, she observed sadly.

Not knowing what to say, and disappointed by his lackluster reaction, Zaynab compelled herself to take her seat when all she wanted to do was run upstairs to the refuge of her bedroom, where she could cry the heartbroken tears she was holding back right then.

CHAPTER TWELVE

ONCE AGAIN ARA was destroying a good thing he had going with Zaynab.

He'd already ruined his marriage, and now he was demolishing the good impression that he had worked hard to achieve in the short time they had lived together once more. And even though he knew his actions were hurting her, and he wanted to stop, apologize and grovel his way back into her good graces, Ara just couldn't bring himself to do it.

Like a train careening fast toward a break in the tracks, all he had to look forward to was the promise of a steep plunge and the fiery wreck awaiting him in the end.

And the end appeared to be the baby shower Salma offered to host on his and Zaynab's behalf.

"Here are the parents-to-be!" Salma announced their arrival to the guests now all gathered in the spacious and well-tended back garden and patio of her parents' home.

Having arrived for their visit a couple days ago, Anisa and Nasser were the only guests on his side. And aside from her mother, who Ara had flown in for the party, everyone else who came up to congratulate them were friends of Zaynab's.

He recognized her friend Neelima from the restaurant, and then there was her octogenarian client, Opaline. With

Opaline was the man who'd been in Zaynab's resort suite in Mauritius, and whom Ara now knew after researching was Opaline's grandnephew, Remi. Though he had no right to it, certainly not after how he'd been acting toward Zaynab as of late, Ara still tensed up when Remi's friendly smile shined down over her and his hand touched her arm, lingering there as he passed his well wishes on her soon-to-be motherhood.

Zaynab smiled back at Remi, looking far more relaxed in that one moment than she had with Ara in a long while. Not since he'd been slowly retreating from her and the warmth and happiness she made him desire so very badly. Happiness that he frankly felt no right to, not when he was so confident that he'd end up hurting her.

I've hurt her before, haven't I?

He had pushed her to the point of divorcing him. It had to have been a last resort for her. Knowing Zaynab, she wouldn't have married him at all if she'd thought it would end in the dissolution of their marriage a year later.

No, Ara thought. He'd forced her hand with his cold attitude, and he was doing it again now.

"Are you all right?" Zaynab quietly asked him at one point as they were taking pictures beneath a white trellis wrapped by pretty, vibrantly bright flowering vines. She was alternating between looking at him and the phone cameras guests were holding up at them, smiling for everybody else, but the light of the gesture didn't truly reach her dark eyes as she peered up at him. "Because if you're not, you can tell me."

"I'm fine," he gritted out the lie.

Zaynab's glare could have frosted the blooming flowers above their heads. "Really?" she said, her voice low, her words only for his ears. "You could've fooled me. It looks like you'd rather be anywhere else."

"Zaynab…"

She narrowed her eyes at him as though quietly warning him off telling her any more falsehoods.

With possibly the worst timing, the professional photographer Salma had hired for the baby shower instructed, "That's a good pose! Get in a little closer and just hold it there for a few seconds, please."

Ara froze as Zaynab turned into him, smoothed her hands over the lapels of his suit jacket and gazed up at him, heeding the photographer's instructions to the letter. To everyone else they must have appeared like an adoring couple eternally in love. She might have even fooled him if he wasn't chilled by the emptiness looking up at him now. Like she'd utterly given up on trying to reach him, and somehow, that thought withered his already low opinion of himself.

"Perfect," the photographer called out, aiming their lens at the other guests in attendance and giving them a break.

Zaynab quickly removed her hands from him and turned to walk away. He took a step after her instinctively but faltered in the follow-through and let her go in the end.

She didn't look back at him once as she mingled with the guests, smiling warmly at everyone but him. Zaynab strolled through the garden in her beautiful pink dress and warmly welcomed the people who had taken precious time out of their day to celebrate with them. He should have been by her side doing the exact same thing, but instead, he stood apart from the party and general merriment, and merely spectated the festive mood all around him.

He could have been admiring the lengths that Salma had gone to in making this party a beautiful affair.

Gold and white balloons and streamers festooned the wooden fence cordoning off the backyard and the sliding glass doors into Salma's parents' home. Upbeat pop music played from someone's portable Bluetooth speaker, and a catered buffet spread was ready to be enjoyed on two long folding tables. It was all very thoughtful of Salma to prepare for him and Zaynab, and given all the tireless effort that went to making this party happen, Ara only felt more villainous for not enjoying it as fully as he ought to have.

As he watched Zaynab from the sidelines, Ara was transported back to when he'd met her for the very first time.

He had walked up behind her as she looked out over the Indian Ocean from the bow of his yacht, the golden ribbons of sunset mirroring off the blackening waters holding his ship afloat. Sensing him before he announced his presence, Zaynab had turned slowly and, with a shy smile, she'd immediately captivated him.

She was weaving that same magic now on the party guests, her smile just as entrancing today as it was that day on his yacht.

Ara could envision her hosting his business dinners, welcoming potential new investors and helping him seal many lucrative deals for his company. Beyond that, he had selfishly wanted that smile of hers in his life forever. It was why he'd desired her from the start. Why he had chosen to make her his wife.

And why I'm in love with her.

At least to himself, Ara had never denied his strong affection for her, but it was becoming clearer to him more every day that his attraction now felt more like infatuation. He loved Zaynab, always had, and it was why he was working so hard now to keep her from getting any closer.

Discourage her from loving him back. Protect her from the pain he knew he'd cause her.

Because love did that.

He'd loved his parents, and they had been killed and taken away from him. He had even deeply cared for her father before Sharmarke had been revealed to be a monster. No matter how alluring it was, loving her could only lead to his suffering. Maybe not today... *But someday.*

A muscle in his cheek hardened when Zaynab was by his side again to open the presents their guests gifted them.

She tried to avoid his eyes, but he could see that the enthusiasm she presented to her friends and mother was not as wholehearted as it might have been, and that was wholly his fault. She deserved to be happy, on this day especially. The only thing that comforted Ara right then was the knowledge that he was doing this for the good of his family. For Zaynab and their baby.

If that was the closest he could do to loving her outright then so be it.

Like any first-time expectant mother at her baby shower, Zaynab would've thought the occasion would have been a happy one. Instead, she had spent the few hours impatiently and guiltily waiting for the party to end.

And it was all because of Ara.

For over a month now she had been aware that he was acting more like the colder version of himself that she'd gotten after they first married. She'd made excuses for him quietly. *He's busy working. He just wants to help people. He'll go back to giving our relationship priority soon enough.*

But those excuses were slowly unveiling themselves to be threadbare reasons for her to overlook his off-putting and distancing attitude. And that was her mistake for not nipping it in the bud as soon as it became apparent to her. If she had, Zaynab wouldn't have had to sit through his embarrassing glacial impression in front of all the family and friends who had showed up with gifts and well wishes for their baby shower.

It would've been fine if she was alone in noticing how he was acting. Sadly, she'd had to endure several guests coming up to her and asking whether Ara was feeling all right.

She told them all the same made-up story, that he was feeling a little under the weather and that was why he appeared sullen. Since no one caught her on the barefaced lie, Zaynab assumed that Ara hadn't revealed it to be so. Unfortunately for him she couldn't find it in her heart to be thankful to him for not outing her deception as she wouldn't have been placed in that awkward position in the first place had he not forced her hand.

And had he not made her fight back from biting his head off multiple times during the party.

Managing to hold her frazzled emotions together until they were in the privacy of his vehicle was the hardest thing Zaynab had done in a long while. It was almost as difficult for her as when she'd gone to ask him for a divorce at his sister's engagement party.

Sometimes she'd questioned whether she should have gone in person all those months ago. If she had just called him to ask for the divorce instead, then they wouldn't have ever ended up in her hotel room...

And I wouldn't be pregnant.

She would never regret having their baby now, but then it wouldn't have led Ara to talking her into living together, and by that logic they wouldn't be here now, sharing the back seat of the chauffeured car with an oppressive tension settled between them.

Zaynab was just grateful now that her mother had chosen to stay behind and help Salma and her family with the party cleanup. And she was just as relieved when Anisa and Nasser had said that they were going to explore the city after the party and would find their own way home later.

With their houseguests all preoccupied, she and Ara would have the house to themselves to argue if it came to that. And she sensed that it *would* come to that. Though the luxury car had a privacy screen that would make it impossible for the driver to hear their conversation, Zaynab had hoped to wait until they were home alone together before she broached the subject of how he'd acted at the baby shower. But almost as soon as they were on the road her frustration and anger bubbled to the surface and spilled out.

"You humiliated me," she said, refusing to look at him and staring out her window instead. Not that she was paying any mind to the buildings and streets they passed on their short journey home. She just didn't want to see anything on his face that might make her stop. This was something Zaynab had to do. She had to let him know how awful he was making her feel lately. It still didn't make it easier to spit out the bitter words that felt and tasted like gravel in her mouth. "Almost everyone asked me if you weren't feeling well, and I said 'yes.' I lied to them *for you.*"

Ara's long drawn-out, deep sigh snapped her head around to him, her anger blistering hot and choking her up.

"They're my friends and family, and they just hosted a party for us and our baby! Doesn't that mean anything to you?"

"Of course it does," he said calmly but his cool tone only incensed her more. "I appreciate—"

Zaynab scoffed, not caring that she interrupted him. Leaning in closer over the console between them in the back seat, she glared incredulously at him. Because surely he wasn't trying to argue that he hadn't been abjectly rude at the party. "Did you, really? Because your actions said otherwise. My God, Ara, you were sulking. *Sulking!* At our baby shower!" She shook her head, the rage fading as quickly as it surged, heartache and disappointment taking over. "How could you?" she accused him softly.

Then, unable to stare at him a second more without crying, Zaynab looked away, bit her trembling lower lip and fought the tears pinching the corners of her eyes. Sobbing in front of him would only undermine the point she was trying to get him to see; that he was acting terribly, and that if Ara didn't change back to the kind, sweet, thoughtfully attentive version of himself she'd seen of him, then they might not last the two months left of their six-month arrangement.

That she would have no choice but to continue with their divorce and break their family up.

As she discreetly wiped at a tear that leaked free, Zaynab was glad that Ara had read her body language perfectly and didn't attempt to reengage her in their unfinished conversation. Because they would still definitely need to talk. She only needed a moment to gain her composure again and iron out the weepiness that gripped her now. Using the rest of the car ride to do just that, Zaynab didn't speak again until they were walking through the front door of their home.

"Zaynab, I'm… I'm sorry."

Ara's apology drifted from behind her as she stormed

toward the sitting room. It was spacious enough for her to pace angrily while they hashed this out.

Sensing that he followed her, Zaynab scowled and finally looked at him, her heart racing and her chest heaving.

"What are you apologizing for exactly?"

Ara's brows slammed down in consternation. "For the way I acted…" he said slowly as though testing the waters with her, and when she didn't snap his head off, he continued, "If I offended you, your mother and friends in any way, I am sorry for that. It wasn't my intention."

"Wasn't it though?" When he didn't answer, she gave her head a vigorous shake, an embittered laugh tumbling out. "I don't know what's worse—the fact that you've been acting so standoffish lately, or the lie."

"Lie?" he echoed, his eyes growing as hard and cold as hers had to be.

"Yes, your lie. I ask if you're fine, and you keep telling me that you are, but that's a lie."

She tried not to balk when he slid a step closer to her, bearing down as he gritted out, "That's not a lie."

"It is!" she retorted.

Taking another step, and then another, and backing her into the coffee table, Ara stopped his advance and glared at her. "Fine. You're right. I wasn't the consummate guest of honor. I just…"

"You just didn't want to be there," she said, punching her chin up and meeting his glare fearlessly. She wouldn't be intimidated or guilted into silence.

Not that she believed that was what he was doing. Ara had never made her fear him physically, not once. The only risk he truly posed was to her fragile emotions. *To my heart*, she thought bitterly. And that was because she loved him.

I do love him.

She wouldn't have married him if she hadn't. And even though she'd asked for the divorce, it was to save her heart from shattering any more than it was being around him and knowing that he didn't and probably wouldn't ever return her love.

That was why they had to move through this, right now. Zaynab was tired of walking on eggshells and waiting for him to wake up and realize that he was pushing her away. Because he was, and unless he was doing it on purpose, and this was all some calculated ploy to chase her out of his life, Ara was risking her really walking away from him this time and for good.

"I am right, aren't I?" she said far more quietly. "You didn't want to be there at the party today. And you… You don't want to be here with me now, do you?"

When he blew a harsh breath and spun away from her suddenly, Zaynab's heart gave a lurch. Inhaling sharply, she squeezed her eyes shut at the sight of him retreating, feeling a fresh wave of new tears welling forth. Before the overwhelming sadness warped her voice and made it impossible for her to speak without sobbing, Zaynab sniffled and asked, "Why did you marry me?"

Silence answered her, and so certain that he must have walked away and left her, she blinked open her eyes, chancing the tears that flicked from her lashes and trailed down her cheeks. Only to see that Ara had simply moved a few feet away and was looking at her with this inexplicable fury twisting his handsome face.

It was when he spoke that she understood none of his unconcealed wrath was for her at all, but for himself instead.

"I'm not worth your tears, Zaynab," he growled, the

rumbling of his self-directed anger coming through clearly. "I never will be, and I shouldn't have married you."

Zaynab sucked in a whistling breath, her lungs burning and her vision of him blurring with the tears now fully wetting her face.

"So Sharmarke was right when he said you were spying on him," she said, hating to admit anything that had to do with her father, especially now that she had to accept that, like her parents, she'd failed her marriage.

"He told you that." Ara unbuttoned his suit jacket and loosened his tie, his expression far more menacing if that were possible. "He shouldn't have. It was a problem between us, him and me. There was no need for him to involve you."

"I'm your wife. His daughter. Why wouldn't it involve me? Maybe he was trying to protect me from being hurt by you." She lobbed that last part in a fit of pique, annoyed with him in part but also just devastated by their argument.

And Ara took it personally. His scowl was fierce and his eyes dark slits of irritation. "Is that what you think? That his intent was to protect you, and that you needed protection from me. That I would ever want to hurt you, Zaynab?" His big shoulders heaved and then fell, and he didn't look quite as enraged by the mention of her father when he said, "I… I have hurt you, I know, but it was never with intention. Never part of some plot to inflict pain on you. *Never.* I swear it."

Swallowing around the jagged edges of brittle emotions, Zaynab shook her head, exhausted and defeated, and knowing that pretending Sharmarke was ever concerned for her and hadn't only been working to preserve his own reputation would be a waste of time.

This isn't about my father and what he's done wrong.

This was all her and Ara, and the wall of thorns he kept around himself, the feelings and thoughts he kept from her.

Smiling sadly, Zaynab forced herself to look at him as she blinked more tears. "You must have only married me for your cloak-and-dagger mission."

Ara couldn't believe it, but her hurled accusation was swirling in his mind, reverberating loudly as if Zaynab were uttering it over and over again.

And yet as much as it pained him to confess, there was a half-truth in what she believed of him.

"I did think that your father might be less inclined to be suspicious of me if I agreed to his suggestion of an arranged marriage." Before she could crow with triumph—not that Ara thought for a second that gloating was her aim since she looked generally stricken at his confession—and knowing that he was hurting her made the next words easier to speak in the hope she would take even the slightest comfort in them. "I did *not* know that Sharmarke meant to give his own daughter away."

"But you took the opportunity that landed in your lap anyway," she said bitingly.

She meant that he'd used her to get to her father. Hearing that she still believed that of him pulverized his confidence that she might have learned to trust him since living together again. *Why would she? I've isolated her again, and in our own home, and I made her feel this way. Made her want to lash out at me.*

The fault was entirely his and his alone.

And yet recognizing that, Ara couldn't give her what she wanted. What he could clearly see would soothe her.

Because even though it would be true if he told her that he loved her, he wasn't willing to give in to it. Refused to participate and set himself *and* Zaynab up for any future torment if their love didn't last. *Or if it was killed.*

No, he hadn't changed his mind, and after all of this, Ara was only that much more determined to keep from fully loving her and protect her from loving him.

"You're right," he said, unclenching his jaw to force out the hateful words and lying to her, "I saw an opportunity in marrying you, and I took it. I believed it was my only chance to protect the public from your father's criminal actions."

"You never loved me."

"I… No, I never loved you, not like that." The lie fell from his lips smoothly, but inside he was a writhing mass of agony. Masking it as long as possible, Ara looked away from her and delivered what he hoped was the final blow to his ongoing misery, and what he prayed made Zaynab see the light and run far, *far* away from him. "We should divorce."

He expected her to agree.

Maybe not immediately, as the quiet stretched on after he had proposed the suggestion, but eventually Zaynab would see that it was the best possible solution for her. He was a difficult husband. Unloving to her, and cruel for it, and she had always been right in her instinct to leave him.

Ara was bargaining on her still wanting the divorce, but she confused him when she asked quietly, "What did you say?"

"I'll leave. Give you the divorce, move out, but I only ask that you allow me to help you with whatever you need for the baby." Their child. Ara had wanted to be there when she gave birth, and had even once, not too long ago, secretly longed to remain by her side and watch their baby grow up with Zaynab.

Now he'd have to settle for visits and updates from her.

He could still be a good father and protect Zaynab and their child from afar.

It wasn't ideal, but it kept love out of the mix.

"I don't want a divorce."

Baffled, Ara didn't think he heard her correctly, until Zaynab made it clear that he had as her hands cradled her pregnant belly and she said, "I won't let Button grow up without a father. You owe it to be in their life."

"And I will be," he agreed vehemently.

"I know what it's like being a child of divorce." Her voice dropped an octave above a whisper, her gaze far-off, no doubt reliving the memories of hardship after Sharmarke abandoned Zaynab and her mother. "It's not easy. Questioning yourself. Rationalizing that it was somehow your fault even though it couldn't have been." She sucked in a shuddery breath, blinked and looked at him far more clearly. More than that, he noticed how she straightened her shoulders back as though preparing herself for battle. But since they were alone, her only opponent could be him.

"That's why I don't want a divorce anymore. We have to do better for our baby. Better than my father did for me."

"Zaynab, I—"

"No, Ara, listen to me. I *want* this. Need it. If you can't…" She broke off, and he knew he'd never hear what she might have said because she moved on with only the softest of hitches in her breathing, "If *we* can't make our marriage work in any traditional sense, I'm open to stay together for our baby. For Button. Please…"

Her plea broke him.

He had barely nodded when Zaynab moved toward him. Ara watched her until she was standing before him, her warmth pulling at him, and the temptation to lean into her nearly overcoming his higher reasoning.

But he also couldn't stand there any longer and withstand her dark eyes on him, her cheeks still wet from crying, and her sweet perfume infiltrating his staunch barriers.

"What are you…"

And before he could say more, she pushed her face up and pressed her lips to his. Shocked, Ara stood frozen as she kissed him. The salt of her tears mingled with the kiss, at both sweet and bitter. Though his surprise didn't last long, she didn't give him time to react, take her in his arms and return the kiss.

It was only after she pulled away that he realized why she'd done it.

"There. I think that's intimate enough to break the iddah and undo our divorce," she said, breaking his heart as she let him go. Zaynab walked around him then. And though technically he could hear her footfalls padding away, somehow Ara felt far lonelier than he had when she'd first left him in that big house of theirs in Berbera all alone.

CHAPTER THIRTEEN

ZAYNAB HAD ALWAYS thought leaving Ara would be hard, but now she knew that staying with him after learning that he didn't love her was going to be far tougher of a challenge for her.

I have to though.

For their baby's sake, she had to stay. The last thing she would wish on her own child was a distant, if not fractured relationship with their father. And despite how hollow and bereft she felt being with Ara right then, Zaynab never doubted he would be a good father. He'd keenly cared for their child from the moment she'd told him she was pregnant. He'd moved to London when she hadn't wanted to uproot her life, and he had even gifted her a lovely home as not only a dowry but to raise their child in.

It must have been why she'd thought he had a change of heart where their relationship was concerned.

I thought he cared.

More than that, Zaynab had really felt that he loved her. Clearly though she had deluded herself into seeing signs that weren't there.

And now since she had decided to remain married to him, she'd have to learn to be stonyhearted like him. Even the thought daunted her. But if it meant that Ara was more comfortable with the idea of staying married to her and not loving each other in the traditional sense, then Zaynab had to make it work somehow and some way.

It didn't help that her decision to end their divorce talk happened only about a couple days ago.

Two days in and she was already beginning to waver in her resolve and question her ability to maintain this cold front with him. It was downright exhausting to tiptoe around him, but she'd managed it. She had asked him to stop giving her rides to and from work, not wanting to be confined in the car with him if not necessary. And though they still had meals together, Zaynab no longer exerted herself in getting him to open up to her, not even when the silence that accompanied their meals only made her nervous enough to deal with indigestion all night long.

Their guests were still with them, so Zaynab at least had some company besides Ara's.

And yet Nasser and Anisa were busy touring the city and doing some shopping for their wedding, and Zaynab's mother was fully enjoying her retirement and spending time catching up with friends that she'd left behind when she had moved from London. They couldn't be with Zaynab every waking hour to keep her from thinking about Ara and what their lives might have been like had he loved her.

She was having one of those quiet, pining moments when her mother dropped in on her in her bedroom. Zaynab hadn't expected her to be back so soon, so she couldn't dash the tears away fast enough.

"Zaynab! What's the matter?" Her mother hurried to her side and hugged her. "Why are you sitting in here alone and crying?"

Zaynab looked around her, afraid that her mother's voice might have carried through the house. Anisa and Nasser were still out, but Ara was, as usual, shut up in his office. Zaynab quickly realized that she was fretting for no reason though. The chance of him having heard anything once he was absorbed in his work was merely hopeful on her part. And she also didn't have to worry about any of his security cameras catching her crying as none of the bedrooms were being monitored.

"Are you sick?" Her mother paused, her face crumpling more with worry as she lowered her voice and asked, "Is it the baby?"

Zaynab shook her head. Though her mother heaved a sigh and whispered, "Alhamdulillah," she still clutched her chest and gazed at her uneasily.

"But if it's not the baby, and you're not sick, then what's wrong?"

Her mother was the last person she would've chosen to confide in. After surviving her battle with cancer, Zaynab had only wanted to shield her from worry, and she had for a year now. It was almost as tiring to avoid Ara as it was to keep the problems with her marriage from her mother.

Perhaps that was why she opened her mouth and blurted, "It's Ara."

And apparently that was all that needed to be said for her mother to bundle her back into her arms. Clinging to her, Zaynab buried her face in her mother's shoulder and cried more of the seemingly never-ending tears that had plagued her recently. Her mother quietly patted her back and rocked her the way she had when Zaynab was younger. When she was soothed enough to pull back and wipe at her face, Zaynab didn't see any judgment in her mother's eyes. Just the same open concern and love for her.

"Now, tell me what's wrong," her mother urged, taking Zaynab's hands and squeezing comfort into her.

Needing to unburden herself, Zaynab told her everything. Starting with the reasons that had led her to asking Ara for a divorce and ending with her choice to remain with him in the end.

When she was done, her mother tsked. "Why didn't you tell me you were thinking of a divorce?"

"I didn't want to worry you."

Laughing, her mother gently cupped and stroked her cheek. "You will always worry me, Zaynab. Now that you will be a mother, you will understand what that feels like."

"That's why I'm staying with him. For the baby."

Her mother nodded. "I know. It's very noble of you to sacrifice for your child," she told her, her smile sympathetic.

"Is it?" Zaynab said. "It feels awful." Like her heart was breaking over and over again, and there was nothing she could do to stop it. *Because I can't make Ara love me.*

"It should since you love him."

Zaynab bit her lip, not even bothering to argue what she knew was true. She loved Ara, but that was her problem. "How do I stop?" she said pleadingly.

Her mother laughed again and smoothed her hands over Zaynab's, lovingly caressing some of the tension from her.

"You know, I loved your father very much. And I know that, once, he cared for me too. But we grew apart, your father's heart turned away from me, and we weren't the same people who had fallen in love and chosen to be married. It's why I left him."

"You left him?" It was the first Zaynab heard of this. She'd just assumed it was her father who had wanted to separate from her mother. That it was *his* fault Zaynab's childhood wasn't what it should have been had her parents remained married.

Her mother inclined her head. "It's true. I demanded it, in fact. I sensed the end of our relationship was coming, and I wanted to beat your father to it," she said with a sad smile.

"How did you know that... Well, that you didn't love each other anymore." Although it wasn't the same for her and Ara, considering he never had loved her, Zaynab was still curious how things could have gone so wrong for her parents if what her mother was saying about their love was true.

"Besides your father saying it to me, I just looked at him one day and didn't recognize him as the man I'd loved once."

Zaynab didn't know what to say. And her mother seemed to understand because she wrapped her in another embrace, and while holding her, she said, "It was hard, of course, and I had my moments of regret, but in the end, now more than ever, and certainly whenever I look at you, I know that leaving your father was the best decision I could've made.

"As for you and Ara, I can't choose what's best for either of you. As a mother, I want you both to be happy, even if that means living apart from each other and raising your child like that," her mother said and kissed her cheek. "Just know that I will support you in whatever decision you make, always."

It was like something clicked in her head, and Zaynab drew back, gazed into her mother's eyes, and quietly said, "I don't think I made the right decision..."

After hearing her mother loving fiercely and then bravely embracing her choice to divorce Sharmarke, Zaynab had gained a missing piece of clarity. It struck her just then that she'd never told Ara how much she cared for him, not once. She'd asked for a divorce and hadn't told him why she had been unhappy with their relationship. And now she was doing the same thing by choosing to remain quiet, staying with him and accepting a loveless marriage.

"But I think I now know how to fix it," Zaynab said to her mother, and for the first time since she and Ara had argued, she didn't have the urge to cry hopelessly.

Not for the first time, Ara had hurt Zaynab, and since it was becoming so frequent he had to accept it wasn't unintentional. Because he'd been trying to push her away for a while now with his coldly indifferent attitude. He'd closed himself off to her purposefully in the hopes that she would leave him. Spare her the grief of loving him and being committed to their relationship when he didn't think he could give her what she wanted and deserved: true love.

I would've broken her heart someday.

The way he saw it, better that the heartache and grief come earlier than having either of them be invested in each other even more.

Of course Zaynab likely didn't see it that way. Her stricken expression was branded into his memory, and even though several days had passed since she informed him that she'd changed her mind about the divorce and pleaded for them to remain married for the baby, the whole dramatic scene might as well be imprinted onto his soul. At this rate, he likely wouldn't ever forget the disappointment and heartbreak in her eyes when she'd looked at him. And he certainly wouldn't be able to scrub away the taste of her tears when she had kissed him.

Something told him that his injury to her this time might even be irreparable. That he'd well and truly broken her patience with him.

Ara just didn't think anyone else was aware of that fact until Anisa sighed and asked, "Okay. What did you do to upset Zaynab?"

They were strolling the popular shops of Notting Hill

on her request. She'd wanted last-minute souvenirs and, though Nasser was free to go with her, Anisa had asked Ara specifically to come along with her. And now he knew why as she led him into a bookshop, the cool, hushed atmosphere prompting him to lower his voice as he answered her.

"What do you mean?" he said.

Turning her head away from perusing the books, Anisa raised a brow in challenge. "I mean that there's a weird tension between you two, and don't you dare try to say there isn't."

Ara closed his mouth, having planned to do exactly that. He hadn't wanted to talk about it, not only because he didn't wish to burden his sister with his relationship troubles, but also there was the fact that he didn't know how to make Zaynab happier and yet protect them both from the torment that love carried with it.

"She's *upset* with me."

"Why?" Anisa tossed back over her shoulder as she walked down the corridor of bookshelves.

She led him to the back of the shop, to a seating area with two armchairs and a sofa, the chintzy material of the furniture pairing well with the homely feeling of the bookshop. There weren't a lot of patrons in the bookshop, and so they had that area to themselves.

He must have looked confused as to how she knew about the seating area because she explained, "Nasser and I visited this bookshop yesterday." She then nudged him good-naturedly, adding, "Don't think you can change the subject. Now I know you're used to giving the advice, Ara, but I might actually be able to help you if you'll let me."

Sighing heavily, he palmed his beard and, after an anxious pause, said, "We argued."

"Is this about the divorce?"

Right. He'd almost forgotten that Anisa had overheard him speaking to Zaynab about it.

It happened when Zaynab had left him a year ago after he'd discharged himself from the hospital in Mogadishu and returned to Berbera alone. Anisa had been there waiting for him, and Nasser with her, after Ara had tasked him to guard his little sister. Though he and Anisa hadn't been on speaking terms at the time, he'd wanted her to be safe, and Nasser had proved himself capable of delivering security guarantees. And Ara had been correct in trusting his instincts and choosing Nasser to protect his sister. He just hadn't known that he was also inadvertently the reason they had met and fallen in love. Now, because of him, they were about to be married.

Meanwhile he couldn't help but be reminded that the same happiness that Nasser and Anisa shared couldn't be said of him and Zaynab.

"Yes, and no. We're not getting divorced any longer."

"So, what's the problem then?" Anisa tilted her head, her bafflement understandable. "Shouldn't we be celebrating?"

Far from feeling in a celebratory mood, Ara bowed his eyes, gripped his beard punishingly and growled, "There's no divorce, but we're only staying together for the baby."

Anisa was silent for a while, but then she snorted and said, "Well, that's stupid."

Ara jerked his head up fast, sharp and angry words forming quickly on his tongue. But before he had the chance to utter them, and deal his sister any harm, she held up a hand to stop him and acknowledged his outrage.

"I'm sorry to have been so blunt, but what I meant is

that you don't have to be with each other to raise your child together."

"We know that. But Zaynab... She wants it this way." He didn't know why Zaynab would bind herself to him when Ara was giving her the chance to leave him and be free of the emotional turmoil he was causing her. And maybe, though the thought pained him greatly, she could even find happiness with someone else and be loved as wholly as she deserved.

"Did you think that this might not have to do with the baby? At least for her."

Ara went rigid, nostrils flaring and his mind turning over what Anisa had just said. "Then what would it have to do with?"

"Oh, I don't know..." She tapped her chin and rolled her eyes before giving him a sharper look than he could ever. "Could it be that, perhaps, she loves you? That she doesn't want you to end your marriage because she thinks it's her only connection to you."

He was shaking his head even before Anisa finished, unable to digest what she was insinuating. That Zaynab loved him wasn't the bombshell news here, he always knew she'd cared for him, but that she loved him to the point of accepting the passionless union he could only offer her— Ara was dumbstruck that it could be true.

"Do you love her?" Anisa asked and touched his arm and snagged his attention.

He'd been staring off into the distance, far beyond the walls of the bookshop; the shock that Zaynab's love could be so strong for him blanking his mind to any other thought. But he'd heard what Anisa had said and now he was having trouble sorting out a response.

"I... Yes." He wouldn't lie because admitting it wouldn't

change that he had been right. If what Anisa proposed was true, and Zaynab's love for him was causing her torment, then Ara had reason to be worried. His fear for love hurting either of them, or even *both* of them was now real. Which was why he said, "It doesn't matter. I can't give her what she desires. I can't love her the way she should be loved."

"Why not?"

"Because," he snapped. *Because love causes untold measures of pain that ripple through life. It's a short burst of happiness that can only end in misery.* Instead of telling her all of that, he grumbled again, "Just because."

"This is about hooyo and aabo."

Hearing Anisa mention their parents only incensed him more. But he was too angry and too distraught to tell her she was wrong. *Or maybe she's right...*

Anisa didn't give him time to decide which it was. "I know what you're feeling, Ara. It might not be the same for me as it is for you. You knew them better than I did, and I was so young, that sometimes... Sometimes I can't even remember their faces it feels like." She smiled sorrowfully at him and tightened her hold on his arm. "I get so sad knowing that they won't be with me at my wedding, and they won't ever meet Nasser."

"Anisa," he rasped her name, taking her hand over his arm and squeezing her fingers.

"I want them with us so badly, it physically pains me." She looked up, breathing out slowly and fanning her face with her free hand to stave off the tears he saw glimmering in her eyes.

Instinctively, he reached for her and drew her into his arms. Anisa hugged him back as tightly as he was holding on to her. It felt like a while before they pulled apart and his sister wiped at her face, her smile wobbly but not as colored by the profound loss that changed both of their lives.

"I miss them, too," he confided, chuckling when Anisa stared wide-eyed at him. She had a right to be surprised, it wasn't often that he shared his feelings. His humor dissipated soon enough though, and with it came a hollow realization that Anisa was correct. At least about the part that their parents' deaths had forged his trust issues with love. If he were being honest with only himself, losing them had shaped who he was today more than he cared to admit.

And it had undoubtedly influenced his decision to keep Zaynab from getting closer now.

Though he survived his parents' passing away, Ara couldn't say the same for Zaynab. "I don't want to love and lose her. I won't survive that."

Anisa grasped his hand. "I won't say that losing her isn't possible. But what I will tell you is that when I first met Nasser, and as I gradually got to know him, I didn't know how I felt until he walked away and I allowed him to leave.

"The thing is, him leaving wasn't what I regretted most. It was my not speaking up about how it broke my heart, and I was only heartbroken because I loved him. And he felt the same way. But if Nasser and I hadn't loved each other, we wouldn't have fought to be together."

Normally Ara wouldn't have cared to hear about his sister's love life in detail, but in this instance it was illuminating.

The question though was, did he want to fight for Zaynab, their marriage and their family?

To fight for their love?

Ara seemed to have his answer when he asked Anisa, "How would I even fight for her?"

CHAPTER FOURTEEN

"ARE YOU GOING to tell me where we're going?" Zaynab asked, nervously plucking at the ruffled trim of her beige tunic before forcing her hands into the lap of her long black skirt. She glanced over at Ara as he sat behind the wheel and confidently steered through the thickest parts of London traffic. They were nearing the Thames, and it was busier than usual on that temperate spring night.

The smile lifting up a corner of his mouth should have caused her some alarm, mostly because they barely spoke to each other these days. She'd hoped to change that since speaking to her mother a couple days ago, but every time she set out to talk to Ara, she had a flash of his coldly unreadable features when he'd told her that he would sign off on their divorce and her heart froze from fear to see that look on his face again.

Despite that, now all she felt was an answering flutter when he turned his dark eyes from the road and briefly settled the force of his gaze on her. "I could, but I'd rather you see it for yourself."

She saw what he meant a short while later after they parked and walked from the footpath between the dazzling London Eye and the Thames to a pier where an impressively long boat floated gently on the dark river waters. Encased by a glass roof and walls, and lit up so brightly that it glowed, it reminded her of a giant, buoyant snow globe.

Only as they neared it Zaynab could see it wasn't a snow globe at all but a restaurant, warmly lit and redolent of polished refinement and a menu that had to be seriously pricey. But that wasn't why she hesitated halfway up the pier to the boat, looked at him warily and wondered, "Why are we here?"

It wasn't like she and Ara were on the best of speaking terms right then. Although she didn't mind the promise of dinner, Zaynab also couldn't pretend everything was normal with them either. *It's far from normal...*

She'd thought that she could remain with him and learn to be as emotionally detached in their relationship as he was, but it wasn't as easy as she presumed it to be. Worse, starving her love for him was starting to feel impossible. And it made her wonder whether she had doomed herself to forever pining away for Ara in secret, never having her love returned and never being happy with him again.

"I just wanted a change of scenery for dinner, and this restaurant came highly recommended from Anisa. Apparently she and Nasser dined here recently."

Though his explanation didn't fully settle her nerves, Zaynab nodded slowly and moved along.

At the boat, waitstaff ushered them in with smiles and guided them to one of the tables on the empty boat. Besides figuring that they arrived earlier than anyone else, she thought nothing of their being the first guests aboard the floating restaurant, except for the fact that she was now briefly stuck with Ara.

It should have been the perfect window for her to tell him how she felt about him had her tongue not anxiously tangled up on her.

I don't want a marriage that's empty of passion.

That was all she had to say, but that one sentence was full of the incomparable weight of her love for him. She couldn't just blurt it out... Could she?

Before Zaynab tried, Ara stood up from their table near the center of the boat and he left her to walk up to the glass walls of the ship.

In his well-tailored charcoal gray striped three-piece suit, he looked the same as always. But with his back to her, his hands locked behind him, and the view of nightlife teeming along central London in front of him, Ara didn't sound like himself as he said, "Besides dinner, there's another reason I invited you here, Zaynab."

Ignoring the way her heart took a nosedive like an anchor heaved off the side of a ship and into the murky depths below, she gulped.

"I've been thinking about the divorce. About us."

She curled her hands into fists in her lap, her nails indenting into her palms.

"But before that, I have to tell you something about me. Something I hope will help you understand my reasoning and my actions lately." She heard him sigh, the sound gratingly loud in the quiet of the boat. Even the staff appeared to have made themselves scarce. And with the ship covered in glass, it truly felt like they were trapped in their own little bubble right then.

"Since my parents died, I've always carried this feeling that I should have been with them. That if I had been, I could have saved them."

Zaynab pinched her lips together and stopped the comforting words that rushed up in her, and though she forced herself to remain seated, she gazed at him with a longing to give in to the need to embrace him.

"And I might have, had I not allowed an argument to keep me away from them. I let my anger get the best of me, and although I know it didn't kill them directly, it held me back from being with them in their time of need. It's a regret I will live with for the rest of my life." She believed what he said. The grief in his voice heavy and thick, and pressing down on her lungs as though she was grieving with him. And, in a way, she was. Her love panged for him. Made her want to run up behind him and wrap her arms around his shoulders and hug him until he forgot the tragedy that both disfigured his past and shaped him into the man he was today.

She hadn't wanted to interrupt him, sensing that he needed to expunge his feelings, but Zaynab couldn't help herself from trying to console him.

"I'm sure that's not true…"

"It is," Ara intoned. Behind his back, he tightened his hands, his fingers locking around his wrist, knuckles jagged against his deep brown flesh. "Because I *should* have been there, Zaynab. I… I had time off school. A holiday break. And when most of my friends left to visit their homes, I had remained on campus to avoid the inevitable arguments I knew awaited me if I returned home to my parents. An argument about my leaving my business program and pursuing being a chef, of all things.

"It was stupid," he breathed out harshly. "And though it felt so important to me then, I wish it hadn't been. More than anything I wish—*Allah*, how I wish I had taken the time to go home, be with them, even if it was one last time."

She knew he was done when he hung his head and his shoulders drooped suddenly as if burdened by an invisible pressure. And he held perfectly still, like a beautiful statue after that, the silence no longer holding her curiosity as he'd given her a peek into what he was thinking and feeling.

But she couldn't feel relieved knowing that he was hurting.

Only before Zaynab could rise from her seat and go to him, Ara glanced at her over his shoulder.

"I hurt them with my selfishness, and I promised myself I wouldn't do that to anyone I love again. But I did, with Anisa when she moved away. Because I wanted, selfishly, to have her by my side where I could protect her. I allowed four years to pass without speaking to her, and I almost lost my remaining family because of it."

Zaynab's breathing staggered at the ardor tightening across his handsome face right before he looked away from her.

"I want to be selfish," he said, his words spoken to the glass wall in front of him, but they were aimed at her entirely. "I'm fighting against the thoughtlessness of keeping you with me. But if I lost you—Zaynab, I can't lose you. I won't. Not even if I have to act inconsiderately and make you hate me."

Hate him? The notion couldn't be further from her mind, not especially when her love for him surged up in her more powerfully than ever before.

"I loved my parents, and their deaths nearly destroyed me. If I hadn't needed to care for Anisa, needed to step up and be the remaining family she had, I don't know where I would be today. And it's because I loved them that I'm still hurting so much."

"You're right," she said, finally finding her voice and feeling like she had to speak up. "About love. I loved my father, and it pained me when I finally realized that he didn't love me back."

"It's his loss," Ara remarked.

Zaynab smiled at his quickness to defend her, not that it was needed. *Though it's appreciated.* And because she believed that she now understood where he was going with this, she said, "I know it's hard to care about someone and question if they care much back."

"I do care for you," he rasped, "love you even—"

She had already been on the edge of her seat the entire time, so she rose up fairly quickly.

"What did you say?" Walking slowly over to him, she glimpsed her reflection hovering behind him and saw the uncertainty that gripped her heart crinkling her brow and trembling her lips. She touched his shoulder when he wouldn't turn around to her, when he wouldn't repeat what he'd just told her. But that small bit of contact worked in rousing him, and Ara gave her what she wanted. What she'd always ever desired from him.

"I love you, Zaynab," he said.

"I always did," Ara said, lifting his hand to where she touched his shoulder, his palm enveloping her fingers. "That was never in doubt, at least not for me."

"I thought… You said you didn't, *couldn't.*"

"I lied."

"Why?"

"Because I didn't want you getting hurt by your father's crimes. And then because I didn't know how to be a husband to you." Telling her all of this after bottling it up inside for so long was at once terrifying and relieving. He hadn't felt freer in all his life, even though a part of him still wanted to cower from Zaynab behind the last shreds of his usual defenses.

I want to show her this.

He needed to at this point.

"After Sharmarke was imprisoned, I'd hoped that maybe—" he paused and grasped her hand a little tighter "—we could live together and I could learn to be a better life partner to you."

"You did?"

He could see Zaynab's eyes widen in her reflection. Although he'd finally opened the floodgates on his thoughts and feelings, Ara still hadn't looked at her fully. This was the most vulnerable he'd been in a long while. Not since his parents died and he'd equated love and any other emotion like it as a security risk to his mind and heart.

"I did. But then you asked for the divorce, and I wanted to give you what you wanted. I didn't want you to force yourself to stay with me. When I signed the divorce application for you, I'd thought it would be the last time I ever saw you."

Then she'd messaged him that she was pregnant, and Ara's every primal-charged instinct was to claim his family.

"The baby was my second chance at making amends to you," he said.

"Ara, I… I didn't know you felt that way." She took her hand away and he let her go, but he still didn't turn to face her, not even when he felt her stepping back away from him, her sandals moving soundlessly over the carpet. From what he could see in the glass wall's reflection, she was pacing behind him.

"At the hospital in Mogadishu, when you were in a coma, I was worried that you'd never wake up. We were married for two months then, and I was already thinking about a divorce, but then you were injured so badly and all I kept thinking was that I wouldn't speak to you again—and I knew, I just knew then that I loved you."

It wasn't news to him that she loved him. He'd begun to suspect that she did from how sad she would become because of him, but it was another thing to hear her say it aloud.

She loves me.

And she was concerned that she'd almost lost him. It was exactly the distressing kind of situation he'd wanted to avoid inflicting on her; the whole reason he had suppressed his love for her and refused to tell her of it. To think that his worst fear had already happened a while ago and that he hadn't known about it.

Ara's heart constricted, and he waited for his usual doubts to creep in and ruin this special moment with her. When nothing happened he was surprised but pleasantly so. He knew that he owed it to Zaynab. Talking to her was helping, and had he known that it would, he might have braved telling her all of this a while ago.

As if reading his mind, she sighed and said, "I wish you would've told me all of this a long time ago."

"I do too." And knowing how much he regretted it the first time Ara didn't want to suffer the remorse of another missed opportunity. "That's why I want to ask you to give me another chance."

By his side now, Zaynab touched his hand.

"I'm scared that if I do, that it might not be enough," Zaynab said far more quietly, the fear threaded in her words clear to him, touching that final part Ara hadn't even realized was closed up in him. He hadn't looked her at her properly when they'd been talking this whole time. Now, desperate to remedy that, he gently took hold of her wrist and pulled her around him, trapping her between him and the glass wall, and taking her face in his hands.

"I love you," he said, seeing the tears beading at her eyes and knowing that she needed to hear it again. *That we both need it.* "I've always loved you from the moment I first saw you. I might have struggled to get to this point, but Zaynab, it was never because I didn't care for you. Never because I didn't love your heart, your smile, everything about you that made me want to ask you to marry me."

She closed her eyes and her lips parted on a whimper.

"If you give me this chance, I swear I'll use it to show you this time." He paused, gathering his courage for this last part. "But if you can't trust me, I'll understand. I just can't give you what you've asked of me. I won't condemn us to a marriage where we're not in love."

Her eyes fluttered open at his ultimatum, a blend of a cry and laugh coming from her. "Are you saying you'll divorce me?"

"Maybe," he said, smiling stupidly as her sparkling eyes softened his heart completely.

"I don't know what to say to that."

"Say yes," he urged her and watched her chin tremble anew. Only now it wasn't because she was unhappy with him. Rather, with her eyes shining, Zaynab kept him on tenterhooks until the very last moment.

"All right," she whispered.

Ara expelled the breath he had been holding in anticipation.

"But only if you promise to speak to me. Tell me how you're feeling and let me in up here," she said, touching his temple before smiling serenely and moving her hand to his chest, her palm pressing down over his heart, "so that I know how to protect this."

Feeling his own eyes watering after that, Ara lowered his head and kissed her, giving them what he knew they both wanted and needed. Almost all too naturally, he slid his hands down to her hips and she wrapped her arms around her neck. Their kiss was at once both soft and sweet and fiercely passionate, but it was also everything in between. It was the perfect reflection of the ups and downs they'd gone through together, and now standing there, with Zaynab in his arms where she belonged all along, Ara wouldn't have had it any other way.

He would've kissed her to breathlessness just to prove his adoration for her, but they broke apart as noises filtered over to where they stood in the restaurant alone. Ara suspected that would be changing soon as the sounds crystallized into individual voices.

"I was beginning to think we might have the restaurant to ourselves," Zaynab said, her brows knitting together like the thought of sharing the space now displeased her.

"Are you disappointed that we won't?" he teased.

Still in his arms, she swatted at his chest lightly but laughed. "A little. Aren't you?"

"Oh, most definitely." Ara then bussed her lips quickly, playfully. "But I actually rented out the restaurant for the evening."

That grabbed her attention, her face switching to confusion in the blink of an eye.

"Then who else could be here?" she asked as the noises only grew louder, the voices headed straight for them.

Ara spun her in his arms and pointed out the glass wall, his head hovering by hers, lips brushing the heated tip of her ear. "Take a look for yourself."

And she did, gasping, "Is that my mother and your sister? Salma? Oh, my God, Ara, did you invite Opaline and Remi?" She looked away from their family and friends to goggle at him. "Why?"

"Simple. They're as much a part of our lives as Button is," he said and drawing her back against him, he settled his hands over the taut swell of her belly and smiled when her hands gripped his.

She leaned into him with a little frustrated moan falling from her soft, kiss-swollen lips. "That's sweet of you, really, but I still would've liked it if it were just the two of us."

Ara laughed, never thinking he'd ever feel this lightened of burden… *Or this happy again.* With Zaynab though, he suspected he'd be happy eternally.

EPILOGUE

A few months later

IT ALL FELT full circle standing on Ara's yacht, gazing out at the horizon where the deep blue of the Indian Ocean met the cloudless blue skies of that sunny and warm late October afternoon. Zaynab didn't think there could be a more perfect day for a wedding.

Standing off at the bow by herself, she smiled at the swell of laughter and cheers sounding from behind her where Anisa and Nasser's reception was in full swing, but it was the strong arms snaking her waist from behind that had her giggling full-on. Flushed with happiness, she pushed back against Ara, knowing she'd never tire of his embraces, or stop longing for him to hold her the way he was now.

"Are you hiding from me?" he asked, nuzzling her ear and kissing her cheek.

Arching her head back and resting it on his shoulder, laughing when his lips teased along her jawline, Zaynab stroked her hands over his arms and murmured, "Maybe, but only because I know you'll have us scandalize the wedding guests."

"Not my guests," he said between little nips, "not my problem."

Zaynab snorted and let him have his way a little longer before she wriggled enough to get him to loosen his arms and allow her to turn to face him, her gaze lovingly roving over his features. She was still getting used to seeing him without that big beard of his. He'd grown it for as long as possible and then, right before she'd given birth, Ara had suddenly decided to shave it all off. Now he kept his jaw mostly clean-shaven, except for the occasional dark stubble of his five o'clock shadow.

But without the beard, the scar he'd gotten from his brush with death stood out to the world starkly.

Tracing the scar with her fingertips first, she followed it by kissing that little imperfect part of him that still, somehow, was flawless to her.

"What are you doing out here all alone?" he asked.

It must have looked strange to anyone who'd noticed her standing alone since the party was nearer the stern of the ship and spilling along the port and starboard. She had the front of the boat all to herself before Ara had sneaked up on her.

She hummed noncommittally. "Just thinking to myself, that's all."

"Are you having doubts about moving back to Berbera?"

Less than a week ago, they had settled back in his house right on time for Anisa and Nasser's wedding.

She shook her head and said, "No. Not one single doubt in my mind that we've made the right move for us."

He smiled at her and, not even bothering to see if anyone was looking in their direction, he swooped down and kissed her deeply and thoroughly. Once he ravished her into a panting, blushing state, he gestured for the shore of Batalaale Beach in the distance and where they could make out the hulking shape of the fortified stone enclosure that circled their home.

"We should head back. I miss Aasma."

"I miss her, too," Zaynab said, her heart sore at the thought of being apart from their little girl. Named in honor of Ara's late mother, little Aasma was only three months old and already she was their whole world and had them wrapped around her tiny baby fingers. "But we can't just leave your sister's wedding. What would everyone think? Besides, my mum wouldn't be too happy if we showed up early. Because then that would mean less time for her to coddle her granddaughter."

Her mother had come along to help settle them in for their new lives here. Though Zaynab was still unsure of when she and Ara and little Aasma would return to London, she was ready for it to be anywhere from a month to several years, as long as she had her family and they were all happy together.

"Though if you want to incur the wrath of your sister *and* my mother, then by all means. Just leave me out of it."

Ara mock-shuddered before grinning. "Put like that, I suppose it would only make sense for us to wait it out a little longer."

Zaynab snorted with laughter, her humor lingering but muted when he took her in his arms again, her hands wrapped around the railing of his ship, the ocean spread out before them and Ara grounding her from behind with his firm hold. "Remember when we first met."

"How could I forget?" he rumbled affectionately into her ear. "You were standing right about here and you were looking out at the ocean, gazing at the sunset. And then you turned, and looked right at me, and I knew that we were meant to be."

"Oh, did you now?" Because for a while it had felt like they would never have made it this far. That they would never have this at all. And yet they'd persevered together, and now here they were, as happily fated as Ara believed they were.

"I did," Ara said, so solemnly that Zaynab looked back over her shoulder at him, his face right there, his lips sealing hotly over hers.

And when he moved back, his hooded gaze shifted from her mouth up to lock eyes with her. "It's because, Zaynab, I loved you from that moment onward."

If she hadn't seen that love shining back at her so openly she wouldn't have believed it.

Touching a hand to his smooth jaw, Zaynab leaned in and kissed him sweetly, injecting all the boundless joy he gave her into the gesture. Yet still not enough, she drew away and said, "I love you, too, Ara. From the moment I saw you, maybe, but certainly now and forever."

"Forever," Ara agreed resoundingly, and Zaynab had no doubt that their love would be everlasting.

* * * * *

MILLS & BOON®

Coming next month

SECRET FLING WITH THE KING
Susan Meier

'You're not a prince.'

'One better,' Mateo said, studying her eyes. 'I'm your king.'

The way he said it was possessive and primal enough to send a zing of electricity through Jessica. Struggling with the urge to lean into him, she didn't know what she thought she was doing, moving around a ballroom floor as if she was dancing. 'There's no music.'

He laughed. 'Okay.' He began to sing the music of the *Blue Danube Waltz*. 'Da Da Da Da Da…Da Da, Da Da.'

Their slight moves became the wide swirling motions of a waltz.

And it felt wonderful. Before she could stop herself, she wished for a full skirt to bell out when they twirled. She wished for real music and the noise of a crowd celebrating in this wonderful room.

He reached the end of the song and when his humming stopped, he stopped dancing. She caught his gaze. Expecting to see laughter there, she smiled. But he didn't.

His dark eyes searched hers. A shower of tingles rained through her. Her chest tightened.

Continue reading

SECRET FLING WITH THE KING
Susan Meier

Available next month
millsandboon.co.uk

LET'S TALK

Romance

For exclusive extracts, competitions and special offers, find us online:

- **f** MillsandBoon
- **X** @MillsandBoon
- **⊙** @MillsandBoonUK
- **♪** @MillsandBoonUK

Get in touch on 01413 063 232

For all the latest titles coming soon, visit
millsandboon.co.uk/nextmonth

afterglow BOOKS

Afterglow Books is a trend-led, trope-filled list of books with diverse, authentic and relatable characters, a wide array of voices and representations, plus real world trials and tribulations. Featuring all the tropes you could possibly want (think small-town settings, fake relationships, grumpy vs sunshine, enemies to lovers) and all with a generous dose of spice in every story.

♪ @millsandboonuk
⊙ @millsandboonuk
afterglowbooks.co.uk
#AfterglowBooks

For all the latest book news, exclusive content and giveaways scan the QR code below to sign up to the Afterglow newsletter:

SCAN ME

afterglow BOOKS

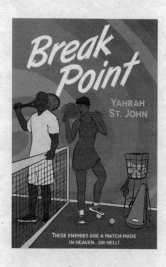
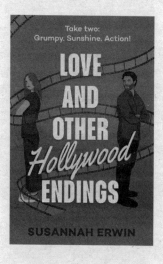

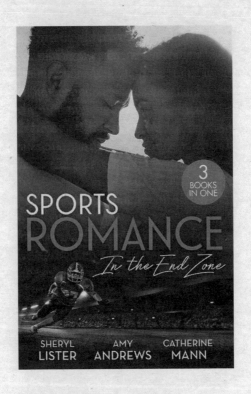